IMPACT

BOOKS BY PAUL LEVINE

THE JAKE LASSITER SERIES
To Speak for the Dead
Night Vision
False Dawn
Mortal Sin
Riptide
Fool Me Twice
Flesh & Bones
Lassiter
Last Chance Lassiter
State vs. Lassiter
Bum Rap
Bum Luck
Bum Deal
Cheater's Game

THE SOLOMON & LORD SERIES
Solomon vs. Lord
The Deep Blue Alibi
Kill All the Lawyers
Habeas Porpoise

STAND-ALONE THRILLERS
Impact
Ballistic
Illegal
Paydirt

IMPACT

2020 Edition

Paul Levine

HERALD
SQUARE
PUBLISHING

AUTHOR'S NOTE

The Story Behind "Impact"
How To Steal a Case at the Supreme Court

Readers often ask, "Where do you get your ideas?"

Sometimes, a real event inspires a fictional retelling. That's true with my Jake Lassiter series where "Bum Rap" is based loosely on the South Beach Bar-Girls racketeering case, and "Bum Deal" is modeled after a New York murder trial where a physician was charged with killing his wife, despite the absence of a body or any forensic evidence. "Cheater's Game," a 2020 title, closely aligns with the college admissions scandal that shined a light on unsavory practices of our leading universities, not to mention shady conduct by parents and their teenage kids. (Previews of both "Bum Rap" and "Cheater's Game" appear in these pages immediately following "Impact").

"Impact" combines two disparate stories, one real and one imagined. I've long been fascinated with the crash of United Airlines Flight 232 in July 1989 at Sioux City, Iowa. The DC-10 suffered both a catastrophic failure of its huge, tail-mounted engine and the loss of hydraulics systems needed to control the plane. The disaster was caused by...wait a second! No spoilers. The bizarre events that led to the crash are the underpinnings of "Impact."

I've also long been interested in the U.S. Supreme Court and these questions: *How could you steal a case? How could you bribe, extort or buy a case at the highest court in the land?*

Without giving too much away, I concluded that you needed to "own" a law clerk. Why? If the justices are the sorcerers mixing the stew of law and facts that decide cases, their law clerks are the sorcerers' apprentices. Some clerks wield outsize influence with their justices. With a plane crash lawsuit worth several hundred million dollars, how great would the temptation be to plant your own law clerk on the court?

The result is "Impact," which also inspired something on its own. The interplay between justices and their law clerks was the idea behind "First Monday," a CBS legal drama I co-created with Donald P. Bellisario. It starred James Garner, Joe Mantegna, and Charles Durning, but unfortunately, only lasted one season.

"Impact" was previously published in hardcover with the title, "9 Scorpions." Why? Because Justice Oliver Wendell Holmes, Jr. referred to his brethren as "nine scorpions in a bottle." I tried to capture the buzz and sting of that imagery. I hope you enjoy the result.

Paul Levine
Santa Barbara, CA
January 2, 2020

PROLOGUE

THE SILKEN SKY WAS ENDLESS, the stars infinite, the breeze sweet with a thousand promises. On a night like this, the past is forgotten and the future is forever.

Tony Kingston loved flying at night, the huge aircraft slicing through the tar black sky like some tri-masted sailing vessel on a great adventure. Which is what Kingston thought when feeling poetic, when he let the drone of the three massive engines wash over him, playing their serene song.

Other times, burdened with the reality of a discount air carrier in the era of deregulation, he thought he was flying a bus, an over-crowded, undermaintained, ancient clunker of a bus. Now, as he acknowledged instructions from Miami Center and descended to eleven thousand feet he felt the big jet's power under his hands. It was still a remarkable beast, four hundred thousand pounds of muscle, one million separate parts in all. Looking as if it shouldn't be able to get off the ground, this huge aircraft was a testament to man's genius, he thought, just as surely as man was a testament to God's genius.

Hell, the fuselage of the DC-10 looks like one of those fat Cuban cigars—the Robustos—I bring back from Havana.

Tony Kingston looked through the V-shaped windshield and into the night. To the left was the vast darkness of the Atlantic Ocean. Below and to the right were the twinkling lights of Florida's Gold Coast, Palm Beach merging with Ft. Lauderdale and farther south, Miami Beach. In less than twenty minutes, they should be pulling up at the gate at MIA. Listening to the soothing white noise of the slipstream, he took the measure of his own life, calculating credits and debits, figuring he was solidly in the plus column.

A former combat pilot, Kingston sometimes missed the action, the camaraderie of the flight squadron. But he overly romanticized it, he knew, and flying a fighter was a young man's game. What he had now was a career: chief pilot for Atlantica Airlines. The title almost sounded military. So why did the job often leave him wanting more?

Because commercial aviation is to flying what elevator music is to Mozart.

But what had he expected? Surely not the same rush he got from his beloved A-6 Intruder rocketing off the deck of a carrier, a load of HARM missiles slung under its wings.

"Miami Center, this is Atlantica six-four-zero at eleven thousand," said copilot Jim Ryder into the radio.

"Roger, six-four-zero. Maintain eleven thousand," came the scratchy reply.

In a few moments, they'd be handed off to Miami Approach Control, which would guide them from the ocean to the airport for landing. With a steady easterly sea breeze, they would make a sweeping loop over the Everglades to the west of the city and come back again, landing into the wind. It was routine. Tony would line them up with the radio signals that indicated the descent profile and the runway center line, then ease the big bird to the ground. Copilot Ryder would keep up the chatter with Approach Control, and Larry Dozier, the flight engineer, would scan the myriad gauges, which assured that hundreds of mechanical, electrical, and hydraulic systems were performing as intended. Within minutes, the passengers would be heading to their hotels or homes or cruise ships.

"Atlantica six-four-zero, expect Harvest Three approach for runway nine left," Kingston heard in his earphones. On his right, Ryder opened the approach chart.

"Confirm intercept altitude at fifteen hundred feet and decision height two hundred," Kingston told his copilot.

"Roger that," Ryder said, consulting the chart. "Final approach fix is Oscar."

Kingston looked forward to the landing. Even with all the computerized help, it still took a warm body to bring the plane home. For all its drawbacks, being a commercial pilot still beat a suburban commute and a nine-to-five job.

So why did he miss the adrenaline jolts he remembered from the Gulf War? He could still feel the G forces on takeoff from the *John F.*

Kennedy that sunny and windy January day, the heightened heartbeat as he approached the target. One of the "Sunday Punchers," he dropped a missile down the smokestack of the Iraqi cargo ship *Almutanabbi*, docked at a Kuwaiti port. The American public watched the whole thing on CNN, including an interview afterward with Kingston on the deck of the carrier. He was unshaven, his dark hair tousled by the wind. Behind him, a navy seaman was painting a hash mark in the shape of a ship on the nose of his fighter. Kingston smiled and spoke comfortably into the camera, his crooked grin and pugnacious chin seeming to symbolize American fortitude.

When he watched the grainy, black-and-white videotape of the bombing, Kingston was riveted by something he couldn't see from his fighter: two men walking on the products jetty alongside the *Almutanabbi*. They paused and looked up. So strange. They must have heard the jet or the whistling approach of the missile.

One man said something to the other and shrugged. Then they continued walking. Several seconds later, the blast rocked the freighter, and the two men disappeared in a fiery cloud.

Why hadn't they dived for cover? Why hadn't they run?

Now Kingston derived a tranquil satisfaction from flying the fat Robusto filled with tourists. With all the computers and automated gear, he knew he was no longer so much a pilot as an operations director, troubleshooter, and systems manager. But in an emergency, he carried the lives of three hundred people on his strong shoulders. He was good at his job and figured he had finally grown up. He no longer needed the rush of a catapult takeoff from the deck of a carrier. He no longer needed the *Top Gun* macho swagger, the envious looks from men, the adulation from women. He had been a womanizer, a fault common to combat and commercial pilots alike. Now he had a committed relationship with a wonderful, intelligent woman, and if she was also beautiful and twenty years his junior—so what, some things don't change.

"Atlantica six-four-zero, good evening," Miami Approach welcomed. "Turn right heading two-two-zero. Descend and maintain eight thousand."

Ryder acknowledged the message, and Kingston turned the aircraft toward the west. In a few moments, they were over Miami heading toward the Everglades. Both men listened to conversations between Approach Control and other aircraft. At forty-four, Kingston was older than his first officer but in better physical shape. Jim Ryder had grown a paunch from too much hotel room service. Tony Kingston still had a military bearing and rock hard gut.

"Atlantica six-four-zero, you're number thirteen for approach."

"Jeez, we'll be halfway to Naples before they bring us back," Ryder said. He turned around in his seat to face the flight engineer. "Hey, Larry, you want to hit South Beach tonight?"

"Sure. Berlin Bar, maybe Bash, finish up at Amnesia," Larry Doziev said. "How about you, Tony?"

"No thanks. I've got to finish my report for the union."

"That's what happens when you get married," Ryder said.

Kingston laughed. "I'm not married. *You're* married."

"Yeah, but you're acting married ever since you and the mystery woman got together. When you gonna show her off?"

"Maybe *she's* married," Dozier said.

Not yet. But I'm going to change that.

He had never before committed to one woman, always thinking the next one was the fantasy creature who would fulfill all his needs. Now, with the passage of time and more women—flight attendants, models, executives with one-night layovers—in his past than he could remember, he finally had someone whose needs he wanted to fill, a woman he loved more than he loved himself.

Lisa. Lisa Fremont.

The girl from down the hill in Bodega Bay who had traveled so far. He'd known her practically all her life, but he had been blind to the hell she had endured at home. Maybe if he hadn't been stationed so far away, he could have done something. For starters, he would have thrashed Harry Fremont.

Lisa. How have you done it?

Abused child to teen runaway to underage stripper, then with the guidance of an older man—not him, damn it—a new path, summa cum laude at Berkeley and now law school at Stanford. He was awed by her inner strength, her accomplishments, and he loved her dearly.

I've found a soul mate, not a cell mate, and I'll be faithful to her until the day I die.

"C'mon, Tony," Dozier said. "Just one drink."

Kingston scanned the airspeed and altimeter readings. "Sorry guys. Like I said, I've got work to do. Maintenance laid off another dozen workers last week. We've got twenty percent fewer mechanics and thirty percent more planes than we did—"

"I know, I know, but you're pissing against the wind."

Behind them, facing the starboard bulkhead, flight engineer Dozier swiveled his chair toward the front of the aircraft. "Hey, Tony, you might as well give up. Max Wanaker's gonna cut costs till bodies pile up, and then he'll make changes."

"Tombstone technology," Ryder said. "It's an old story."

"Or they'll say the equipment was fine," Dozier added, "so the accident must have been—"

"Pilot error!" Ryder shouted in mock glee.

"It's one thing to drop the olive from the salad," Kingston said, referring to a famous cost-cutting move of another airline several years earlier. "But laying off maintenance people, rushing inspections, and making us fly planes that ought to be in the shop or—"

"Scrapped!" Dozier interrupted, tapping his control panel. "This baby's older than some of the girls Tony screws."

"*Used* to screw," Kingston protested. There was so much he couldn't tell them. Lisa's relationship with Max Wanaker, president of Atlantica Airlines was one thing.

What could she have ever seen in him? But then, she was still a kid.

"Tony was a helluva lot more fun when he chased women instead of FAA inspectors," Ryder said, getting in one last shot.

Kingston was thumbing through the flight manual, preparing to call out the landing checklist. "You guys want to land this plane or bust my balls?"

"We just want the old Tony back," Ryder said.

Cowboys. All pilots begin as thrill-seeking cowboys. Late nights, high speeds, and fast women. I'm damned happy to have matured.

"You know what I want?" Tony asked, then answered his own question. "Joe Drayton. He knows his people have been pencil-whipping inspections they never perform. He's gonna sign my report."

Ryder laughed. "No way. Drayton's three years from a vested pension. If he goes public, he'll be refueling DC-3s in Addis Ababa."

"You're wrong," Kingston said. "He's already slipped me the paperwork."

Now Dozier was chuckling. "Hey, Tony, you're the one creating most of the paperwork. Every time an engine coughs, you do an occurrence write-up. Every time we're hit by a microburst, you write a memo on inadequate training for windshear conditions."

"I'm just doing my job," Kingston said. "Three days ago at O'Hare, I spot an oil leak on my walk-around. Some rent-a-temp mechanic comes over and wipes it with a rag. I refuse to fly the ship and I get written up. A couple months ago, they forget to replace the O-rings after doing a master chip inspection on an L-1011. The plane barely gets back to Atlanta after the captain sees the oil pressure gauge light up. Plus they're covering up their mistakes. Did you read the bulletin on the 757 Tom Ganter flew out of Miami last week, the one where the instruments went haywire?"

"Yeah. It had a wasps nest in the static sensors," Dozier said.

"Bull! That's the cover story. Ganter took a look at the static ports after he got her back down. They were covered with duct tape for Christ's sake! The maintenance crew had polished the plane and forgot to strip off the protective tape. I'm telling you guys it's only a matter of time before we kill a shipload of people."

It was a recurring nightmare, a plane falling from the sky, the panicked cries from the passenger cabin, the thunderous explosion and raging firestorm that would silence every scream. He was not afraid for himself. Tony Kingston had confidence he could handle any crisis, as long as the ship didn't fail him.

"Lighten up, Tony," Dozier said. "Atlantica's never had a fatality. Not one."

Jim Ryder took off his headset and turned toward the captain. "Larry's right. You're crying wolf so often no one pays attention. No one cares."

"I care!" Kingston thundered.

જ્જી

Rita Zaslavskaya stood awkwardly to let the man to her right get out of his window seat and open the overhead compartment. He grabbed a weathered brown leather jacket and slipped it on, then crunched her right foot under his wingtips as he slid back into his seat. Rita had a fair complexion, dark, curly hair, and a strong face that was more handsome than beautiful. She was a large-boned woman in her mid-thirties who stood six feet one and played volleyball with other Russian immigrants on Sundays at a Jewish Community Center in Brooklyn. She'd asked for an aisle seat in an exit row because her bum knee did not take kindly to cramped quarters. One of these days, she'd have it scoped. It was on her list of to-dos, along with getting contact lenses, having her hair straightened, and finding a husband. The last on the list was inexorably linked to the first two, she thought, and would be considerably easier if she would refrain from spiking the ball off the heads of every eligible bachelor in

Bensonhurst, including a handsome but frail cantor from Minsk who had flirted with her ten minutes before she deviated his septum with a particularly vicious kill.

Maybe it was for the best. He was such a shmendrick.

"Excuse me," her seatmate said, lifting his foot from hers. He'd been in and out of the overhead ever since they had left LaGuardia. When he wasn't popping up and down, he was staring out the window in grim silence.

"No problem," Rita replied, glancing at the old leather jacket, which the man had zipped all the way up to his Adam's apple. "Isn't that a little warm for Miami?"

"I'll take it off as soon as we're inside." He was a small, paunchy man in his thirties with wispy pale hair and wire-rimmed glasses. He wore a wedding band, she noticed out of force of habit.

"Nice-looking jacket," she allowed. "Good material."

"It's an authentic re-creation of the Army Air Force A-2 jacket from the Second World War, right down to the seal brown horsehide, the wool cuffs, and brass zippers," he said, pointing to the sleeve patch with its winged logo boasting of the 9th Bomb Group. "Steve McQueen wore one in *The Great Escape.*"

Rita didn't know Steve McQueen from Butterfly McQueen, but her sense of logic was offended. "So why put it on now if you're just going to take it off when you get inside the terminal?"

"The A-2 isn't just for warmth. It'll protect you in case of a crash or enemy attack."

That made her smile. "I live in Brooklyn. Maybe I should get one."

"I'm talking about fire. The danger is greatest on takeoff and landing, which is why I always bring this along, too." He bent over and reached into his carry-on bag, drawing out what looked like a SCUBA mask. "My personal smoke hood. It'll filter out the toxins."

He pulled the mask down over his face, tested his breathing, then slid it onto his forehead, as if he were about to explore some exotic tropical reef. "Some people might regard my safety consciousness as ..."

Meshugeh, she thought. *Crazy.*

"Excessive," he said, placing a pillow between his bulging belly and the seat belt, then cinching the buckle hard. "Do you know the correct bracing position in the event of a crash landing?"

Before she could answer, the man bowed forward, as if in prayer.

Tony Kingston guided the aircraft on the downwind leg, occasionally looking out the windshield at the pitch-black Everglades, a prehistoric creeping river of sawgrass, alligators, and marshy hammocks. The three men in the cockpit reviewed the landing checklist and waited for instructions to turn left and begin looping back to the airport.

Suddenly, an explosion reverberated behind them, a booming rumble accompanied by the discordant shriek of shearing metal.

"Jesus, what was that!" Ryder shouted, instinctively looking back toward the cabin.

Kingston tightened his hands on the yoke as the airframe shuddered. "Larry, what do you see?"

The flight engineer scanned his gauges. "Pressure on engine two has gone to zero. Fuel flow is zero. Shit, we must have blown the aft engine."

"Perform engine shutdown checklist," Kingston ordered. As Ryder ran through the items, turning off the fuel to the tail engine, idling the throttle, the aircraft rolled slightly to the right. Kingston fought the yoke to level the plane. "Ailerons not responding."

Dozier checked the gauges. "Double shit! Hydraulic pressure zero. Hydraulic quantity zero."

"Can't be," Ryder said. "We've got three redundant systems. You can't lose them all just blowing one engine."

Kingston struggled with the yoke, which trembled under his hands but wouldn't turn. He locked his hands on the wheel, took a breath, and threw his shoulders into it. Nothing. The aircraft continued to tremble.

Ryder's fingers danced over half a dozen switches as he scanned his gauges. "Elevators, ailerons, and rudder all inoperative," he said, his voice strained.

"It can't be," Dozier repeated. "How the hell are we gonna turn? How are we gonna control our descent?"

We're not, Kingston thought, rapidly analyzing the situation. Without flight controls, it would be virtually impossible to land. He tried to activate the speed brakes. "Spoilers not responding either," he said after a futile try. He increased thrust on the left engine and the wings leveled off, but the aircraft continued vibrating, and a few seconds later, the nose pitched up and the airframe shuddered.

"We're gonna stall!" Ryder warned, his voice breaking.

Kingston gave it more power, hitting the right engine harder. The nose came down, but the aircraft rolled slightly left.

"Miami Approach, this is Atlantica six-four-zero," Kingston said into his mike, while fighting the roll. His voice was calm, but the words were clipped with urgency. "We've lost the two engine and all three hydraulic systems. We declare an emergency six-four-zero."

The voice in his headset was equally composed. "Roger six-four-zero. We'll vector everyone else out of there. Descend to fifteen hundred. Turn left to two-seven-zero and prepare for final approach."

"That's a problem," Kingston responded. "Gonna have to use asymmetrical thrust from number one and three to try and turn."

His matter-of-fact tone masked the tension building inside him. Inconceivable as it seemed, they simply had no control over the aircraft.

How the hell are we going to land this big fat bus?

"Copy that, six-four-zero. Advise when you're ready to turn into final."

"When and if," Ryder muttered.

There was a knock at the cabin door, and Larry Dozier opened it. Senior Flight Attendant Marcia Snyder, a divorcee who had just put her third child through college, rushed in and slammed the door. Her face was pale, and her words came rapidly. "I was in the aft galley. The explosion was right over my head."

"Did you see anything?" Kingston asked.

"No. At first, I thought we'd hit a small plane. There was a puff of smoke, but no fire I could see. I think part of the tail is gone."

"Prepare the passengers for emergency landing," Kingston ordered. "Short briefing procedure. We don't have much time. And get me a souls-on-board count."

"Already did," she said. "Two hundred seventy-five passengers, thirteen crew."

Kingston nodded his thanks. Marcia was already out the door, heading back into the first class compartment, when Kingston turned to his first officer. "Jim, deploy the ADG. See if we can get some power out of it."

The copilot yanked a lever, and a small propeller-driven generator dropped a few feet out of the aircraft into the jet stream. Dozier kept his eyes on his control panels. After a moment, he said, "We're getting power. But without the hydraulics, it's not going anywhere."

"We have to do it manually," Kingston said.

"How?" his copilot asked.

Kingston didn't know. There was no procedure for this. He'd have to make it up as he went along. "Grab your yoke. We'll work them together.

Larry, get up here and handle the throttles. Let's try to turn left. Ease off on number one and give some power to number three. Jim and I will pull like hell on our yokes. Let's go!"

As the pilot and copilot tried turning their two-hundred-ton aircraft with the power in their forearms and wrists, the flight engineer crouched behind them, one hand on each of the working throttles.

The aircraft yawed shakily to the left, and the right wing tilted upward. "Too much!" Kingston warned, his voice rising for the first time. Excessive roll and the plane could flip over. One thing the DC-10 was not was an acrobatic aircraft.

Dozier eased back on the right engine and gave more power to the left. The aircraft rolled in the other direction, leveling off, but the nose pitched upward.

"Miami Control, this is six-four-zero," Kingston said, forcing himself to calm down. "We can't control the aircraft. When we correct pitch, we start to roll and vice versa, and we're yawing like a son of a bitch. Don't know how we'll line it up with the runway."

"Copy that six-four-zero. Got you on radar, forty miles west of the airport. We'll have equipment waiting."

Again, the big aircraft yawed to the right, this time the left wing tilting upward.

Equipment.

The controller meant fire-rescue, paramedics, and enough foam to float a battleship. But without the ability to turn, without a way to control the pitching, rolling, and yawing, they would not so much land as cartwheel across the runway. In that case, the only equipment they would need would be hearses.

"We can't turn your way and we don't have any brakes," Kingston replied, "so I don't know how we'd stop this thing even if we get it there." He pictured the crammed apartment buildings and condos west of the Palmetto Expressway. "We don't want to drop it into a neighborhood." He glanced at his two crewmates and pointed down toward the ground. They both nodded. "We're going to have to ditch." He sighed audibly and signed off, "Six-four-zero."

Below them, in the darkness, was the primordial slough. Kingston hoped for a soft, level spot, not a strand of mahogany or live oak trees. It wasn't the ideal terrain for ditching but better than the side of a mountain.

Dozier was hurriedly thumbing through the flight manual. "Nothing here. Nothing for loss of all hydraulics."

"It's not supposed to happen," Kingston said softly.

&

He said his name was Howard Laubach. Rita Zaslavskaya said she was glad to meet him, but she wasn't glad at all. She had heard the explosion and felt the plane shudder. Now, the right wing kept dipping and the nose of the plane was sliding back and forth. She'd asked a flight attendant what happened, but the woman hurried past her and headed toward the cockpit, the color drained from her face.

"It could have been anything," Howard Laubach said, a hopeful note in his voice. "A flock of birds could have been sucked into the engine. Heck, that's brought down planes before. But the captain seems like he has this one under control."

It didn't seem under control to Rita. It seemed as if the plane would veer to one side, then overcorrect and swerve to the other side like a wobbly drunk attempting to walk a straight line. Other passengers were chattering nervously or praying or simply grasping their armrests with bloodless hands. Rita felt queasy, as if she'd eaten piroshki made with spoiled meat, and the look on the flight attendant's face had frightened her. Something was very wrong.

She turned to her seatmate. "You're pretty calm for someone who brings his own oxygen aboard." She was annoyed that the man could be so oblivious to the situation.

"It isn't oxygen," Laubach said, testily. "I'm just prepared. If there's a fire, you'd wish you were, too." He clutched his smoke hood, as if she might steal it.

"What's that noise?" Rita asked, jerking around in her seat.

"Landing gear," Laubach said. "He's setting her down."

"Where? Here?" She leaned past him and peered out into the blackness. All she could see was the startled face of an insane woman. It took her a moment to figure out that she was staring into her own reflection.

&

Suddenly, a horn blared on the Ground Proximity Warning System. The nose angled up again, and both pilot and copilot pushed forward on the yoke. Tony Kingston already had given the tower his count: 288 souls on board. It helped the authorities when it was time to count bodies.

"Six-four-zero, please advise," Miami Control said through the headset.

"We're about to put the world's largest tricycle down in the swamp," Kingston said.

"Roger that, six-four-zero. We've got you on radar and we're dispatching rescue vehicles."

"Tony, I can't keep the nose down," Ryder said. "I'm having a real nose-up moment here." His voice was cracking.

"More power, Larry."

Dozier pulled both throttles back. "C'mon baby," he coaxed her. "Level, level, level."

The aircraft picked up speed and the nose came down.

"You're gonna have to back off some more," Kingston said. "We're going too fast."

"Without flaps or slats, I can't slow it down without stalling," Dozier said, sounding desperate.

It's not hopeless, Kingston told himself, but he knew the odds were against them. At over two hundred knots, they'd likely break up on impact.

Dozier eased up on both throttles.

Too much.

A puff of smoke, a sputter, a cough.

"Oh, shit!" Ryder shouted. "Number one quit."

They were flying on one engine. Dozier immediately increased the power, but it was too late. The number three engine smoked, choked, and stalled. They coasted in total silence, the huge aircraft a glider.

"Okay, fellows," Tony Kingston said. "We're taking her in."

For several seconds there was nothing but the sweet, sad rush of the slipstream past the windshield. Then the left wing dipped, and the plane rolled hard, the wings virtually perpendicular to the ground. Loose papers flew across the cockpit. Without the lift from the wings, they had only a few seconds before they would plunge nose down into the ground.

Tony Kingston fought the yoke, his cramped arms futilely trying to right the plane. He heard screams from the cabin, just as in his nightmares. Next to him, his copilot whispered a prayer.

Kingston wanted to draw out the last moments, to arrange his thoughts, pull up memories from the recesses of his mind. But there was no time. He saw her then, her face flashing by, beautiful but heartbroken, and for the briefest moment, he felt a stabbing pain, knowing of her anguish when she heard the news. He said it then, knowing the cockpit voice recorder would pick it up, and she would hear him or at least read the words. He told her he loved her.

A few jumbled images raced through his senses: his father, long buried; a cold Minnesota lake where he swam as a child with his sister; and then the black-and-white grainy videotape of the two men walking along the jetty in Kuwait just before the bomb hit.

What did they say to each other? Why didn't they run?

======

IN THE CIRCUIT COURT OF THE ELEVENTH JUDICIAL CIRCUIT IN AND FOR DADE COUNTY, FLORIDA

CASE NO: 96-00136 CA 04 (11)
GLORIA LAUBACH,
individually and as Personal
Representative of the Estate
of HOWARD J. LAUBACH,
deceased,
Plaintiff,
vs.
ATLANTICA AIRLINES,
a Delaware corporation,
Defendant.

_____ /

COMPLAINT FOR DAMAGES FOR WRONGFUL DEATH
(EXCERPT)

Plaintiff GLORIA LAUBACH, individually and as personal representative of the estate of Howard J. Laubach, deceased, sues Defendant ATLANTICA AIRLINES (hereinafter "ATLANTICA"), a Delaware corporation, and alleges:

1. This is an action for wrongful death brought pursuant to the Florida Wrongful Death Act.

2. ATLANTICA is a common carrier engaged in the business of transporting fare-paying passengers on regularly scheduled flights in aircraft owned, leased, operated, managed, maintained, and/or controlled by ATLANTICA and its agents and/or employees. As a common carrier, ATLANTICA is obliged to provide the highest degree of care to its passengers.

❧

14. At all times material hereto, ATLANTICA was the owner, lessee, and/or operator in control of a certain DC-10 aircraft, a dangerous instrumentality, bearing registration number N1809U, which was used to transport passengers as a common carrier.

15. Plaintiff's decedent was a paying passenger on board the subject aircraft, a flight in domestic transportation between New York City and Miami, Florida, and was one of 288 persons killed when the aircraft crashed in the Florida Everglades on December 27, 1995.

16. ATLANTICA, through its agents and employees, breached the duty of care owed to decedent by negligently failing:

    a. To furnish an airworthy aircraft;

    b. To properly navigate and operate the aircraft;

    c. To properly train its flight crew as to the procedures in the event of loss of flight controls;

    d. To properly inspect, overhaul, and replace worn-out and unsuitable components;

    e. To provide sufficient security to prevent the placement of bombs or other explosive devices on the subject aircraft;

    f. To operate the aircraft in a safe and competent manner, thereby resulting in the fatal crash in question.

∾

27. As a proximate result of the crash, ATLANTICA is liable to PLAINTIFF for damages as follows:

    a. Pain and suffering of the decedent prior to death;

    b. Pain and suffering of the survivors, beneficiaries, and heirs;

    c. Loss of society, companionship, guidance, and services of the decedent;

    d. Loss of support;

    e. Lost net accumulations, lost value of life, and funeral expenses.

WHEREFORE, PLAINTIFF demands judgment against ATLANTICA AIRLINES, INC. for compensatory damages, plus interest and costs in an amount in excess of two million dollars ($2,000,000.00), and further demands trial by jury.

Respectfully submitted,

Albert M. Goldman, Esquire

======

PART ONE

"Nine scorpions in a bottle."
—Description of the Supreme Court of the United States by Oliver Wendell Holmes, Jr., Associate Justice, 1902-1932.

CHAPTER 1
Study by Day ... Strip by Night

ON THE NIGHT BEFORE HER INTERVIEW at the Supreme
Court of the United States, Lisa Fremont did not know if she could go
through with it. She wanted the job all right—what newly minted lawyer
wouldn't?—but then, the thought of corrupting the position, of using it
to repay an old debt, was antithetical to everything she thought she had
become.

*But have I really changed? Am I Lisa Fremont, magna cum laude from
Stanford Law or Angel from the Tiki Club in the Tenderloin?*

Until today, she thought she could handle it. But that was before she
visited the Court to get the feel of the place. What she felt was reverence,
a sense of awe, even piety.

*I got goosebumps for God's sake! How do I explain to someone like Max
that marble statues and musty law books and the weight of history give me
goosebumps? He only gets excited when the Dow Jones jumps.*

Using his own key, Max Wanaker had breezed into her apartment just
after 6 P.M. He kissed her hello, poured himself a Scotch, and made her
a Gibson, heavy on the vodka, light on the vermouth. Then he loosened
his tie and tossed his Armani suit coat over a chair. He kicked off his black
Italian loafers, polished to a high gloss.

Lisa wore a cropped stretch lace camisole and high-cut briefs, both
white with satin trim, under a soft pink chenille bathrobe that made her
golden red hair glow a buttery copper under the track lighting. She had
put on the robe when Max turned the air-conditioning down to sixty-five.
It didn't matter if it was her apartment or his hotel suite, everything was
always done to Max's specifications. Now, in early autumn in Washington,
D.C., there was a manmade cold front settling into the living room.

In more ways than one.

They hadn't gone out to dinner. Too risky. Not because Max's wife, Jill, might discover them. Jill was blissfully alone in Miami, well aware of Max's long-term relationship with Lisa.

No, the risk was bigger now. There could be no connection—no nexus, to use the legal term—between Atlantica Airlines and her. If there were, and it became known, she'd be no use to Max, and his big plans would be blown.

If I can go through with it at all.

For a moment she wondered what Tony would have done, but that was easy. Tony Kingston was the Eagle Scout, the *Top Gun* navy pilot, a yes ma'am, no ma'am, guy who didn't jaywalk, litter, or cheat on his taxes. But Tony was gone, and now the plaintiffs' lawyers said he'd been negligent. Lying bastards! Vultures picking at the flesh of the dead. A part of her wanted to help Max tank the case just to shut them up, but she realized that was irrational, and hadn't she spent all these years locking her brain into a lawyer's sense of logic and reason?

After dinner, she told Max she didn't think she could do it, and they argued until 2 A.M.

"An ethical problem?" Max asked incredulously as he paced around her small living room. "Three years of planning, and now you have an *eth-i-cal prob-lem.*" He dragged out the words, as if trying a strange new phrase in Tagalog or Punjabi.

"Yes, Max, I realize that's a foreign concept to you."

He stopped pacing long enough to absorb the insult, then ignored it. "Are you worried about being disbarred?"

"It would be one of the shortest legal careers in history," she said, ruefully. "I could go to jail, too."

"So that's it! You *are* afraid." He laughed, the told-you-so, condescending chuckle he used when the joke was on someone else. "I remember a time when you could walk, buck naked, into a party of drunken investment bankers and show no fear. You could control every man in the place with your wits and your poise, and now you're afraid of what, being subpoenaed by some two-bit G-twelve assistant attorney general who drives a Chevy?"

Vintage Max, measuring a man by his net worth.

"If he drove a Porsche," she said, "would he be more worthy of respect?"

Max glared at her, a black-eyed scowl that could terrorize a corporate VP or send a secretary home in tears. In the old days, Lisa was intimidated by him, too. Not anymore.

"What are you going to do, Max, fire me? Too late. I've got tenure. I know where the skeletons are buried."

"Not all of them," he said with a coldness that sent a shiver up her spine.

They stood looking at each other, Max Wanaker and Lisa Fremont, former lovers and current coconspirators. He was frowning, his gray mustache turning downward. He was handsome and dark-complexioned with salt-and-pepper hair swept back and moussed. A jogger and tennis player in his younger days, Max was starting to put on a little weight around the middle. Too many business dinners, too much booze.

She remembered the way he looked when they first met, ten years ago. Why did it seem like another lifetime? He had been thirty-nine, and she was seventeen.

Jesus, it was another lifetime.

She knew how much she had changed. But what was different about Max? Not just his graying hair. In those days—before Atlantica—he was on his way up. Big dreams, boundless energy and optimism. He'd scratched and clawed until the dreams came true. So why was he so unhappy now? There was the crash of Flight 640 three years ago and the lawsuit, of course, but she knew there was more, and lately, Max wasn't talking.

She poured him another Scotch, hoping to mellow him out. "I went to the Court today, just to look around. Jesus, Max, you walk through these giant bronze doors with scenes of ancient Greece and Rome molded into them. Then there are marble statues and busts everywhere. Lady Justice, Moses, Confucius …"

"Confucius?" he said, puzzled.

"I went into the library. All hand-carved wood, giant arches, a quiet, peaceful place. It's almost holy, like a church or a cathedral."

"Exactly!" he agreed, smiling now. "That's what they want you to think. Like all those churches you hauled me to in Italy. Why do you think they built them like that? For the glory of God. Hell, no! They did it to scare the shit out of the peasants. You walk into a church, what's the first thing you do? You lower your voice, you whisper. Same thing in your fancy Court, right? The judges are the priests— they even dress like priests— and everyone else is a peasant. They want to scare you into thinking you're on hallowed ground, that they're doing sacred work. Hypocrites! They don't want you to know what they're doing under the robes."

Lisa walked to the window, looking past her balcony into Dumbarton Oaks Park and the creek beyond. Max had chosen the apartment, but unlike the old days, he wasn't paying for it. At least not on the books. Two years ago, when she was still in law school, he began erasing the paper trail—the canceled checks, airline passes, credit card receipts—that would link her to him. It was his idea that maybe one day she'd be able to help him in a way no one could know about. It sounded crazy at first, just as crazy as taking a money-losing air-freight forwarder with three aging jet props and turning it into Atlantica Airlines, poster child of deregulation and booming international air carrier ... until the disastrous crash of Flight 640.

"You're very persuasive, Max," she said, at last. "You should have been a lawyer."

Max laughed. "No way, baby! That's why I spent a hundred grand on you."

"I don't think I'll get the job," she said, softly. "I think Justice Truitt will look at me and see I don't belong there."

Or is that what I want? The easy way out, sparing me the hassle of refusing to do Max's dirty work.

"That's where you're wrong. You belong anywhere you want to be. You're the most powerful woman I've ever known."

"I learned from you," she said.

"No! You had the power as a seventeen-year-old but didn't know it. All I did was mark the trail for you. You climbed it all by yourself." He studied her for a moment, and she averted her eyes, her shyness a childhood trait. He smiled. "Anyway, don't worry. The judge will take one look at you and want to adopt you."

"Max, he's your age."

"Even better ... he'll want to screw you." He laughed again, his mood softening, maybe pleased she was confiding her fears. She so seldom showed any insecurity.

"Stop worrying," he said. "You're going to get the job. You're going to be the sexiest smartest law clerk in the history of the Supreme Court."

"Maybe," she said.

"You're being interviewed by a man, and deep inside, we're all alike."

No, Max, you're not. You and Tony were not alike. And I doubt you and Sam Truitt share much in common despite the same configuration of x and y chromosomes.

She'd never told Max that she'd become Tony Kingston's lover after their breakup her first year in law school. As far as Max knew, Tony was just the navy pilot she'd introduced him to, the hometown hero she said would be a great addition to the Atlantica fleet. Well, she was right, wasn't she?

"It's different on the Supreme Court," Lisa said. "You know what they taught us first year in law school?"

"Probably how to overcharge your clients."

"*Jus est ars boni et aequi.* Law is the art of the good and the just."

"And the meek shall inherit the earth," Max responded in the sarcastic tone she knew so well. He walked to the window and wrapped his arms around her from behind. "If the law worked so damn well, O.J. would have sucked gas, Klaus von Bulow would have been stuck full of needles, and"—he paused a moment, as if not sure whether to continue—"and your father would have been hung by his testicles."

She turned around in his arms to face him. "And the victims of Flight six-forty would have hit Atlantica for several hundred million in verdicts," she added.

"Sort of proves my point, doesn't it?"

It did, but his cynicism irritated her. If Max were right, then why had she just spent three years studying law and another year clerking for a federal judge? Just to be another manipulator of the system? But even if he were wrong, how could she turn him down? Max had never denied her anything. He had supported her, nurtured her, helped her grow into an adult. In return, she had been his lover for most of the past decade. He'd been understanding when she left him during law school and comforting when she'd come back after Tony's death. And now, for the first time, he wanted something more, something that collided head-on with everything she had learned the past four years.

"If justice is such a rare commodity," she said, "maybe I should work for it. Maybe I should help put criminals in jail or defend the wrongfully accused."

"You're too smart for that. That's sucker talk. I don't see you in the Justice Department or in some public defender's office with a metal desk and stale coffee."

"I remember the first time you told me how smart I was," she said. "It was endearing then. Now, it sounds like an insult."

"There's smart," he said, "like book learning, which can open some doors but otherwise doesn't mean shit, and then there's street-smart, which you can't buy with a degree. You got both, which knocks my socks off."

No one had ever expressed admiration for her intelligence before Max came along. Not her teachers, not her mother, not her father. Especially not her father, whose praise was limited to her physical assets.

Max had told her she could be anything she wanted, and she believed him. He gave her confidence and a chance at a new life. Now that she had that life, she didn't want to risk losing it.

"Do you remember when you told me I was smarter than you?" she asked.

"Sure. It was the night we met."

ↄ

Max Wanaker walked into the Tiki Club and sat down on a bar stool in front of the stage. It had a rusty brass go-go pole, chains hanging from the ceiling, a scratchy sound system, and a number of missing bulbs in the multicolored lighting system. In the back was a darkened lap-dancing lounge with black satin couches. The place smelled like a mixture of stale beer and cheap perfume, moist mildew and industrial strength cleaner.

A connoisseur of strip joints, Max preferred the sophisticated atmosphere of Ten's in Manhattan, where fifty-five exotic dancers stroll onto the stage in full-length sequined gowns, strobe lights blasting, smoke machine billowing. Tonight, he was slumming. Mainly because he had been bored, he told the limo driver to stop when he saw the flashing neon sign, LIVE GIRLS.

As opposed to what? DEAD GIRLS?

The sign, as effective as the Sirens' songs that lured sailors onto the rocks, brought Max into the club. Now he approached the small stage, scanning the room. The strippers all looked as if they'd been ridden hard—the meaty redhead slouching on stage, out of step with Aerosmith, already down to her ratty gold panties, oversize tits barely bouncing; the two in lingerie at the bar, cadging drinks—all of them with big hair, six-inch nails, and siliconed melon breasts. He had one watery Scotch and was ready to leave when Lisa came on the stage to the music of Billy Joel.

Jesus, she's just a kid.

She looked like a cheerleader. Small breasts, sleek reddish blonde hair, clear blue eyes, long legs, a full mouth, little makeup other than painted-on whiskers, something he didn't get until he realized she was wearing a tight leopard skin dress with little leopard ears. She seemed embarrassed, and he was enchanted.

She could dance. She moved smoothly to the music, closing her eyes, which he knew was a no-no. It occurred to Max that he knew more about her business than she did.

You're supposed to make eye contact, baby. You're supposed to make every guy in the joint feel like you've got the hots just for him.

She was so young and so obviously new at this that Max felt a stirring. Not just to bag her. Hell, he'd bedded down half his company's secretaries, more than a few strippers, plus his daughter's fourth-grade teacher. This one was different. She looked like she didn't belong here.

What's a nice girl like you …

The old male rescue fantasy took hold even before he talked to her. What he could do for her!

And vice versa.

The leopard dress was off now, and she was holding on to the brass pole, each leg astride it, grinding her hips in time with the music, humping that lucky pole, her firm ass moving rhythmically in time with his pulse. Her eyes wide open now, she looked at Max and seemed to blush.

Now there's a first.

Then she smiled shyly at him, swung away from the pole, and drifted up to the edge of the stage. He slipped a twenty-dollar bill into her garter where it joined a number of singles. The garter was all she wore, other than the high-heeled shoes. Her strawberry nipples were erect, her mouth set in an innocent, yet seductive smile. She never said a word. She just turned around and bent over, putting her hands on her knees and arching her back. She wiggled her ass clockwise, as if on coasters, stopped and wiggled counterclockwise. With impressive muscle control, her buttocks quivered in time with the music, and he felt the contractions in his own loins.

Later, when her set was done, back in her slinky leopard dress and little leopard ears, Lisa wobbled up to him on six-inch heels and inquired with her whiskered smile and cat eyes if he'd like to buy her a drink.

"What's your name?" he had asked, "Jellylorum or Mistoffelees?" for he had just taken his wife to see the musical *Cats* in London.

"Rumpleteazer," she said without missing a beat.

"You've seen the show," he said, surprised.

"No way! My boyfriend thinks live theater is watching three lesbians in leather and chains."

"Then how—"

"When I was a kid, I read the Eliot poems. *Old Possum's Book of Practical Cats.*"

"When you were a kid," he repeated, smiling.

"Yeah. I thought the poems were silly. I think Eliot should have stuck to 'The Waste Land.'"

"Really? You read a lot?"

"I'm taking classes. That's all I do. Study by day, strip by night."

He watched her size him up, noting the manicured, polished nails, the gold cuff links, the dark suit. She wasn't even subtle about it just taking inventory, probably calculating her tip by the pedigree of his watch. Cocking her head the way the older girls must have shown her, she said, "So you want a private dance or what?"

He laughed. "You really are a rumpleteazer, aren't you?"

"I'm not J. Alfred Prufrock."

"What's your name? You never told me."

"Angel," she lied.

"Nah. I'm your *angel*."

And he was. Max Wanaker, who at that time owned a Miami freight forwarding company and had just beaten back a Teamsters strike, rescued Lisa Fremont teenage runaway. He spirited her out of the Tenderloin and put her in an apartment on Nob Hill. It was there—where little cable cars climb halfway to the stars—that Max made an amazing discovery. Lisa wasn't like the others, which is to say, she wasn't after money. This brainy stripper read Dostoevsky in the dressing room between sets, picked up her high school degree in night school, and was about to enroll in community college when Max bulldozed his way into her life and suggested Berkeley instead.

"You're smarter than I am," he told her that first night. And then repeated it time and again until she believed it was true.

⁊

Lisa poured Max another stiff shot of Glenmorangie, the pricey single-malt Scotch he ordered by the case. He twirled the golden liquid in the glass, sniffed it took a sip. The ritual done, he turned to her. "So what's the bottom line? Are we on the same page here?"

Speaking in corporate jargon when it's my life!

"I can't do it, Max. I can't prostitute myself."

Max's face reddened. He stared at her in disbelief. "What!"

"I would do anything for you, but not this."

"*This* is the only thing I've ever asked."

"I'm sorry. I want to help, but …"

Max had been wonderful. If it weren't for him, where would she be now? But what he had given her—the education, the belief in herself—

had changed her. She didn't know precisely when she had rejected Max's way of life, but somewhere between the Tiki Club and the Supreme Court, she had moved on. "You're asking too much, Max."

"After all I've done for you," Max said, his voice a razor despite the mellow whiskey, "don't you think you owe me this?"

He'd never said that before, not even close. Anger boiled up inside her. Her look was lethal, her voice icy. "Why not just total up my bill, and I'll pay you back with interest. What's the prime rate these days, Max?"

"It's not the money and you know it. I just resent this attitude of yours, like you're looking down at me."

Lisa padded barefoot to the bar and dumped her drink into the sink. "From the curb to the gutter, Max. It's not that far."

Max looked wounded, like it was his blood going down the drain. "You stopped smoking. You're not drinking. Is there anything else you're not going to do, anything I ought to know about?"

She didn't answer, just stood there, stone-faced.

"The new, improved Lisa Fremont," he said, sarcastically.

"Don't you like me this way?"

♋

No, Max Wanaker thought. He didn't like her this way at all. Christ who had she become? Maybe it served him right. He had wanted Lisa to grow, had encouraged her independence, but look what happened. The roses still bloomed, but they'd grown thorns. He liked Lisa the *girl*, not Lisa Fremont, Esq., the *woman*, the goddamnn lawyer. She's been a tough kid. Hell, she had to be to survive. Now she gets misty-eyed looking at statues and books. How long until she learns that her precious oaths and credos are just faded ink on rotting paper?

Max struggled to control his anger and mask his desperation. He wanted to tell her just how important the case was to him. He wanted to tell her that it wasn't just about money or even the survival of the company. He wanted to tell her the truth.

If we don't win, I'm a dead man.

No, if he told her that, she would want to know everything. And if he laid it all out, what would she think of him? If he told her the crash had been his fault, that he had ordered the maintenance records falsified, that he had perjured himself before the NTSB, that blood was on his hands, would she help him? Maybe, if he told her the spot he was in.

Oh, he could rationalize it. Every airline cuts corners. It didn't take Mary Schiavo, the big-mouth blonde from the Department of Transportation, to tell him that airlines would rather have their insurers pay off wrongful death verdicts than spend the money to fix known dangers. Simple cost-benefit economics, babe.

He just never thought it would happen to him, to his airline. And he never expected the guilt, the nightmares, the pills, the late-night sweats.

No, he could never tell Lisa the truth. He tried a different approach. "Why do you think we've been together so long?"

"Inertia, Max. We're used to each other."

"No. Because deep down inside, we're alike," he said.

"If that's supposed to be a compliment—"

"We both see things the way they really are. We take the cards we're dealt, and if it means sliding an extra ace up the sleeve to get what we want, then damn it, we do it. We don't play by somebody else's rules."

"That's not the way I see myself," she said, sounding defensive, a measure of doubt creeping into her voice.

"A leopard can't change her spots," he said with a smirk.

"I didn't cheat in college or law school," she said angrily. "I worked like hell in the appellate clerkship. I'm proud of my accomplishments. I'm proud of who I am."

"Dean's list doesn't mean shit in the real world, Lisa. You got good grades? So what? I got MBAs from Harvard making my coffee. Sometimes I wonder where you get off. I mean, Christ, I remember where you came from. I remember the bartender. I remember the bruises."

⁂

She remembered, too. Crockett was the day-shift bouncer and occasional bartender, a ponytailed bodybuilder with a hot temper and delusions that he was the next Arnold Schwarzenegger. She'd moved in with him a week after the one-way journey south from Bodega Bay, and he'd gotten her the phony ID and the job at the Tiki Club. She gave Crockett her tips, but they were never enough to pay for his hash and steroids.

"Some guys I know are having a party tonight," he told her one day as she was leaving for the club.

"What guys?" she asked.

"Businessmen from out of town. They got a room at the Ramada by the airport."

"So you want to go?"

"Not me! Ain't my ass they wanna see."

"I don't do private parties. Sheila told me—"

"Sheila don't know shit. Who'd pay to see her saggy tits? This is four hundred plus tips."

Lisa was shaking her head when he grabbed her, his huge hands digging into the flesh of her upper arms. She tried to twist away, but he held on, pressing harder, slamming her into the wall but never letting go, using his size and strength just as her father had done to imprison her and break her will.

"I put a roof over your head," Crockett said. "I get you a job. I protect your ass from guys who'd slice you up and eat you for breakfast. You owe me!"

Thinking back now, here it was again.

Max, Crockett, dear old Dad. How many men do I owe?

She went to the motel that night, carrying a boom box, getting paid up front, then stripping for three drunken salesmen, all the time palming a miniature can of Mace, a trick Sheila had taught her. One of the scumbags, a paunchy forty-five-year-old wearing a wedding band, lunged for her. She sidestepped him, and when the other two tried to tackle her, she sprayed one squarely in his open, dumb mouth and kneed the other in the groin, a direct shot that sent him tumbling to the floor, vomiting.

The first man took a wild swing at her and missed. Lisa turned to run for the door, but he tripped her, then dragged her to the floor, clawing at her thong, drawing blood from her hip with his fingernails. He was about her father's age, and those memories, so fresh then, came racing back, filling her with fear. She had vowed it would never happen again.

I'd kill a man before I'd let him ...

She was on her back with the man above her when she worked an arm free and hit him with a blast of the Mace. He howled and toppled backward, his hands tearing at his eyes. Lisa scrambled to her feet, picked up a table lamp, and bashed it across his forehead, quieting him. Adrenaline pumping, she made it out of the motel room with her backpack and money but left the boom box behind.

"Dumb bitch!" Crockett yelled when she got home, backhanding her across the face, cursing her a second time when he counted the money, discovering the roll of bills was really a single twenty on top with nineteen two-dollar bills underneath. "Stupid jailbait bitch!"

Three nights later, Max Wanaker rode up to the Tiki on his white horse or was it a white limo? Whatever his flaws, Lisa now knew he had rescued her. She had been one step away from the streets. Cocktail waitress, stripper ... hooker was not far behind. Max seemed to know everything in those days. He saw right through the Dermablend makeup she used to cover the bruises.

"Who did this to you?" he had asked.

"My boyfriend, but he didn't mean to hurt me."

"Where can I find him?" Max asked.

Even now, she could remember his voice. Grim and determined.

Where can I find him?

It would be that simple. No further explanation needed. She knew Max wouldn't do it himself. The soft hands and manicured nails did not belong to a thug. But he knew people, had dealt with the Teamsters. In Max's world, everything could be arranged. She saw the bartender only once more. He was trying to get up Russian Hill on crutches.

Yes, Max, I owe you, but maybe that makes me resent you even more.

"Sometimes you really piss me off," she said.

"I'm sorry," he said, backing off, sounding sincere. "You know how I feel about you ..."

How? Say it!

How many times had he said the three magic words? Twice, she recalled, once after too much champagne and once when he thought he'd lost her.

In fact, you did lose me, Max. I was tired of sneaking in and out of hotels.

She had just started law school and felt like she was getting somewhere. So why was she stuck in this nowhere relationship? She wanted her independence, and Max was surprisingly understanding. He gave her time and space. He was secure enough to let her go, telling her he hoped she would return.

It was the best time of her life. She found Tony Kingston, or rather, he had found her. Discovered the babysitter had grown up. Lisa had taken care of Greg, Tony's son, since she was twelve, helping around the house, admiring the photos of the handsome naval aviator in his spiffy flight suit. Tony had never been married, and when the child's mother— Tony's teenage girlfriend—took off, he was left with a son to raise. Lisa remembered her adolescent excitement when Tony came home on leave, duffel bag slung over a shoulder.

So strong and decent, so unlike my own father.

She had learned enough psychology to know Tony was the father she had never had. But he was so much more, too. Tony didn't rescue her as

Max had done; he treated her as an equal, something Max never did. Tony was everything. And then, suddenly, he was gone.

Just as Max had hoped, she came back. He told her she had changed, that he liked the old Lisa better. The old Lisa is dead, she said. He didn't ask who she had been with, and she never told. The past and the future both remained unspoken.

Now, pacing in the apartment overlooking the park, he said, "I'd leave Jill for you in a second if you'd ask me to ..."

She let the bait dangle. Ten years ago, she prayed to hear those words. Now, they left her confused and troubled.

"God, Lisa, I love you. I always have."

Whoa! What did he say? And why now?

"Do you love me, Max, or do you just need me more?"

"When the case is over, I'm going to ask Jill for a divorce and we can get married."

"Max, please ..."

"Okay, I won't pressure you. But you're right about one thing. I need your help. I wouldn't ask if I didn't. Hell, I'm begging you. This is even more important than you know."

"Tell me."

"I can't. Not now."

She thought about it. Hard as it was for Max to say it, he did love her. She never doubted it. And he had helped her when no one else cared whether she slept under a bridge or went hungry. Now he was asking her to choose between him and some flowery notions of right and wrong.

No one would ever know. It was just one case.

But what about her beliefs? What about the new, improved Lisa Fremont, to use Max's mocking phrase? Could she put her new ideals on the shelf just this once? And how deeply did she believe them anyway?

The marble statues and bronze doors notwithstanding, justice was an ethereal concept, a divine ideal, which like sainthood was rarely seen on earth. Justice was the pearl in the oyster. Keep on shuckin' and good luck huntin'. Despite the lofty notions she'd learned from the law books, her views were shaped by her own experiences. Weren't everyone's? What was it Justice Cardozo had said? "Try as we might, we can never see with any eyes except our own."

And what my eyes have seen.

Now, after four years at Berkeley, summa cum laude—thank you very much—three years at Stanford Law, magna cum laude with a prize-winning law review note, and one year clerking for a federal court of appeals judge in the D.C. Circuit, she had all the credentials. So why did she consider herself a fraud?

She wanted to believe, but damnit, Max had pressed the right buttons. She was a priest without faith, a pagan inside the holy tabernacle. To Lisa Fremont, the law was not majestic. The slogan carved into the pediment— equal justice under law—was a benediction for the Kodak-toting tourists. The law was as cold as the marble of its sanctuary.

Disregarding the lofty symbols and images, she thought of the legal system as a dingy factory with leaking boilers, broken sprockets, and rusted cogs. The law was bought and sold, swapped and hocked, bartered and auctioned, just like wheat, widgets ... and girls who run away from home.

In the upcoming term, she knew the Court would be asked to consider nearly seven thousand cases but would issue fewer than one hundred rulings. Law clerks, whose first function was to summarize and analyze the petitions seeking review, frequently complained about the workload. No problem, Lisa thought.

If I get the job, I'll read them all. I'll plow through the research, draft the justice's opinions, and make his coffee, if that's what he wants me to do.

She'd know the legislative history of the statutes and the precedential value of the cases. She'd master the procedure and the substantive law. She'd write pithy footnotes and trace the source of a law back to Hammurabi. She'd prepare incisive pool memos for the judicial conferences and brilliant bench memos for her boss. She'd stay up all night with the death clerk on execution stays, and she'd be at work at 8 A.M. sharp.

She'd be prepared to search for the truth, to do justice.

She'd do all of those things in every case ... except one.

The case of *Laubach v. Atlantica Airlines, Inc.* would be different. She already had read the file. She knew the issues and the arguments on both sides. Even more important, she knew who had to win.

ဢ

"I'll do it, Max. I'll do it for you."

"Great! I knew you wouldn't let me down." The tension drained from him, and he smiled triumphantly. "We make a great team, Lisa. When your clerkship's up, you should come into the airline's legal department. Pete Flaherty's going to retire in a couple of years. How would you like to be general counsel?"

"Max, please stop planning my life. Let's just get through this."

"Whatever you say, darling."

His smile was still in place. He had done it. And he hadn't even used his trump card: the truth. If Lisa knew that his life was tethered to such a slender thread, she would have rushed to help him. But this way was better.

She's doing it for love, not pity.

Max felt invigorated. Oh, there was much more to be done. She had to get the job, and she had to convince her judge—the swing vote, according to Flaherty—to go their way. But he had great confidence in Lisa. He would trust her with anything, a thought that made him smile, for he was doing just that. He was trusting her with his life.

☙

Late that night, lying in bed, staring at the liquid numbers of the digital clock melting into the enveloping darkness, as she listened to Max snoring alongside her, Lisa confronted the stark, bleak truth. Yes, she would do what Max had asked. Not because she loved him, for at this point, she didn't know what she felt. Not because she owed him, because that was never part of the bargain.

She would do it because her loyalty to Max outweighed her newfound principles. Max had been right all along.

She didn't believe in the words carved into stone.

Her soul was as barren as his, her heart as icy.

Deep inside, she was just like him.

======

NTSB FAILS TO FIND CAUSE OF CRASH

WASHINGTON D.C.—(AP) The National Transportation Safety Board announced yesterday that it could not conclusively determine the cause of the crash of Atlantica Airlines Flight 640, which claimed the lives of 288 persons in a fiery crash in the Florida Everglades in December 1995.

Citing contradictory evidence and the failure to recover all the essential parts, the NTSB said in a lengthy report that it could not state with certainty what caused the aircraft to lose its hydraulic systems on approach to Miami International Airport. However, Board Chairman Miles McGrane pointedly stated that there was "substantial evidence" to support the widely held belief that a bomb was detonated inside the tail-mounted engine of the DC-10, causing engine fragments to sever the hydraulic lines.

"Traces of PETN were recovered from the nacelle of the number two engine, but many of the engine parts, including the stage one rotor fan disk, were not found," McGrane said. "Presumably, they are buried in the muck of the Everglades and will never be recovered. Without these parts, we cannot perform the metallurgical tests needed to reach a definitive conclusion."

PETN, or pentaerythritol tetranitrate, is a component of plastic explosives. McGrane added that there was no evidence of pilot error or mechanical failure, other than loss of flight controls, which followed the apparent explosion in the number two engine.

Pressed by reporters, McGrane expressed frustration with the months of delays and endless speculation about the cause of the crash. On the day of the accident, armed U.S. Navy jets were conducting flights from the Key West Naval Air Station. He discounted the theory that a ground-to-air missile or an errant heat-seeking missile from a military jet downed the aircraft. None of the jets reported firing a missile.

Two weeks prior to the crash, a Cuban exile group in Miami threatened violent reprisals against Atlantica Airlines which, through a foreign subsidiary, had begun charter flights from Mexico City to Havana. Two members of the group, La Brigada de la Libertad, were arrested for allegedly spray painting anti-Castro slogans on the fuselage of an Atlantica aircraft after climbing a fence to gain access to a hangar at the Miami airport. The group vigorously denies all responsibility for the crash of the New York-to-Miami flight.

=======

CHAPTER 2

The Junior Justice

OLIVER WENDELL HOLMES JR. SAT HERE. Oh, not in this chair. Not even in this building, if we're being tediously literal about it, Sam Truitt thought.

But Holmes sat *here*, at the far end of the bench, to the Chief Justice's left, when he was the junior justice on the Supreme Court of the United States.

So what the hell am I doing in old Ollie's chair?

Which was also, at various times, figuratively at least, the chair of Brandeis, Cardozo, Black, Frankfurter, and Brennan. Giants of jurisprudence whose thundering pronouncements were engraved in stone for the ages. Men of soaring intellect and towering integrity.

How will I even begin to measure up?

It was a rare moment of insecurity for Sam Truitt, who frequently was described as egotistical and vain, even by his friends. His enemies called him a left-wing, Ivy League intellectual snob who was out of touch with the real world. But friends and enemies alike agreed that he was brilliant and eloquent. His opponents feared that eventually, with a long enough tenure, he would be worth two or three votes on the Court, using his superior intellect and persuasive skills to sway others.

At the moment, though, Truitt wasn't capable of persuading cats to chase mice. Deep in a crisis of confidence, drowning in waves of self-doubt, he was an imposter, a graffiti artist in the Louvre, a trespasser in a shrine.

Though he was a broad-shouldered man, over six feet and two hundred pounds, a former athlete still fit at forty-six, at the moment, he felt he was a dwarf in the imposing, marble-columned courtroom.

Sam Truitt still had not recovered from the confirmation process. Looking back now, the stinging vitriol of the personal attacks had caught him by surprise. On CNN and before the Senate Judiciary Committee, the Republicans hauled out their hatchet men, and the sound bites dug deep wounds. He remembered his discomfort at being grilled by Senator Thornton Blair of South Carolina, mouthpiece for the right-wing Family Values Foundation.

"So if ah git this right, Per-fessor Truitt," Blair droned, waving a fistful of Truitt's *Harvard Law Review* articles on civil liberties, "you'd hire gay teachers but ban the bible in our schools. You'd give away condoms to our innocent children and take away guns from our law-abiding citizens. You'd have federal marshals protect baby-killing abortionists but leave the public defenseless against rapists and murderers. Does that about sum it up, Per-fessor?"

"That's a fallacious representation of my views," Truitt said, sweating under the lights, sounding uptight and uncool, even to himself.

"Fal-la-cious, is it?" the senator asked rhetorically, making the word sound obscene. "When's the last time you attended church, Per-fessor?"

"I don't see the relevance of that," Truitt said, backpedaling, trying to keep his feet on a rolling log in a treacherous river.

"Didn't think you would," Blair said, turning to the committee chairman. "With lawyers as thick as fleas on an old hound, you'd think the President could find one that reads the Good Book on Sunday mornings."

The hate mail delivered to his Cambridge office had shocked Truitt. Protesters spewed invectives and picketed in Harvard Square, calling him a card-carrying ACLU leftist and a pornography worshiper who cared more about spotted owls and snail darters than jobs and families.

Despite the uproar, the Senate had confirmed him, and if the 53-47 vote was not exactly a resounding vote of confidence, it should no longer matter. He was appointed for life, or more precisely, in the words of the Constitution, during "good Behaviour."

With a capital B.

Sam Truitt intended to lead an exemplary life on the Court. He would do nothing to attract the attention of the Family Values Foundation, which had begun a "Truitt Watch," promising an impeachment petition at his first lapse. He had a single blemish in his past "Behaviour," one that attracted the attention of the FBI when he was on the President's short list for the nomination. Ten years earlier, a law student named Tracey had filed a sexual harassment claim against him after he slept with her, but nonetheless gave her a C in constitutional law. He had remained true to his academic virtue—if not his marital vows—but Tracey believed he had not held up his end of the unstated bargain.

In truth, she had seduced him, but still, he had violated university rules. Stupid.

With a capital S.

In case he didn't know just how stupid, his wife, Connie, had fixed him with that icy, New England smile and said, "Next time you screw a student, Sam, spare me the humiliation and give her an A."

Before the misconduct claim could be heard, Tracey dropped out of law school, sparing him an ethical dilemma. Would he have told the truth?

Sure I screwed her, but she wanted it.

Oh, brilliant. Just brilliant. Want some more, Dean? The *Veritas*, the whole *Veritas*, and nothing but the *Veritas*.

While I was grading her paper on the legality of strip searches at border patrol stations, she came into my office and pulled up her skirt. "Want to pat me down, Officer?" She was young and willing and hot, and God help me, I'm just a man.

With a small m.

Or would he have lied?

I never touched her. She is obviously a deeply troubled young woman with an overactive imagination.

That would have violated his principles, but thankfully, he never had to confront the question. Ironic, he thought, how his personal life did not live up to his professional standards.

Now, he had taken a vow of monogamy, which in his marriage was akin to a vow of chastity. When he told this to Connie, she laughed and said, "Don't forget poverty. You've taken that vow, too, and dragged me with you."

Poverty to Connie meaning the inability to afford a summer home in the Hamptons.

But he was serious about living a blameless life. No scandals in or out of Court. No ammunition for the Foundation's muskets. He wanted a long, productive career, writing cogent opinions that would live forever in our jurisprudence. He wanted to join the thirty-year club with Marshall, Story, Holmes, Black, Douglas, and Brennan.

I'll drive my enemies crazy and then out-live them.

But that morning Truitt was worried about getting through his first day, not his first decade on the Court. He felt as if he had sneaked into the ornate building. Just after dawn, he'd come up the steps and paused before the giant six-ton bronze doors. Even earlier, he'd sat on a bench on the oval plaza, the Capitol glowing behind him in the rosy early morning light. At the base of the flagpoles, he'd noted the scales of justice, the sword and book, the mask and torch, the pen and mace. He'd gazed up at the two marble figures flanking the steps, seated as if on thrones, Justice on one side, Authority on the other. Above him, sixteen huge marble columns supported a towering pediment with a sculpture of an enthroned Liberty guarded by other symbolic figures. Atop it all was engraved the lofty phrase, EQUAL JUSTICE UNDER LAW.

In a place where the figures were carved from marble, he had feet of clay.

It was a building to be entered triumphantly on the back of an elephant, following a cavalcade of golden trumpets and shimmering banners. Instead, he felt like a thief in the night.

And now, Samuel Adams Truitt—at least the name sounded like he belonged here—sat in Holmes' chair at the wing-shaped bench of gleaming Honduran mahogany, looking toward the heavens, or at least toward the four-story-high coffered ceiling, when he heard the voice of God.

"Justice Truitt!" the voice boomed.

Chief Justice Clifford P. Whittington both sounded and looked like God, if you pictured the Creator as a sixty-seven-year-old Iowan with a barrel chest, a rugged profile that, like the statues, could be carved from marble, and long, wavy white hair swept back and curling up at the neck.

Startled, Truitt swiveled toward the front of the courtroom. "Chief," he answered.

The Chief Justice strode toward the bench. He looked vigorous enough to vault the bronze railing that separated the public section from the lawyers' gallery.

"Getting a little head start on the rest of us?" the C.J. bellowed, his deep voice resounding in the cavernous chamber. "Or just walking the field before the game?"

The game.

The sole point of common ground between the two men, Truitt thought, was that they both had played football in college. Whittington had been a lineman at Yale in the days before face masks—though some liberal academics claimed he played too long without a helmet—then went to Oxford as a Rhodes scholar. He was a Renaissance man, a throwback, a midwestern farm boy who beat the eastern intellectuals on their turf at their game. He liked to think of himself as a common-sense judge with traditional values. Truitt considered him rigid, small-minded, and mired in the past.

Truitt also knew that the chief had huddled with Senator Blair, feeding him damaging questions for the Judiciary Committee hearings. If there was one man in America that Whittington did not want on the Court, it was the glamour boy from Harvard who appeared on even more news shows than the biggest publicity slut on the Court, Whittington himself.

"It's customary for the Chief Justice to chat privately with a new member of the brethren," Whittington said, somewhat ceremoniously. By this time, Truitt was making his way down from the bench. It didn't seem proper to have the Chief looking up at him.

"Can we still call ourselves brethren when we have two women on the bench?" Truitt asked with a smile.

"I don't know," the Chief replied with a malicious grin. "I hear you're the expert on sexual harassment, Professor."

Touché.

"I just figured you were doing some field research," the Chief continued, eyes twinkling.

"Actually, I've written extensively about sex discrimination," Truitt said.

"So you have. I read your piece on the male-only military college case. You didn't much care for my dissent."

"I just thought it was too late in the day to allow a public college to bar women. The states can no longer discriminate based on gender, race, or sexual preference."

"'No longer'? I rather like that term. It implies that the Court has changed, which it damn well has. But the Constitution hasn't changed, except for those twenty-seven amendments. So, how do you explain it Sam? How did we get so far from the framers' original intent?"

"We haven't. They simply weren't faced with these questions in the context of the current era. If Madison or Jefferson were alive today, I doubt they'd disagree with giving women the right to vote which took an amendment to their Constitution. I wrote a piece called, 'Whose Original Intent?' in which—"

"Read that one, too, and didn't agree with a damn thing. As for your forays into legal realism, inviting judges to ignore precedent and use the social sciences to shape our lives, well it's just plain dangerous. Then there's your essay on legal pragmatism. There are no grand foundational principles, eh Sam?" The Chief raised his bushy eyebrows. "Being a legal pragmatist means never having to say you have a theory."

"That's a bit of an oversimplification."

The older man beamed a photogenic, white-toothed grin. He was still tan from a summer at Martha's Vineyard, where he enjoyed tweaking the noses of Boston's liberal establishment at clambakes and cocktail parties. Truitt looked directly into the Chief Justice's eyes. The two men were the same height, six two, though the Chief probably weighed twenty-five pounds more than Truitt.

"You probably think I'm a troglodyte," the Chief said.

"I think you like getting a rise out of people, particularly the junior-most justice."

"Well, you're not wrong about that, but I mean what I say. You know what makes me a good judge, Sam ... hell, a great judge?"

"Modesty?" Truitt ventured.

Whittington laughed. It was a big man's laugh, water tumbling over a falls. "Because I don't have an agenda. I don't give a rat's ass if a woman has an abortion. But I object to this Court finding a constitutional right of privacy when the sacred document doesn't mention the word."

"Needless to say, I—"

"Save your breath, Sam. I know your position."

Truitt wondered what the judicial conference would be like, the Chief's thunderous voice shouting down all dissent. He was reminded of Samuel Goldwyn's famous line to a young screenwriter: "When I want your opinion, I'll give it to you."

"I'll tell you something else," the Chief rumbled. "*Miranda* is a disgrace. Hell, now the cops have to urge a defendant *not* to confess. I'd overrule the so-called exclusionary rule, too. If the constable blunders, why should the criminal go free?"

"I suppose you'd like to do away with the Fifth Amendment privilege against self-incrimination."

"Not entirely," Whittington said, without a trace of irony. "But what's the trial judge required to do when a defendant doesn't take the stand?"

The old buzzard's treating me like a first-year law student.

"The judge instructs the jurors that they're not permitted to draw an adverse inference from the defendant's failure to testify," Truitt said, straining to keep the annoyance out of his voice.

"Doesn't that just fly in the face of common sense? Why shouldn't the jury consider just why the little weasel didn't even try to contradict the evidence against him?"

"Because this Court held that such an instruction compelled the defendant to be a witness against himself."

"A ridiculous decision!" Whittington roared. "I'd overrule it if I had the votes."

A door opened, and a marshal in a blue blazer—perhaps attracted by the noise, most of which came from the Chief—stuck his head inside, saw the two men, and ducked out again.

The Chief lowered his voice and moved closer to Truitt, as if ready to share a great secret. "Sam, you know the tobacco case on the docket?"

"I haven't read the briefs yet, but I know Blue Cross claims the cigarette companies manipulated nicotine levels to keep smokers addicted."

"That's the one. Just part of the modern-day trend to blame big business for our personal weaknesses. If people want to smoke, should the law stop them?"

"But that's not the issue, Chief. Blue Cross wants reimbursement for medical payments based on—"

"Paint it with any brush you want, but it's just another example of using the Courts to change social policy. You're not inclined to favor the plaintiff, are you, Sam?"

The question jolted him. "I'm not inclined either way until I read the briefs and listen to oral argument."

The Chief coughed out a *harrumph*. "Don't get so damned self-righteous. We're all *inclined* one way or another and on rare occasions can be persuaded to go against our predispositions. I was just hoping to count on you on this one."

So this is how it's done. Horse trading like congressmen in the cloakroom. So much for the holiness of the temple.

"You're not lobbying for my vote, are you, Chief?"

"I'm just trying to see where you stand, but I'm getting the feeling that you and I are going to disagree on damn near everything," Whittington said. "I can tell from your writings that you're plaintiff oriented."

"Only when the law and the facts are on their side," Truitt said.

"The law is whatever the hell we say it is," the Chief said with a crafty smile, "and the facts can be read any which way we want. Oh, hell, Sam, let's not get into a fuss yet. I just want to lay my cards on the table." The Chief paused and seemed to appraise the younger man. "I suppose you know I opposed your appointment."

Truitt chose to stay as quiet as a little weasel invoking the Fifth.

"Well, I did," the Chief said, "and you probably think it was on political grounds, but you're wrong. The Court is split into too many camps now. It's hard as hell to put together a consensus. Too many plurality opinions, too many concurring opinions on different grounds, way too many dissents."

"'Nine scorpions in a bottle' was the way Oliver Wendell Holmes described it," Truitt said.

"On this Court, we've got field mice, gnats, and maybe a horse's ass."

"Which one are you, Chief?"

Whittington's face froze for a second, but then he laughed drily, like a log crackling in a fire. "I'm the old lion, the king of the jungle. And who are you, Sam? Tell me why you're here, and don't give me any B.S. about answering your country's call. I know you hustled like a son of a bitch to get the appointment."

"I want to make my mark. Fifty or a hundred years from now, I'd like scholars to read my opinions and say, "Damnit, he was right, and he was right before anyone else'"

"Just as I thought, you want to be a star. That makes you dangerous because the quickest way to be noticed is to ignore precedent and strike out on your own."

"I respect the past, but I'm not irrevocably bound by it. Jurisprudence must recognize that the law changes with society. All the great justices, Holmes included, did just that."

The Chief looked toward the back wall, where a sculpted marble frieze depicted a winged female figure of Divine Inspiration flanked by Wisdom and Truth. "When Teddy Roosevelt finally appointed Holmes to the Court, the Great Dissenter was sixty-one, which is what, fifteen years older than you. He'd been a Civil War soldier, a lawyer, a professor, and a judge in Massachusetts who'd already written a thousand opinions. He was the foremost legal mind in the country. He'd been tempered by experience, and I assure you of this, when he taught at Harvard, he didn't prance around the stage like some"—the Chief Justice searched for a phrase—"some vaudeville comedian."

Vaudeville? This guy probably thinks Bob Hope is a bright new comic.

"John Jay was only forty-three when Washington appointed him the first Chief Justice," Truitt said.

Whittington grinned, as if he'd just filled an inside straight. "I knew John Jay. John Jay was a friend of mine. And trust me, Sam, you're no John Jay ... or Oliver Wendell Holmes, either."

"I get the point," Truitt said. "You don't like my style."

"I don't give a dog's dick about your style! All I care about is the Court. This isn't a classroom or a burlesque hall. Don't expect to hear applause or be rewarded with adulation. And don't be impatient about writing opinions. You know I give the assignments."

"Only when you're in the majority."

"When it counts, I make it my business for the majority to be with me. With all the different factions diluting the voice of the Court, we're weakened as an institution. You're way out there, and I predict a string of showy one-man dissents aimed at your Harvard Square and *New Republic* friends."

"I suppose having eight other justices is a real nuisance," Truitt said, measuring his words. "It would be a lot more efficient if you could just decide every case, maybe assign the opinions to one of your admirers."

Whittington barked out a laugh. "Well, you don't scare easy, I'll give you that." He looked around, as if someone might be watching, but the courtroom was deserted. "I like you, Sam. As a man, I like you. Hell, you and Curtis Braxton are the only judges I've got who can break walnuts in your fists or chop down a tree with a one-handed axe. Maybe someday you and I should Indian wrestle to decide a vote. Or should I say, 'Native American wrestle,' so as not to offend your sensibilities?"

"Chief, just out of curiosity, how long are you planning to bust my chops?"

"Not long, Sam. Ten or fifteen years at most. And in case you're thinking this old billy goat is going to retire before then, I'll remind you that Holmes was still on the Court at ninety-one, Bill Douglas they had to push out of here in his wheelchair. I never cared much for Douglas' seat-of-the-pants jurisprudence, but he was a tough monkey. Christ, after his stroke, he drooled on the briefs, but he was there voting at conference, irritating the hell out of his chief."

I think I'm auditioning for that part.

"Douglas used to call Warren Burger 'Dummy' behind his back," the Chief continued. "When Douglas was too ill to read the briefs, a clerk asked him how he'd be able to vote. You know what he said?"

"'I'll wait to see how the Chief votes and then vote the other way,'" Truitt said, figuring it might be a good strategy for him, too.

"You got it," Whittington said, nodding.

The conversation had wound down, and the Chief looked as if he was ready to dismiss the younger man. As he turned to leave he said, "Stop by my chambers this afternoon for the formal orientation and a glass of brandy."

"I'm still interviewing for my final law clerk," Truitt said.

"My assistant will call you," the Chief said, as if he hadn't heard. Or cared. He turned back toward the junior justice. "One other thing, Sam. I read the FBI files on you. It's all hearsay, double hearsay, and innuendo, of course, but you have a reputation as having an eye for the ladies."

An eye for the ladies. Vaudeville. Burlesque. Maybe I should crank up my Model T.

"Now, in my younger days," Whittington said, "I cut a pretty wide path through the hay field, so I understand. I don't care if you were humping one-legged midgets in Faneuil Hall, but you're on my Court now. The Court of Jay, Marshall, Taney ..."

And Whittington.

"I don't know what you're getting at Chief, but I think you're way off base."

The Chief Justice ignored him and plowed ahead. "Your father-in-law's an old friend. I don't agree with his politics, but he's a fine poker player. You never would have been appointed without him, and you sure as hell never would have been confirmed."

"Senator Parham's retired," Truitt said.

"He still has friends on both sides of the aisle. So, it seems to me, a young man like you, a man who married into a prominent family, owes something to his wife, Sam."

Truitt reddened with anger. He fought the urge to grab the Chief by the lapels and tell him to mind his own business. "Chief, I'd appreciate it if you and I could confine our conversation to Court business," he said, grimly.

"This *is* Court business! Frankfurter once said that the Court had no excuse for its existence unless it is a monastery. Now, he meant that we should be isolated from outside influences, but I think the analogy extends to personal lives, too. Do you follow me, Sam?"

Like a duck behind its mother.

"With all due respect, Chief, I think you're out of line."

"Can't I get a simple yes from you, Justice Truitt?" the Chief Justice snapped.

"Yes, sir," Truitt replied, feeling like a noncom responding to a superior officer. "I know how to comport myself, and I don't need anyone to remind me."

"Don't use that tone with me! Can't you see I'm trying to help you? You've got enemies out there, and if you screw up, they'll ship your ass back to your ivy-covered tower."

"Then I should thank you for your guidance," Truitt said, gritting his teeth, getting the message.

If I roll over for the Chief, give him my vote, he'll toss me a line, drag me out of the deep water. If I don't, he'll let sharks like Senator Blair and the Family Values Foundation devour me.

"You're welcome," Whittington said. "Good to have you aboard. You have my full support, but if you ever do anything to bring disrespect on this Court ..."

The Chief paused, his eyes aflame, his smile menacing. "I'll have your dick on the chopping block before you can zip up your fly."

======

IN THE UNITED STATES DISTRICT COURT FOR THE
SOUTHERN DISTRICT OF FLORIDA
Miami Division

Case No. 96-00148-CIV-Schenkel
GLORIA LAUBACH, individually
and as personal
representative of the
Estate of Howard J. Laubach,
deceased, et al.
Plaintiffs,
v.
ATLANTICA AIRLINES, INC.,
a Delaware corporation,
Defendant.
_____/

ORDER GRANTING DEFENDANT'S MOTION
FOR SUMMARY JUDGMENT

Defendant Atlantica Airlines, Inc. ("Atlantica") has moved for
summary judgment on two grounds as to the wrongful death claims
asserted against it by Plaintiffs in these consolidated actions.

Procedural Background

This action arises from the devastating crash of Atlantica Flight 640 in
the Florida Everglades in December 1995. Howard J. Laubach was one of
the 288 persons on that flight, all of whom died. In January 1996, Mrs.
Laubach, acting as personal representative of her husband's estate, filed
this action in the Eleventh Judicial Circuit Court in and for Dade County,
Florida. Atlantica timely removed the action to this Court pursuant to
28 U.S.C. 1332 and 1337. Numerous other lawsuits involving the same

incident were transferred to this District and consolidated with the instant action in accordance with the multi-district provisions of 28 U.S.O. 1407.

Laubach's widow and personal representative filed this action pursuant to the Florida Wrongful Death Act, sections 768.16-27 of the Florida Statutes. She contends that Atlantica was negligent in several respects, including failing to furnish an airworthy craft, to navigate and operate the plane properly, to train its crew properly, to inspect and maintain the aircraft, and to provide sufficient security to prevent the placement of explosive devices on the airplane. She contends that the Airline's negligence directly caused her husband's death, and that she has sustained pain and suffering and economic damages as a result of his premature death. Mrs. Laubach is seeking damages in excess of $2 million from Atlantica. The complaints filed by numerous other plaintiffs have been consolidated herein on the issue of liability.

Factual Background

On December 21, 1995, Flight 640 left New York's LaGuardia Airport bound for Miami with 275 passengers and 13 crew members aboard. The first two hours of the flight were uneventful. On its approach to Miami International Airport, there was an explosion in the number two engine and a resulting loss of all flight controls due to severed hydraulic lines. The aircraft crashed, killing all on board.

The cause of the Flight 640 disaster has not been determined, and may never be determined, because much of the aircraft is buried in the Everglades and cannot be recovered. The only evidence of record concerning the cause of the crash is that traces of explosive components commonly found in terrorists' bombs were discovered on engine parts recovered at the crash site.

Standard of Review

In considering Atlantica's motion for summary judgment, this Court must draw all inferences from the evidence in favor of Plaintiffs, the nonmoving parties. *First Union Discount Brokerage Services, Inc. v. Milos*, 997 F.2d 835 (11th Cir. 1993). Summary judgment is appropriate if the record shows "that there is no genuine issue as to any material fact and that the moving party is entitled to a judgment as a matter of law." Fed. R. Civ. P. 56(c). However, in order to demonstrate a "genuine" issue of fact, Plaintiffs "must do more than simply show that there is some metaphysical doubt as to the material facts." *Matsushita Elec. Indus. Co. v. Zenith Radio Corp.*, 475 U.S. 574, 586 (1986). Rather, they "must come forward with 'specific facts showing that there is a genuine issue for trial.'" *Id.* at 587.

Discussion

First, Atlantica correctly notes that the federal government exclusively regulates matters of air safety and flight operations. This federal regulatory scheme was enacted to ensure the safety of all passengers by centralizing rule-making authority and promulgating uniform federal airline regulations. Atlantica further points out that the 1978 Airline Deregulation Act includes a preemption provision "prohibiting the States from enforcing any law 'relating to rates, routes, or services' of any air carrier." *Morales v. Trans World Airlines, Inc.*, 504 U.S. 374 (1992) (finding that this clause preempted state consumer protection law restricting the advertising of airline fares). Atlantica contends that this action involves questions of airline "services," which are controlled by the federal law and therefore are outside the scope of state law. The Court agrees. Because federal law does not provide a private cause of action, Plaintiffs have no remedy. Although this result may seem harsh, this Court has no authority to create such a cause of action; it is a matter for Congress to consider and address.

Moreover, Plaintiffs' claims against the Airline fail for the additional reason that they have not presented any evidence of negligence. While not conclusive, the evidence of record is that the crash of Flight 640 appears to have been caused by an explosive device planted by unknown third parties. There has been no showing of any error of commission or omission on the part of Atlantica that contributed to the planting of such a bomb. It is Plaintiffs' burden to demonstrate such evidence.

Because Plaintiffs have failed to demonstrate a genuine issue of fact as to the essential element of negligence, their claim fails on this ground as well.

WHEREFORE, the Court grants Atlantica's motion for summary judgment as to all claims raised in the complaint.

Norman T. Schenkel, Judge

======

CHAPTER 3
One Giant Step

LISA FREMONT STIRRED, CRAWLING THROUGH the cobwebs of sleep, grasping at the fragile tendrils of an early morning dream. Through the fog, she saw herself stretched between Max Wanaker and Sam Truitt, who were playing tug-of-war with her.

"I love you," Max was saying, pulling at one arm.

"But I respect you," Sam Truitt countered, pulling the other arm.

"I need your help!" Max pleaded.

"But your loyalty is to the law," Truitt said.

I want it all, she thought, waking up with a ferocious headache.

She had a breakfast of three Tylenol and black coffee. Max was gone, having left early to meet the lawyers for another session at the FAA, contesting a surprise inspection report.

Lisa had slept restlessly, her mind churning at the prospect of the job interview. She awoke several times, and now another dream came back to her. She and Max were in New York at a Broadway show. While in the office, he was a gruff corporate executive snarling at underlings, but take him to *Les Miserables*, and he'll burst into tears the first time Fantine sings, "I Dreamed a Dream."

Maybe that's why I still care for him. But is it love or a mixture of debt, gratitude, and nostalgia?

Which made her wonder.

If I'm trying to change, if I'm trying to be different from Max, why do this? I want to believe in ethics and fairness and all the flowery words in all those dusty books. Why don't I? Why can't I?

She'd gone through so many changes that her life, which had once seemed so simple—should I wear the black fishnet stockings with the see-through toreador's jacket?—had become incredibly complex. Including the really big questions.

Who am I? What do I believe in?

She didn't know.

Late last night, they'd ordered Thai takeout and watched a movie. Just like being married. They had made love, but her heart wasn't in it. It had become a mundane duty. A routine parting of the legs and disengagement of mind from body. *Really* like being married, she supposed.

Lisa wanted more. She wanted a man she would long for when they were apart, cherish when they were together. Sure, it sounded like soap opera stuff, but she'd had it once, oh so briefly, with Tony.

Lisa proceeded to get dressed, or rather to get dressed and undressed several times. She began with the double-breasted navy blazer. Three of them, actually, spread across her bed. One had natural shoulders and white buttons, the second padded shoulders and gold buttons, both with three-inch lapels, while the third was collarless.

After modeling them all in the bedroom mirror, she chose the one with gold buttons, a nautical flair.

If he hires me, I'll probably get all the damned admiralty cases. And if he doesn't, I will have let Max down, something he never did to me.

She stood in front of the mirror, holding the jacket under her chin. The strong, dark color suited her fair complexion and blue eyes. Okay, so they weren't really blue. They just took on whatever color framed her face. They became emeralds if she was dressed in her Sherwood Forest aerobics outfit, as she called the kelly green tights and leotard. They looked like the shallow, turquoise water off St. Kitts if she wore the light blue silk scarf knotted at her neck. In the mustard business suit she bought on sale at Saks, an instantly regretted purchase, her eyes assumed a hazel cast.

She held up two blouses, both silk and pearly white, one with a mandarin collar, the other a V-neck. She had a good neck, so why not show it. Of course, under that theory, she should also show her ass.

She tossed the clothing onto the bed, the silk blouse sliding to the floor, the blazer joining a jumble of suits, dresses, and jackets already modeled, critiqued, and discarded. Now she was naked, studying herself in the mirror. It had been ten years. Strange, she looked younger now than she had as an underage dancer —*"never say stripper, you're an exotic dancer"*—in her black garter belts, matching thong, and that awful red satin bolero jacket. And the makeup! Thick eyeliner on top and bottom lids, smeared upward to give a catlike look of sexual ferocity, her lips painted a deep crimson.

Who was I then? Who am I now?

"I'm Lisa Fremont," she said to the mirror, extending her right hand to an imaginary interviewer.

"Ah yes, Ms. Fremont," dropping her voice to a masculine timbre. "I've reviewed your curriculum vitae, and I must say, you have an impressive background."

She laughed. "You don't know the half of it, Justice Truitt."

She gave good interview—top of the class, a first-rate law review note on the right of privacy, and street-smarts that her Ivy League competitors couldn't match—so why was she so nervous? Another interview came back to her. In her last semester at Stanford, she had applied to one of San Francisco's largest and stuffiest law firms. She'd gone to lunch with the senior partner and two young male associates—all suspenders, cuff links, and pearly California teeth. They were at the Big Four, a mahogany mausoleum honoring four railroad tycoons, a place so masculine that testosterone replaces the vermouth in the martinis. The old coot was rambling on about the glory of representing insurance companies, banks, and manufacturers with an unfortunate predilection—his lawyerly term—for producing exploding tires, collapsing ladders, and toxic pharmaceuticals. She listened politely, ignoring the two boy-toy lawyers whose leers suggested they couldn't wait to bend her over a stack of Corpus Juris Secundum. She wasn't halfway through her Dungeness crab cocktail when the boss patted his worsted wool suit pocket and turned to her apologetically. "It appears I've left your curriculum vitae in the office. Could you orally refresh me?"

The two associates snorted vichyssoise up their nasal cavities, faces turning the same color as their power burgundy ties.

"No," Lisa answered, politely, "but I have a couple of girlfriends who'd love to."

She didn't want the job, anyway. Or rather, Max didn't want her to have the job. He was already talking about the court of appeals job, a great stepping-stone to clerking for the Supremes.

Lisa Fremont, clerk on the United States Court of Appeals for the District of Columbia. That had seemed like the top of the world. But now, this …

After a year clerking on the appeals court, she applied for a job with Samuel Adams Truitt, the newest Justice on the Supreme Court, whose vote Max's lawyers said they needed if they were to win. Neither Max nor his deep-carpet mouthpieces could help her now. To be a law clerk on the Supreme Court of the United States, you had to earn it.

She studied herself in the mirror. She had long legs with more than a hint of muscle in the calves, a legacy of the dancing. Her stomach was flat and her bottom tight, countless squats in the gym compensating for sitting on her ass the last twelve months in the chambers of Judge Mary Alice O'Brien, a sixty-six-year-old Reagan appointee who sipped bourbon during recess.

Still looking in the mirror, Lisa arched her back and stood, hip shot, an old pose from the club. Her firm, high breasts were too small for her prior line of work, Lisa had thought, until Sheila, the mother hen and oldest stripper, told her, "It ain't what you got, honey, it's what you do with what you got."

From the Tiki Club to the Supreme Court. One small step for a woman, one giant leap for a stripper.

Now, she put on her makeup, a light foundation that covered the sprinkling of freckles across her narrow nose. Her cheekbones, already strong, took on new contours with a light dusting of blush. An almost invisible application of mauve eye shadow and a coral lipstick followed. She'd already blow-dried her short, reddish blonde hair that, like her eyes, changed color in different surroundings, taking on golden red highlights at times, becoming a flaming forest fire in direct sunlight. She'd gone through law school and her one-year clerkship with a shoulder-length layered shag. She cut her hair after her visit last spring to Harvard, a week after Professor Sam Truitt's appointment but before his grueling confirmation hearings. She'd sat in the back of the lecture hall, listening and watching ... and learning. Not about natural law versus positive law—she'd already read Truitt's articles—but about the man.

The hall had been packed. No Socratic inquiry this day. It was a straight lecture, or rather a performance. The tall, handsome, broad-shouldered professor, a youthful, sandy-haired forty-six—as different from his faculty colleagues as she was from her fellow students bounded across the stage, taking the class on a trip, dramatically tracing the history of the law, the entire range of rights and responsibilities from the Code of Hammurabi to modern teenage curfews. Playing several roles, Sam Truitt became Madison and Hamilton tackling federalism, Zola shouting *"J'accuse!,"* John Marshall Harlan dissenting against segregation, and Clarence Darrow pleading for the lives of Leopold and Loeb: "Why did

they kill little Bobby Franks? They killed him because they were made that
way, and that calls not for hate but for kindness."

Affecting a Boston accent, standing ramrod straight, he became Oliver
Wendell Holmes Jr., the magnificent Yankee: "When the people want
to do something and I can't find anything in the Constitution expressly
forbidding them, I say, whether I like it or not, Goddamnn it let 'em do
it!"

He drew raucous laughter as Dickens' Mr. Bumble, who, having been
told that the law presumes a man to control his wife's actions, responded,
"If the law supposes that, the law is an ass, an idiot!"

Near the end, he became Willy Loman, telling his boss, "I put thirty-
four years into this firm, Howard, and now I can't pay my insurance. You
can't eat the orange and throw the peel away." Then he asked his students
to consider the moral and legal issues of Willy's suicide and whether the
life insurance company should pay his widow. Before anyone could think
it through, he was George in *Of Mice and Men*, shooting Lennie to spare
him from a lifetime of imprisonment, asking what George should be
charged with, and what are the moral differences between his actions and
those of Dr. Kevorkian?

Cooking a stew of history and law, morality and philosophy, fact and
fiction, Truitt mesmerized the students. Here was a professor who was
witty and entertaining, profane and profound, charismatic and charming.
It was a breathtaking performance, and afterward, the students stood and
applauded for several minutes, whistling their approval, stomping their
feet, crowding around him, peppering him with questions. Many of the
women—Lisa included—desired him. She had to remind herself that this
was a job, that Sam Truitt was her mark, and what she had to sell was
herself instead of a seventy-five-dollar bottle of carbonated champagne in
the Tiki VIP room.

But he was so damned smart and so damned sexy. What a powerful
combination. In the tepid tea of academe, Truitt was a bracing shot of
vodka on the rocks. Law professor as rock star.

She allowed herself a small fantasy. She was in the library of the
Supreme Court, deep in the tall stacks, searching for some obscure
precedent among the dusty volumes. She stood on tiptoes and stretched to
pull down a volume, but it was too high. Standing behind her, Sam Truitt
reached up and plucked the book from the shelf. Their bodies touched.
She turned, and his arms slipped around her waist, pulling her close. She
rubbed against him, an affectionate cat, and they kissed, a magical kiss

that swept her away. Away from her past, from Max … from reality. She even tried out the name, Lisa Truitt, repeating it silently, then chasing the thought away. How juvenile! Sam Truitt was one of the elite. What would he see in her? Besides, dummy, he's married.

The day after the lecture, Lisa hung around the student lounge, where several female students were sipping coffee, when one gestured toward a tall, short-haired blonde with pouty lips who breezed in, sat down, crossed her long legs, and pulled a cellular phone from her briefcase.

"Guess who's cutting Truitt's con law seminar," said one of the women, the apparent leader of the group.

"Teacher's pet," another answered, a plump young woman in round glasses. "God, he likes that Eurotrash, just-back-from-Monaco look. Remember the research assistant last year? Another short-haired blonde."

"Why go to class," the first one said, "if you can get briefed up close and personal?"

"He does like that lean and hungry look," an Asian woman agreed.

"I'm having fantasies about Sam Bam Truitt," the first woman said, "and they don't have anything to do with the due process clause."

The other women giggled.

She turned toward Lisa. "We're going to play the desert island game. Are you in?"

"Sure. What are the rules?"

"We determine the world's sexiest man by the process of elimination. We start with two men, and you have to choose who you'd rather be stranded with on a desert island. We eliminate the other one and keep going. I'll begin. John F. Kennedy Jr. and Sam Truitt."

"Ooh, tough one," the plump one said. "Does Truitt get a bonus for passing the bar the first time?"

"Up to you. It's your fantasy."

"I'll take Sam Truitt," Lisa broke in. "He reminds me of a cross between Harrison Ford and Jeff Bridges."

"No, he's more wicked," another said. "Like Nick Nolte."

"Yeah," the plump one said, "and most of the profs look like Pee-Wee Herman."

More laughter, and Lisa moved on. The day she returned home from Cambridge, she went to a trendy Georgetown salon, Curl Up and Dye, and had her hair cut into a shorter, layered "Princess Di." She did it partly to look more professional, like a network television anchor, and partly to appeal to Sam Bam Truitt's tastes.

If he's attracted to me, it will be easier.

But she was also attracted to him and wondered if that would make what she had to do even more difficult.

Now Lisa finished dressing, putting on the white silk blouse, then a taupe-colored skirt, a below-the-knee number with four darts that clung to her waist and flattered her shape. She tucked the blouse under the narrow waistband of the skirt, then stepped into closed Ferragamo pumps with three inch-heels, maybe just a touch higher than necessary.

She lifted her chin and draped a double strand of South Sea pearls around her neck—a gift from Max—latching the chain carefully, then put on the matching earrings, a tasteful single pearl on a solid gold post. She slipped into the blazer and placed a silk pocket square in the breast pocket, smoothing it with her hand. She put two extra copies of her curriculum vitae in a soft-sided burgundy briefcase, imagining it stuffed with certiorari petitions, legal pads, and weighty briefs.

"I'm going to get this job," she sang out, putting a tune to it. She was heading for the door when the phone rang.

"I need a babysitter," said the male voice.

"Greg!"

"Just called to wish you luck. Today's the day, right?"

"In twenty minutes."

"Go get 'em. You're the best."

"Thanks, kid."

In her mind's eye, she still saw little Greg Kingston in the Giants cap pounding his first baseman's mitt, asking her for a game of catch because Dad was away, stationed in Germany or Florida or somewhere that sounded a million miles from Bodega Bay. She pictured the white clapboard house up the hill, gray smoke swirling from the chimney, Greg's grandmother in the kitchen baking fruit pies.

She remembered running out of her own house one night, her drunken father diving for her legs as she flew off the porch, his calloused fisherman's hands clawing at her. She stumbled and scraped a knee, then scampered up the hill where Greg's grandmother took her in and dribbled iodine on the wound. For a time, at least, she'd found a haven from fear, a place where she could close her eyes without fear of what she would see upon awakening.

At twelve years old, she was Greg's babysitter but soon became part of the family. Greg's mother had long since taken off, and Tony was still on active duty, so the skinny eight-year-old boy with the hair falling in his eyes became the little brother she never had. Although he was now a handsome, lanky twenty-three-old with a mischievous grin, he would always be the kid wanting to play catch.

When she was in law school and had broken off with Max, Lisa returned home to visit Greg and found Tony there. He was nineteen years her senior, though still slightly younger than Max. She caught Tony's look when they said hello.

No, I'm not the babysitter anymore.

She could still remember the feeling when their eyes locked. It was intense and immediate. Spontaneous combustion, the moment charged with electricity, and best of all, it was mutual. She recalled that first night, a full moon over the Pacific, wine and cheese on the bay in an old Boston Whaler. Sitting at anchor, the wind rippling across the water, they became lovers, their desire for each other unquenchable. Even now, with eyes closed, she could hear the anchor line stretching tight as a violin string and see the flashing channel buoy, keeping time with her heart.

The physical soon became more, and while the lust quotient never wavered, they grew together until they belonged to each other in a deep, encompassing way that she had never known. What was it about Tony that was so different? His honesty and decency, his capacity for giving more than he took. He loved to have her around, to listen to her, to share his dreams, his hopes, his fears. Their rapport was natural, their bond unbreakable.

My God, I didn't know such a man existed!

Life, which once had been so bleak and gray, became a kaleidoscope of luscious colors. She had a family.

A man to love, a kid brother, Jesus, even a grandmom baking cherry pies. If only it could have gone on forever.

Now, Tony was gone, but the boy was still a part of her life, and she adored him. Just hearing Greg's voice, so much like his father's, sent waves of anguish through her.

"Where are you, Greg?" she said into the phone.

"Miami."

Damn. When's he going to give it up?

"I thought you were going back to school this semester."

"I got a job driving a forklift."

"Where?"

"Atlantica. I'm in the engine shop."

No! You're going to foul up everything.

"Greg. When are you going to drop this? It's been nearly three years. A bomb brought down the plane. Your dad's dead, and there's nothing you can do to change it."

There was a silence on the phone, and she recoiled at the sound of her own words. But it was true, wasn't it? What difference did it make what caused the crash? Dead was dead.

"I've been drinking beer with some of the guys in maintenance," he said, after a moment, "keeping my mouth shut but listening, picking up dirt. The incompetence around here is pretty amazing."

"Legally, it's irrelevant," Lisa said. "It doesn't matter if all the mechanics were drunks with two left thumbs—"

"It's not just them," he interrupted. "You ought to hear how they talk about Max Wanaker. Dad thought he was a real turd, too."

She never told Greg that his father might have had other reasons for despising Max. "Greg, I don't think it's healthy for you to still be obsessed about the crash."

"We deal with our loss differently. You can close your eyes to it, but he was my father."

"I loved him!" Lisa shot back, "and all this does is twist a knife into the wound."

"I've got to find out what really happened."

She listened while Greg ran through a list of what he'd been investigating the past three years. They'd been through it all before.

Her mind wandered. She didn't want to acknowledge it, but the kid was right. Ever since the accident, she had repressed it, trying not to think about her loss. She forced herself to forget his face, his smile, the way she felt in his strong arms. God, how she missed him! Her lover, her hero, her pilot.

What she had just said to Greg was the God's honest truth.

Tony Kingston was the only man I ever loved.

CHAPTER 4

Scoreless in October

SAM TRUITT CAME OUT OF HIS CHAMBERS to greet her. He was wearing a blue oxford cloth buttoned-down shirt with a green tie that he wasn't sure matched. The tie had little orange patterns shaped like the state of Florida, a gift from the governor to the first Floridian ever to sit on the Supreme Court. Truitt had left his suit coat in his chambers, purposely setting an informal tone, trying to put the young woman at ease. He'd shaken enough sweaty palms the last few weeks to know just how much pressure his young charges were feeling.

Truitt made a mental note to put his suit coat back on when he went out to lunch. A memo from the Chief that very morning announced with considerable distress that certain justices had been seen in the corridors in their shirtsleeves. Truitt toyed with the idea of putting on a powdered wig and flowing robe for his promised meeting with His Holiness.

He approached the young woman, who sat demurely in a chair in his outer office. "I'm Sam Truitt." He smiled and extended his hand, getting his first look at her. Startled by her beauty, he nonetheless maintained a judicial demeanor.

She rose from the chair and gave him a polite, how-are-you smile. "I'm Lisa Fremont" said the stunning woman in the navy double-breasted blazer. Her handshake was firm, dry, and warm. She had a fair complexion, eyes nearly as blue as her blazer, golden red hair, and what appeared to be a great figure underneath the conservative outfit.

No way will I hire her. No way. Too good looking. Way beyond attractive. Connie would kill me.

"I see you've met Eloise," he said, gesturing toward his secretary, a plump woman in her sixties who was perched in front of a word processor, eyeglasses dangling on a rhinestone chain looped around her neck. "Elly was with me in private practice, at legal services, at Harvard, and now here. She keeps track of my appointments, corrects my misspellings, and warns me when I have gravy on my tie."

"At Harvard, you didn't wear a tie," Eloise said, without looking up from her keyboard, her voice disapproving. "Blue jeans and chambray shirts, you looked like a cowboy in a Marlboro ad."

"Elly remembers when I couldn't find the courthouse door."

"His first trial was a pro bono criminal case," Elly said, momentarily stopping her typing. "His presumably innocent client stuck a firecracker into the ear of a friend."

"A couple of drunks in a bar," Truitt explained.

"Boys will be boys," Lisa said, easily working her way into the story.

"Exactly," Eloise agreed. "So here's young Scrap—that was his nickname before he got so high and mighty—dancing around the courtroom like Fred Astaire, cross-examining the victim." She dropped her voice a couple of octaves and sang out, "Isn't it true, Mr. Fiore, that you suffered no permanent injuries?"

"And the witness looks at me," Truitt broke in, "and says—"

"I beg your pardon," Lisa interrupted, cocking her head and putting a hand to her ear.

Truitt looked at her in astonishment.

"That's right!" he said, impressed.

The story was meant to loosen up the applicant as well as test for a sense of humor. This was the first time anyone had the courage or intuition to beat him to the punch line. It did not occur to Sam Truitt that Lisa already knew his often-told tale from reading an obscure legal newspaper that had profiled him.

If only you weren't so distractingly, maddeningly beautiful I could be as chaste as one of the Chief's monks in the monastery, but with my reputation, he'd still think I was shagging you.

Nearly all the 532 resumes Truitt had received were from qualified candidates. Top students from the best law schools, they could all write, research, and analyze. For his three clerks—he was entitled to four but wanted a smaller staff—Truitt sought a team with camaraderie. They'd have to put in long hours, but they should also be able to have a beer together. He admired hard workers, and perhaps because of his own background, appreciated those who did not have a law school education handed to them as a legacy. He also wanted at least one woman, and someone from west of the Mississippi.

So far, he had hired two men. Victor Vazquez came to Florida from Cuba with his parents on the *Mariel* boatlift, attended Miami High, worked two jobs at Tulane, then earned a free ride at the University of Michigan Law School, where he was editor in chief of the *Law Review*. Next was Jerry Klein, whose IQ was off the charts and who had dropped out of medical school to enroll at Yale Law because he thought it would be fun. He won the job by telling Truitt that the only difference between the two professions was that lawyers merely rob you while doctors rob you and kill you, too.

"I think W. C. Fields said that," Truitt responded, testing the chubby young man.

"Actually it was Chekhov."

"I know," Truitt told him. "I just wanted to see if you'd correct me. You're hired."

Either Klein had chutzpah, or he lacked the natural instincts to be wary of correcting his boss. Either way, Truitt liked him. He sensed that Lisa Fremont had the same self-confidence. Only difference, the obese, pimply Klein looked like a sausage stuffed into an ill-fitting suit. This goddess standing before him looked as if she just stepped off the cover of *Cosmopolitan*.

Ten years ago, hell five years ago, he would have relished the sexual tension, the flirtatiousness that is a constant companion in the workplace. But there was a difference between a university faculty and the Supreme Court. The Chief Justice, bless his scurrilous heart, was right about that. The tabloids would love to have another scandal as juicy as the President and the intern.

Truitt was determined to be polite but brief with Ms. Lisa Fremont, then dismiss her and continue the search for the female equivalent of Jerry Klein.

"Let's go into my office and talk," he said. "If you're up for it, Elly makes a potent *café Cubano*. Any that's left over, we send to Cape Canaveral for the booster rockets."

"Sissy," Elly called at him.

"I'd love some," Lisa said. "I missed my morning coffee."

It was the first lie she would tell that day, but by no means the last.

ᕫ

Sitting primly with legs crossed in an antique chair more handsome than comfortable, Lisa sized up Sam Truitt's office. It had that messy, genius-at-work look. Trial transcripts, pleadings binders, the official records of a hundred cases covered the mahogany desk, a brown leather sofa, and portions of the plush blue and gold carpet. Somewhere on that desk or on a wooden cart nearby, Lisa knew, would be the consolidated cases of *Laubach et al. v. Atlantica Airlines*. There would be copies of the pleadings, the summary judgment dismissing the cases, the one-sentence affirmance in the Eleventh Circuit Court of Appeals, the plaintiffs' petition for certiorari, and the Supreme Court's four-to-four decision—prior to Truitt's confirmation—to hear the case. Although it would take five of the nine justices to overturn the summary judgment, under the Court's time-honored Rule of Four, a majority had not been necessary to grant review.

Lisa had already read the file, courtesy of Max's lawyers. She knew the facts. She knew the law. All she did not know was how to convince anyone—much less the humane and sensitive Sam Truitt—to close the courthouse door to nearly three hundred grieving families. But that would have to come later. First, she had to get the job, and she was beginning to feel the butterflies. She tried to chase away a recurring thought—that she didn't really belong here. That all the higher education, and the fine clothes and the superficial gloss that came from flying first class and staying in penthouse suites, couldn't hide who she really was. Draping a streetwalker in mink didn't make her a duchess.

All this time, I thought I'd come so far, but have I? Why do I feel like the same scared kid who ran away from home?

She feared that Sam Truitt would see right through the façade, that she would be humiliated and never get the job. For a moment, Lisa felt lightheaded and thought she might faint. Then she sipped the demitasse of Cuban coffee, waiting for the caffeine to surge into her veins. As she half-listened to the justice explain the law clerk's duties—all of which she knew—she forced herself to calm down and concentrate.

Max is counting on me, and I can't fail him.

She studied the chambers, looking for clues to Sam Truitt, the man. Floor-to-ceiling bookshelves covered one wall. The books contained every decision of every federal court since the founding of the Republic. The latest edition of the United States Code, the federal statutes, were there, too, as were the tens of thousands of regulations of federal agencies. A computer at the desk was linked to databases that could research in seconds what would have taken days or weeks in earlier times. In the corner, half-a-dozen cardboard boxes remained to be unpacked.

A mahogany stand-up reading desk stood against one wall. An American flag with gold fringes was lodged on a pole in the corner. A framed black-and-white photo of a football team, the players and coaches sitting on bleachers, rested on an oak credenza, as did a partially deflated ball. Antique books with cracked golden bindings were displayed behind glass, and a portrait of Chief Justice John Jay hung over the fireplace mantel.

Truitt went on for a while about the pool memos the clerks prepare to help the Court to determine whether to review lower court cases. With little enthusiasm, he mentioned the importance of writing objective bench memos for him, fairly summarizing each party's position, and listing similar cases that may have been omitted from the briefs. It was a mechanical speech he seemed to have given before.

Omigod! He's bored. I don't even have his attention. He's already dumped me in the reject pile.

"Tell me about yourself," Truitt said, leaning back in his leather chair and sneaking a quick look at his wristwatch. "Skip all the legal stuff. I've already read your transcripts and I've spoken to Judge O'Brien, who gives you a glowing recommendation. Tell me about Lisa Fremont, the person."

He's just being polite before showing me the door.

Lisa fought the urge to speak quickly, to cram a lifetime—and not an entirely honest one—into a minute. She took a deep breath to relax and began at her own pace. "I grew up in Bodega Bay, California."

He nodded and said, "*The Birds.*"

"Right. They made the Hitchcock film there, but that was before I was born. I think of the place more as *The Old Man and the Sea.* My father was a fisherman."

She paused, just as she had rehearsed, then watched as he nodded with approval. Tilling common ground, or rather, fishing the same waters, the son and daughter of humble men facing each other in the palatial Courthouse, one block from the Capitol, with the Library of Congress and the Senate offices on either side.

The Justice, the law clerk, and Joe DiMaggio ... all children of fishermen.

"He was a shrimper mostly," she said. "Crabs, too, depending on the season. For a while, he crewed on someone else's boat, but usually he just worked alone."

When he worked at all. When he wasn't drunk, sprawled across the convertible sofa with the popped springs, the sofa he hauled onto the front porch to her everlasting shame, the sofa where he lay, unshaven and reeking

of sweat and beer and vomit, tossing bottles at passers-by, the sofa where on a
dark night when no one heard her screams, he ...

"It was a hard life," she said. "Neither of my parents even graduated
from high school. In fact, Mom was in tenth grade when she got pregnant
with me. I knew I had to get out of there. I left home for San Francisco
and went through a series of minimum wage jobs that convinced me of
the need for higher education."

"I don't recall those early jobs on your CV."

Let me orally refresh you.

"Just some waitressing, barmaid work, that sort of thing. One summer,
I had a job at Yosemite, clearing trails."

"Really?" he said, perking up, paying attention. "I spent a summer as
a park ranger at Fort Jefferson."

"Where's that?" she asked, seemingly with real interest.

He told her that the Civil War fort was in the Dry Tortugas near
Key West, but she knew that. She knew Sam grew up in Everglades City,
that his father, Charlie, had piloted a stone crab boat and that he died
of lung cancer at fifty-seven. She knew that Sam had camped out in
Ten Thousand Islands as a young boy and fished off Shark Point. She
knew he drew pictures of all the animals he spotted—water moccasins,
manatees, ospreys, and alligators—and that he could imitate the caw of
a mockingbird and build a fire from two pieces of wood. She knew he
skippered a homemade airboat through the Everglades and built his own
fishing hideaway in the islands at age sixteen. She knew he had won two
hundred dollars in the eleventh grade for an essay about preserving the
Glades and was rewarded with a trip to Tallahassee, where his picture was
taken with the lieutenant governor.

She knew that the local Rotary Club had taken up a collection to help
him buy books for his first semester at Wake Forest, that he worked two
jobs and was a walk-on with the football team, which never did give him
a scholarship. She knew he took a year after graduation to work with the
Peace Corps in Central America, went to law school at the University
of Virginia, and afterward spent two years with Legal Services, helping
migrant workers in Florida's sugar cane fields, before a short stint in private
practice and then on to Harvard to pick up an LL.M. degree.

Lisa Fremont knew all these things because she had read the three
books and ninety-eight legal articles he had written and seven hundred
sixty-seven newspaper and magazine articles that had mentioned his name.
Thanks to the very same software that could find every reference to the

phrase "capital punishment" in every judicial opinion over the past two hundred years, she could find all published references to Samuel Adams Truitt, including last August's social columns in a Nantucket weekly where the newly appointed justice and his wife, Constance, enjoyed grilled lobster and sweet corn at Senator Parham's summer home. For the early material that wasn't stored on a hard drive, she had dug up copies of his high school and college yearbooks and student newspapers. Lisa Fremont was nothing if not a great researcher.

Now she maintained eye contact as Sam Truitt spun his personal history with the enthusiasm of a man who loves life and doesn't mind talking about it.

At least I've got his attention. Now, be appealing but not seductive, smart but not arrogant.

After telling his abbreviated version of his trip from Everglades City to the Supreme Court, with various stops en route, Truitt said, "I appreciate the fact you've had some real jobs. I confess to having a bias against people who were groomed from infancy to become lawyers. It's a great asset to have some life experiences."

Does erotic dancing count? You wouldn't believe what I used to do with my "great asset."

"Do you have any underlying legal or moral philosophy?" he asked, and she was caught off guard. She knew that he'd written with admiration of the humanism of Jean Calvin, whose teachings provided the bedrock for the protection of individual liberties. She could memorize and take tests and research the law, but ...

What do I believe?

It was the same question that plagued her last night. Though she wished it were otherwise, she didn't believe the slogans on the pediments. At best she had an ideology that came from listening to Max Wanaker's theory of enlightened self-interest.

Do unto others before they do unto you.

"I'm not sure I have a clear, discernible philosophy," she said, sounding lame, hating her answer, knowing it disappointed him.

"If you were a judge," he asked, giving her a second chance, "what moral and ethical framework would you bring to the courtroom?"

She bought time by finishing her Cuban coffee, feeling the caffeine rush. She needed to wing it, to spin bullshit into gold. Wasn't that a large measure of lawyering? She'd won moot court at Stanford by keeping her poise and cleverly answering the unexpected question, but just now, she lost her concentration. Her mind flashed back to Max and the way he looked last night, how desperate he seemed about the case.

"This is more important than you know."

Why? And why wouldn't he tell her more? Sure, the case was important. Jesus, nearly three hundred people had died. Damage claims could exceed half a billion dollars. But that's why every airline carries massive amounts of insurance. Other than a quick spurt of adverse publicity from a megabucks verdict if Atlantica lost the case, what was the crisis?

Regaining her focus, Lisa was aware of Justice Truitt staring at her, waiting for her answer. "I'd just call them the way I saw them," she said, using the sports cliché, falling deeper into the pit she had dug. The look on his face told her he was dissatisfied.

"Let's try it this way," he said, patiently. "What's your view of Calvinism?"

She forced herself to focus. That she could be sitting here, in this majestic building, being asked to judge the work of a sixteenth-century French theologian struck her as both quaint and oddly moving. Sam Truitt, a man whose own words would be studied and critiqued by scholars a century from now, actually sought her opinion.

And I have none.

Oh, she could recite Calvin's belief in the ultimate power of the moral law. She could ace any test on Aquinas or Aristotle, Bacon or Bentham. She was smart with what Max derisively called "book learning."

But beneath it, she had no core, no body of beliefs that shaped her. She was an empty vessel, and realizing it, she suddenly felt chilled and frighteningly alone.

The justice waited for her reply. The easiest course would be to agree with his well-known written work. But she knew that he hated bootlickers. She needed to get back on track, back to the job she had promised Max she would do.

Oh Max, what have you gotten me into? I can't hack it here.

Struggling to control her emotions, she pushed away the anxiety and the dread. "You probably don't agree," she said, haltingly, "but I've never thought that there is a natural law arising independent of governments. I take the view that all moral obligations are artificially realized, imposed by governments."

"Aha!" he said, rising to the challenge, and in fact rising out of his chair and beginning to pace in front of the credenza. "You're with Hobbes! You're a bloody Royalist."

"He was more realistic than Calvin," she said. "Hobbes understood that moral obligations require laws, not the goodwill of men. It's the sovereign that sets the rules, not our own consciences."

She gave him a half smile and cocked her head. In another setting, it would have been flirtatious. Here, in the midst of a polemical quarrel that Cromwell and Charles the First might have had, if they spoke at all, it was an intellectual challenge.

"I think you have it backward," he said. "'We, the people—'"

"To coin a phrase," she interrupted, beginning to feel more comfortable in the ebb and flow of a dialectic debate she was prepared to win or lose, as the situation required.

He laughed and continued. "The people give the government its rules, but those rules arise from natural laws. Take the Decalogue of Exodus. Thou shall not kill. Thou shall not bear false witness ..."

Thou shall not commit adultery.

Funny how that popped into her head as she watched the judge—her judge—stalk around the perimeter of his chambers, a smaller stage than in Cambridge. He had the enthusiasm of a young boy and the wisdom of a philosopher. Not to mention the body of an athlete and the easy grin of a man who finds the world amusing.

A damned intoxicating combination in the person of Samuel Adams Truitt. If only you weren't married, if only this weren't a job.

Truitt carried on for a while, attacking Hobbes for his view that government could prescribe an official religion and ban all others, which she admitted was a mistake.

"A mistake this Court unanimously followed in 1892," he said, shaking his head sadly, "when it held that the government can prohibit the exercise of religions other than Christianity. Four years later, the Court upheld laws prohibiting blacks from riding in the same railroad cars with whites. The decisions were wrong because they violated the natural law, as codified in our Constitution. Under Calvin, citizens can resist immoral laws because the sovereign is beholden to the natural law."

"But who determines what the natural law encompasses?" she asked. "In the 1870s, the Supreme Court said it was the 'law of the creator' that women be barred from becoming lawyers. These days, a lunatic in Florida says God tells him to kill a doctor who performs abortions. Does he have the right to ignore the lesser law of the government?"

"No, because the most basic natural law of all is not to kill."

And so it went, teacher and student, judge and clerk, man and woman, traveling through the centuries on the magic carpet of their mutual knowledge, Truitt noting that being "endowed with certain rights by their Creator" came from Calvin, Lisa responding that the "pursuit of happiness" came from Hobbes.

She was focused now and ready to impress the justice with her erudition on a number of subjects, all of which interested him, she knew from her research.

I'm rallying. I think he likes me.

Truitt sat down again, and they spoke easily for another forty minutes, Lisa working into the conversation a cross section of popular culture. She mentioned novels that moved her, films that resonated, and rock music she loved, the songs invariably stemming from Truitt's era. She moved the conversation toward the American musical theater and why didn't they write shows like *Guys and Dolls* anymore? He agreed, telling her he had acted, though not very well, in a college production of the show about a thousand years ago.

"You must have been a wonderful Sky Masterson," she said.

"Actually, I was Big Jule."

"No!" she said, feigning surprise. She'd already seen the yearbook photo of young Sam, brawny in a gangster's pinstriped double-breasted suit with exaggerated lapels and enough shoulder padding for an offensive lineman. He was hoisting Sky Masterson up by his somewhat narrower lapels, holding him two feet off the stage floor with one hand. "I really would have thought you'd have the romantic lead." She blushed, her face seeming as red as her hair. "Oh ... I didn't mean ..." The more she stammered, the redder she became, a trick that required holding her breath, or at least not inhaling while she spoke. "I'm sorry, I mean ... If I said anything inappropriate ..."

"No. That's all right. I was just the biggest guy in the University Thespians. It was either play the heavy or haul the scenery around."

She quickly regained the composure she had really never lost. The blushing, stuttering episode had been rehearsed in front of a mirror just as Sam Truitt had rehearsed "Luck Be a Lady" so many years ago. It had seemed to her that being too polished, too poised, might come off as artificial and, well ... rehearsed. So the momentary slip had the dual purpose of making her seem human and letting him know she found him attractive. *I like her,* Sam Truitt thought. *She's bright and beautiful, articulate and interesting, but beyond all that ... I like her.* Obviously, she can do the work. And she'd be fun to have around.

If only she weren't so damned sexy.

"Is there anything you want to ask me?" Truitt said.

"I was looking at the football you were holding. Did I read somewhere that you were captain of your college team?"

"No, I wasn't good enough for that. I was captain of the special teams."

"What made them so special?"

He laughed. At least she wasn't an expert on everything. "At Wake Forest, nothing, I assure you. I was the long snapper."

"Sounds like a fish," she said with a feminine shrug.

"I spent all my playing time looking between my legs, snapping the ball to the punter or field goal kicker. It's a knack, seeing the world upside down and putting a tight spiral on the ball, getting it to the punter, nose up, in seven-tenths of a second, thigh high, so he can think just about the kick. A good snapper gets the ball to the punter faster than the quarterback can throw it the same distance."

"Really? I guess it's much more complicated than most people realize," she said, encouraging him.

"It sure is. You fire the ball with the right hand, guide it with the left. Before the snap, if you squeeze the ball, or cock your wrist, the defensive linemen will time their rush and get a jump on your linemen. So no hitches, no nerves, and most important, you've got to have the perfect stance. You've got to keep your ass down." He laughed and went on, "Which, come to think of it, was the President's advice when he appointed me to this scorpions' nest. 'Keep your ass down until you get the lay of the land.'"

"Sounds smart. You're here for life. Why be impatient to make your mark?"

"I've never been good at laying low," he said, then walked to the credenza and picked up the partially inflated football. Although he didn't ask her to, she rose from the chair and joined him there, putting her hands on the cracked leather. It was, in its way, an intimate gesture, each of them touching the other, through an intermediary, the old football. She ran her fingers across the chipped white paint that spelled out, WAKE FOREST 16 – FURMAN 10.

She has beautiful hands. What's happening? Jesus, Sam, act like a judge, not a schoolboy.

"It was my last game, my only game ball. A reward for playing three years without a bad snap. That and some tackles on the kickoff team. Unfortunately we didn't kick off much."

"I know enough about the game to understand that. You didn't score often, right?"

"Often? The Demon Deacons were scoreless in October."

"'Scoreless in October,'" she repeated with a laugh that trilled like a pine warbler in the Carolina woods. "Sounds like a movie title."

"Or a lonely fraternity boy's lament," he said, chuckling.

"Or the number of opinions the junior justice writes his first month on the bench," she said, keeping the ball in the air.

"I'm afraid the C.J. would agree with that," Truitt said. "It's going to take me a while to get used to being the new kid on the block. I was playing basketball with Justice Braxton yesterday, and he started calling me 'Junior' just to mess up my jump shot. Did you know there's a basketball court above the courtroom?"

She nodded. "The highest court in the land."

"Right again. You seem to have a feel for this place."

And for me. What am I going to do? She's almost too good to be true.

∽

Lisa watched him squeeze the old football, seemingly lost in a private thought. "You speak very fondly of your football team," she said, "even though …"

"We were really abysmal," he said, finishing her sentence.

"But winning wasn't everything to you, was it?"

"I haven't thought about it much, but you're right. We lost ten games in a row before beating Furman. I loved the game and I loved my teammates, even though we were probably the worst team in the history of college football."

"No!" she said in mock disbelief.

"You can look it up," he said, but of course she already had.

"In 1974, we were shut out six games in a row by a combined score of two hundred and ten to zero," Truitt said. "North Carolina, Oklahoma, Penn State, Maryland, Virginia, and Clemson."

"Wow, is that some kind of record?"

"Maybe. We even lost to William and Mary, and I suspect Mary could have done it all by herself."

She laughed, knowing he'd used the line many times before. She was turning the tables on him, becoming the interrogator. "What did you learn from all the losses? About life, I mean."

"No one's ever asked me that," he said, seeming to think it over.

C'mon, Sam. Every man I've ever known loves to talk about himself.

"The value of hard work, patience, and discipline," he said after a moment. "That to win you have to sweat and sacrifice and put the team first and even if you do all of those things, you may still lose, but that it's no disgrace to lose with honor. Most of all, I learned that you've got to play the game within the rules, and that surely goes for life, too."

The rules. Max Wanaker makes his up as he goes along. Sam Truitt follows the ones engraved in the marble.

The phone buzzed just as Truitt was telling how he got the nickname "Scrap" and how the little-used kickoff team was called the "Scrap Pack."

"The Chief says you're to come to his chambers right away," Eloise said over the speaker.

"Tell the Chief I don't work for him," Truitt replied.

"No, sir!" Eloise screeched over the intercom. "We're not going to start off seeing who's got the biggest bulge in his briefs. I'll tell him you're in conference and will be there the instant you're free."

The intercom went dead, and there was a moment of silence as interviewer and interviewee tried to remember exactly where their conversation had ended.

"That's probably the only time anyone will catch you quoting Justice McReynolds," Lisa said.

"You picked up on that?" Truitt asked, astonished. "That's a really arcane bit of Court trivia."

He looked at her with something approaching awe, and Lisa smiled.

"Back in the 1930s," she said, "Chief Justice Hughes left a message with McReynolds' secretary. 'Tell the justice to come to my chambers at once, and wear his robes.' McReynolds responded with ... well, just what you said. 'Tell the Chief I don't work for him.'"

"McReynolds was a real misanthrope, a racist, and a bigot," Truitt said. "But you probably know that, don't you?"

"I know he wouldn't appear for the Court photo because he didn't want to be in a picture with a Hebrew. That's what he called Brandeis."

Showing off now. Put a lid on it, Lisa.

"That was him. And you're right. It's the only time I'll quote the bastard." Truitt glanced at his watch. "Whoa. We've been at it for nearly two hours."

Sensing that was her cue, Lisa said, "I want to thank you so much for your time, Justice Truitt."

"I've enjoyed this. I really have," Truitt said. He paused a moment, as if she shouldn't leave just yet.

Sam Truitt couldn't pinpoint the moment he changed his mind about Lisa Fremont, couldn't even say exactly why he had. She was smart and savvy, and they seemed to have great synergy, and he was tired of interviewing candidates. There was such a relaxed nature to their conversation, he felt as if he had known her forever. So without ever actually consciously deciding, Truitt reached the conclusion that she'd be perfect. He would hire her *despite* her great looks, though he didn't think his wife would buy that for a second.

What is he thinking? Lisa wondered. Am I overstaying my welcome? Should I curtsy and head for the door?

"Once the session begins," Truitt said, breaking the silence, "I'm afraid there won't be time for what Elly would call 'high-falutin' gabfests.'"

As if I already had the job.

"And from now on," he continued, "it's just plain 'Judge.' That's what Vic and Jerry call me. Ask Elly for the forms you'll need to fill out, then get ready to roll up your sleeves."

Omigod! What did he say?

"You mean I'm hired?"

"Didn't I say that? No, I guess I didn't. I must have thought you could read my mind."

"That would be a pretty good attribute for a law clerk," she said, beaming. "I'll work on it."

"Along with about a thousand cert petitions." He stood and extended a hand. "Welcome aboard."

For the second time that day, Lisa Fremont shook his hand, and their eyes locked. This time his expression seemed to come from a deeper place, and for a moment, she felt he was trying to look deep inside her. At the same time, he clasped both hands over hers. There was nothing inappropriate about it, nothing sexual, overt or otherwise. It seemed to be a gesture of comradeship, a recognition that they were about to spend the next year together embarked on a great adventure.

Wow! I did it. I'm a clerk on the Supreme Court of the United States. Me! Lisa Anne Fremont from Bodega Bay. And Max didn't do it for me.

She allowed herself just a few seconds of elation. Then the realization set in. She wasn't just Sam Truitt's law clerk. She was also working for Max Wanaker and Atlantica Airlines, petitioner in one of the biggest cases of the new term. In legal jargon, she had a major conflict of interest. Her job was to subvert justice, not to achieve it. She tried not to think about the cruel paradox, which threatened to ruin the moment.

She focused a businesslike smile on Sam Truitt. In the past two hours, she thought, they had learned all about each other. Or had they? She'd already known him. And he only thought he knew her. For a moment, looking into his blue-gray eyes, she thought there was a glimmer of recognition, that he saw through the gaps in her resume and in her life, that somehow he glimpsed the abyss that separated who she had been from who she had become. But if he had sensed anything wrong, why had he hired her?

She broke eye contact, and he released her hands. "Thank you, Judge. I'll try to live up to your expectations."

"You and me both," he said, laughing, giving her a warm smile. Then his voice dropped nearly to a whisper and his brow furrowed. "Lisa, we have a chance to do wonderful work here. Not just to resolve individual disputes, but to set the tone for civilization, to draw boundaries for conduct, to define fundamental rights and responsibilities, and to right wrongs. We're the conscience of society and the buffer between the government and the governed, striking the balance between the state and the individual. We protect against anarchy on the one hand and dictatorship on the other. Our job is to breathe life into that glorious two-hundred-year-old document they keep under glass a few blocks west of here. God help me, I hope we're both up to the task."

Lisa stood in stunned silence. What could she say? Oh, I'm sure you'll combine the wisdom of Solomon with the compassion of Gandhi and the strength of Zeus. And I'll be right there beside you ... corrupting the process, violating everything you believe in.

She had never known anyone like Sam Truitt. He was truly afraid of falling short, of failing to live up to his own standards and those who came before him. Here was a Galahad whose greatest fear was that he could not attain the Holy Grail.

She admired and respected this man who was honest and devoted to principles, not to the accumulation of power and personal wealth. He was everything Max Wanaker wasn't. What a sad irony that she had to betray Sam Truitt's trust and tarnish his beloved bronze statues. For a moment, she felt such shame that she could not look him in the eyes.

He guided her toward the door, grabbing his coat for the walk down the corridor to the Chief's chambers. "Wait!" he said at the last moment, and she tensed.

What is it? Has he seen through me? Maybe he's the mind reader!

"I've completely failed to ask what substantive areas of the law interest you," he said.

With the self-discipline and poise that had brought her so far, she chased away the guilt and the fear. "Aviation law has always fascinated me," Lisa Fremont said.

======
IN THE
SUPREME COURT OF THE UNITED STATES

GLORIA LAUBACH,
individually and as
representative of the
Estate of Howard J. Laubach,
deceased, et al.
Petitioners,
vs.
ATLANTICA AIRLINES, INC.,
Respondent.
ON PETITION FOR A WRIT OF CERTIORARI TO THE
UNITED STATES COURT OF APPEALS FOR THE ELEVENTH
CIRCUIT

PETITION FOR A WRIT OF CERTIORARI
QUESTIONS PRESENTED

Whether the 1978 Airline Deregulation Act bars Petitioner's claims under the Florida Wrongful Death Act for the death of her husband in the crash of a commercial aircraft, and if there is no such federal remedy, leaves Petitioner without the right to sue for money damages?

Whether Petitioner presented sufficient evidence as to Respondent's negligence so as to preclude the entry of summary judgment and to permit jury consideration of that issue?

∾

REASON FOR GRANTING THE WRIT

The decision below (a) radically departs from established case law; (b) subverts the intention of Congress; and (c) immunizes the tortfeasor from liability, thus permitting a wrong without a remedy, an abhorrent result in a case involving the deaths of nearly three hundred persons.

Respectfully submitted,
Albert M. Goldman, Esq.

======

CHAPTER 5

Reservoir Dog

LISA DROVE AROUND FOR HOURS before heading back to the apartment. She passed the Washington Monument, the circle of American flags crackling in the autumn breeze. She drove by the elm trees and the Reflecting Pool, and just as the lights came on, she curled behind the Lincoln Memorial with its distinctive Doric columns resembling the Parthenon. She slowed the car and fought the urge to join the tourists and walk up to old Abe—now dramatically backlit—and soak up all that corn-pone Americana. Thinking about it, she felt like a character in a black-and-white movie, *Ms. Fremont Goes to Washington.*

What she was feeling now was every bit as hokey as the old Frank Capra tearjerker. A vague disquiet settled over her as she considered notions of justice and honor and the young Scrap Truitt sweating on the football field in a noble but losing effort.

How could I do it? How could I sit there and smile and wow him with my intellect, all the time planning to sabotage his treasured work? How low can I go?

She crossed the Arlington Memorial Bridge and headed to the national cemetery, parking the car and sitting there in the enveloping darkness. Scattershot thoughts raced through her mind, but one kept returning, kept nagging at her.

"Tell me about Lisa Fremont, the person."

No. You wouldn't like Lisa Fremont, the person. But I can change. I want to believe all the flowery phrases about duty and justice and principle. Sam, I want to be like you!

She *didn't* want to be like Max. She was angry with him for manipulating her.

"After all I've done for you, don't you think you owe me this?"

No! Not this.

She believed there was a time in a person's life when one decision affects everything else. You head down that crooked side road one mile too far, and you'll never get back on the highway. But it wasn't too late to play it straight, and this time there was nothing Max could say that would change her mind. When she got back to the apartment, she'd tell him. Not only wouldn't she try to sway Justice Truitt's vote on the *Atlantica* case, she'd recuse herself from even preparing the bench memo.

Her cellular phone rang, startling her. It was Max, wondering when she'd get home. She told him she'd gotten the job; she left for later the rest of the day's news.

Max didn't congratulate her, just mumbled *uh-huh*, like it was no big deal.

Like every day a poor girl from Bodega Bay, a teenage runaway, an underage stripper with no future gets to be a law clerk on the Supreme Court of the United States.

Now, she had prospects. Entree into the biggest and best law firms. Before taking the clerking job on the D.C. Circuit, she'd been interviewed by a Chicago firm with offices in London, Paris, Moscow, and Rome. Hadn't the managing partner told her to keep in touch, to call him when her clerkship was over? Well, a year from now, she could waltz right in there. Law firms fall all over one another competing for young lawyers who have sat at the foot of the throne.

Hey, Max, guess what. A leopard can change her spots.

"I'll be there in ten minutes," she said on the cellular. "We have to talk."

"Yeah, we do," he said.

&

Two men in suits were waiting inside Lisa's apartment. Max Wanaker was sleek in his jet-black Armani with a thin pinstripe. Theodore Shakanian wore a baggy charcoal gray Wal-Mart special and brown shoes. A cigarette dangled from his mouth, and Lisa shot him an angry look. She didn't let Max or anyone else smoke in her apartment. Lisa knew little about Shakanian, other than the fact that his office was adjacent to Max's in Atlantica's Miami headquarters and he was an ex-cop from New York. Ever since the crash in the Everglades, the two men seemed to be spending a lot of time together.

Max looked grim, his face drawn. "I think you know Shank," he said, gesturing toward Atlantica's head of security, a lanky man with three days of black stubble sprouting from an acne-scarred face.

"I do," she said. "I just don't recall inviting him over."

Max forced a laugh and smiled apologetically at Shank. "Lisa's always been territorial. Like a cat."

"What's going on?" she asked.

"Put your briefcase down and relax," Max said. "Shank will explain it."

She tossed the briefcase at Max, who caught it just before it clipped him in the forehead. He gently placed it on a sofa of white Haitian cotton.

"Congratulations on getting your new job," Shank said, his voice gravelly, like tires crunching loose stones.

"Thank you," she said without enthusiasm. "What's going on?"

Why the hell was Max spreading the news?

She'd seen Shank several times in the last few years but had never exchanged more than a casual greeting. A sullen, homely man, he stood perhaps an inch above six feet and had a Sergeant Joe Friday flattop that was so out of date it had come back into style. He looked to be between forty and fifty, there was no way to tell. Either he owned only one suit, or he had a closet full of the gray ones, which he always wore with a white shirt and a gray and black tie. She had only seen him once without the suit, in Max's hotel suite in Paris at the annual air show. He was speaking on the phone in a combination of English and what sounded like Japanese and was wearing jeans and a polo shirt. Lisa had been surprised at the size of his arms. In a suit, he looked rangy, even underweight. In the snug, short-sleeve shirt, she could see thick wrists and powerful, cabled forearms. On one forearm was the tattoo of a knife slicing a heart down the middle.

"Right now, you've got the most important job of anybody at the airline," Shank said, exhaling a plume of smoke, "and your enterprise falls under my jurisdiction."

Lisa wheeled toward Max, the anger building. This was supposed to be between the two of them. Now it was an *enterprise*. A phrase came back to her from criminal law class: the RICO statute and "racketeering enterprises." She pictured the FBI, the U.S. attorney task force, and a grand jury all probing into their little enterprise.

"Damnit, Max, I thought I was doing a personal favor for you. Now, it's a corporate job? Who else knows? Did you put it in the shareholders' report?"

"Calm down, Lisa," Max said. "Let me fix you a drink." He walked to the liquor cabinet and tossed some vodka over ice, pouring in bottled orange juice from the mini-refrigerator below the wet bar. Then he poured another for himself, his hands trembling. He wouldn't look her in the eyes.

"I don't want a drink," she said angrily. "I want you out of my apartment."

Max shrugged, chugged one of the screwdrivers, and appropriated the other, carrying it to the sofa where he sat down, apparently content to sit out the dance.

"*Your* apartment is paid for by Atlantica," Shank said with a sneer, "so I tend to look at it as corporate property and you, Ms. Fremont, as a corporate asset."

Lisa fought to control her rage. She had worked so hard to be independent, to be free of anyone else's control, that she felt violated by the man's presence in her home. "You can't invade my privacy like this! You can't take over my life."

Shank didn't move. He looked amused, watching her as a fleck of ash fell from his cigarette to the red and gold Persian rug.

Lisa wheeled toward Max, waiting for an explanation, for something that would make sense. After a long pull of the screwdriver, he said, "A matter as sensitive as this, I had to bring in Shank."

"And who else?"

"The general counsel, but no one else."

"You told Flaherty! Why not just take an ad in the *Post*?"

"Flaherty had to know. He's the one who ran the projections. All the judges' opinions were run through the computer and stacked up against the facts of our case. The vote came out four-four. Truitt's new. He's the swing vote. If we get him, we win. If we don't, we lose."

She walked toward the faux fireplace, turning away from both men to gather her thoughts. "Then you're in a lot of trouble. Has Flaherty read Truitt's law review articles, his speeches? Does he know Truitt was a card-carrying member of the ACLU when he was a young professor? That he did a stint in the Peace Corps? Does he know that every Thanksgiving he still dishes out sweet potatoes at a homeless shelter? In a dispute between corporate executives and widows and orphans, which way do you think he'll vote?"

"Everyone has his price!' Max said.

"Wrong! Everyone *you* know has his price, but you don't know Sam Truitt. He really believes the stuff that's carved into the marble, the basic decency of people, the rule of law. Trust me. He's not the kind of man you can buy."

Shank cleared his throat. "That's exactly why you're so important, Lisa."

It was the first time he'd ever called her by her given name, and for a reason she couldn't articulate, she didn't like the familiarity.

"We're counting on you to persuade your boss that Atlantica should win," Shank said. "Simple as that."

"When two hundred eighty-eight people die in a plane crash, it's not so simple." She was growing even more furious.

"The trial court ruled for us," Shank said, smirking, "and so did the appeals court. It's not Atlantica's fault if some crazy Cubans bombed the plane."

"Shank's right," Max piped up. "The trial judge found we weren't negligent."

"Then you have nothing to worry about, do you? You don't need my help."

Shank smiled, or at least, he bared his teeth, small and jagged like eroded slivers of rock. "Maybe not, but we like to think we've bought some insurance."

"Sorry, I'm not for sale."

Shank's teeth vanished, and little vertical furrows appeared on his sloping forehead. "Max led me to believe you'd already been paid for."

Damn him!

"Max," she said, casting him a murderous glance, "is behind the times. Here's a news flash. I didn't go to law school to join some conspiracy that could put me in jail. I don't work for Atlantica, and I don't work for Max. As of today, I'm an employee of the United States government, and I'm not going to prostitute myself for you or anyone else."

"What!" Max was staring at her, wide-eyed. "Lisa. Lisa, darling, I thought we had a deal."

"There are no more deals, and there never will be. Now, you two are conspiring to obstruct justice, and I want you out of here."

Shank's laugh crackled like dead leaves underfoot. "Hey, Max. Call a cop. We're obstructing justice here."

Looking worried, not laughing at all, Max hurriedly stood and walked toward Lisa, who stiffened and folded her arms across her chest.

"Lisa, just hear Shank out," Max said, agitated. "Please. For me."

She'd never seen him this way, so nervous and unsure. There was a shift of power going on here, but why?

Jesus, Max. You're his boss. Why are you deferring to this glorified security guard?

"You've got five minutes," she said, "and then the two of you can get out of here."

Max nodded thankfully and returned to the sofa and his drink.

Shank ground out his cigarette in a crystal bowl on the coffee table and said, "We need you to use whatever legal mumbo jumbo you can come up with to win the case."

Mumbo jumbo? Oh, that's clever. Try to fool the guy who's maybe the smartest legal mind in America.

"But if you can't persuade him with the law," Shank continued, "we have a backup plan."

"Really? And what would that be?"

His smile was a leer. "Max showed me your bedroom, all frilly and smelling of powders and perfumes."

"Are you out of your mind?" Lisa exploded. "What do you think I am?"

"I don't know," Shank said. "What do you think you are?"

She was so astonished by his tone, by the insinuation, that she was momentarily speechless. Who was this thug to insult the boss' girlfriend, to throw his weight around with Max standing right there? Jesus, she didn't have to take this. Incensed, she turned to Max. "Are you going to let him talk to me like that?"

Max looked as if he might have a stroke. "Lisa, please—"

"It's not enough that you're planting an agent on the Court you want me to seduce Truitt, too."

"We're just counting on you to do what you do best Lisa," Shank said.

"And what would that be?" she asked, eyes narrowing. "Say it!"

Shank moved closer, drilling her with his dark eyes. His face was just above hers, invading her space, making her skin crawl, as if she'd just walked into a cobweb. She fought the urge to flinch and turn away.

Max, how could you let this lowlife bully me?

When Shank was close enough for Lisa to see every acne crater and smell his sour breath, when he filled her entire range of vision, when she felt both a distinct revulsion and a palpable fear, he spoke in a snarl, "You'll fuck him, Lisa. You'll fuck him real good."

"Bastard!" She whirled toward Max. "Did you hear that? This has gotten way out of hand. Since when am I taking orders from your rent-a-cop flunky?"

Shank laughed again, the sound of a Rottweiler barking. "Is that what you told her, Max, that I'm your flunky?"

"Now see here, Shank ..." Max said, making a jerky gesture with his arm and spilling his drink, his voice trailing off.

Lisa looked at Max in astonishment.

"Now see here?" Like some effete character in a tux straight out of Noel Coward.

"Get the hell out of my apartment, both of you!" Lisa shouted.

Seemingly amused again, Shank turned to Max. "How 'bout it, boss man, should we leave? Should we vacate the premises?"

Max started to say something, but nothing came out. He seemed to be nailed to the sofa and to have lost the power of speech. He meekly turned his palms upward in a gesture of surrender.

"Max is plumb out of ideas," Shank said, "so I'll do the talking. In case you missed it the first time, you'll fuck the judge till he's blue in the face. 'Til he's cross-eyed. 'Til he's deaf, dumb, and blind. You'll turn him upside down and inside out and suck him dry. And when he's so dizzy he doesn't know his own name, you'll get his vote because he'll do any damn thing you ask."

Stunned, a flood of bitter memories swept over her: her father telling her that she'd always be able to make a living on her back, the guys at the Tiki offering her wads of bills to meet them in the parking lot after closing, Crockett trying to pimp for her, then beating her up when she wouldn't go through with it. Max had protected her then; now, he was pushing her into it. The realization came to her with sickening clarity. After all these years, Max had become her pimp!

"In short, Lisa," Shank went on, seeming to enjoy every moment, licking each word with his tongue, "you'll do the judge just like you did old Max here, though frankly, jailbait pussy was probably sweeter. That so, Max? Was it better in the old days?"

"Now Shank, there's no need for that," Max said, standing up but not moving toward the other man. Not leaping across the room and decking the foul-mouthed pig, which is what Lisa imagined Scrap Truitt would have done. She pictured Truitt slugging the swine, breaking his jaw, citing some principle of natural law that empowers a man to defend his woman's honor.

"Oh, ex-cuse me," Shank said, dragging out the words, taunting them both. "You two were in love. The horny executive whose wife didn't understand him and the stripper with the genius IQ who could suck the chrome off a trailer hitch."

She slapped him, the *cr-aack* of hand on skin seeming to echo in the apartment. Finally, Max moved, dancing around the coffee table, coming up to Shank, apologizing, begging forgiveness, the girl doesn't get it yet, it's not her fault, Jeez Shank, it'll be okay.

"Shut up, Max," Shank said with a certainty that his order would be followed.

It suddenly occurred to Lisa that if Max was afraid of Shank, she probably should be, too. *Who was he, anyway?*

Shank turned back to Lisa and lowered his voice to a frightening whisper. "You're not fully aware of the situation here, Lisa, and I'm taking that into account. Max has protected you, and I let him. I didn't want to embarrass him, to cut off his balls in public, so I always walked two steps behind him, like the wife of the Japanese emperor. But now, you gotta know exactly how it is, to appreciate Max's position and your own."

He's talking about Max as if he weren't here. But then, he really isn't.

Shank smiled at her, but it was the smile of the wolf contemplating the hen. Then his right hand shot out, quick as a snake, and seized her by the wrist. His left hand grabbed her above the right elbow, and he twisted hard, spinning her around, bending the arm painfully until the back of her hand pressed against her shoulder blade. She couldn't see his face as he spat out the words, "You're nothing but a little slut who's forgotten where she belongs. You think you're smart, but if you were, you would have sized up the situation long ago. You would have shown respect. You would have had fear."

He cranked her arm higher, and a searing pain shot through her shoulder. She thought of a chicken's wishbone snapping in two.

He leaned even closer to her, brushing his lips through her hair, exhaling foul breath. "Do you know why they call me Shank?"

"It's ... it's your name," she said, confused.

"No! My name is Shakanian. A shank is a blade that cuts fast and deep. I'm a knife, and I'll cut right to the meat of you. Do you understand?"

"Yes." But she didn't understand. It was beyond comprehension.

"What do you know about me, Lisa?"

"Nothing," she said, her voice barely a whisper.

"So let me tell you. I live alone. I don't have a wife or a friend or a parakeet. What I've got is a lot of time to think. Lately, I've been thinking about you and how much you owe Max here, which really means how much you owe Atlantica. Do you follow me, Lisa?"

Wordlessly, fighting the pain, she nodded.

"Good." He released the pressure on her arm slightly but did not let go. "Do you like the movies, Lisa?"

Whether it was the pain or the fear, or the utter inanity of the question—for a second, she thought he was asking her out—Lisa couldn't answer.

"I'll bet you do," he said. "I'll bet you like foreign films with subtitles or love stories with sappy endings. Me, I go to the movies by myself, and I like to laugh, forget my troubles. So I see the comedies. *Reservoir Dogs, Bad Lieutenant, Natural Born Killers*. Ever see any of them?"

"They're not comedies," she heard herself say.

"Sure they are. Take the scene in *Reservoir Dogs*. One of the robbers has a cop tied up. He wants to know who's the informant in the gang. The cop won't tell him, so the robber cuts his ear off."

With his free hand, Shank roughly grabbed Lisa's ear, twisting it, painfully. "Now, here's the funny part. I'd already done it. I cut a guy's ear off maybe ten, twelve years before I saw the movie. So I'm watching it, thinking you don't get that much blood from an ear. That wasn't realistic. But the screams. The screams were real."

He's a madman, and he's going to cut me.

She knew a girl from the Tiki whose jealous boyfriend slashed her breasts to keep her from dancing. Lisa was paralyzed with fear. Her eyes searched frantically to see if he was holding a knife.

He let go of her ear and his hand brushed against her neck, seductively, stopping to fondle the single pearl earring. Then he kissed her neck, and unleashing his tongue like a serpent, he licked her. With a repulsive slurping sound, his tongue slithered up the slope of her neck.

I'm going to throw up. Jesus, if he doesn't stop, I'm going to …

His tongue withdrew and his teeth clenched the pearl earring, holding it there a second, freezing her with terror. Then he wrenched his head downward, ferociously tearing the post through her earlobe, yanking it free with a twist of his head like a pit bull mauling its prey.

She screamed as the pain shot through her, the sensation of her own shredding skin terrifying her.

Max stood, frozen in place.

Shank twisted her arm even higher against her shoulder blade. "Do you have fear now, Lisa? Do you have respect?"

Blinking through tears, she begged him, "Please! Please stop."

"Say it, bitch!" Again he twisted her arm, until she thought the ligaments would tear loose from the bones.

"I have fear," she cried, eyes squeezed shut, her shoulder screaming in agony. "I have respect."

He let her go. Her arm throbbed. Her ear stung. Blood dribbled from her earlobe. She felt faint.

"Good," Shank said, pocketing the bloody earring like spare change. "I've got confidence in you, Lisa. When you're through with the judge, he'll vote to revoke the Constitution if you ask him to. You do your job, Lisa, we've got no problems." He flashed a smile as jagged as a cracked eggshell. "You don't, I'll take your other earring and the ear, too."

He said it softly, matter-of-factly, without anger. Max hurried to Lisa's side and wrapped his arms around her just as her legs buckled.

Still speaking in a hushed voice, Shank said, "Now why don't you take a little walk so Max can bring you up to speed?"

Silently, Max guided her to the door. She was too shocked, too much in pain, to protest. As she stepped into the corridor, Lisa took one look back inside the apartment. Shank was lighting another cigarette. He took a deep drag, then tossed the match onto her Persian rug.

CHAPTER 6
The Shoe Box

SAMUEL ADAMS TRUITT MAY HAVE BECOME A JUSTICE of the Supreme Court but at home, he still carried out the trash. And walked the dog, a russet-haired mutt with retriever and shepherd blood named Sopchoppy, Sop for short. And verbally sparred with his wife, Connie, she of the patrician good looks and slashing wit. And on regular cycles, for the past two years, he gave his wife twice daily injections of Pergonal plus a 5 A.M. blood test, all aimed at increasing her egg production so that with the help of a fertility expert, a Petri dish, and divine intervention, they could enjoy the benefits of parenthood.

So far, the in vitro fertilization had not worked. All the ultrasounds, all the drugs with their chaotic mood-altering side effects, all the hours in the doctor's office squeezing her hand while a scope was inserted through her abdomen into the ovaries, all the needles depositing fertilized eggs into the uterus ... all for nothing.

For a while, he thought the experience brought them together. It was one of the few remaining areas of common passion or even interest. They laughed over Truitt's discomfort at walking into the OB-GYN's waiting room filled with suspicious women, then disappearing into a restroom to masturbate into a plastic cup.

"Was it good for you?" she had asked.

"My hands were too cold," he replied, "so the nurse helped."

Connie had shown him endless wallpaper patterns, paint chips, and photos clipped from *Architectural Digest* as they set about planning the nursery. Sam Truitt didn't know calico from chintz, and in fact spent several years of bachelorhood with window coverings of old bedsheets, but he took an interest in the mythical nursery for the mythical baby because it made Connie happy.

But lately, after so many misses, after Connie's headaches and nausea, exuberant hopes followed by deep despair, after more than twenty-thousand dollars in medical bills, there was little talk of babies and bassinets. Connie's moods had become both extreme and unpredictable. She would burst into tears at the sight of a pregnant woman or laugh hysterically at inopportune times.

Today, Truitt knew, Connie had been to the doctor to see if the latest implant of a fertilized egg or "pre-embryo," in Dr. Kalstone's lingo, had taken hold.

God, let her be pregnant.

Sam Truitt wanted to be a father; he wanted Connie to be happy; and he wanted to preserve his marriage. At the moment, all three were in jeopardy.

He had just stuffed a bulging garbage bag into the plastic curbside container. He had walked and pooper-scooped Sop, fed and brushed him, and told him he was sorry there were no game birds to chase in the neighborhood.

Carrying the recycle container to join the garbage at the curb, Truitt opened the gate in the black wrought iron fence to what was laughingly called their front yard. It was a rectangular space of dry brown grass roughly large enough for a single grave. One block away was the old Chesapeake and Ohio Canal, the narrow manmade waterway where tourists now rode in mule-drawn boats and locals hiked and jogged along a towpath lined with giant sycamores and willows.

The cramped townhouse was only twenty-seven feet wide—fifteen feet shorter than his snap to the punter—but stood three stories high. It was, Connie told him, a shoe box standing on end.

But it was in Georgetown, which is where she wanted to live. Insisted on it, really. Her family's second home had been here when she was growing up, when her father was a U.S. Senator from Connecticut. That house was three times the size of this one. But property was cheaper then, and her mother's inheritance fueled not only Daddy's political career but also a lifestyle far in excess of what an elected official could provide.

Truitt walked up two flights of stairs to the bedroom, eager to hear about Connie's visit to the doctor but apprehensive at the same time. She sat at her vanity applying makeup, seemingly oblivious to his presence.

If she's silent, does it mean she's not pregnant? No, the husband is not permitted to draw an adverse inference from the wife's failure to testify.

At thirty-eight, Connie was a striking woman whose fine bone structure, manner, and posture spoke of cultured breeding and expensive schooling. Truitt did a fancy sidestep to get around her without banging her elbow. "At home, I had my own sitting room," she said in greeting, as if reading his mind about the tight confines of the townhouse.

At home.

Home being Waltham, Massachusetts. Home being where they had spent the bulk of their not entirely happy marriage. Home *not* being where they now lived.

"It's the nineties," he replied. "Downsizing is in. I read it in *USA Today.*"

"Sam, you don't read *USA Today.*"

She kept her eyes on the mirror, where she was smoothing a glistening liquid on her lips. Whatever happened to simple lipstick? He could not keep up with women's fashions. Sam Truitt could tell you what Thomas Paine had for breakfast the day he wrote, "These are the times that try men's souls," but he was oblivious to what his wife wore to the Kennedy Center last Saturday night, coincidentally, to see a revival of *1776.* Or, for that matter, the names of the two couples—her friends not his—with whom they shared an après-theater supper, her expression, not his.

He dodged around the bed and opened the door to what the broker had called the walk-in closet but which would not accommodate anyone with shoulders wider than the average coat hanger. Connie's clothing took up all of her side and most of his. He stripped down to his underwear, straight-armed a number of her cocktail dresses, and hung up his suit. Feeling claustrophobic and not wanting to jitterbug past Connie like Emmitt Smith squeezing through the off-tackle hole, Truitt sat on the edge of the bed with its duvet of roses and hyacinths and looked at his wife in the vanity mirror.

He couldn't stand it any longer. "How did it go today?"

"I had lunch with Stephanie," she said, her eyes meeting his in the glass.

Objection! Not responsive. Your Honor, please admonish the witness to answer the question.

"They're building a gazebo in their backyard," Connie continued.

Truitt pondered this tidbit of news. Just what does one say to a wife whose sister is building a gazebo in the backyard of her showy two-million-dollar home? That it will be a nice addition to her Jacuzzi, lap pool, and sauna? That it must be nice being married to a lobbyist whose basic claim to fame is being the son-in-law of a former senator—fame enough to make $850,000 a year, more than five times the salary of a Supreme Court justice.

"Gazebos are nice," he said, prudently.

"She showed me the plans. It has a gas grill, a microwave, dishwasher, full-size refrigerator, plus an ice-cream fountain and a wet bar with two beer taps."

Why is she dragging it out? Am I going to be a father or not?

"What, no roller coaster?"

"There's no need to be sarcastic," she said. "Or a snob."

"What!"

"A reverse snob, actually."

He was stumped. "What does that mean, that I look down on people who are better than I am?"

"No, you look down on people who have attained goals which you think are"—she paused to find the right word, searching the breadth and depth of her Bryn Mawr-Sorbonne vocabulary—"inconsequential or frivolous."

"I cop a plea," he said. "Guilty as charged. What are the sentencing guidelines for a repeat offender?"

"Life," she said, "without parole."

He smiled with real pleasure. That was the old Connie. In the fencing match that was their life, a parry was usually followed by a thrust. Sometimes he yearned for the early days when they made each other laugh and competed to see who had the sharper wit. Connie usually won.

He watched his wife lift her long, chestnut hair into some impossible upswept pile that she clasped with several silver barrettes. Most of the time, she wore her hair parted in the middle, where it fell, long and swingy, across her shoulders. It made her look like a college coed. Now, with her hair up, she looked regal, Princess of the Capitol, with a long, slender neck and prominent cheekbones, her dark hair set off by flawless porcelain skin.

He pondered the nature of their relationship. Did he love her? Maybe it wasn't a raging passion, but there was still care and affection and, occasionally, warmth.

Sam Truitt had met Constance Parham at her family's third home, the summer cottage on Nantucket. Truitt was an assistant professor at Harvard Law with no particular interest in politics, but he had a professed animosity toward many of President Reagan's appointees to the federal bench. Senator Lowell Parham was the senior Democrat on the Judiciary Committee, and after reading one of Truitt's diatribes in *The New Republic*, he began calling on him to draft questions for judicial appointees considered unqualified.

Truitt was not ordinarily an introspective man, but he thought now of the forces that had brought him to Connie. Constance Parham was eight years his junior, just finishing up a graduate degree in art history when they met. He remembered the instant attraction to this tall, sassy brunette with a quick wit and a lethal tongue. She had the clean WASP features of her mother, a high forehead with a widow's peak, a wide smile, and the gift of her father's laughter and intelligence. Connie could hold her martinis, crack wise, and beat most men at tennis.

Looking back now, Truitt thought he fell in love with the family. The senator was a liberal without being a sissy, a Harvard intellectual who liked to hunt, fish, and drink bourbon. His wife was a descendant of Massachusetts Puritans who made several fortunes in New England textile mills and had the foresight to shift their wealth into Arizona real estate just before their businesses succumbed to foreign competition. Alice Parham adored her husband, who returned her love in both public and private displays of affection. Constance Parham grew up with the benefits of status and privilege; boarding school in Europe, a college curriculum that required a commute to Paris, and an endless supply of eligible suitors, some Cabots, some Lodges, some Kennedys. And one Truitt.

৩

"It'll be nice for the kids," he said, after a moment.

"What?"

"The ice cream bar. Maybe the beer taps too, for all I know."

"What are you implying?" Irritated now.

"Nothing, just that the gazebo will be nice for your sister's children, our nieces and nephews, the little blond platoon of well-fed Virginia storm troopers."

Actually, there were only four of them, all in braces, all in private schools, all with their own horses in their own stables. The orthodontics and tuition alone must be astounding, he thought, not to mention the oats and carrots. Harold Bellows, his brother-in-law, had an eighty-acre estate in Virginia. In the basement of the sprawling home was an English pub. A real one, the stained glass and dark wood stripped from a country pub in the Cotswolds. To Truitt, it represented the essence of ugly-American acquisitiveness. Taken from a place enjoyed by an entire village, the old scarred wood bar—ripe with the wet scent of a hundred years of spilled ale—was now used, if at all, by one pudgy, overpaid apologist for sugar growers, oil companies, and heaven help us, handgun manufacturers.

"You're attacking me," she said angrily.

"What? How?"

"You're reminding me in a cheap and cowardly way that we don't have children, that I can't have children, that my tubes are scarred, but your sperm count is in the top one percent. You're a first team All-American sperm machine with a wife who can't complete a pass."

Oh no. God no.

His heart sank. She had answered the question of the day, the question of the decade, the question of their lives. He walked over to the vanity and put his arms around her. Her shoulders felt like pillars of ice. "Connie, I'm sorry. I'm so sorry."

She glared at him in the mirror. "If you were truly sorry, you wouldn't have used Stephanie's children to disparage me."

He wondered if every marriage had one wound that would never heal. "I didn't! Sometimes a gazebo is just a gazebo. I was just making conversation about our spoiled nieces and nephews and a goddamnn gazebo that's probably bigger than our house."

"Exactly! You were striking out at me because of the gazebo. You thought I was belittling the amount of money you make in comparison to Harold, so you brought up the children to hurt me, to remind me that I'm defective, that I'm not a whole woman."

"No! I swear—"

"It's your fault as much as mine," she fired back. "You're the bastard who knocked me up back on the island."

The ferocity of her words startled him, and he backed off, retreating to the bed. His head throbbed. Their arguments were becoming more severe, Connie's attacks more cutting.

"Connie, what can I say to you? You're not defective. You're a bright, witty, breathtaking woman, and I don't care how much money Harold makes. I don't care if he moves the Smithsonian into his gazebo and invites the Washington Redskins to play in his backyard. So let's just forget it."

In the mirror, he saw her eyes brim with tears. There would be no more playful banter today. She had brought back the memories, which hung over them like the stalled thunderhead of a summer storm. At the time, Connie was just finishing her master's degree, still writing her thesis on French impressionism. They'd just starting going out, and one August night, after a swim in the cold Atlantic at dusk off Siasconset on Nantucket Island, wrapped in a blanket on the beach, they'd made love. He remembered even now her salty taste, her long wet hair falling into her face, his body grinding into her with the urgency and passion of new lovers.

My God, the heat we brought to each other.

He could still picture the fusion of their bodies, each of them heedless of the scraping sand and incoming tide, seeing only the first stars of evening, the rising moon, and the fire in each other's eyes. What he wouldn't give to re-create that with her now. For longer than he cared to admit, their lovemaking had been infrequent and perfunctory.

But then ... oh Lord, then the sex had been synchronized with the pounding of the waves. He had sung out her name on the sea breeze, exploding into her with a thunderclap from within, watching bolts of lightning through closed eyes.

He had also exploded into her without protection, an event that just now prompted Connie to refer to her husband not as "Sweetheart" but rather as "the bastard who knocked me up back on the island." Actually, he *had* used a condom, but it burst because, in his feverish haste, he had neglected to squeeze out the air pocket in the tip, which then detonated in the midst of their furious coupling. Sam Truitt's manual dexterity, it seemed, was limited to putting a spiral on the long snap.

Connie became pregnant. Their first crisis, the one that would launch all the others. Just like the chaos theory the physicists introduced to popular culture. The flap of a butterfly's wings in Brazil can cause a typhoon in the Pacific. And, he supposed, the explosion of a condom on Nantucket can cause an October freeze in Georgetown fifteen years later.

At the time, they handled the situation surprisingly well. He was sensitive, caring, understanding. She was thoughtful, mature, and decisive.

He said it was her choice all the way. He believed, then as a man, and now as a judge, that the woman had all the votes. There was no talk of marriage. After all, they barely knew each other. But if she chose to have the child, he promised to be there for them both. He'd visit, bring birthday presents, pay for everything right up through college. He gave himself an A for his hypothetical parenting skills, which she reminded him, were considerably greater than his actual contraception skills.

The abortion was quick and apparently without incident. Well, not without psychological incident. Connie became depressed. He felt guilty.

He'd never heard the term back then, but now he supposed they were snared in a codependent relationship. He wouldn't leave her, not like that. He was captured in the web of her moodiness, sinking in the quicksand of her unfulfilled needs.

They were married six months later, and the artificiality of the closeness that carried them through the abortion soon evaporated. For reasons neither they nor the doctors could understand, this healthy, athletic, screw-every-damn-night couple could not conceive. Several years later they learned that the abortion had caused an infection, which scarred her fallopian tubes.

Complicating their lives, hanging over them like an unseen ghost, was the child they never had. They did not even create an illusion, a fantasy child to sustain them like the playwright Albee's ineffectual George and vicious Martha, locked in a perpetual embrace of psychological cruelty. Their life together had begun with the act of conceiving an unwanted child on the shore of an ocean, and in what Sam's Southern Baptist relatives would have considered an act of biblical retribution, they cried a sea of tears trying to duplicate the feat.

"Do you know what really angers me?" she asked, finally.

Everything, he thought.

"The fact that you don't see the connection between your words and the source of your feelings," she answered herself.

He had to get out of there. The bedroom was growing smaller by the minute. He stood and tried to escape, squeezing between his wife and the bed, banging his shin into an open vanity drawer.

"Damn! *Plessy versus Ferguson!*" When he was angry, Truitt tried to confine his profanity to the names of horrific Supreme Court decisions. Sopchoppy responded with a quiet *woof.*

"I told you this house was too small," she said as he fled, hopping on one foot.

The Truitts' two-hundred-year-old farmhouse near Waltham was ten times larger, Connie frequently reminded him. They had eighteen gently rolling acres with a stream on one side of the property and a duck pond on the other. But Connie was unhappy there, too, always complaining that the house was too big, too drafty, too old, too far from Boston.

Washington was going to be their move to the city. Embassy parties, dinner at Citronelle, shopping for antiques.

Sam Truitt cared nothing for black tie dinners or sautéed foie gras with poached figs in port wine sauce. His tastes were simpler, preferring cut-off jeans and a meal of plain grilled snapper and boiled swamp cabbage, a legacy of growing up in Everglades City. It took him thirty years to find out that his momma's swamp cabbage was called heart of palm when served in fancy restaurants, including The Palm, and an appetizer portion could set you back eight bucks. He used to eat about a pound of the concoction for supper. His mother, a Florida Cracker, would slice open a palm tree with a machete and cook the fibrous meat with sow's belly or ham hock in a fifty-five-gallon drum on an open fire. They'd eat, year-round, at a picnic table under a live oak tree, zebra butterflies flapping over their heads, causing typhoons in Tonga, he now supposed.

Washington was also going to rejuvenate the marriage, and who knows, maybe lead to a magical fertility that had escaped them farther north. So far, all it had accomplished was to bring them into closer confinement.

Two scorpions in a shoe box.

He preferred the open spaces of the wetlands where he grew up. Connie insisted on referring to the Everglades as "the swamp," despite his insistence that it was really a slow-moving freshwater river some sixty miles wide. Just after his nomination to the Court last spring, he returned to Florida for "Sam Truitt" day, which the local weekly termed the largest celebration the town had ever seen, if you didn't count the annual seafood festival. The volunteer fire department led a parade, with the high school band playing off-key Sousa. A chugging John Deere tractor hauled Sam and Connie down Conch Avenue on a float with papier-mâché pillars representing the Supreme Court, Connie choking on the diesel fumes that hung in the humid air.

In the sweltering Fishermen's Hall, Truitt made a speech, tracing his success to values learned in the sloughs and creeks of the Ten Thousand Islands, and Connie stood there in a yellow sundress, fanning herself with a commemorative poster, complaining about the heat, picking over the supper of fried catfish, hush puppies, and key lime pie—washed down with sugar-laden iced tea. Later, manhandling bottles of tequila, Truitt and some of the good ole boys, now leathery fishermen with scarred hands and squinty eyes, swapped lies about their youth and who built the fastest airboat from broken airplane propellers and old Chevy engines.

Truitt hadn't been home since his mother's funeral eight years earlier. His father had died three years before that. This time, as he clasped hands and slapped shoulders of old friends and acquaintances, he kept an eye on Connie, studying her discomfort. While he felt at home, she looked afraid of stepping in something squishy and repulsive.

That night in their motel room, as they settled onto opposite sides of the lumpy bed, Connie said, "I didn't know I'd married Huck Finn."

"Yes you did," he replied.

Sam Truitt knew that Connie would have been happier married to a real estate developer who made millions building condos in protected wetlands, or an investment banker who knew the value of the deutsche mark when the markets opened each day—anyone whose net worth equaled her appetite for consumption.

To Truitt, status was achieved by deeds, not dollars. His love of the law was paramount over building a net worth. It also took priority over personal relations, something he acknowledged as a flaw in his character. When they first moved to Washington, he realized that he was more concerned about the needs of migrant workers than those of his newly migrated wife.

He accepted the fact that Connie grew less affectionate each year. Hell, he deserved it. Sam Truitt was, after all, a man who had difficulty expressing his emotions, much less fulfilling the emotional needs of another person. Who could blame Connie if she longed for a man who would pamper his wife instead of illegal aliens?

So Sam Truitt understood half a dozen years earlier when she had her first affair, with the tennis pro at the club, of all the mundane clichés. He responded with an affair of his own, an adoring law student, in violation of university rules and his own ethics. I'll see your cliché and raise you another. They weathered those storms and stayed together.

At first, Connie had seemed happy when he received the Supreme Court appointment. No more faculty teas with their dreary gossip washed down by watery punch. Life in Washington would be different. But she must have been thinking of her father's social whirl as a senator, always making the rounds of chic parties and Georgetown dinners. She was not prepared for the more monastic life of a Supreme Court justice. Boredom set in quickly. After not having worked for years, Connie began an interior decorating business. Now, her fondest hope was for the defeat of the Democratic president in the next election, both to punish him for appointing her husband, and to bring wealthy Republicans to town with an insatiable desire to redecorate.

His shin still throbbing, a truce having been declared by his retreat from the bedroom, Truitt was sitting at the small desk in the study when he heard Connie's voice. "Did you hire the third law clerk, Sam?"

"Yes," he called back, as he thumbed through the briefs for the first oral argument of the new term. "She's a real winner. Lisa Fremont."

"Tell me about her." Connie was moving around in the bedroom. They were talking to each other now separated by the landing at the top of the stairs—and years of missed connections.

"She's from the West Coast. Berkeley, Stanford, then a year clerking on the D.C. circuit."

"A California beach bunny?"

"She's a fisherman's daughter and smart as hell."

"I'll bet she's pretty."

He could lie, of course. "She looks like Howard Stern in drag."

But the first time Connie had the clerks over for dinner, she'd brain him with a lamb chop. "As a matter of fact, she's quite attractive," he said.

"I thought you had a bounce in your step when you came home today."

"I had to pee."

She walked into his study from the master bedroom. She was wearing a sleeveless black silk cocktail dress, a triple strand of pearls, and matching earrings.

"My God, you're beautiful," he said.

"Look at you!" she cried. "You're not ready."

"Ready for what?" he asked, even though it occurred to him that she was dressed for a party while he was wearing a twenty-year-old Wake Forest sweatshirt with holes in both Ds of Demon Deacons.

"The reception at the Watergate. It starts at seven. Hurry up. I'll find your tux."

"What reception?"

"The benefit! The one Stephanie and Harold invited us to, bought our tickets, a thousand dollars each."

"Not the one sponsored by the National Association of Manufacturers," he said, vaguely recalling having told his brother-in-law thanks but no thanks.

"Who cares who's sponsoring? It's for the hospital. It's nonpolitical, nonsectarian, nonoffensive even to a holier-than-thou associate justice on the Supreme Court."

"I told Harold we couldn't go," he said guiltily, realizing he'd forgotten to tell Connie.

"What! Why?"

"NAM is amicus curiae in a major case on punitive damages, and they're involved in another half dozen cases with cert petitions pending. Besides, I can't accept a gift from a lobbyist."

"You must be kidding. Do you think you'll be compromised by eating their goat cheese on endive?"

"No, but my attendance makes it appear they have access to the Court."

Holding her high-heeled black shoes in one hand, Connie waved her hairbrush at him with the other. "Don't do this, Sam! Don't do this to me. I'm going stir crazy in this damn shoe box."

"I know it seems silly or quaint, or just plain stupid, but a Supreme Court Justice has to live like a monk." He thought of the Chief, who wasn't right about many things, but on this one, he was. "Some justices won't even attend the President's State of the Union address because of separation of powers. Even those who go refuse to applaud."

"You're right, Sam. It is stupid. Now, are you getting dressed or not?"

He looked into her eyes, which were ablaze with hostility. All the disappointments and frustrations of a life that didn't turn out the way she planned seemed to be reflected in her glare, in her bearing, in the way she pointed the hairbrush at him as if it were a Saturday night special manufactured by one of her brother-in-law's clients.

"I can't, Connie. I'm sorry, but I can't"

She threw the hairbrush at him. He slipped his head to the side like a boxer dodging a punch, and the brush clattered against the wall. She hastily pulled on her shoes, smoothed her dress over her flat stomach, and looked at him, her upper lip quivering with anger. "All right, Mr. Supreme Court Justice," she said, spitting out the words. "Be a monk. Be a bishop or a cardinal or the damn pope for all I care."

She turned dramatically and left the room, looking like a leading lady playing her big scene in her shimmering black dress. She started down the narrow staircase, two flights to the ground, her stiletto heels clapping against the wooden stairs like rifle shots. "But I'll tell you this," she called out, "I'll be damned if I'm going to be a nun!"

CHAPTER 7
A Deal with the Devil

THEY WALKED ALONG A WELL-WORN, dimly lighted path in Rock Creek Park, Max holding on to Lisa, who was still shaken. The tennis courts were empty. A man in a warm-up suit struggled to control a giant Irish wolfhound on a leash. Man and dog disappeared around a bend in the path. The only sounds were the rusting leaves on the ancient oak and maple trees and the gurgle of the nearby creek.

Max wrapped an arm around her and dabbed at her bloodied earlobe with a white handkerchief. He'd failed her and could only imagine how disappointed she must be in him. He felt puny and weak in front of the one person in the world who had always seen him as being so strong.

He knew he had lost her, that it could never be the same, and that was the worst part, worse even than the humiliation and the fear. She thought he was a coward, but she didn't know the truth, didn't know of his pain and guilt over the crash. How could she? He had kept the truth from her.

When did it all start to go downhill? It didn't happen all at once, and I didn't see it sliding away, inch by inch.

"Lisa, I'm so sorry," he said. "If I could turn the clock back—"

"You can't! None of us can. If I could, I'd turn it back so far we never would have met."

"Lisa—"

"Get away from me! Or if you really want to help, call a cop. Have the bastard arrested for assault and battery."

Jesus, now he didn't have a choice. He had to protect her from her own instincts. Fighting Shank was suicidal. The only way out was to cooperate.

Max still needed Lisa's help, but she despised him. He had to win her back one last time. He considered what to tell her and settled on the truth.

"I know you're upset, but—"

"Just let me alone. Go tell that maniac that he just bought himself a ticket to jail. Now, are you going to call the police, or do I have to do it?"

"No! Lisa, you don't understand."

"I understand you're not the man I thought you were," she said. "I always knew you played fast and loose in business. I knew you had no respect for the law, but to let another man hurt me ..."

Her voice trailed off and tears welled in her eyes.

A knot tightened in Max's stomach. She was right. What could he say? There were many ways to fail a woman but none so shameful as what they had just been through. He was filled with a self-loathing and disgust that he had never known before. He had put her in the line of fire without explaining the risks. He had neglected to tell her she didn't have a choice to turn down the job. Now there was only one way out, but she still didn't see it.

"If you go to the police, I can't protect you," he said.

Her laugh was filled with contempt. "Protecting me does not seem to be your strong suit, Max."

But that's exactly what I'm doing. Please listen to me.

"You can have FBI baby-sitting you round-the-clock, and they'd still get to you," he said.

"What are you talking about? Who are *they*?"

He brooded silently, head down. He would tell her everything, but where to begin? "I never expected it would go this way. I hate what I've done and I hate what I've become. I'm so sorry to have put you in this position."

"Max, you're babbling. What did you do?"

గు

Her tone had changed. For the moment, at least, the anger subsided and she seemed willing to listen.

"I made a deal with the devil," Max Wanaker said.

He began with Shank, the symbol of everything that had gone wrong, the nightmare sprung to life.

He told her that Shank had been a young detective on the NYPD back in the 1970s. He was a member of the Special Investigations Unit assigned to narcotics. Unfortunately for the populace, Shank was more interested in lining his own pockets than in capturing criminals. He had boasted to Max about a game the SIU detectives played with drug dealers. If the DA was planning to abandon an investigation because of insufficient evidence, Shank would sell the case, telling the dealer he could make the investigation go away.

"I was dumping a case that was gonna be dumped anyway," Shank had told him. "What's the big deal? It's more like point shaving than throwing a game."

But of course, it didn't stop there. Soon, Shank was illegally wiretapping drug dealers to find out when and where a sale was going down. He would show up, bust the guy, seize the heroin, then sell it back and never press charges. Or Shank would plant drugs on a suspect, arrest him, then extort him. If he paid, the file would disappear. But that wasn't the worst of it.

"He killed people, too," Max said. "Drug dealers, mostly. Says he did a service to society."

"'The savage in the service of civilization,'" Lisa said.

"Huh?"

"Victor Hugo's description of Inspector Javert in *Les Miserables*."

"Great music," Max said, and she let it pass, then listened intently as Max told her everything he knew about Shank.

After years of Internal Affairs investigations ranging from police brutality—"customers' complaints"—to official corruption, the DA put together a case that could send Shank away for bribery and several other major felonies. The day before the hearing, the witnesses—two guys who saw hand-to-hand exchanges of money—both disappeared. They turned up three weeks later, their bodies composting on a truck farm in New Jersey. With teams of cops, FBI, and DEA agents trailing him, taping him, attempting to set him up, with the Knapp Commission ferreting out corruption on the force, Shank turned in his badge.

"He became a bodyguard," Max said, "working for a company that protected foreign dignitaries. Then he formed his own company. On the surface, it was a limo service, but the drivers were ex-cops like Shank, and the clients were drug dealers. Not street punks, but Colombian cowboys, Asian heroin traffickers, that sort of thing. The drivers were bodyguards, guys who knew the city and could get them around."

Somehow, Max didn't know exactly how, Shank ended up in Japan, working for this consortium that invests in businesses in the West.

"They' re the ones who loaned Atlantica money when my back was to the wall four years ago," Max explained.

"What loan? I thought business just turned around."

Max laughed, but there was no mirth in the sound. "Yeah, that's what the annual report said."

"You cooked the books," she said. "You show a loan as revenue, so you have an undisclosed debt. That's securities fraud, Max."

"The SEC is the least of my worries, I assure you."

"Who gave you the loan?"

"Actually, it's more of an investment, though not the kind you learned about in corporate law class. My Asian buddies aren't lenders looking for prime plus two points. They want fifty percent of my profits or my head on a stake."

"Gangsters?" she asked.

"Yeah, sort an investment banker version of Shank, except they don't shake down drug dealers. They suck the blood out of companies in trouble. There's no paperwork, no liens on aircraft, no nothing except the knowledge that I've got some new partners, or more accurately, new bosses."

"This consortium," Lisa said. "What's its name?"

"No name. No address. No phone number. I deal with a man in Osaka named Katsushika Koshiro."

"I can't believe this. You're probably dealing with the Yakuza." She looked alarmed.

"Yakuza, Tongs, Triads. How the hell would I know the difference?"

"You wouldn't if you closed your eyes to it. You're laundering dirty money, aren't you Max?"

"I suppose. I didn't ask questions."

"Max! How could you? And how could you drag me into it?"

"Lisa, you don't know what it was like then."

"You never told me."

He thought of everything he'd done to save the airline. Shit, he'd worked his ass off, scrambling for financing, playing the angles, cutting corners till they were round. When he was acquiring his kingdom, Max considered himself a combination of Donald Trump and Machiavelli's Prince. Somewhere he'd read that Trump could not pass a mirror without stopping to admire himself, often repeating his mantra: "You're a king ... You're a killer." Max had longed to be both, and if he was not born to royalty—of either the real estate or Renaissance variety—he had learned to wear the crown. He pushed himself to excel, to win, to destroy the opposition. Within the orbit of his own universe, he'd become a king.

*But look at me now. A figurehead CEO with a big desk, a bigger debt,
and my life hanging by a thread.*

"It all happened after you stopped seeing me," he said. "Expansion
had eaten up our credit line, and our bond rating was so low that 'junk'
would have been a step up. We'd put all those reconditioned DC-10s on
line, the price wars were killing us, and we got slaughtered on the Miami-
London route. All the wise guys were selling us short, and our stock was
in the toilet. We were days away from a bankruptcy filing when I closed
the deal. I wouldn't have done it if there had been any other alternative. I
would have lost everything, and I'd already lost you."

"What are you saying? That you engaged in a criminal conspiracy
because I broke up with you?"

"No, but if we'd been together, who knows, you might have talked me
out of it."

He immediately regretted what he'd said. The way it sounded. Whiny
and weak. My mistress left me, so I went to pieces. But there was a measure
of truth in it. Lisa was in her first year of law school. He remembered the
determined look on her face when she told him it was time she moved on,
grew up. He'd been expecting it, but it still hurt. Who could blame her?
He had a wife and two kids back home. Lisa had been with him for six
years, and he'd been faithful to her, if that's what it's called when a married
man has only one girlfriend. He loved her. He hadn't said it often, but he
was sure that she knew.

So he'd let her go, praying she'd come back. She was going through
a phase, he thought. Tasting independence, testing her wings. There was
another man, he was sure. But then, hadn't he told her she was free to
date? What was he going to do, lock her in her apartment? She'd told him
about the football player at Berkeley and the young lawyer who taught in
the clinical program at Stanford. She never lied to him or hid anything.
Until the breakup. He knew then that she'd met someone. Someone
who mattered. Max remembered traveling to San Francisco on business,
driving down to Palo Alto, and sitting in the car outside her apartment
building one Friday night. All night. She never came home.

From San Francisco, he had flown to Japan and closed the deal, selling
his soul, coming home with a check. So maybe, in a way, it was Lisa's
fault. Had he not been so distraught over losing her, maybe he wouldn't
have done it. If she'd been home that Friday night, making frozen pizza or
doing her laundry, lonely and dejected, maybe she would have invited him
in. They'd have made love and talked, and she would have convinced him

to file for Chapter 11 reorganization, instead of dealing with Katsushika Koshiro, who smiled like a piranha and handed him cashier's checks with strings attached ... to his throat.

Lisa came back to him nearly a year later. She never mentioned who she'd been with, what had happened. It was after the crash, and she was different. Older, sure. A year of law school under her belt. But more world weary, too. He told himself she'd simply grown up, that she was still the same Lisa, but of course she wasn't.

Who is the same? Am I?

When they got back together, she seemed sad, resigned. The sizzle they had created so long ago was missing. But she was back, and that was enough. It had to be.

He picked up a branch that had fallen from a tree and used it as a walking stick. Ahead of them, a squirrel dashed across the path, an acorn clamped in its mouth. The squirrel hopped onto a tree, scooted around the back side, and disappeared. A reminder that winter was coming, as if Max needed a reminder. No, what he needed were more acorns.

∽

Something didn't make sense to Lisa. There were still missing pieces. She forced herself to focus, to be analytical.

"What does Shank do for the consortium?" she asked.

"I'm getting to that," he said.

"And why is he so insistent that I help you win the appeal? I know the case is important but lots of airlines have survived devastating crashes with huge damage awards. The insurance pays off the judgments and life goes on."

"It's not that simple," Max said.

It never is, she thought.

"For about a year, everything was okay," he said. "We were getting this influx of money, breaking even on a cash basis, turning things around. Then some assholes blow up flight six-forty, and the world turns to shit. Bookings drop twenty-five percent and never fully recover. We get sued, the FAA grounds three of our other DC-10s for so-called maintenance problems, and the publicity is killing us. Then came the coup de grace." He lowered his voice, as if the words were too painful to say aloud. "In the middle of the litigation, our insurer goes belly up."

"What! You never told me that. I knew Lloyd's was having problems with some of its partnerships, but I'd never heard of them defaulting."

"They didn't. I switched the coverage to a Bermuda trust, a reinsurer supposedly with a billion dollars of assets."

"Oh, no."

Oh yes. Max told her how his Japanese partners had wanted to see some return on their investment, because fifty percent of zero was not making them happy. With the cost of insurance skyrocketing, he had a brilliant idea. He could cut the premiums in half by going the Bermuda route. It was a risk, sure, but Atlantica had never had a crash. Paying those huge premiums was like burning money. The one thing he hadn't counted on was the trust going bankrupt. It turned out to have been a scam. Max Wanaker, a sharpie himself, got taken by a couple of Australians who phonied up the books. They had an insurance company, sure, until there was a claim. Then they disappeared.

The enormity of the situation was beginning to sink in. Atlantica had no coverage! They'd been flying bare when 640 went down. Which meant that judgments of, say five hundred million dollars, which was roughly equivalent to the net worth of its assets, would wipe out the company.

"My Japanese pals would lose everything," Max said.

"How much is everything? How much do you owe?"

"Initially, it was twenty-five million to keep operations going. A few months later, another twenty-five. After the crash, we were hemorrhaging money. I kept turning to Koshiro, and the money kept flowing. They had no choice. It was either that or lose their investment. The total now is two hundred ten million."

"Oh my God!"

"Yeah, it's a lot, particularly when it's got my personal IOU on it. Shank is their attack dog. Director of security is just the title we came up with to explain his presence. He watches me and, frankly, tells me what to do, following instructions from Koshiro. Basically, his job is to get their money back, either by turning around the airline, or more likely, selling off the assets. To do either one, we've got to win the case."

"I don't see why you're taking all the heat," she said. "It's their fault for letting you drop the Lloyd's insurance."

"You don't get it, Lisa. They didn't authorize it. They didn't know about it. It was my little secret."

Oh, Jesus! Now, it was coming clear. He'd bet the farm. Only it was somebody else's farm and he never told them he'd slid all their chips into the pot.

"Max, oh Max."

It was incomprehensible to her. He had missed one rung on the ladder and was sliding straight down to a crash landing. How could he have taken such a risk, one misstep compounding another, first the foreign racketeers, and then the insurance? She was softening, her anger turning to pity. Her heart ached for him. This man who had once rescued her, who had saved her from the streets, was drained of all his life, an empty shell of a man. Suddenly, she hugged him, tucking his head against her shoulder. It was a comforting embrace, one of compassion and empathy, not romance. They'd been through so much together, and now this.

She broke the embrace and appraised him. He had aged more than she had realized. His eyes were puffy, his forehead creased, the shoulders slumped. She forced herself to think like a lawyer. Max had a problem and needed her help. How could she do it without compromising the principles she had so recently adopted?

"And there's no paperwork?" she asked. "No promissory notes, guarantees, memos."

"No, what difference does it make?"

She was quiet a moment. It was fully dark now. The wind was picking up, and the temperature was dropping. She still wore the double-breasted blue blazer and taupe skirt, her interview uniform. Her shoulder ached from Shank making a pretzel out of her arm, her ear burned as if stung by a wasp, and her feet were beginning to hurt in the new pumps she'd bought to match the blazer.

"The debt is probably not enforceable," she said. "It violates so many laws it probably could be voided."

Max's laugh was a small, dry cough. "Lisa, darling Lisa, I think law school melted your brain. What happened to those street smarts? They won't take this to court. *I'm* the collateral. If we lose the case, they foreclose on *me*. Shank will make sushi out of me."

"Which he wanted me to know," she said, sorting through the whirlwind of developments since she had opened her apartment door barely an hour earlier.

Max's head on a stake!

It wasn't hyperbole. He had meant it.

"That's part of it. Shank figures you won't cut and run if you know my ass is on the line. He's betting you'll flip Truitt for him rather than let me go down for the count."

Damn! Life was so unfair. This was not her battle. She shouldn't have to do this. She wanted to run, to get away from Max, from Shank, from the creeping shadows of her past. She could head back to California. To Tasmania. To hell with the clerkship!

"Was Shank right?" Max asked, his voice pleading. "Will you help me?"

"Oh Max, poor darling Max. I'm trying to let go of the past."

"I won't beg you Lisa."

Yes you will, damnit! That's just what you're doing.

"But I need your help more desperately than I've ever needed anything. If I mean anything to you ..." He stopped, appraised her a moment. "Are you letting go of *me*, too?"

She hadn't thought of it in those terms before, but he'd nailed it, hadn't he?

I want a new life, and as much as you mean to me, as much as I owe you, I've moved beyond you. I've shed that old skin.

But, looking at the rusted relic of the man who had done far more for her than any other person on the planet, she couldn't run away. Last night, Max had said he'd only marked the trail for her. *"You climbed it all by yourself."* But she knew she would never have taken the first step without him. Her eyes brimmed with tears.

"No, Max, I'm not letting go of you," she said, hating herself for caving in.

Damn, damn, damn it to hell. I can't abandon him.

She would stay and do what had to be done to get Sam Truitt's vote. She would repay the old debt ... with interest. "Max, you rescued me once and changed my life forever. I won't let you face this alone."

The tension seemed to drain from him. He smiled broadly, a bright sun emerging from gray clouds. "Great! Maybe we can start over. Do things right this time."

"Max, don't. Please. I'll do everything I can, but when the case is over—"

"Just hear me out. My kids are nearly grown. Jill couldn't care less if I come home or not. I can just end it ..."

He was going on about their new life, excited, relieved, hopeful ... but something Max had said was echoing in the back of Lisa's mind. *"That's part of it."*

"We can get a place on the beach," Max was saying. "We can get married and—"

"What do you mean 'part of it'?" she interrupted.

"What?"

"A few moments ago, I said that Shank wanted me to know how much trouble you were in, and you said, that was part of it."

"Yeah."

"So what's the rest?"

၏

Max didn't want to answer, didn't want to say the words. Didn't even want to think it. But she had asked, and she ought to know, probably would have known half a dozen years ago, before all that academic double-talk dulled her instincts and filled her head with useless ideas.

"I'd thought it was clear," he said. "I thought you'd already figured it out."

"What?"

"If we lose, Shank will kill you, too."

CHAPTER 8

The Sorcerer's Apprentice

SHE WOULD DO IT. SHE DIDN'T HAVE A CHOICE.

Shank had frightened Lisa to the core of her being, and she had the torn flesh to prove it. Last night, in the midst of a restless sleep, she'd had nightmares of a featureless man with a foot-long razor, sharpening the blade on a leather strap, which popped and snapped under the smooth steel. Behind the cardboard mask of a face, the man said she had cute little ears, then emitted a piercing laugh, which awakened her.

She had nowhere to turn. Even if she could go to the police, what would she say? *I was part of a conspiracy to corrupt the Court, and now that I've backed out, my life has been threatened.*

At best, she'd be fired; at worst, disbarred. No, strike that. At worst, Shank would kill her.

So she would do it for Max. And for herself. And then she would be free.

It wouldn't be easy. The case cried out for reversal. Even the math was against her, as the Court routinely reversed eighty percent of the cases it agreed to hear.

She rationalized what she was about to do.

Hell, it's only one case. I'll make up for it somehow.

She tried to focus on the future, life after Atlantica, life after the Supreme Court. In a year, she would get glowing recommendations from her justice, whom she would call "Judge," and maybe later, "Scrap." Then she'd take that law firm job in Chicago with a good shot at one of the European offices.

All of these thoughts kept intruding, clouding her mind, distracting her from the dozen law books spread across the long, polished table in the ornate third-floor library of the Supreme Court. She was wearing a three-piece Calvin Klein outfit, expensive as hell, a V-neck soft jacket in steel blue feathered crepe of wool and nylon over a gray washed silk georgette wrap blouse and a matching wrap skirt.

She looked down at the open volume of annotated Supreme Court opinions, but her mind was floating on gentle breezes in a vast ocean. The South Pacific. Tasmania.

Tasmania being a symbol, she knew. The end of the world. Escape. She was in the sixth grade when she'd read about the islands. New Guinea, New Zealand, Bora Bora ... Tasmania. She was also in the sixth grade when her drunken father first lurched into the bathroom when she was in the tub. He'd wanted to scrub her back, but she said no. He muttered something about her being just like her mother and left, saying he'd be back. She started taking baths only when he wasn't home. Just the thought of Tasmania then seemed like a trip to another solar system. So exotic, so remote, so safe. She didn't need a shrink to tell her the connection.

For a moment, she thought she smelled cigarette smoke, but it was the wisp of a cruel memory drifting back to her now. She was twelve years old and dreaming the dreams of a child when she smelled the smoke. She opened her eyes and saw the glowing tip of a cigarette and the silhouette of a man standing at the foot of her bed.

"Daddy?"

Harry Fremont sat on the bed, grinding out the cigarette between calloused fingers, then dropping it on the floor. He leaned over in the darkness and brushed back Lisa's bangs from her forehead.

"You're home," she said sleepily.

"Man goes where the fish run, comes home and finds no supper ready."

"Do you want me to make you some macaroni and cheese, Daddy?"

"You're Daddy's little girl, aincha?" he said, his breath a mixture of smoke and bourbon, his clothes reeking of fish and seaweed.

She wanted to be Daddy's little girl, but the way he'd been looking at her lately frightened her.

"You look like your Momma, but you ain't gonna get fat like her, are you?" he said, tracing a finger down her forehead, across the bridge of her nose, and then around the outline of her lips, tickling her until she twitched her nose like a rabbit

"Momma's pretty," she said.

"She's passed out on the porch, snoring like a pig. Woman never could hold her whiskey."

"It's cold outside, Daddy. You should take her a blanket."

"She's falling down on the job. You know what happens when a woman don't do her job?"

Lisa shook her head no, in the darkness.

"Then it's up to her little girl to do it instead."

"Do what, Daddy? I cook and clean and do my errands."

He pulled the sheet down from under her chin. "I'll show you, baby."

There were other nights—endless nights—in the next five years before she ran away. A picture came back to her from that day. She was hugging Greg Kingston, each of them crying on the other's shoulder, then the skinny thirteen-year-old grabbing a baseball bat and begging her not to run away.

"You don't have to leave," he told her. "If your old man touches you again, I'll brain him. I'll squash his head."

Greg tried to call his own father, but Tony Kingston was three thousand miles away at Hulbert Field in the Florida panhandle. Lisa barely knew Tony then. He was, after all, a grown man, and she was seventeen. She remembered the gilt-framed photo of Tony on the living room wall. He was standing on a carrier deck in his flight suit a proud, heroic warrior with a crinkly-eyed grin. To Lisa, the photo seemed to say, this is a *man*!

Looking back, she realized that the best part of her own stunted childhood and adolescence—hell, the only decent part—was in the Kingston home; she remembered spending as much time as she could with Greg and his grandmother, Mary Kingston, a plainspoken woman who waited tables in a waterfront restaurant and made delicious salmon soup at home. Lisa did the dishes and looked after Greg, basking in the warmth and love she never received at home. Sometimes, sitting in the small, neat living room after dinner, Mary would talk about her son while they folded laundry or just watched television. For a time, it had seemed Tony would never get out of Bodega Bay, Mary Kingston told Lisa. His senior year in high school, Tony had gotten his high school girlfriend pregnant. They never married, and the girl moved away, leaving the infant Greg with Tony. Tony was reluctant to leave town, to take the college scholarship he'd been offered, but Mary pushed him to go. He joined Navy ROTC, then made the grade in flight school after graduation. Mary stayed home and cared for her grandson.

Despite the distance, Tony was a caring, loving father. Several times, Lisa answered the phone when he called from some remote air base, sometimes with the roar of jets in the background. Tony would always ask how she was doing, and he always seemed to care.

One image of Tony kept coming back to Lisa whenever she thought of her childhood. Home on leave, Tony stepped off the bus from San Francisco with an olive green duffel bag slung over a shoulder. He wore camouflage fatigues bloused inside black combat boots, a red scarf at the neck, the insignia of some special squadron that seemed so exotic to Lisa. It was as if he had materialized from within a movie screen, a mythical hero come to life. How could she have known then that Tony Kingston, father figure, would become her lover, her soul mate, the man who made her complete? How could she not love this strong man whose eyes filled with tears when he spoke of those his bombs had killed on his Gulf War missions? How could she know he would always be there for her ... until the day he died?

But he wasn't there that night when she was seventeen and scared to go back home. Only Greg was there to protect her, baseball bat in hand. She kissed Greg good-bye and hitched a ride to San Francisco, setting up housekeeping with the steroid-freak Crockett in a roach-infested Daly City apartment, bringing Tasmania with her in the form of a poster of the Cataract Gorge. That poster was long gone, but only today she'd hung another above her desk in the Supreme Court building. This one was a montage of shots of the island's rocky coastline; Blowhole, Devil's Kitchen, and Tasman Arch. Symbols die hard. Maybe someday she would go there. Maybe she wouldn't have a choice.

A few months after Lisa ran away, Harry Fremont's pickup truck—filled with stolen crab pots—plunged off a cliff on a desolate section of the Shoreline Highway. Many times, she envisioned the truck, soaring into space, tumbling in slow motion, crashing onto the rocks seventy-five feet below. Unlike the movies, there was no explosion or fire. Instead, the coroner later told her, her father had been conscious—his hands raw from clawing at the twisted metal that trapped him—before dying sometime after dawn from loss of blood and shock. So there is a God, she thought, hoping her father had not been so drunk as to be anaesthetized from the pain.

Lisa was still an undergraduate at Stanford when Tony left the navy, looking for a job in commercial aviation. She was with Max at the time and told him about her neighbor from home, a ruggedly handsome combat hero from the Gulf War who looked like a poster boy for *Top Gun* pilots. Atlantica was growing wildly, adding routes, aircraft, and crews.

Impressed, Max called Tony personally, and the triangle was formed. Later, after Lisa left Max, she and Tony became lovers. After Tony's death, she went back to Max without ever telling him of the one love in her life that meant so much.

Now, Lisa looked around the library's vast, quiet reading room, a place with the hushed solemnity of a cathedral. Huge wooden archways framed the room, with figures at the spandrels representing science, law, and the arts. The faces of a dozen Greek and Roman lawgivers were inset into carved medallions. Overhead, antique chandeliers hung from the ceiling. It was a room of such dignity and formality as to demand respect and even reverence.

The library's bookshelves contained 450,000 volumes, though at the moment, Lisa could not focus on one. She was supposed to be double-checking citations in a brief filed by a pro-life group seeking to invalidate an ordinance barring protests near abortion clinics. In his 8 A.M. conference with the clerks, Truitt said he thought the plaintiffs had misstated the holdings of several First Amendment cases. He gave her the job of reading the cases and doing a memo. It was scut work for the new kid. Any decent second-year law student could finish the job in thirty minutes. Why was she having so much trouble?

Shank.

She couldn't stop thinking about him, and every thought terrified her.

At the next table, Jerry Klein's pudgy body was hidden somewhere between twin mountains of books. Every few minutes, Lisa heard a "gotcha!" from inside the valley of treatises, as if Jerry either had made a stunning discovery or squashed an invading bug. Victor Vazquez was back in his clerk's office, using the computer to research a challenge to the Brady Bill's requirement that state police do background checks on gun buyers.

The print in the casebook became blurry, and Lisa realized she was nodding off. She needed sleep. She couldn't focus. Her mind was moving too quickly, flashing from horrific images of a downed aircraft to her nightmares of a razor-wielding assailant.

The airplane.

She had suppressed her pain ever since the crash. Max had kept things from her, and she had her secrets, too. She had come back to Max—a safe port—in her despair, but the loss of Tony was hers alone. Now the pain flooded back along with the certainty of her own jeopardy. Her life was threatened and there was nothing she could do about it. She had not felt trapped since escaping the hell of an abusive father. She felt safer with Crockett, who beat her, than with Harry Fremont, dear old Dad, who pried her legs apart. *"It ain't my fault if you're such a sexy little thing."*

Now she faced a different kind of terror.

Just thinking about Shank made her shiver with fear. She had little doubt he would fulfill his threats. "He's a killer," Max had said. "And worse, I think he enjoys it. He told me how they used to bust up guys with a sap, an old nightstick weighted with a lead core. It's like hitting someone with a sledgehammer. He'd toss guys off roofs, dunk their heads in toilets, throw them out of moving cars." Max paused, and Lisa pictured a man cartwheeling out of a police sedan onto the highway. "Of course, he knew I'd tell you all his stories," Max continued. "He could be just trying to scare you."

"Well he did a good job."

Now she sat there, reading a case on the historical underpinnings of the right to freedom of assembly. Trying but not succeeding to relate the decision to the abortion case. Looking up when footsteps approached. Aware of movement around her. Unfocused. Lost.

She checked her watch. Nine-thirty-five. She wanted to be in the courtroom for the oral arguments beginning at ten.

C'mon, concentrate!

∽

Lisa had a few minutes to spare before oral arguments when she ducked into her office to drop off her notepads and briefcase. A young man in a windbreaker and baseball cap stood at the window, staring out at the Senate Office Building across Constitution Avenue. He turned as she walked in.

"Greg!" she gasped, then broke into a wide smile.

They rushed to hug each other, Greg Kingston lifting Lisa off her feet and swinging her around a full 360 degrees. "How's my babysitter?" he asked.

"Still learning the territory. This place is a little intimidating to a girl from Bodega Bay."

"Nah. You can do anything."

Greg was a little under six feet, lanky and loose limbed. His smile was startling, so much like his father's. With the same strong jawline and lock of unkempt dark hair falling across his forehead, he was looking more like Tony all the time.

"I'm glad you're here," Lisa said. "I was worried about you playing private detective at Atlantica."

"They don't kill the forklift drivers," he said. "Only flight crews and passengers."

There was bitterness in his voice. Ever since the rumors of faulty maintenance began circulating, Greg was convinced that someone was to blame for his father's death, someone other than nameless, faceless terrorists.

"You should go back to college," she said, changing the subject, trying to get his mind off the case.

You don't know what you're getting into. I've got to protect you.

"Gee thanks for the mothering," he said, grinning.

It was an old joke between them. When little Greg would become frustrated with Lisa's rules and regulations, he once told her, "Jeez, I wish you'd get married and have a kid. If you were a real mom, you'd have someone else to boss around."

It was true, she thought. Greg brought out her mothering instincts.

"Tell me about the job," he said. "What are the judges like? Do you have to kiss their robes?"

"Supreme Court justices are sorcerers," she said. "They're given impossible questions, so they boil a witches' brew and find magical answers in its broth."

"Whoa! Sounds like English lit. And what do you do?"

"I'm the sorcerer's apprentice."

"Neat! I'm thinking about law school myself."

"Our deal still stands. I'll coach you for the LSAT, but first you've got to get your bachelor's—"

"Do you know who Joe Drayton is?" he interrupted.

That again! How can I get him off that?

"Of course I do." She remembered the day Max Wanaker brought her the files, eleven cardboard boxes stuffed with pleadings, discovery, expert witness reports, and the personnel records of everyone with any connection to the crash. It felt creepy thumbing through the crew files, reading letters of commendation for the flight attendants, the first officer, the flight engineer, and then, her heart thundering, opening Tony's bulging file. She remembered an eight-by-ten glossy photo sliding onto her desk, the official Atlantica shot of Tony in cap and uniform, a flood of emotions engulfing her. Love and loss, pain and regret, the cold alarm at knowing she would never see him again. She had forced herself to calm down as she studied the face of the pilot with the crinkly eyes and dusting of gray at the temples. She closed her eyes and tried to conjure him up, putting life to the photo. She remembered the day she rode in the jump seat on one of Tony's flights. Before takeoff, she leaned over his shoulder and he showed her how to start up the engines. "In case you ever have to be my copilot," he said, smiling. "Easy as one, two, three. Fuel valve, starter, ignition. All there is to it."

But life isn't by the numbers. Who'll show me the way now?

She had read the file, thumbing through a stack of Tony's memos alerting management to lackadaisical training and bad parts, warning of shoddy maintenance and security flaws. Reading his words, she could hear his voice. Impassioned, determined, and she pictured Tony banging away with two fingers on an obsolete typewriter, determined to do what was right.

"Joe Drayton was Atlantica's maintenance chief," she said to Greg, after a moment. After her surreptitious review of his file, Lisa was reasonably certain she knew more about Drayton than either the plaintiffs' lawyers or Greg. Before coming to Atlantica, Drayton had a spotless record at Delta for fifteen years. Nobody in the industry had anything bad to say about him. He was an aeronautical engineer by training who paid equal attention to design and maintenance. Years earlier, he'd been featured in *Jet Propulsion* magazine when he'd discovered why the early 727s were experiencing premature touchdowns. Instead of pilot error, as was widely presumed, there was a design flaw in the tail that caused an excessive sink rate.

"Drayton took early retirement after the crash, and the plaintiffs couldn't find him," Lisa continued, "so you conspiracy theorists got all hot and bothered." She sat down on the corner of her desk and watched Greg pace, another of his father's traits.

"According to the guys in the engine shop," he said, "Drayton took his pension in a lump sum, then disappeared."

"As far as I know, that's not a crime."

"But if prosecutors could grill him under some hot lights, there might be evidence of one," he replied.

"You watch too much TV," she said. "This is just a civil suit, not a criminal investigation."

How can I get him off the case? Greg, go home! Go somewhere safe.

She was plagued by the fear that he would somehow stumble into Shank's path.

Greg was still pacing. "I think Atlantica stashed Drayton somewhere so he couldn't testify. Like they couldn't trust him or something."

"C'mon, Greg, we've been over all this. Drayton wasn't available for deposition, so Atlantica substituted his top assistant. What's the problem?"

"I went to the courthouse in Miami and read the file. Isn't it suspicious that Atlantica claims it doesn't know where Drayton moved after he retired?"

"No, and even if I did, I couldn't discuss it with you. The case is on the argument calendar."

"Hey! We're family."

She laughed, looking at him with real tenderness, marveling at how much Greg resembled his father in ways having nothing to do with their looks. Both shared a willingness to fight for what they believed. An unwillingness to give up. Both were tough minded, stubborn, and focused. Greg would make a great lawyer. Or would he? Maybe he'd be frustrated by the compromises, the deals, the shortcuts that bypass justice for expediency.

"C'mon Greg. I have to abide by the ethical rules."

"No you don't," he said, lowering his voice to a conspiratorial whisper. "Don't you see? You're in a great position to help the victims, give them a chance at a trial."

"That would be unethical," she said, fully cognizant of the irony. Greg would never suspect that she could be working for Max Wanaker. He had no idea of her past involvement with the man his father had despised. She would do anything to shield him from that knowledge. She vowed to keep him away from Max, and more importantly, from Shank.

"If I can come up with new evidence," Greg said, his voice rising with excitement, "the good guys can win. Plus, if you tell me where to take the stuff, the FBI, or wherever, I'll bet we can get the feds looking up Max Wanaker's ass with a flashlight."

"It's too late to come up with new evidence," she told him. "The Court will look at the record at the time of the summary judgment. Besides, what can you find that the plaintiffs' lawyers and all their investigators couldn't?"

"I already found Joe Drayton," Greg Kingston said.

℘

Actually, Joe Drayton had found Greg, he told Lisa. Someone at the engine shop must have gotten word to him that Tony's kid was poking around. Over the past few months, small packages with no return address, all postmarked Mendocino, California, began arriving at Mary Kingston's house in Bodega Bay. "You know Granny," Greg said. "They were addressed to me, so she wouldn't open them. Finally, she bundled them up and sent them to Miami. You won't believe what's there."

He reached into a nylon backpack, pulled out several sheets of construction paper, and spread them over her desk. Each page contained a meticulous ink drawing. She sat down and Greg leaned over her shoulder, pointing to the first drawing, which appeared to be a file cabinet, its drawers open, papers strewn on the floor. A neatly printed caption read: "Follow the paper, but the paper lies."

"The maintenance records," Greg said. "It means they've been fabricated."

"Not in a court of law. Who'll authenticate it? Who'll define it? Who'll tie it specifically to the crash? As evidence, it's meaningless."

He waved her off and pointed to a drawing of a fat pencil with an oversize eraser and something coiled around the pencil.

"Looks like a snake," she said.

Greg tapped a forefinger on the desk. "A whip. 'Pencil whipped' means they filled out safety forms but never did the work. I learned that drinking beer and throwing darts with some of the mechanics."

Lisa remembered the transcript of the cockpit voice recording, Tony talking about fabricated records. *"Joe Drayton knows his people have been pencil whipping inspections they never perform."*

Greg uncovered a drawing that looked like a broken propeller. He read the caption aloud: "'Where's the stage one fan rotor disk?'"

"Buried in the mud and the muck of the Everglades," Lisa said, studying the illustration of the propeller with half its blades missing.

She'd read all the reports. Federal investigators had scoured the Everglades, searching miles from the crash site, where the explosion occurred. In the turgid language of the NTSB, the accident resulted from the "separation, fragmentation, and forceful discharge of the stage one fan rotor disk following a catastrophic failure within the number two tail-mounted engine."

Disk fragments, propelled like shrapnel, had cut through the hydraulic lines, destroying all flight control systems. To conclusively state that a bomb had caused the "catastrophic failure," investigators needed the disk itself for testing, but it was never found. Although the NTSB failed to reach a definitive conclusion as to the cause of the crash, the report strongly suggested that a bomb caused the explosion. Two months later, a federal judge in Miami granted summary judgment for Atlantica Airlines.

Greg pointed toward a dark stain on the drawing of the ruptured fan disk. "Take a whiff."

Lisa sniffed at it. "Liquor?"

"Kentucky bourbon," Greg said confidently, the kid trying to sound worldly.

"This isn't evidence," she said, sharply. "It's a parlor game. Anonymous notes and secret clues are not evidence. You don't have facts! You don't have documents! You don't have witnesses!"

"I can find the evidence."

Oh, Greg, I've got to protect you because this Sherlock Holmes shit can get you killed.

"The way I figure it, Drayton's plagued by guilt," Greg said, trying to sound mature. "He wants to do the right thing, but he can't without implicating himself and probably some friends who still work there. But he liked Dad a lot, and he's torn up over what happened. Now, he's trying to lead me to the truth."

"The truth is that a bomb brought down the plane," Lisa said. She believed it, but then she had to. If it weren't the truth, she was an accomplice in the cover-up, and that was too difficult to face. "Even if Atlantica's maintenance was shoddy, a bomb killed your father. The investigators found that chemical—"

"PETN, a nitrate. But PETN is a fuse material. Where's the RDX or Semtex or nitroglycerin? Where's the twisted metal patterns?"

Lisa looked at him in astonishment. Was this the kid who so recently had only cared about baseball and girls?

He shrugged and said, "You're not the only one who spends time in libraries."

"You just want someone to blame. You want someone to suffer just like you have. When you can't find the terrorists, you go after the airline."

"I didn't show you the last drawing," he said, pulling out one more. It looked like a black bowling ball with a fuse growing out of it. A cartoon bomb, Elmer Fudd trying to Mow Bugs Bunny out of his hole. A large red X was drawn thickly—angrily, Lisa thought—through the bowling ball.

"What's he saying?" Lisa asked, but it came to her even as Greg spoke the words.

"There was no bomb," Greg Kingston said.

PART TWO

"This is a court of law, young man, not of justice."
—Oliver Wendell Holmes, Jr.

CHAPTER 9

Samson and Delilah

LISA BARELY LISTENED TO THE ORAL ARGUMENT. She was worried about Greg. He had left for the airport, headed for San Francisco. He told her he'd stop in Bodega Bay to kiss Granny and get a decent meal, but then it was back on the Shoreline Highway for the drive north to Mendocino.

There was no phone listing for Joe Drayton in California. Greg had checked, just as the plaintiffs' investigators had in all fifty states, plus quite a few offshore islands. Greg didn't know Drayton's address, but he was sure Drayton wanted to be found … if only by him. Why else send the packages, he asked Lisa, all postmarked Mendocino, a postage stamp coastal town?

While working in the engine shop at Atlantica, Greg had hung out with the mechanics, keeping his mouth shut, his ears open. One of the senior guys, a supervisor, had visited Drayton on a trip out west but didn't say where.

"Old Joe's taken up painting," the supervisor said one day after work in a Miami Springs tavern.

"Houses?" a younger mechanic asked.

"Pictures. He sits all day long on a cliff, painting pictures of the ocean."

"Kinda dull, isn't it, unless he puts some ships in the pictures."

"No ships, no whales. Just waves and rocks. Joe don't hardly say a word. Just paints and sips Jack Daniel's from a pint bottle."

Mendocino. Cliffs. The ocean. Drayton wouldn't be hard to find, Greg told her. Then he kissed Lisa, smiled the smile of the young and innocent, and headed for the door.

"Wait!" she called after him.

She agonized over what to do. She wanted to tell him of the dangers. Shank might have someone watching Drayton. It was a fool's mission anyway, thinking an old drunk could solve the mystery that hundreds of FBI and NTSB investigators couldn't.

She gripped Greg tightly by the shoulders and looked into his dark eyes that so resembled his father's. "I've got to tell you something."

He cocked his head, waiting.

What can I say? I want to tell him the truth, but what would he think of me?

"Yeah?" he asked after a moment.

"I love you," she said. "Be careful."

He grinned, kissed her on the forehead, and was gone.

ᴄᴏ

Lisa tried to concentrate on the argument, but her mind was wandering again. Later today, Sam Truitt would assign the bench memos for the December docket. There were dozens of cases.

But for me, there's only one.

She didn't even think about the search and seizure cases, the FCC case, the census count dispute, or any of the others. All that mattered was *Laubach v. Atlantica Airlines*, and before she could sway Sam Truitt's vote, she had to get the clerking assignment.

She refused to think about the consequences if she weren't chosen to review the briefs and prepare the bench memo. There would be no opportunity to convince the judge if Jerry or Vic got the case. Then she would have to face Shank, a prospect that sent waves of panic through her.

Lisa considered directly asking Truitt for the case, but that could backfire. He liked to balance the high-profile cases with the dull ones, giving each clerk a fair sampling. He had already told the clerks he didn't want to be lobbied.

She watched Truitt perform from his perch at the end of the bench. He exuded natural charm, bringing his fierce intellect, quick wit, and sly grin to this hallowed chamber. He was a man's man with more than enough magnetism to attract women without really trying. In a world where the frogs all think they're princes, he was one of those rare men who didn't realize how damned desirable he was.

"Isn't it true that an ER nurse in your county hospital would be guilty of a crime if she spoke Spanish to a patient?" Justice Truitt asked.

"Technically, yes," admitted the county attorney, shuffling his feet at the lectern, his accent betraying a south Texas upbringing.

"Even if the patient's appendix has burst and his only language is Spanish, the nurses and doctors must speak to the man only in English, correct?"

Jamming it home. Overdoing it a bit, Lisa thought.

The county attorney cleared his throat. Buying time. The bleat of the sacrificial lamb facing the blade. "Yes, but in such a case, I doubt there would be a prosecution."

"That's not our concern, is it?" Truitt asked, closing in for the kill. "We're concerned with the facial validity of a law that requires public employees to speak English while on the job. Now, what compelling state interest is served by this astonishing restriction on free expression?"

From her seat in the clerks' gallery, wedged between two marble pillars, Lisa watched her boss set up the hapless county attorney. Too easy. Lisa shot a glance at the Chief Justice. Old Whittington was drumming his fingers, glaring toward Sam Truitt, the junior-most justice with the senior-most mouth.

The three clerks and their boss had talked it over this morning at their breakfast conference. Lisa had pleaded with Truitt not to monopolize the questioning. It would only piss off the Chief.

Victor Vazquez and Jerry Klein hooted at her in that male way, raising their voices, as if they could win an argument by sheer volume.

"Don't listen to her!" Klein implored. "Go for it, Judge."

"Yeah, show everybody it's not Whittington and the eight dwarves anymore," Vazquez agreed. "You can go *mano a mano* with his sorry ass any time. The Supremes are singing to a new beat."

Immature jerks. Why is it that men have to paw the earth and lock antlers to prove their manhood?

"The County Commission enacted the English-only ordinance after a referendum of the voters approved it," the county attorney said. He couldn't have been more than thirty-five, a tall, gangly man wearing rattlesnake cowboy boots with his dark blue suit. He probably shot quail or ducks or wild boar or whatever the hell they shoot in Texas, Lisa thought. "The ordinance represents the will of the people that English be codified in order to preserve our heritage and tradition."

Truitt looked past the lawyer, his eyes locking on Lisa. She saw a playful smile forming, the gleam in his eyes.

Don't do it. Don't try to show how damned clever you are.

"It seems rather ironic that Rio Grande county," Truitt sang out, trilling the words—*Rrrr-io Grrrran-day*—"where Spanish conquistadors once roamed, which even today has a forty percent Hispanic population, claims that the English language is its heritage and tradition."

Laughter from the gallery. A glare from the Chief Justice, who waved his gavel menacingly but didn't slam it home. Enjoying the titter of approval from the audience, Truitt seemed oblivious to the Chief's reaction.

Macho lunkhead.

Next to her, Jerry Klein squirmed with delight. On the other side, Vic Vazquez whispered, "Way to go, boss."

વ્

The rest of the morning passed quickly. Next came the Blue Cross suit against the tobacco companies for reimbursement of medical costs. The defendants had appealed orders forcing them to disclose their top-secret cigarette formulas.

"Isn't there such a thing as a trade secret?" the Chief boomed at the plaintiffs' lawyer. "Should Coca-Cola have to give up its formula every time it gets sued? Should Mrs. Fields have to give up her cookie recipe to a competitor?"

To Lisa, the questions were classic non sequiturs inasmuch as the plaintiffs claimed the formulas were needed to prove that the tobacco companies manipulated nicotine levels to keep smokers addicted, but that was the Chief for you. All bluster, no substance.

After lunch came a challenge to the constitutionality of the Brady Act's requirement that state police check backgrounds of handgun buyers. And finally, a spirited argument over the law requiring cable television companies to carry local stations, with the solicitor general, decked out in his cutaway morning coat and striped trousers, arguing that the law was necessary to protect small TV stations from financial ruin.

Lisa sat there in the palace of the law, a courtroom of grandeur and majesty, from the red and gold drapes reaching toward the four-story recessed ceiling to the twenty-four Ionic columns of Sienna marble. The walls were Spanish marble, the floor beneath the carpeting Italian and African marble. A marble frieze ran around the upper third of the walls with carved figures peering down at them. One was a handsome godlike character, sitting bare-chested on his throne, a lawgiver in some ancient society. He had a defined, muscular chest and a six-pack of abs, and Lisa could not help but fantasize that it was Sam Truitt, powerful, noble ... and sexy.

She drifted into a daydream, Sam holding her in his strong arms. With a start, she realized she'd been suppressing her feelings. With all that was going on, how could she feel anything? But there it was, the sizzle of electricity inside her when she looked at Sam Truitt, when she heard his deep voice, when she imagined him stripped of his black robes, bare as the marble god on his throne. Eyes closed, her legs crossed, she squeezed her thighs together. The warmth of her fantasy spread through her like a surging tide.

This is crazy! I'm supposed to seduce him, and I'm the one with the schoolgirl crush.

She chased the thought away. Coming on to Sam Truitt was too risky. He could reject her or fire her. Anyway, none of that mattered if she didn't get the Atlantica assignment today. That was the greatest urgency, something that was, quite literally, a matter of life or death.

I need the Atlantica case, Sam. I've got to have it!

She wished she could tell him why. The judge wouldn't be afraid. She pictured Truitt beating Shank to a pulp with his bare hands. The image of that monster, bloodied and bowed, comforted her. But Truitt was a judge, a man who believed in the rule of law. Someone's harassing you, get a restraining order. That wouldn't work on the streets.

If she were still in the Tenderloin, in the world of the Tiki Club, she could turn to someone equally as tough as Shank, equally as cruel. But she was far removed from that subterranean place, and in this world, there were only books and briefs and words ... and they could not protect her. Besides, if somehow she could make Shank disappear, there would be someone else following in his place. From what Max told her, the Koshiro crime family was well organized, well financed, and well armed.

She would have to take care of herself. She would have to get the case and then get Sam Truitt. Surveying the courtroom, she took stock of the hard, cold marble everywhere. In another frieze, a man wrestled with a snake. Subtlety was not the strong suit in the Court's allegorical figures.

If this is the Garden of Eden, am I the snake?

She turned her attention back to Truitt—the living breathing justice, her boss, her target—not a figure of stone, but a man whose shoulders amply filled out his black robe. Sam Bam Truitt, the women at Harvard had called him. She drifted off again, daydreaming through the oral argument, picturing her boss as Samson, spread-eagled between the pillars, bringing the great building down.

Which makes me Delilah.

Truitt was more subdued after the first argument, no longer strutting and showing his feathers like a male peacock. Gwendolyn Robbins, one of two female justices, dominated the questioning in the gun control case. She was a wrinkled, well-dressed, chain-smoking, profane Texan who enjoyed telling risqué jokes about her ex-husband, a prominent oil man. Robbins clearly supported the Brady Act restrictions. Taking the other side, the Chief Justice badgered the government lawyer, while Curtis Braxton, the Court's sole black justice, seemed to side with Robbins. Braxton was a moderate conservative who was third-most junior after Truitt and Victor Small, a former attorney general from Maine, a conservative Republican who seldom said a word in conference or on the bench. All the justices wore identical long black robes except the Chief Justice, who sported four gold stripes on each sleeve.

Because of the historic seating arrangement alternating away from the Chief Justice—right, left, right, left—according to seniority, Braxton and Truitt sat next to each other on the bench. Once during the abortion protest argument, Lisa saw her boss pass a note to Braxton, who smiled, wrote something, and passed it back. Truitt read it stifled a smile, balled up the note and tossed it into the antique brass spittoon behind him. A couple of boys in the sixth grade, Lisa thought. One day, they're hurling spitballs, the next they're sitting on the Supreme Court. Why did she feel so much more mature than men nearly twice her age?

She knew Truitt liked Braxton, whom he called "General." The two men worked out together in the court gym and shared a table at lunch in the justices' dining room. Braxton had played college basketball before entering the army, which sent him to law school, then made him a JAG prosecutor. He became commandant of the JAG school at the University of Virginia and eventually judge advocate general of the army before being appointed to the bench by the previous Republican President. At fifty-three, Braxton still had a washboard stomach and a ramrod military posture.

If I corral Truitt's vote, would he be able to bring Braxton along?

Lisa sized up the other justices, searching for the dynamics of picking up another vote or two. The senior associate justice, Guido Tarasi, with his neatly trimmed gray beard, was a former U.S. Attorney from New York and was even more conservative than the Chief and considerably brighter. William Hubbs was a short, bald, lumpy man with squinty eyes who resembled Yoda and was a Life Master in contract bridge.

He had an impressive ability to quote prior decisions verbatim but an unfortunate habit of misapplying them to current cases. Powell McLeod had worked his way up from the federal district court in California to the Ninth Circuit Court of Appeals and then, thanks to scoring a perfect 100 on a Conservatives for America ranking, was elevated to the Supreme Court by President Reagan. He usually voted with the Chief Justice. The most liberal justice was Debora Kaplan, a petite, quiet scholar who, as a lawyer, had argued on behalf of abortion rights in several cases as amicus curiae for the Women's Rights Project of the ACLU. There was no way Atlantica would get her vote. Same with Gwendolyn Robbins. Though her iconoclastic views defied categorization, she could be counted on to side with widows and orphans.

After her quick run-through of the others, Lisa concentrated on her boss. Notwithstanding all the prior research, she was still getting to know him. She needed to find his weaknesses. Maybe that was her great skill, her witchcraft, plumbing the depths of men for their failings.

Her thoughts turned to Max. She wondered why she didn't hate him for getting her into this mess. Maybe because she remembered so clearly when he had been her only friend, her gallant knight in a chauffeured limo. He had always helped her, starting the first night they were together.

⁂

"I'm a dancer, Mr. Wanaker. Not a hooker."

Jesus, we've just had sex, and I'm calling him Mr. Wanaker.

She was seventeen. Max had walked into the club, slipping twenties into her garter belt. She'd been there only six weeks but she'd heard every dumb line in the book.

"You should be an actress. I'm a producer. Here's my card ..."

"My friends and I want you to come to a party. You can trust us ..."

"You've got small tits for a stripper, but that's okay. I like small tits ..."

Max was different. Three nights in a row. The tips kept coming, but he never asked her out, never tried to bullshit her, never tried to touch her. He even got some bonus points for telling her he was married. She'd seen enough ring-finger tans to know most guys weren't as honest. On the fourth night, he said he was going back home the next day. Miami. What time did she get off?

"It's against house rules to date a customer," she told him. "Too many wackos out there, plus if a girl propositions a guy, even off premises, and the guy's a cop, they could pull our liquor license."

But he persisted in a gentlemanly way, and she said yes. He wanted
to take her for drinks to the Top of the Mark, then dinner at some fancy
place with the best abalone, or maybe hit Chinatown for moo shu soup, or
a trendy new place in the Embarcadero for crab ravioli in scallion ginger
relish.

*Scallion ginger relish? They didn't put that stuff on the double cheeseburgers
at the all-night joint where the girls gathered after work to separate the singles
from the tens and twenties.*

At 3 A.M., a limo was waiting, and she ducked inside to find Max
Wanaker and a chilled bottle of Dom Pérignon. The chauffeur drove to
a secluded spot where they looked down at the Golden Gate Bridge as
the fog piled up over the twin towers, enshrouding the spidery cables,
blurring the cars' headlights into ghostly beacons lost in feathery steam.
Maybe it wasn't Tasmania, but it was as close as she ever figured to be.

They sat there, sipping champagne and talking. Max told her of his
dreams. He owned an air freight company at the Miami airport. Sure, he
made good money, but he wanted more. He wanted his own airline, and
with deregulation, he could start a discount carrier with leased planes,
subcontracted mechanics, borrowed pilots … and on he went as the night
turned to dawn, the early sun tinting the fog crimson and orange. Tinting
her hair a fiery red, too, or so Max told her.

"My God, you're so beautiful," he said, holding her hand, just after
sunrise.

Four hours and he hadn't tried to touch her.

"What are your dreams?" he asked. "What are your hopes? Where do
you want to be in five years?"

She didn't know. No one had ever asked.

Until then, life had been day to day. She had no plans beyond the
weekend. She wanted shoes that didn't give her blisters. She wanted a
leather mini with a brass zipper up the side. She wanted a dressing room
with a working toilet, an apartment without roaches, a boyfriend who
didn't hit her.

How stupid. How sad.

"I have no dreams," she admitted.

"Sure you do," Max Wanaker said. "We'll just have to find them, and
then we'll just have to make them come true."

We. First person plural.

She had never experienced "we."

They went back to his hotel room. A suite at the Fairmont atop Nob
Hill. He took her to bed. He was more gentle, more patient than Crockett.

Max wanted it to be good for her. And it was. So was the fresh orange juice and steaming coffee and eggs Benedict from room service. And when he said he'd be coming back to see her, she knew he was telling the truth.

Max Wanaker only made one mistake. As she was gathering her things, and there wasn't much to gather, he tried to sneak five Ben Franklins into her purse.

"I'm a dancer, Mr. Wanaker, not a hooker," she told him, angrily. "I did this because I wanted to, not because ..."

She started crying. He apologized, told her it wasn't payment that if he had the time, he'd go to a jewelry store, buy her a gift but he was rushing to the airport, so please just take the money and buy whatever you want.

She refused.

"Okay, okay," he said, wiping her tears with a silk handkerchief. "Will you accept a gift, instead?"

She nodded, sniffling.

He handed her the little box of chocolates the maid had left in the room. "And if you keep calling me Mr. Wanaker, I'm going to start feeling like your grandfather."

She laughed and tucked the box in her purse. When she got home and reached in for a nougat, she found five hundred-dollar bills.

෴

So how would she get to Samuel Adams Truitt? she asked herself, as the gun control argument wound down. How would she get the Atlantica assignment she so desperately needed and then get Truitt's vote? What were his weaknesses? She needed a strategy, a method of persuasion. Would he vote for Atlantica if she brought out the "Bam" in Sam? No, he wouldn't roll over in the conference room just because she did in the bedroom. In fact, he might go the other way just to prove his damned rectitude.

Okay, lust was not a surefire bet. What were his other sins? Pride certainly. She'd seen him at Harvard and she'd seen him today. It was not enough to toil anonymously on the High Court. He needed to be a star, the star he never was when bent over the ball, snapping to the punter. He needed to be adored by the intelligentsia, quoted by CNN, benighted by historians.

How could she turn that on its head? The lower court decision in *Atlantica* had been bitterly criticized by virtually every commentator. She had clipped a *New York Times* editorial, griping that the trial court "slavishly applied legal technicalities to callously slam the courthouse door in the faces of victims' families, a result so Kafkaesque as to invite universal scorn."

Kafkaesque, indeed?

Truitt's vote in favor of the families of the crash victims was laughingly predictable. Reversing the dismissal of the lawsuits would be wildly popular. But let's turn that around. How heroic it would be, what moral courage it would take, what intellectual integrity would be required, to go against the emotional outcries, for Justice Samuel Adams Truitt to uphold the law, no matter how seemingly egregious the outcome? *Sheesh.* That was a tough sell, and she didn't think Truitt would buy it.

She would work on it, just as soon as she got the assignment. Today was the new-case conference, and there was no margin for error. Just that morning, Shank had called her at the apartment. The terror of their first meeting had never left her, and the sound of his voice seemed to compress her chest as if caught in a vise. "I'm keeping your earring as a souvenir," he had said with a grunt. "Don't give me a reason to add to my collection."

CHAPTER 10

Heavy Lifting

JERRY KLEIN MUMBLED, PROBABLY BECAUSE of the difficulty of speaking clearly with three caramels stuck in his jaw. "Juhst great bohst," he managed, through sticky teeth.

"You kicked some serious butt today," Victor Vazquez agreed.

Truitt lay flat on his back on the bench in the gym one floor above the courtroom, his hands gripping the bar with six forty-five-pound plates along for the ride. He wore gray cotton shorts and a torn Wake Forest T-shirt in the school colors of black and gold. The clerks were dressed in their conservative court duds and carrying yellow pads while their boss sweated, grunted, and groaned.

Victor Vazquez was standing above the justice, spotting for him, hands lightly cradling the bar. Klein looked ill at ease, as if at any moment a giant weight might fall from the sky and crush him. Lisa stood off to one side, admiring the sheer physicality of her boss, from his well-muscled arms to the size and shape of his calves. She was quite sure he had the best legs of any member of the Court, perhaps in Court history. It seemed unlikely that John Jay, John Marshall, or Roger Taney did many squats or lunges.

While the justice worked through his reps, the two male clerks kept up the patter, reliving the glory of each piercing question from the first argument. Lisa remained quiet until Truitt looked her way, a bit sheepishly, she thought. She didn't say a word.

Let him ask.

Like an actor who's unsure of his own performance, he seemed to want her approval. Making men wait was part of the game. They were such babies, such puppy dogs, leaping at your legs, begging to be petted. Okay, here's a bone, judge.

"You'll be quoted in the *Times* with that Rio Grande crack," she said.

Still at the bench press, he lifted the bar from the rack, lowered it to his chest, then extended his arms fully, hoisting 300 pounds, all told. Smoothly, he did it again, his arms pistons, the triceps popping out, his pectorals straining against the front of his T-shirt. She liked him even more out of his robes, sweaty and pumped.

"But you don't approve?" he asked, exhaling sharply.

"The Chief nearly hit you with his gavel," she said, evenly. "It's your first day on the bench, and you're like the kid in class with all the answers, the kid who can't stop waving his hand."

"Four ... five ... six," Vazquez called out, counting each rep.

"The kid everybody hates?" Truitt said, reluctantly agreeing.

Klein scowled at Lisa, annoyed that she had killed the festive mood. "Seven, eight. Four more!"

"It's not just that you're being overly aggressive," Lisa said, and she heard Klein suck in a breath, as if he'd been hit in the solar plexus.

"Nine, ten. C'mon, Judge."

But Truitt dropped the bar into the rack with a metallic *clang*. "Damn," he said. "I'm getting weaker."

Oh, Samson, such beautiful hair.

"What else, Lisa? I have a feeling you weren't finished."

"With all due respect, Judge, the English-only case is a slam dunk, either seven-two or eight-one to strike down the ordinance. But Whittington will never assign the opinion to you. You'll be lucky to get one on taxation of pension plans. He'll punish you until you fall in line. You have to decide what's more important, being quoted in the newspaper or having your ideas cut into the cloth of our society, carved into the marble of our jurisprudence."

Truitt stood up and draped a towel over his shoulders. He looked at her, poker-faced.

Klein and Vazquez exchanged worried looks.

Lisa waited patiently.

Finally, Truitt said, "Your metaphors are strained, but your reasoning is sound. Lisa, I'd appreciate it if you'd remind me when my head gets too big for my helmet. Okay?"

She nodded. "Sure, as long as it's not a full-time job."

He laughed heartily, and Lisa let out a breath she didn't know she'd been holding.

"All right," Truitt said. "Let's do some heavy lifting."

೧

For the law clerks, there were two tricks at the bench memo conference that took place among the barbells, Nautilus machines, and racks of free weights in the otherwise deserted court gym. The first was to keep up with the boss as he raced through his super sets, taking no breaks, combining the anaerobic workout of pumping iron with the aerobic exercise of maintaining a high pulse rate. From the incline press to the decline press to flies with dumbbells and cable crossovers, Sam Truitt sped through a burning series of chest exercises. Then, breathing hard, his face flushed, it was on to the military press and dumbbell side laterals for the shoulders. All the time, Truitt was firing orders at his clerks as Vazquez ran through the docket, reading from a blue-backed file.

The second trick was to get the cases you wanted without asking for them. If you directly asked for a case, Truitt had promised to assign it to one of the other two clerks. Justice was supposed to be administered blindly, without fear or favor and basically without any self-interest on the part of judges or their clerks.

Veins popping in his arms, sweat streaming down his face, Truitt divvied up the first dozen cases in rapid-fire succession. To Lisa, it was somewhat bizarre. She felt like a voyeur at a fraternity initiation, or perhaps some ancient male bonding ritual.

Victor Vazquez got the juicy search and seizure case on the December docket: Can the government confiscate a car that's been used to transport drugs even if the owner was unaware of the criminal activity? A related case fell his way, too: Does seizing a drug dealer's property after convicting him of a crime constitute double jeopardy?

Jerry Klein complained that he wasn't getting anything to tax his intellect, especially after Truitt gave him a humdrum case involving adjusting the census figures to compensate for undercounting minorities. "Judge, there's no constitutional basis for forcing an adjustment," Klein whined. "This is a no-brainer."

"Then the Chief should write it," Vazquez said.

Back on the bench now, doing triceps extensions with the barbell, Truitt scowled at both of them. "No prejudging, Jerry. Do your research. And Vic, show some respect."

Next Klein got a case on the constitutionality of a law limiting liquor advertising, but he still bitched that truthful advertising is obviously protected speech under the First Amendment, so his prodigious talents were being wasted.

Lisa waited, concealing her impatience.

C'mon, judge. Atlantica, Atlantica.

Truitt gave her a case challenging the practice of using race in shaping congressional districts, and she graciously accepted.

Damn! I don't care about the redistricting case. I only care about the one that can get me killed.

"Oooh, that's a good one, Judge," Klein moaned.

"If you want to trade," Lisa said, "it's okay by me."

"No trading," Truitt said, straining to get the barbell raised, his left arm trailing a bit. "Believe it or not, there's a method to this." He turned his head to catch a glimpse of his clerks. "What's next?"

"The Decency Act case," Vazquez said, thumbing through the folder. "How far does free speech go in cyberspace? Can Congress police the internet?"

"Oh, Jeez, that's the case of the year," Klein mewled. "The Christian Coalition on one side, the ACLU on the other. It's Jerry Falwell versus Larry Flynt all over again."

Truitt was looking at Lisa.

Don't give it to me! Sure, it's a great case, but if it will shut Jerry up, give it to him, and save Atlantica for me.

She said, "Judge, if Jerry wants—"

"This one goes to Lisa," Truitt interrupted.

Oh no. This isn't working. Jerry's going to whine until he gets a hot case … my case!

"Jerry, stop your lobbying," Truitt ordered. "And let's get this over with. I have judicial conference in twenty minutes." He stood and massaged his right thumb deeply into the tendons in his left forearm. "What's next, Vic?"

Vazquez scanned his list. "Whoa, almost missed Atlantica Airlines. That's been expedited by the clerk's office. Oral argument the week before Christmas."

She was unwilling to sit back and wait for him. "I have an expertise in aviation law," Lisa said, taking the risk.

Keep it casual. Don't be too eager.

"I remember your telling me that," Truitt said.

"Oh sure," Klein groused, "give her all the good cases."

Victor Vazquez laughed. "Hey, Jer, do you have to act like the guy who was always chosen last in Little League?"

"Settle down, everybody," Truitt ordered, double-timing it toward the preacher's bench for some bicep curls. Vazquez and Klein scurried after him, Lisa following at her own pace.

"Well, it's true, Judge," Vazquez said. "Just 'cause Jerry got sent to right field where he counted daisies, he makes everybody suffer now."

"I never played Little League," Klein said, then turned to the judge. "*Atlantica's* not really an aviation case."

"No?" Lisa asked, trying to sound skeptical, believing it was jump-on-Jerry time. "What is it, then?"

"Well, of course it's an air crash, but the case was never tried," Klein said. "The issue is whether Congress preempted all state remedies when it passed the Airline Deregulation Act. In other words, in its haste, did Congress eliminate all actions against airlines for wrongful death by taking jurisdiction of aviation cases from the states but failing to provide a federal remedy?"

"Well stated," Truitt said, bent over the bench, lowering the bar onto its rack. "That's the threshold issue."

"Judge, I wrote a law review note on preemption," Klein added, polishing the teacher's apple.

"I know, Jerry. I read it. You attached it to your resume, along with letters of recommendation from your con law professor, your rabbi, and your piano teacher."

"The law gave the federal courts sole jurisdiction over fare litigation, frequent flyer programs, lost luggage, all that junk," Klein said, "but Congress wouldn't have taken crash cases away from the states without providing a federal remedy."

"That inference doesn't hold up logically," Lisa broke in. "It's just as likely that Congress screwed up by simply failing to preserve a litigation remedy. The question then is whether it's the Court's job to straighten out the mess and correct Congress' mistake."

"Hey Lisa, get real," Vazquez said, jumping into the fray. "Do you think this Court is going to rule that two hundred eighty-eight people got killed and their families can't sue?"

Two against one. Maybe three if the judge wants in. I've been outnumbered my entire life.

"Every week, more people than that die in car accidents with uninsured drivers," she said. "Every day, more than a thousand people die from cigarette smoking. Nobody ever said life was fair."

"Without prejudging the case," Truitt said, standing up and toweling the sweat from his face, "isn't it this Court's job to help make life fair?"

"Respectfully, sir, that's not your job at all," she fired back, then took a breath.

Slow down. Don't be overzealous. Don't let him see your fear.

"It's the Court's job to fairly apply the existing law," she went on, "not to change the law in misguided efforts to make life easier or more comfortable for those it considers oppressed."

"Whoa!" Klein yelled. "Survival of the fittest. The conservative's out of the closet."

"Lisa was never in the closet," Truitt said. "We needed some balance on the staff, and we got it."

"I just don't believe in using lawsuits to change society," Lisa said. "The whole tort system is riddled with inconsistencies and is based on an illogical theory, that a person can be compensated with money for nonmonetary loss. Will the people who lost spouses in an air crash be 'fully compensated' with a check?"

"Okay, guys," Truitt said. "Time out. This isn't about tort reform. It's a simple question of whether there's any remedy for an air crash in view of Congress' actions."

"I can't believe this," Klein said, picking up one of the justice's high-protein Power Bars from his gym bag, apparently mistaking it for a Milky Way. "Lisa, are you saying you'd vote to affirm and hold that there's no such thing as a case for wrongful death against an airline?"

"It might not be necessary to reach that issue," she said, avoiding the tough question. "Even without the preemption issue, the trial court granted summary judgment on the ground that there was no evidence of negligence."

"Without a trial!" Klein thundered.

"*That's* what summary judgment is for," she said, calmly. "The plaintiffs couldn't point to any evidence on which a jury could find the airline liable for a terrorist bombing. Unlike Pan Am Flight 103, there was no evidence that Atlantica failed to follow its own safety procedures."

"If it was a bomb at all," Klein said, trying to sound mysterious.

That got Truitt's interest. "Do you have another theory, Jerry?"

"The plaintiffs made a bunch of motions for more complete discovery of maintenance records. They seemed to think Atlantica was hiding something."

"They had a year of discovery and couldn't find anything," Lisa shot back.

"It could have been a maintenance defect or pilot error," Klein said.

"Pilot error! What was he supposed to do? He couldn't land without ailerons, flaps, and elevators!"

Saying too much now. Defending Tony. Becoming irrational. Angry at Klein for suggesting that the man she loved did something wrong.

God, Tony, how I miss you! How I need you!

Lisa felt her eyes brimming with tears.

Oh damnit, they'll think I can't handle a debate. They don't know I'm crying for you.

"Ailerons?" Klein said, raising his eyebrows. "Lisa's a regular Amelia Earhart."

"There's no evidence of pilot error in the record," she said, regaining her composure, sounding more judicious. "There is evidence, however, of plastic explosives in the number two engine. A fair reading of the record tells us that there were only two possible causes of the crash, and neither would be the fault of the airline."

"What's the second one?" Jerry said, chomping at the bait even as he chewed on the boss' fiber-enriched Power Bar. "Besides a bomb, what?"

She had Truitt's attention now. He seemed to be studying her, appraising every word. She would wow him with her expertise, leaving him no choice but to give her the case.

"A meteor," she said, "which would also be out of Atlantica's control, or is that pilot error, too?"

"A meteor!" Klein belched out a laugh. "The statistical improbability is staggering."

"Wrong, Jerry," she said.

Vazquez shook his head. "Gotta agree with Jerry here, Lisa. Next you'll be saying some aliens zapped the plane with ray guns. Holy *Independence Day!*"

The justice kept quiet, watching his clerks battle it out. Law school come to life.

"It's in the record, Jerry," she said, "page eleven seventeen."

"What is?" Klein turned toward Truitt. "Judge, why is she reading the record in a case that's not hers."

"It's not your case either," Lisa said, thinking they both sounded like petulant schoolchildren.

"What's in the record about meteors?" Truitt asked, seemingly impressed that she'd mastered such arcane data.

"Affidavits by an astronomer and two statisticians," Lisa went on. "About three thousand meteors large enough to bring down a plane strike Earth every day."

"I think one or two smacked you on the head," Klein said.

Keep talking, fatso. Gonna pick you clean.

"At any given moment, there are about thirty-five hundred commercial aircraft in the sky, covering about two-billionths of Earth's surface. Multiplying the number of meteors per day and the length of the era of modern air travel leads to a one-in-ten chance that a commercial flight would have been knocked from the sky. It hasn't happened yet. Or has it?"

"I don't believe this," Klein said. "Bombs and meteors and a district judge in Miami who's been out in the sun too long. All I'm saying is the plaintiffs should have a chance at a trial. Then let Atlantica prove that a meteor—"

"The burden of proof is on the plaintiffs," Lisa said. "They couldn't come forward with evidence at the summary judgment hearing. So sad. Good-bye."

Truitt shot a look at her. Surprise and disapproval.

Oh shit. Coming on too strong. Too cold. Overplaying my hand with sarcasm. "So sad?" How stupid of me.

"All right," Truitt said. "Put a lid on it, everybody. I'm tired of telling all three of you not to prejudge the cases."

He was quiet a moment and seemed to be pondering the assignment.

C'mon, Scrap. You respect toughness, someone who's not intimidated by you. Don't go for a guy who'll just follow your weepy humanistic agenda.

Truitt stripped off his T-shirt and headed for the men's locker room. Sweat streamed down his back. The two male clerks followed.

Hey guys. He-lo-oh! Where the hell am I supposed to go?

Two steps from the door, Truitt seemed to realize what he'd done. He stopped short, and Klein nearly bowled into him. Turning, he looked at Lisa.

When the jury comes back in, see if they'll look you in the eyes.

"Lisa, too much passion about a case can be counterproductive to an objective inquiry. You'll get your pick of the cases on the January docket."

No! I don't care about the January docket. I won't be alive in January!

"Jerry, you take Atlantica," Truitt said.

Lisa struggled to find a rational argument. "But, Judge …"

"No 'buts,'" Truitt said.

She imagined trying to tell Shank that she'd failed to get the case. His rage would be homicidal. She tasted her own fear, acidic as bile in her throat.

"It looks like Jerry and I are coming from different places," she said, scrambling for a fallback position, her mind racing. "We could each give you memos, Judge. That way, you'd have—"

"No arguing, Lisa," Truitt said. "When a judge rules against you, always say, 'Thank you, Your Honor,' then pack your bag and leave his chambers. You'll be back another day. Now, get out of here, all of you. Go to work."

No, Sam! There won't be another day!

And he was gone, ducking into the locker room, leaving Lisa staring into the grinning, caramelized teeth of Jerry Klein.

"Let's go to work," Klein said, as if it were his idea. Then he began whistling, a feeble, spittle-laced attempt to catch the tune of "Les Toreadors" from *Carmen*. Lisa fought off the fleeting image of a bull jamming its horns up Jerry's fat ass.

As the three clerks headed back to chambers, Lisa was mired in anger and despair.

"You overplayed your hand, Lisa," Klein said smugly as they stepped into an elevator with brass ornamental doors. "You may call it logic and strict construction and all that conservative double-talk, but I think your legal analysis stems directly from your personality. Frankly, I've never met anyone who's so unfeeling, so heartless."

"Jerry," she said, with a glare that could cut glass, "you don't know anything about me ... or my heart."

CHAPTER 11

Lover's Lane

THE CHRYSANTHEMUMS WERE IN BLOOM but the roses were not. The katsura tree with its umbrella of branches competed for space with a giant Japanese maple. Squirrels with pilfered nuts clamped in their teeth scampered up the trunks of beech trees, their heads jerking left and right, watching for cop squirrels tailing them.

Lisa Fremont jogged along the brick path in the early dusk, pumping her knees high, climbing a small slope, working up a sweat despite the evening chill. She wore Reeboks, nylon running shorts, and a Stanford cut-off T-shirt that exposed her flat stomach. It was November, and she was underdressed. She could see her breath in the dim light. Tomorrow, she'd wear a warm-up suit.

Now Lisa was thinking. Planning. Trying to stay calm as well as warm. Trying not to think of Shank, who had called her at home, leaving a message on the machine, his voice stabbing her like a sliver of glass. "We have to talk, lollipop. Dress up real pretty for me and wear some nice earrings."

The rest of the message was a direct order. He told her to come to his room at the Mayflower Hotel after work. She hadn't returned the call, and she sure as hell wasn't going to meet that maniac anywhere, much less in his hotel room.

He wants to frighten me. He enjoys it, and he uses my fear to control me. I will not be afraid!

But the anxiety hung over her like a dark and poisonous cloud. At work, she was strung as tightly as piano wire, jumping at the sound of the phone, afraid Shank might show up just to remind her that he could get to her anywhere.

She had called Max at his Miami office, asking him to tell Shank everything was fine and she didn't have time to meet. Besides, it was too risky. She should avoid all personal contact with Atlantica employees.

Anything to keep Shank at a distance.

Max asked how everything was going.

Fine, she told him, just finished the first draft of the bench memo, and the judge loves it.

One sentence, three lies. Is that some kind of record?

The first draft of the memo was done all right, but Jerry Klein had written it. If that bit of news got back to Shank ... well, just the thought of it filled her with dread. She knew what Shank was capable of and had no doubt he would fulfill his threats.

For the past three weeks, she had tried talking to Jerry Klein, tried convincing him. She'd used flattery, admiring his written work, leaning close to him as he banged away on his computer, watching the monitor over his shoulder.

"I wish I could turn a phrase like you, Jerry," she had said.

"Uh-uh." Without looking up.

She found an obscure Eleventh Circuit opinion that bore on a subsidiary issue in the census count case and gave it to him. He thanked her perfunctorily and went back to work.

She took him to lunch at Union Station, flirted with him, but he didn't seem to notice. Maybe Jerry Klein, the overweight, apparently asexual, overly intellectual blob, had no weaknesses to probe.

Now she ran along the path just inside the red brick wall of the Dumbarton Oaks Gardens, two blocks from her apartment. She liked the solitude at this time of day, this time of year. Few tourists bothered with the place once the summer flowers—the roses, magnolia, lilies, and oleanders—were gone. She preferred the fall, when the trees, not the blooms, had the attention. She passed under a white oak, its leaves a rich purple and red. She jogged up several steps, taking care on the broken bricks, headed through the open-air Orangery building, its outside walls covered with tumbling wisteria, while inside a tentacled fig was pruned to resemble dangling pendants covering the Palladian windows.

She loped past the Green Garden and around the Beech Terrace, where a young woman sat on a blanket in the grass, drawing in chalk in the fading light. She passed the Urn Terrace and headed through the Rose Garden, denuded of flowers, awaiting the coming winter.

Just yesterday, after everyone had left the office, Lisa had sat at Klein's computer, slipped in his password, *Veritas*, truth—the self-righteous prick—and called up the *Atlantica* bench memo. It was still in draft form and missing citations, but there was no doubt where Klein stood. He ridiculed the airline's argument, tossed in a couple of jokes about the intelligence, or lack thereof, of the trial judge, and argued that the spirits of the dead cried out for reversal, which struck Lisa as a bit over the top.

Trying to influence Jerry was useless. She needed to go directly to Sam Truitt, but how? She was desperate. Time was running short. Jerry would be finished with the bench memo in a few days. Then it would be over. She'd be out of the loop, and the memo would only reinforce Sam Truitt's predisposition in favor of the victims.

How can I get to Sam Bam Truitt?

Shank's advice echoed in her mind.

"Do what you do best."

But it could backfire. Truitt had not made a pass at her. In conferences with the clerks, he treated her as one of the guys. Other times, with shirtsleeves rolled up, he would stop by her office and plop down in a chair, lean back, and lock his sandy-haired forearms behind his head. She felt a stirring watching him, but he'd simply ask about her research on the Decency Act case and whether she was enjoying her work. Nothing personal. None of the little lines men drop when they're interested. No inquiries about boyfriends, hobbies, or a drink after work.

My hobby, Judge, is trying to stay alive.

She trotted past the Arbor Terrace, the wind rusting through the pear trees, the branches pruned into an aerial hedge. Darker and colder now. Time to go home, toss a Lean Cuisine into the microwave, and ...

A movement on a ledge off to one side startled her. Just a flash of motion in the dim light, nothing more. She picked up her pace, realizing her legs were loggy. Looking around. No one. The place was deserted.

She swung onto the brick path that would take her back to the R Street entrance. It was only a few hundred yards away. She could hear the traffic on the other side of the eight-foot-high brick wall.

Then, the unmistakable sound of footsteps on loose gravel.

Behind her, she thought, whirling to look, jogging backward now, the chill as much from trepidation as the plunging temperature.

Again, nothing.

She turned around and darted past a massive beech tree.

Then the *cr-aack* of a twig and the rusting of leaves. Someone was out there. Someone was running. Someone ...

In the hedge to her right, what was it?

She began sprinting, knees churning, flying over the path, her fatigue forgotten. A burst of adrenaline, and her heart hammered like a sledgehammer pounding at a tree.

From the shaded darkness, a blur came at her from the right side. She ducked a shoulder instinctively, tried to pivot to the left, took one step off the path, and the weight hit her, buckling her knees, toppling her to the ground. She scrambled to one knee, but his shoulder hit her in the back, knocking her flat to the ground, his weight crushing her, squeezing the wind from her. A hand roughly grabbed her hair and yanked her neck up painfully.

"No! Stop! Who—"

"You talking to me?" The voice out of kilter, a weird combination of puzzlement and threat. "You talking to me?" Taunting now.

She didn't answer. Couldn't answer. The fear enveloped her, struck her dumb, made her body tremble. He pressed down on her, ground her into the cold earth.

"Well, who the hell are you talking to!"

And then she got it, Robert De Niro mocking her, or at least his fan, someone who thinks *Taxi Driver* is a comedy, a warped sicko who sees too many movies and loves to inflict pain and terror.

"'Cause I'm the only one here," Shank said, twisting her head so she could see his pock-marked face leering at her.

She tried to stop trembling and suddenly was weirdly grateful that her attacker was Shank, someone she knew.

He might hurt me, but he can't kill me. He needs me.

"Let me up!" she yelled. "Let me go!" The anger rising to an equal pitch with the fear.

He shoved her head into the ground, her mouth grinding into the dirt. Helpless, unable to move, frightened.

"Don't tell me what to do, slut! I tell you what to do. And when I tell you to meet me, you damn well better do it. Max can't help you. You should know that by now."

"I was just being cautious," she said, trying to hide her fear. "We can't be seen together."

"Bullshit! You're just scared shitless to tell me you didn't get the case."

Omigod! How does he know?

She fought back against the panic, pushing away the realization that he longed for an excuse to hurt her, that he enjoyed it, that it was the popcorn that accompanied the movies in his mind.

"I'm going to get the case," she said, trying to sound confident. "I just need time."

He grabbed her hair and balled it into his fist, twisting it angrily. "Do I look like a bitch?" he bellowed into her ear.

She couldn't answer. Terror gripped her.

"I'm asking you, do I look like a bitch?"

It was from a movie, Lisa thought, but she couldn't place it, couldn't figure out the response he wanted. From someplace beneath the horror, she wondered if Shank could distinguish between reality and the twisted images on the movie screen.

"No," she said, softly, trying to mask her fear, "you don't look like a bitch."

"Then why are you trying to fuck me?"

"Please. Just—"

"'Cause you mess with me, I'll fuck you! Not all sweet and touchy like old softy Max. I'll dig a tunnel in you, you'll feel it for a month."

He pressed her down, and she could feel him through his pants, becoming hard, grinding against her bottom, his hot breath coming faster.

"Please. Just give me enough time, and—"

"Time is what you ain't got. Time is your enemy. Time is a fire licking at your little girlie toes, so don't feed me the shit that you got everything under control. This is your one and only warning. I don't care how you do it, but the next time we talk, you better tell me you got the judge's pecker in your pocket."

But it wasn't the judge's pecker she was thinking about. Shank kept rubbing against her, his hard cock pressing between her buttocks, slipping into the crevice of her nylon shorts. She fought against the panic, which threatened to paralyze her. He kept moving against her, breathing harder.

Jesus, I'm lap dancing again.

He pushed harder against her and a dribble of spittle fell from his mouth to her cheek. He was squeezing the breath from her. She felt her energy draining and thought he was becoming more aroused.

The pig wants to rape me.

A thousand thoughts raced through her mind. She thought about grabbing a handful of dirt, tossing it into his eyes, but from her position, facedown, there was no way. She thought about wriggling her ass, bringing him off, but didn't know if that would satisfy him or enrage him.

He moved his lips close to her ear, and his unshaven face scraped her neck like sandpaper. She stifled a scream, the memories flooding back.

Daddy, ouch, your beard scratches!

She remembered her father holding her down, too. She remembered his sour, boozy breath, and the pain as he split her open. She had escaped that pain, her mind taking her into the Tasmania poster, fleeing into a cleansing, purifying waterfall.

Now, with this animal dragging her down, just as her father had done, she fought for self-control. "I'll deliver him. I'll get his vote. Just trust me."

Shank lifted her head up by the hair. "Not good enough." He got to one knee, keeping a hand in the small of her back. A moment of relief, his weight and his swollen cock off her. Then he stood and hoisted her up.

"Hey," she protested, but he was dragging her along the path, past cast-stone columns, then down three steep brick ledges to an elliptical pool, her ankles banging against the bricks. They were in a miniature amphitheater, a pool surrounded by a wood lattice crawling with honeysuckle and ivy, with towering walnut and maple trees overhead.

"You disappoint me, Lisa," Shank said, "but not nearly as much as you're gonna disappoint old Max. That fool's put his life in your hands. And your life, sweet tits, is in mine." He looked around a moment, then pushed her to the ground at the edge of the pool, the water black, dead leaves floating on the surface like the hulls of derelict boats. "What do they call this place?"

She knew but wouldn't answer.

"Lover's Lane Pool," he said. "Ain't that sweet? Maybe we'll be lovers, just like you and Max. Only Max and me are different. He believes you treat a whore like a princess and a princess like a whore, which in case you didn't figure it out, is why he always treated you like a princess. But me, I treat a whore like a whore."

He grabbed her by the neck and pushed her head down toward the water. His grip was powerful, and his fingers dug deep into the tender skin at the back of her neck. She braced a hand on the edge of the pool, but he tore it free and pushed harder on her neck. She plunged forward headfirst into the frigid water up to her shoulders. She held her breath, her mind racing, as he pushed her deeper.

Don't kill me! Please! I'll do it! I'll do whatever you want. Anything.

Her lungs aching, she blew out her breath, fighting to stay conscious, to keep from swallowing. She tried screaming with the last of her breath, her screams bubbles in the inky water.

Let me go, you freak!

Still he held her under, so she did the only thing she could think to do. She went limp, her head falling to one side, and in a moment he pulled her up and tossed her onto the ground on her back.

Barely conscious, she thought she'd rather die than have him give her mouth-to-mouth. She gasped for air, greedily sucking in breaths, lying in the grass, shells of beechnuts sticking to her wet hair, the noise of her breathing blocking out everything else. She inhaled all the air in the world, exhaling great bursts like the whistle of a punctured tire. Shivering from the cold and the fear, she got to one knee, waiting for the next act of torture, the next taunt. She had no strength. If he wanted to rape her, she could do nothing to resist.

Silence.

She looked around, but he was gone.

ᴄᴐ

"You're going about it all wrong," Max said, his voice hollow on the speakerphone.

"Get off the damn speaker," Shank ordered. He was sitting on the king-size bed in the Mayflower Hotel, his feet up, a cigarette dangling from his lips. As he spoke, he used a remote control to flip through the TV channels.

"There's no one here," Max said.

"I don't give a shit. Pick up the phone." Wanting to hear the inflections in his voice, just like the old days with the police wiretaps, some of them even legal. Eavesdropping on the wops and the spies, all the bullshit and bravado. You listen long enough, you listen close enough, you figure out the players, who's got balls, who's full of shit.

Now take Max. No cajones, or otokoiki, as my Japanese buddies would say.

Sitting there in his penthouse office on Biscayne Boulevard a thousand miles away, acting tough on the phone, like he was really the boss.

"Lisa doesn't respond to threats," Max was saying, his voice still echoing through the speaker.

Shank stubbed out his cigarette and surfed past the news channel, basketball scores scrolling across the bottom of the screen, and flicked over to pay-per-view. Sometimes Max just didn't get it, closed his eyes to the truth, like he didn't want to know. Max would take the money from the devil but didn't want to acknowledge that he'd sold his soul. He kept up the front that it was still his airline and that Shank was just a hired hand.

I am a hired hand, but not yours, Maxie.

He wouldn't give Shank his due, wouldn't recognize him as the long arm of the Yakuza family, which was the de facto owner of Atlantica.

Shank had explained everything, told Max to think of the Yakuza as the Mafia. Instead of the Genovese, Lucchese, and Gambino families, you've got your Yamaguchi-gumi, Inagawa-kai, and Sumiyoshi-rengo-kai. But the Yakuza are tougher, Shank told him. Hell, he'd watched as a tattooed young punk with dead, black eyes had cut off his own little finger as penance for botching an extortion job. Crazy bastards went out of their way to make a point.

They eat poisonous blowfish at four hundred bucks a plate for Christ's sake!

Shank was proud to have been one of the first *gaijin* recruited by a Yakuza family that wanted to expand its businesses to the States. By the time Katsushika Koshiro came to him, the Osaka crime boss had already made several fortunes smuggling crystal meth from Taiwan into Japan and Hawaii. Now he was investing in U.S. golf courses, casinos, and publicly held companies, usually through shell corporations. Shank respected and feared Koshiro, descendant of the *boryokudan*, violent men who trace their roots to seventeenth-century gambling dens. The son of a bitch was smart. He changed with the times. Underneath all that bowing and ritualistic bullshit, Koshiro was a modern businessman in the international mergers-and-acquisitions game.

Years earlier, Shank had provided security for Koshiro when he'd traveled to New York to check out real estate investments. Later, invited to Osaka, Shank proved his mettle as a *jiageya*, a property clearer.

Now Shank smiled to himself remembering how he persuaded homeowners to sell out so Koshiro could knock down their ticky-tack homes and build a skyscraper. A .357 Magnum jammed down the throat broke right through the language barrier. But there was one skinny little guy in his sixties who wouldn't sell. On the third visit, Shank brought along a young Yakuza thug with a tattooed serpent crawling up the back of his neck. The old guy still wouldn't negotiate, so the thug started whirling a samurai sword like Darth Vader with a laser blade. Shank still felt a shiver race up his spine every time he pictured the scene. The sword took the man's arm off at the shoulder, blood spurting to the ceiling.

I don't scare easily, but these bastards pucker my asshole.

When Koshiro's Yakuza family put millions into Atlantica Airlines, Shank was called on to protect the investment. His job was straightforward enough: win the lawsuit by any means necessary. If he won, he'd be in charge of security for all American operations—the casinos, the drug trade, smuggling Asians into the States. He could start building his house on the Costa Rican beach property he'd bought with dirty money. Lose, and his blood would be on the floor. That was the problem with the Japs. You screw up, they expect you to fall on your sword. Koshiro had asked him to guarantee victory. Shank had tried to explain that maybe he could buy a vote, but he sure as hell couldn't buy five. Koshiro pretended he didn't understand. Either you promised to do a job or you didn't take it … so Shank promised.

I gotta win or some asshole with a samurai sword will slice my dick into french fries.

Now, as he screened the previews of the soft-core, fake-an-orgasm channels, Shank listened to the hollow, amplified voice of Max Wanaker. "With Lisa, you have to use reason and logic."

Shank pictured Max at his custom-made desk, an asymmetrical chunk of blue-green glass resembling a glacier, a desk on which he spent God-knows-how-much of their employer's money, the money Shank was now charged with getting back, every sweaty dollar. Max would be there, working late, or what he called working, which consisted mainly of making calls to the West Coast, staring out at the cruise ships in Government Cut, thinking he's a big shot in the fancy office with the Picasso originals and a view all the way to Bimini.

Christ, why is everybody in authority, from precinct captains to company presidents, such dumb shits?

"Max, don't make me tell you again! Drop your cock and pick up the goddamn phone!"

Shank heard the click. "Okay, okay," Max purred, in his soothing corporate tone. "Just remember that Lisa's from the streets. You can't scare her."

"I already did." Shank had seen her fear, was aroused by it. When was the first time he had seen that look in some bitch's eyes? High school. Stephanie, one of the preppies. Student council, teacher's pet, the whole cordovan loafers, college-bound crowd. She was a gymnast. Damn good, too, bouncing along the balance beam, flying off the uneven parallel bars, sticking her landings and arching her back, little titties popping out.

It had bothered him that he didn't fit in. Hell, maybe it still did. He ran with the hoods, losers trying to be tough guys. He tried hanging out with Stephanie's crowd, which wanted no part of him. He started coming around the gym where he found her one day, hands chalky, tears streaming down her face. A girl from Westchester County had been selected ahead of her for some Junior Olympics team. Stephanie was an alternate. "Damnit! I wish she'd break her leg," Stephanie pouted, then stomped off.

It wasn't hard to do. Shank hot-wired a car, drove up to Westchester, walked into the school where the girl's picture was framed in a glass cabinet along with an assortment of ribbons, medals, and plaques. Carrying a tire jack inside his coat, he waited until gymnastics practice was over, and when the little blonde girl came prancing down a corridor to the parking lot where her mother waited, Shank called her by name, then bashed her kneecap. Once to put her down, then once on the ankle, which cracked like a coconut under a machete. The girl was too scared to scream. She just looked up at him with a delicious fear in her eyes that had turned him on big time.

The next day, he told Stephanie. Told her he did what none of those limp dicks in A. P. calculus would have done, put his ass on the line for her. Backing away, looking at him with a mixture of horror and loathing, Stephanie yelled that she'd turn him in.

It shocked him. He had miscalculated. "Not if you want to walk again," he said, figuring his mistake was in not just taking what he wanted instead of trying to win it like some knight on a white horse.

"You didn't hurt her?" Max asked, his voice fearful.

"Not yet," Shank said.

Shank hit the button on the remote to buy a porn flick that had already started, a woman psychiatrist taking notes while her male patient, a businessman who looked like a lifeguard in a thousand-dollar suit, lay on the couch. The psychiatrist was one of those blondes with her hair piled up, real businesslike, wearing glasses and a charcoal business suit, but you could see the pouty lips, and you just knew she was a hot box who probably wore black underwear. Shank had seen plenty of psychiatrists in the courthouses in New York. Most were short Jews with beards and bald spots, not stacked, blonde blow job artists. The sound on the TV was muted, but Shank could fill in the dialogue. The guy probably couldn't get it up, and the lady shrink was gonna solve his problem.

"Damn it, Shank. She's with us."

"No. She's with you. You're the asshole who got us into this jam, and now we gotta depend on her royal highness to get us out." Pissed off now, listening to Max pretend he was still in charge. If they were in the same room, Shank might give him a little *Hustler* treatment, bend his thumbs backward till they snapped. "We should never have relied on her. We should have just bought a fifth vote."

"You don't buy a Supreme Court judge," Max said. "Nobody ever has."

On the screen, the lady shrink took off her glasses and loosened her hair, shaking it free over her shoulders. Just a matter of time now.

"How would you know? I mean, how would anybody?" Shank had personally bribed half a dozen judges in New York and twice as many prosecutors. He'd extorted favors from a judge whose son was arrested buying crack from an undercover narc and took cash from another who was caught cornholing a runaway kid in a Central Park restroom. Shanks' view of judges, like his view of human nature generally, was colored a jaundiced yellow. "Most judges are so crooked, they screw on their socks," he said.

"It's different on the Supreme Court."

"Why, you think those guys are any different than you and me? They don't believe in the rules any more than I do. When I was a cop, I didn't follow *Miranda* or the Marquis of Queensberry, and if some scumbag ended up floating in the Hudson, who gives a shit?"

"If Lisa says she'll get it done, she will."

"Sure she will," Shank said. "She doesn't have a choice."

There was silence on the line, Max maybe thinking that over, Shank watching the lady shrink slipping out of her business suit, reaching around to unfasten her black, frilly bra, then tossing it toward a bookshelf where it landed on a fat book, titled *Male Sexual Dysfunction*. Real subtle. She had big round tits, too big for the rest of her skinny-assed, skinny-armed, model's body. What's the world coming to when you can't even rely on a pair of tits to be real?

"I trust Lisa," Max was saying, sounding wimpy.

Trusting a woman! Trusting anyone.

"I even tell her stuff I keep from my wife. There's such a thing as loyalty, Shank, and she's got it. She'd …"

What'd he say?

"… never do anything to cross me."

He couldn't be that stupid!

"You didn't tell her, did you?" Shank asked. Keeping his voice calm. Not revealing his barely controlled fury, not letting him know he'd be floating in the bay outside his floor-to-ceiling windows if he slipped up.

"Tell her what?" Max asked.

Forgetting about the TV now, as the businessman-lifeguard, apparently no longer limp-dicked, dry-humped the blonde shrink. Plastic tits and simulated screwing for seven dollars fifty cents added to your bill.

Shank cranked up his own volume as he clicked off the TV. "Listen, Slapsie Maxie! I just heard you say you tell Lisa things that you keep from your wife. So I'm thinking maybe you told her what really caused the crash."

"No way! Jesus, Shank, what do you think I am?"

A guy living on borrowed time.

"I'm not stupid," Max said. "I didn't tell anybody," Max went on. "There's only the two of us who know."

"You got a short memory," Shank said, "'Cause you sure as shit know there are three."

CHAPTER 12

Lisa's Laws

JOE DRAYTON STEPPED GINGERLY from one pock-marked boulder to another. Each was larger than a pickup truck and considerably heavier, the legacy of several glaciers and two continental plates grinding against each other. The rocks were slippery with frothy tide and green algae. With each step, Drayton came closer to the pounding surf, the spray cold and salty.

The day was foggy and raw. A pounding squall moved inland, soaking him. Reaching into the pocket of his mackinaw, Drayton drew out a pint bottle of Jack Daniel's, which he tilted to his lips and swigged, letting the golden liquid warm his throat. He'd left his easel and canvas on the cliffs seventy-five feet above the waterline. That morning, he'd painted the sky a lifeless gray, the ocean funereal black, the rocks lashed by angry, foaming waves. Now, he perched unsteadily on the boulder, which had been worn into a smooth ledge by a thousand millennia of waves. A hundred yards offshore was a formation of house-size boulders and beyond that only the vast furious ocean.

Drayton rubbed a knuckle across his chin, overgrown with five days of white stubble. He had always been burly with a barrel chest and a waist to match, but he had lost more than thirty pounds since the crash. Sixty-four years old, he seemed shrunken and withered, his trousers ballooning.

He had come as far as he could go, as far from the tropical hell of Miami as he could drive. The road stopped here, on the Mendocino Coast of Northern California, thick forests of firs and redwoods on the coastal ranges separating him from the rest of the world.

He had escaped the heat and humidity, but not the pain and guilt.

Tony was a good man, and I killed him.

A dozen times, he'd picked up the phone to call Tony's boy, and a dozen times, he'd put the phone down and lifted a bottle instead. He couldn't bring himself to speak to the boy, to give words to his feelings. So he drew the pictures, hoping to remain anonymous, handing out clues, trying to lead the way through the quicksand without sinking himself.

Coward! Chicken-shit coward. If you had the balls, you'd go public. You'd go on Larry King and say, "It was my fault. I brought down that plane."

His days were filled with self-loathing. At night, he barely slept, his bed feeling like a coffin filled with stones.

But he had found a way to end the pain and quell the guilt. Once and forever.

Joe Drayton planned to kill himself.

℘

Greg Kingston had borrowed his grandmother's ten-year-old Pontiac Bonneville for the drive north on California Route One, the Shoreline Highway. He wore a black nylon San Francisco Giants windbreaker, blue jeans, and a Giants' ball cap. His father had been a fanatical baseball fan, calling from faraway places to learn how his team was doing, telling Greg about Mays, McCovey, and Marichal, the great Giants from the past.

It was a gray, rainy day, and Greg forced himself to drive slowly on the narrow two-lane road, the old car's shocks squeaking in protest as he negotiated a series of hairpin curves and steep descents. Before leaving Bodega Bay, he had his best meal in months, Mary Kingston's famous fish soup, a luxurious brew of fresh Pacific salmon floating alongside potatoes, onions, and pickled gherkins in a tomato broth, seasoned with bay leaves and topped with a dollop of sour cream. It was a meal in itself, fit for a rainy, raw November day. He had sopped up the soup with a piece of sourdough and told his grandmother that he was going to find the man who had the answers to the crash.

"Did you tell Lisa what you're up to?" she asked. "That girl always had a good head on her shoulders."

"Sure. She wished me luck."

But that's not what she had said at all. Puzzled, he thought about what Lisa told him.

"Be careful."

She had seemed nervous and troubled.

Be careful of what? I'm looking for the mechanic who knows what happened, why Dad and all those people died. What's the big problem?

It wasn't the Lisa he knew from the time he was a Little Leaguer and champion swimmer. A memory from childhood came back to him. When he was in the sixth grade and starting to hang out with a rowdy group, he'd cheated on a history exam, palming a note card filled with dates of Civil War battles. That night, Lisa found his crib sheet and gave him holy hell.

"If you start cheating now, you'll never stop," she said, forcing him to write "Lisa's Laws" a hundred times in his notebook.

I shall not lie.

I shall not cheat.

I shall not make promises that I can't keep.

"And always choose right over wrong," she told him.

"How will I know what's right?" he asked.

"If you follow Lisa's Laws, you'll know. You'll always know."

Proving who was responsible for the crash was the right thing to do. He was sure of it. So why was Lisa going against her own rules?

ल

The rain was growing heavier, and the cold bit through Joe Drayton's mackinaw. Standing on the rocks, feeling the salt spray douse his pant legs, he was growing weary. How long had it been since he slept through the night? Last night, he awoke from the same nightmare: he was swimming through a web of twisted mangrove roots in a festering swamp boiling with blood and a sickening pus. Suddenly, the roots took on the shapes of bloodied, scabrous arms and legs, the limbs of the damned, and they pulled him under, wrenching him into his nightly hell.

Now he listened to the cleansing sound of the ocean beating at his feet. He could be baptized in the frigid water. He could be reborn. If he had the courage to do it, he could join the 288 others he had sent to their watery graves.

He took another swallow of the bourbon, draining the bottle, then tossed it into the sea, where it washed in, then out, on the pulsating waves. He regretted not calling Tony's son. He would like to have met the boy, to have begged his forgiveness.

Suddenly, a rogue wave washed over the boulder, soaking and freezing him. He should have worn the slicker. The thought made him laugh. In a moment, he would be chilled to his godforsaken soul, so why worry about catching a cold?

How should I do it? Should I leap in or just stand and wait for the incoming tide?

Sometimes, a single wave driven by an unseen fury—a storm a thousand miles at sea—would lash the coast, pushing a hundred yards past the high tide mark, washing away an unwary beachcomber.

He would let it happen. Prayed for it to happen. It would be a sign from God.

If God can part the Red Sea, how hard could it be to unleash a single wave? Where is El Niño *when you need the bastard?*

He wondered for the thousandth time how it had come to this. It was his fault. He had let Max Wanaker dismantle his department in one cost-cutting maneuver after another. Rent-a-temp mechanics, pencil-whipped records, gray-market parts, the whole dirty business. Then, after the crash, he had taken the cashier's check for seven hundred thousand dollars that Wanaker called his bonus. Not "hush money." Not "blood money." A bonus.

Drayton noticed the check was written on a Japanese bank. He always caught the details. His job was made up of them. A loose screw in a control panel, a faulty cold-soldered joint on a fuel quantity processor, a cargo hatch not securely latched, he noticed all of these things. Details led to crew write-ups, action items, trend monitoring data.

You miss details, people die.

Another wave washed over the rock, smacking a crevice, ricocheting a stream of water up his leg. He shivered against the cold like a wet dog.

Why did I take the money? Why did I run? I could have told the NTSB the truth and purged my guilt.

The truth. No one in the world knew as much as Joe Drayton about Ship 102. He recalled being alone in his cubicle-size office in the machine shop, looking over the records less than thirty hours after the crash. It was 2 A.M., and only a skeleton staff was in the building. Drayton poured himself black coffee and opened the file cabinet, filled with shame at what he knew he would find. It was all in front of him in black and white, and only he knew what was true and what was false. The DC-10 was twenty-four years old at the time of the crash. The number two engine had been operated 49,614 hours and 19,575 cycles. The service records revealed no abnormal engine operation prior to the accident. All of this was true.

The same records showed that the stage one fan rotor disk was removed and inspected seven times during its twenty-four-year life span, including a last time eight months prior to the accident. The paperwork said that the disk was disassembled and subjected to Fluorescent Penetration Inspection where ultraviolet light was shone on the hard titanium alloy, which had been coated with a dye. Any excessive penetration of dye would show defects due to metal fatigue, and the disk would have been replaced. The disk passed the test, according to the records that Drayton had signed.

"Follow the paper, but the paper lies."

The records were false! The test had not been performed! Not in April 1995 and not during the prior inspection in 1993.

He clearly remembered the second incident. Wanaker had pressured him to get Ship 102 back on line. The number two engine was indeed disassembled because of corrosion in the high pressure turbine nozzle guide vanes. But time was short; money was short; tempers were short. A plane was needed, so Drayton signed the paperwork, and the FPI was never done.

∽

The rain slanted in gray sheets across the narrow road as Greg drove farther north, the wipers on the old Pontiac squeaking across the windshield without clearing the view. He slowed on the precarious turns, then seemed to plow straight through the low, wet clouds as they scudded over the coastal range, the air ripe with a salty sea breeze.

The winding road climbed over the crests of lush, timbered hills and crossed shallow streams flowing from the redwood-covered slopes to the sea. Greg looked toward the ocean, where rolling waves had carved rock formations into marvelous shapes and the water broke over submerged, unseen ledges. He drove through places with romantic, picturesque names: Mount Tamalpais, Green Gulch, Bolinas Lagoon, Tomales Bay, and Russian Gulch.

Alone with the sound of the rain streaming down his windshield like endless tears, Greg thought of his father. He had been a fearless fighter pilot, and then a conscientious, dedicated captain for Atlantica. As a child, Greg wanted to be just like him. He remembered Dad bringing home a present for his eighth birthday, a kid's size Naval flight suit with a dozen zippers and pockets and squadron sleeve patches. He wore the flight suit every day for weeks until Granny made him take it off so she could wash it.

Greg's thoughts turned to Lisa, and how much he cared for her. At first when his father told him that he'd fallen in love with the girl from down the hill, Greg had stared at him in disbelief.

"Are you okay with it?" his father had asked, forehead wrinkled in concern.

"To tell you the truth, Dad, I'm a little wigged out," he replied, honestly.

Then he thought it through, trying to figure just what Lisa meant to him. He remembered doing laps in the YMCA pool when he was twelve, coming up with a training technique to improve his time. He would picture Lisa at the other end of the pool, waiting for him. Not with her whistle and stopwatch but naked, sitting cross-legged, dangling her toes in the water. Deep inside, Greg supposed, Lisa was always more than the babysitter, more than a surrogate sister. What had she been? A child's fantasy love, he supposed, like having a crush on your fourth grade teacher. When he worked through the memories, suddenly it was okay, his dad and his fantasy girl, even pretty cool seeing the two of them in love. Jeez, they made a great couple.

After his father's death in the crash, he lost touch with Lisa for a time. She had gone back to law school, and he was in college. He remembered her calling on his birthday, but when he asked if she would come by, she made excuses and stayed away. At first he was hurt. But figuring he reminded her of his father, that it was painful for her, he didn't push it. Then, one day he and some buddies from San Francisco State were hitting the bars at the fancy hotels, seeing if they could get older women to buy them drinks at eight bucks a shot. They were already buzzed and had been hanging off cable cars, mooning passers-by, being typical jerk-off college kids, when they dusted themselves off and headed to the Fairmont.

"Check it out!" one of his buddies said on his way up the steps to the lobby.

Greg whirled around to see a couple getting into a white stretch limo. "Is she hot or what?"

He was looking at a young woman wearing a slinky black cocktail dress, her long blonde-red hair piled stylishly. Lisa.

Lisa Fremont at the Fairmont.

She was with an older man in a tuxedo. Greg recognized Max Wanaker from a company picnic where the CEO had made longwinded speeches and handed out awards. His father had despised the man, called him a greedy hypocrite. Now Wanaker had his hand on Lisa's arm, helping her get into the limo in her tight dress.

"C'mon!" Greg told his buddies, turning and heading up the steps. "Let's get drunk."

But the evening was ruined. Why was Lisa with Max Wanaker? Greg never asked her, never mentioned seeing her. But it still troubled him. He tried rationalizing it. Atlantica was having its annual stockholders' meeting in San Francisco. Lisa probably knew Wanaker through Dad, and she was lonely. So if Wanaker invited her to a party or a banquet, there was nothing wrong with it, right? But still, it seemed disloyal to the memory of his father, and he couldn't get it out of his mind.

Now, as the rain fell harder, Greg realized he had underestimated the driving time on the winding road. He still hoped to get to Mendocino before dark, but treacherous fog had rolled in from the ocean. The fifteen miles from Gualala to Point Arena, past ranches on one side, tidal pools on the other, took forty minutes. He drove through dense, blustery clouds on a slippery road from Point Arena to Elk, a stretch of tortuous curves. Farther along, the road to Albion wound along a shoreline of tall cliffs and sea stacks, and farther still, crossing a grassy marine terrace with a glimpse of the headlands, he veered through Dark Gulch on the road to the old lumber town of Mendocino with its wooden water towers. Then he set about finding Joe Drayton.

જી

Joe Drayton was thinking about God. Standing on the slippery rock, balancing against the rush off the oncoming waves, his legs becoming stiff, Drayton looked over the infinite expanse of the ocean, thinking of his Maker.

He believed in a Supreme Being. Only a knowing deity would have sent him to the scene of the crash. Only God would have made him witness the holocaust of his own making, to see bodies without heads, arms without bodies, to inhale the jet fuel, its acrid black taste clinging to him, tingeing him with death.

Now the wind moaned, echoing through caverns in the huge, offshore boulders.

The voice of God calling me home.

He remembered a sense of overwhelming numbness, of deadened feelings when he arrived, touching down in the Atlantica helicopter not long after the Coast Guard and Metro police showed up. There had been a false dawn, a pink sun reflecting off clouds on the eastern horizon before darkness settled again. When the sun rose a second time, Drayton saw body parts floating in the razor-edged grass, stuck in the quicksand-like mud. He waded in the knee-deep murky water, his feet sinking into the dense, spongy peat. The prehistoric slough was alive with egrets and herons stomping through the shallows, stalking their prey, oblivious to the insignificant intrusion of man.

He remembered a wintry warm sun on the back of his neck, but he was clammy with cold sweat. Later, he rode around the crash site on an airboat piloted by an old Florida Cracker, a bearded, smelly, rum-soaked derelict whose nighttime gator poaching had been interrupted by the crash. The roaring airboat navigated around hardwood hammocks overgrown with vines and gumbo limbo trees, some littered with detritus from the crash.

The site soon became a surreal military camp with NTSB divers, wearing NASA-style protective suits, probing the muck while sharpshooters carrying scoped rifles watched for alligators and water moccasins. Searchers combed the wreckage for body parts and airplane parts, finding everything from a bloody femur to a wet but working cockpit voice recorder. Picturing it, he was sure he'd had his first glimpse of hell. Now he was prepared for a longer look.

∽

Greg stopped twice to ask directions before turning left on Point Cabrillo Drive and making his way to a lighthouse above the cliffs. That's where all the artists sit and paint, a gas station attendant told him. He slid the Pontiac to a stop in the gravel parking lot and hustled out. The rain had stopped. Gulls hovered overhead, scanning the tidal pools for supper. A woman of perhaps sixty sat on a stool at an easel, painting a likeness of the lighthouse set against a gray, angry sky. Two hikers, a man and a woman in their forties, bundled against the cold, hurried along the bluff-top trail at double time. A lone man with binoculars stood above the cliffs, looking out to sea, watching for whales.

Close to the edge, he found a stool, an easel and canvas, a partially finished painting of a raging sea. The canvas had been soaked by the rain.

Where are you, Joe Drayton?

Greg approached the cliff and looked out at the surging tide crashing on the rocks below. In the distance, several hundred yards down the coastline, a man in a red mackinaw stood on a smoothed boulder, his island in a tidal pool.

Is that you, Joe?

There had to be a path down the cliffs, but Greg couldn't find the opening. He began walking, then jogging along the trail at the top of the cliff, heading along the coastline toward the man. He called out Joe Drayton's name, but over the roar of the waves, how could he be heard? The path wound away from the shore, and for a moment, Greg lost sight of the man.

Joe Drayton thought someone was calling his name. But unless it was God, it must have been the wind. He let his mind drift back to that hellish day, replaying the scene again and again. It was his penance, to experience the agony, to relish his own torture.

Riding in the old Cracker's airboat, he had searched for engine and hydraulics parts. He pictured himself now, kneeling on the bow, praying that it wasn't a maintenance defect that had brought down the plane. In the first hour, he found three cowl rods, a hydraulic pump, some fan blades, and part of a hose, marking the spots with anchored balloons, letting the NTSB Go-Team do its job of recovery and identification. But no fan disk, until late that day, miles away, the setting sun an orange dagger in the eye. Embedded in a log covered with resurrection ferns, surrounded by a web of white swamp lilies like the centerpiece at a ladies' luncheon, was a triangular chunk of machined titanium alloy, glinting silver in the setting sun. A single piece of the fan rotor disk, barely a foot wide, a gift from the devil.

He knew then what had caused the crash. He knew in his heart even before he saw the small crack in the dull surface of the fan disk. He stepped into the shallow water and lugged the disk into the airboat so he could examine it. There was a small cavity several inches long in the middle of the disk.

I should put it back. I should mark the spot and alert the investigators.

If he did, the metallurgical tests would confirm what he could see: a fatigue crack. The report would be filled with the dry, official language of lab technicians: "Fractographic, metallographic, and chemical analysis of the fatigue region reveals the presence of a nitrogen-stabilized hard alpha inclusion around the cavity."

The investigators would wonder how that could have happened in the eight months since the Fluorescent Penetration Inspection. If the disk had passed the test, it should not have broken apart as it whirled around, exploding and hurling the turbine blades through the hydraulic lines.

The examiners would wash the disk with deionized water, then do a mass spectroscopy test, looking for the presence of phosphates. If the FPI test had been done, as the records he signed swore, the compounds would be present. But they wouldn't be found. The records would be revealed as fraudulent. The Atlantica fleet would be grounded, and unable to service its debt, the company would join Eastern, Braniff, Frontier, and the old Pan Am in the airline graveyard. Joe Drayton would be fired, disgraced, perhaps even indicted.

So he used his cellular phone to call Shank at the makeshift command headquarters, a tent pitched on the higher, drier ground of a mahogany hammock. The security director was rounding up the airline's crisis team, making sure no one spoke to the press without his okay, bossing around workers in the mosquito-infested tent. Drayton remembered hearing the buzz of voices in the background, the tent crammed with Metro cops, paramedics, air rescue crews, Coast Guardsmen, and a smattering of NTSB investigators. Outside, reporters swirled around like vultures, and overhead, real vultures circled in the breeze.

"Deep six it," Shank told him.

Drayton didn't argue. When they got back to the dock, an Atlantica courier was waiting. He had an envelope with ten one-hundred-dollar bills for the old Cracker, who seemed happy enough to take the money and head for the deep water of the Gulf of Mexico to bury the disk. Refusing to accompany him, as if that would ease the guilt, Drayton went home to get drunk.

For the first year, he feared that another piece of the disk would be found. Then he began hoping that it would be, that his corruption would be discovered. But it never happened. The rest of the disk, he supposed, was buried deep in the mud, woven into an endless tapestry of ancient, rotting sawgrass, swallowed whole by a freshwater sea.

Drayton was already in California when he heard that the NTSB had found traces of the explosive pentaerythritol tetranitrate in the nacelle of the tail engine. He had shaken his head in wonder.

It must have been Shank. How had he done it? How had he gained access to the parts and planted the PETN? It was a brilliant distraction. Totally believable, too, what with the Cuban exile group having made the threats. The focus of the investigation became terrorism, not maintenance. The FBI virtually elbowed NTSB investigators out of the swamp. No other evidence of explosives was found, of course. No terrorists claimed responsibility, and the cause of the crash could not be

conclusively established. The luckless widows, widowers, and children lost
their lawsuits. Life for Atlantica went on.

The tide was fully in now, and Drayton's boulder was surrounded by
water. A foamy wave washed across the ledge, soaking through his old,
steel-toed work boots, the spray kicking high enough for him to taste the
salty water. The wind was picking up, whistling through openings in a
giant formation of rocks a hundred yards offshore.

He was trembling in the cold and wished he had another bottle. His
mind was foggy from lack of sleep, too little food, and too much booze.
It was time to act. He'd been on this rock a dozen times before, always
planning to jump into the raging water, just as he had planned to tell Greg
Kingston what really happened. But he'd never had the balls to do either
one. He would rather wallow in his self-pity and self-loathing.

He could ease the pain with one slippery step. He could end the
visions of the great silvery plane plunging into the swamp, the nightmares
of red-eyed alligators devouring arms and legs, a little girl's patent leather
shoe lodged in the fronds of a palmetto tree.

He could end it all now.

If he had the courage.

But if he had such courage, would he even be here at all?

A wave suddenly slapped hard at the rock beneath his feet, surged
past him, then shot back again, out toward open sea. Drayton felt himself
being pushed one way, then pulled the other. His arms windmilled as he
struggled to keep his feet, and then he toppled into the briny, frigid water.

෨

Greg broke into a run, following the trail along the bluffs. He dodged
beneath tree branches, tripping over a twisted root, before emerging from
the underbrush at the cliff's edge. He heard a wail that for a moment
seemed almost human, a mournful plea coming from the sea. It took a
moment to realize that it was the wind, singing through the sandstone
arches and tunnels that had been sculpted by millions of years of waves.

Cautiously approaching the sheer cliff, he looked down at the boulders,
but the man in the mackinaw was no longer there. The water poured over
a formation of rocks, raced into a cove dug into the rock below him, and
tore back out again.

Then his eye caught something out of place.

The wrong color in the gray water, foaming white as it skirted across a
boulder into a shallow tidal pool.

A glimpse of something red floating in the pool near the outcropping of rocks below. Another wave crashed into the cliffs, and whatever it was disappeared. He waited a moment as the water swirled in the pool, spilled over a ledge, then returned to the sea. There it was again, just a flash of dark red, a manmade color in surroundings untouched by man.

There was a steep path cut into the cliff, and he went down cautiously, holding on to the porous rocks. Loose shale and pebbles slid out from under his shoes. Halfway down, a giant wave crashed into the rocks below and shot upward through a blowhole, dousing him, knocking him off balance. He grabbed a slippery cone of hard rock, steadied himself, and chilled by the frigid shower, continued downward.

Greg was nearly to the waterline when he caught sight of the red plaid fabric, which he recognized as a man's woolen coat. Then he saw the back of the man's head and the baggy trousers. The lifeless body was floating facedown, the surging water tugging it toward the shore, then out again. But unable to clear the ledge, it stayed in the pool, a speck of matter at the edge of the endless ocean.

Greg could not see the man's face, but he knew. He had lost Joe Drayton. He lost the one chance to do justice for his father. It was his own damn fault. If he'd found Drayton a year earlier … if he'd gotten here an hour earlier, who knows?

I've failed you, Dad.

Greg Kingston began to cry, his sobs becoming a low-pitched wail that even he could not hear, for he was drowned out by the whistling wind and the tumbling sea.

CHAPTER 13

Black Monday

WHERE WAS THE PHOTO OF HIS WIFE?

Lisa considered the question as she dressed for the dinner party. The invitation was handwritten in fountain pen on the silver-bordered, creamy white personal stationery of Mrs. Samuel Adams Truitt.

So very proper.

Jerry Klein, Vic Vazquez, and Lisa Fremont were invited to what Mrs. Truitt described as the first of oh-so-many annual autumn dinners for the clerks.

"I look forward to our meeting," Connie wrote to Lisa in utterly perfect penmanship. "My husband has told me so much about you."

Really? Has he told you I'm planning to screw him? No, I suppose not. He doesn't have the slightest idea.

Lisa would have expected a gilt-framed photo of Mrs. Truitt on the justice's desk. But there was none. Sam never referred to his wife in their conversations. There was no indication that he was a married man, except for the plain gold wedding band, which looked small on his large hand.

So where was the former Constance Parham, upper-crust daughter of the retired senator, princess of Nantucket, widely renowned for her exquisite taste? Where did the wife fit in?

Somewhere after a shaggy-haired mutt whose framed photo—happily diving into a pile of autumn leaves—stood on the credenza in his masters' chambers.

Whither Constance?

Lisa was out of time and out of ideas. It would have been so much easier if the judge had been flirtatious, if he'd made the first move. But he hadn't, so it was up to her.

The only way to get Sam Truitt's vote is to get into his life and into his bed.

Oral argument was in three weeks. Without the opportunity to write the bench memo, she would have to rely on soft, sweet whispers. She regretted it had come to this, that she had come full circle, that she would have to use her body to survive. A strange mix of conflicting feelings buzzed inside her like a bee against a windowpane. She felt a flood of warmth thinking about Sam Truitt the man, but a leaden sorrow thinking about Sam Truitt the target. She wanted him but hated betraying him. Damnit! Why couldn't she just do her work, start her career, and live a normal life?

Why am I anchored to my past by a ball and chain?

It really was unfair. The first man she'd met since Tony's death who could possibly move her, and she was poised to be the instrument of his destruction. Divorce, disgrace, who knows what this could lead to. Her thoughts turned to the dinner party. She would prefer a quiet dinner alone with Truitt, but he had never asked. Tonight would be an opportunity, though a chancy one. She would have to make her move under his wife's watchful eye.

Assuming she even cared.

Lisa's instincts told her that Truitt's marriage was somewhat better than O.J. and Nicole's and somewhat worse than Ozzie and Harriet's.

Her plan was simple but strewn with pitfalls.

He could turn me down. Or he could screw me and then really screw me by voting the other way.

She opened her closet door and took inventory. In order to rock his boat, it would first be necessary to get his attention. No more blue blazers or pinstriped suits. She needed something to measure whether Scrap still had a pulse. She could wear the fitted riding jacket over the hot pants, or if we're going over the top, the metallic jodhpurs with a matching riding crop. But no, it would be a cocktail dress, and there were plenty to choose from.

Max had always loved France, and he routinely took Lisa to the Chanel show in Paris. It became part of their routine, Milan, Paris, New York, following fashion with the seasons. He had been generous, too, Max enjoying his well-dressed mistress turning heads while being escorted to the best table at La Camanette in Villefranche-sur-Mer.

She pulled several outfits out of the closet, nearly choosing an Ungaro black velvet and georgette slip dress of pure silk. It had bare shoulders and hugged every contour on the way to her ankles. The dress reminded her of the "tube of curving black silk" worn by Marjorie Morningstar in one of her favorite novels from her early teens. The dress helped the heroine captivate a rich boy at a dance while the other girls were faded flowers in taffeta. Now she studied herself in the mirror. Too slinky, too sexy.

So was everything else, the Jean Colonna one-shoulder dress with a python bustier, a see-through metallic knit from Chanel, a Ming-vase patterned, sheer number with an asymmetrical fishtail hem, and assorted other scanty, lacy, funky designs never seen in courthouses or the homes of Supreme Court Justices.

Finally, she narrowed the search to two choices, a skin-tight, ankle length fish-scale embroidered Valentino and a similarly long, clinging leopard print dress slit far up the center, a Givenchy. She tried on both, giving each the same hip-shot pose in front of the mirror.

My God, am I hot or what!

It made her laugh. She hadn't been feeling sexy at all. She'd been terrified at what she faced: the shame and the end of her career if Truitt found out, and worse, what the madman Shank would do if she failed.

The long dresses flattered her height and her figure. Fitting like a second skin, they also set off her small, high breasts, revealed the flattest of stomachs, the perfect proportions of her hips. The leopard print had the added advantage of the front slit. When she moved, attention was drawn to her dark, secret place. She chose the leopard, not only for its promise of forbidden pleasures, but also as a private joke that only she and Max would understand.

"What's your name? Jellylorum or Mistoffelees?"

This time, she'd leave off the little leopard ears and painted-on whiskers. But all the same, she'd practice her *me-ow*.

ço

Wonderful aromas filled the townhouse, and Sam Truitt listened to the clang of pots and pans, the joyful jangle of silverware, and the banging of cupboard doors. While he sat in the study reading briefs and bench memos, Connie attacked the kitchen. She was a ferociously good cook, inventive and courageous, the orchestration of a good meal fulfilling some unmet creative needs. Whether it was nouvelle French, California cuisine, or homemade pasta, Connie could make a meal an event.

Tonight, Truitt had dressed early, putting on a seldom worn dark blue cashmere sport coat, gray wool slacks, a white shirt and blue and burgundy rep tie. Connie, who was still sautéeing, baking, and broiling, hadn't gotten dressed yet.

There would be just three guests. Truitt had told his clerks to feel free to bring dates, but each had demurred. Vic Vazquez was engaged to a law student in Michigan and had made few friends in Washington. Jerry Klein looked like he hadn't had a date since he'd begun using Clearasil in junior high, and Lisa Fremont said there was no one she cared to bring. Which made him wonder why. Of course, they were overworked, and there was little time for socializing. But still, a woman like that. A woman of beauty and brains, poise and polish.

Good Lord, if I were single and fifteen years younger ...

"Sam, are you ready?" Connie's voice called to him from downstairs, reminding him that he was married, forty-six, and susceptible to impetuous decisions where women were concerned.

"Willing and able, too," he called back. "What's for dinner?"

He heard her footsteps on the stairs. "Have you forgotten?" she asked, walking into the room. Her face went slack. "Damn, you *have* forgotten!"

"What?"

"It's Polynesian. I told you we're having Polynesian. What do you think these are for?"

For the first time, he noticed that she was holding several strands of flowers.

"I ordered the red plumeria and white ginger blossoms weeks ago," she said, her voice ragged with frustration and anger. "I spent the morning stringing them." She tossed a lei at him. It landed on his lap, and he immediately slipped it over his head in a meek act of appeasement.

"They're beautiful," he said, confused. "What's the problem?"

"The way you're dressed. You've obviously forgotten you were supposed to dress Hawaiian, which means you also forgot to tell our guests. When I sent out the invitations, I hadn't yet planned the motif. I told you last Thursday to tell the law clerks that it's Hawaiian."

The motif. A rare sirloin, a fat potato, and a cold beer would be a dandy motif for me.

"They're going to feel awkward," Connie was saying. "I'm going to feel awkward. You're supposed to be wearing an aloha shirt."

"I don't own one."

"I bought you one, blue silk with red hibiscus."

"I'll put it on," he said without much enthusiasm.

"No! If the clerks are wearing suits, everything will be out of sync."

Truitt couldn't figure out why his wearing a flowered shirt should take on such significance, but he knew better than to pour oil on the flames of Connie's luau.

"I'm sure the food will be great, and everybody will be happy no matter how they're dressed," Truitt said.

"What about me!" Tears formed and threatened to spill down her cheeks.

What about you? What's the problem now?

"I'll be the one out of place," she cried.

"How?"

"In my sarong, you idiot!"

Lisa was the last to arrive. Jerry and Vic were hanging around the kitchen, sipping their piña coladas, asking Mrs. Truitt if they could help as she checked on the tuna cake appetizers warming on a baking sheet in the oven. She'd made them earlier in the day but had nearly forgotten the lime-cilantro mayonnaise dressing because she'd been so angry at Sam.

Sopchoppy at his side, Sam Truitt answered the doorbell and, for a split second, wondered who was this tall woman with golden red hair, this leggy creature in a clinging leopard print dress that reached her ankles? She wore a choker of black onyx and gold with matching earrings and black high-heeled sling-back shoes. "Lisa!" he exclaimed, as if making a great discovery.

"Judge," she smiled, nodding.

She stepped into the small foyer, the dress opening in front, the slit seeming to reach her waist. His eyes unconsciously darted to the opening without any instructions from his brain. Embarrassed, he looked away. Sopchoppy was not as reticent, sticking his wet nose into the slit and sniffing.

"Sop! C'mere boy!" Truitt ordered. He felt himself blush, and then for no reason he could fathom, said, "He's a bird dog."

"Well, that certainly explains it." Lisa's laugh sparkled like the fizz of champagne.

Truitt shooed Sopchoppy out of the way and steered Lisa toward the kitchen. "Let me introduce you to Connie. She's dying to meet you."

∽

Sam spent much of the next three hours playing Black Monday with his male law clerks, debating the worst Supreme Court cases of all time, while Connie and Lisa exchanged compliments in peculiarly female ways.

It took all of Truitt's powers of concentration to focus on the various conversations at the table.

"*Plessy versus Ferguson*," Victor Vazquez said, "is numero uno, the worst Supreme Court decision of all time. It legitimized segregation."

"I love your dress," Connie cooed. "Givenchy?"

"*Dred Scott* was even worse," Jerry Klein said. "A golden oldie. If the Court hadn't ruled that former slaves were not citizens protected by the Constitution, we never would have had *Plessy*."

Lisa nodded. "A John Galliano design."

"I thought so!" Connie exclaimed. "His work is so bold, so sexy."

So inappropriate, Truitt thought, translating what Connie said into what she meant. After so many years with her, he had broken the Axis code. A product of a Puritan upbringing, Connie would no more wear a slit skirt to a dinner party than crotchless panties to an Episcopal wedding.

When he'd introduced the two women, Truitt saw Connie stifle the look of surprise. On this night, Lisa could turn heads in any glittering nightclub. Here, it was as if she was too radiant, too dazzling, too glamorous to fit into their small house. The two women had swapped hellos, after which Connie poured herself a stiff dark rum on the rocks with a slice of lime, then shot her husband a look which he interpreted to mean, *Who do you think you're fooling, you randy old fox?*

Lisa, an exquisite leopard, was gracious, complimenting Connie on the traditional furnishings. "It's just like being in New England," she said, admiring the dining room filled with antiques. "Is that ribbonback chair a Chippendale?"

"Why, yes," Connie said, "in the Rococo style."

"It's quite elegant," Lisa said.

"It'll throw your back out," Truitt contributed.

"What about it, Judge?" Victor asked. "What was the blackest Monday of them all?"

"Don't forget *Korematsu*," Truitt said, "upholding the incarceration of American citizens just because of their Japanese heritage."

"How about *Truitt versus Truitt*," Connie asked with a wicked smile, "where all the husbands who forget their wives' dinner motifs are sentenced to attend the orchid show in lieu of the Super Bowl?"

"Cruel and very unusual," Sam Truitt said.

They were seated at the dining room table, just finishing what Truitt insisted on calling crabcakes, though Connie told him they were made of ahi tuna.

"They're simply delicious," Lisa said, "and the sauce is wonderful." She wrinkled her brow in thought. "I taste a hint of cilantro in the dressing, but I can't identify something in the cakes themselves. Taro perhaps?"

"Close. It's breadfruit," Connie said, impressed. "You certainly know your food."

Making it sound like an indictment, Truitt thought, as if Lisa had acquired her epicurean habits in fancy restaurants, not by slaving over a hot stove.

"Of course!" Lisa said. "I had a dish like this at Manele Bay on Lanai, but I must say that yours is better."

"Lanai," Connie said, wistfully. "I've tried for years to get Sam to go to Hawaii, but he prefers visiting drafty old courthouses ..."

"The Queen's Bench in London," Truitt said, finishing her sentence.

"Sam would rather watch some cranky old solicitors in their wigs—"

"Barristers," he corrected her.

"Whatever. Sam, do you know we've never been to Hawaii?"

"We've never been a lot of places," he said. "Buenos Aires, Bogota ..."

Bodega Bay.

For a reason he couldn't quite figure out, he was thinking about Lisa Fremont and her hometown. He wondered what she'd been like as a child, as a teenager. He wondered if she had a lover back in California. Why was this breathtaking, brilliant woman seemingly alone? He glimpsed at Connie, who gave him a sardonic, sideways glance, looking like a 1940s movie star in her sarong with an orchid in her hair.

Damn, she can always read my mind. After dinner, she'll tell me I was in my Jimmy Carter mode, lust in my heart.

Lisa caught the look in Sam Truitt's eyes. She noted that he had gone through several changes during the evening. At first, greeting her at the door, he was stunned, a tongue-tied schoolboy. Later, he tried to disguise his interest, looking away whenever their eyes met. Once, she could swear he even blushed. But now, warmed by the alcohol and the glowing logs in the fireplace, he had grown more bold.

It's okay, Sam. You can look. You can touch, too.

She had no doubt that his appetite was whetted, and not by the tuna cakes. With the hook baited, all she needed was one moment alone with him to reel him in. She was prepared for him to resist. "I'm married, we work together, my position ... blah, blah, blah."

But tonight she felt irresistible. She could have any man in the world. And truth was, the only man she desired sat six feet away smiling at her both earnestly and longingly.

ↄ

They worked their way through the entree, a wok-seared ono with banana curry, Connie telling Lisa the difficulty of finding ti leaves to steam the bananas. The two women were involved in a discussion of the importance of a very hot wok, while Vic and Jerry debated the relative merits of the inscription "Equal Justice Under Law," engraved above the pillars of the Court's entrance, Jerry arguing that it was redundant because justice must be equal if it's truly just, Vic calling him anal retentive. The odd man out was Truitt, who could not take his eyes off Lisa. For the first time, it seemed, he noticed the details of her face, the startling blue-green eyes, the expressive mouth, a few loose tendrils of hair, like spun silk, flashing red in the candlelight.

"I need a drink," he said and headed to the kitchen. He kept a bottle of Finlandia vodka in the freezer, and it was a fine time for a blast of its frigid heat, taken neat. He had been fantasizing about his law clerk, and his fantasies had nothing to do with her bench memo on the Decency Act case. If anything, his mind was taking him squarely into Indecency. He was enchanted by her astonishing beauty, drawn by the promise of the front-slit dress, energized by her youthful optimism, and amazed by the depth and breadth of her knowledge.

Tossing down the vodka, a hot blade in the throat, he compared Lisa to Connie. So unfair. When a man and woman live together, they inflict wounds and leave scars. He knew all of Connie's weaknesses, as she knew his. Lisa seemed so unscarred by the world, so free of baggage.

By the time he rejoined the table, Connie and Lisa were discussing, of all things, a lawsuit, rather than furniture and food.

"Sam, we need a judicial opinion," Connie said, her words just sloppy enough to reveal she'd been hitting the rum all evening. "There was a story in the *Post* today about a junior high school football coach who was fired for refusing a mandatory drug test. He sued to get his job back."

"I abstain," Truitt said. "What do you two say?"

"Make 'em pee in a bottle," Connie loudly proclaimed, her Boston veneer slipping under the influence of demon rum. "How can we get drugs out of the schools if teachers are stoned?"

"But there's no probable cause this teacher used drugs," Lisa said. "Besides, what if the man's an excellent teacher and coach, but he likes to smoke a single joint on a Saturday night. The test is a blatant invasion of privacy."

"Heavens, you sound just like my husband," Connie said.

"I am committed to personal liberties, just as the judge is," Lisa said.

"Doubtless that's why he hired you," Connie said.

Translation: he hired you because you look like a supermodel instead of a library rat. He hired you because he wants to screw you from here to the Ninth Circuit.

"There's another similarity," Connie continued. "You're both so damned sure of yourself. So filled with self-righteousness."

For a moment, no one spoke. Then Truitt laughed and said, "You see, even a Supreme Court justice can be overruled at home."

His wisecrack broke the tension and covered up what he was feeling. An inner rage. Anger at Connie and at himself as the realization sunk in. He had always repressed the truth of his marriage. He had refused to acknowledge all those wasted years, two people grating on each other, punishing each other for the past. He had sold his life short. And so had Connie, her life as barren as her womb.

Lisa Fremont had become, in one evening, a symbol and a beacon. She symbolized lost youth, both of theirs, and simultaneously shined a white-hot beam on the dark, unspoken secret of his marriage: that it was a loveless, joyless accommodation, two stubborn people unwilling either to make their marriage better or to cut the cord that bound them together like two knife fighters in a saloon.

～

Later, when Truitt walked Lisa to her car, he yearned to say something, something other than an innocuous remark about her work. But he couldn't do it. He would keep his feelings under lock and key. He would never act on what he was feeling. Saying good night, he saw the shadow of Connie standing at the bedroom window, doubtless watching him through the partially opened drapes.

What does she expect? That I'll get to my knees and bury my face inside her dress like Sopchoppy the bird dog?

He felt awkward and ill at ease. Shaking hands would be so stiff and formal. A hug or peck on the cheek was out of the question. He simply grasped both her hands in his, just as he had done that first day in the office. But this time, it was different.

◈

Lisa cocked her head and smiled at him. Her lips trembled as their eyes locked, and now that the moment was here, she wondered if she had the courage to do it.

It would be easier if I didn't want you so much.

It was so confusing, wanting him ... but not this way, not with subterfuge and ulterior motives. When she spoke to him, would she be Lisa who desired him or Lisa who desperately needed his vote? Would she be his lover or Max's coconspirator?

Silently, their hands still joined, she slid her thumb into his palm and stroked him with a soft, slow, circular motion. It was an unmistakable gesture, and if he was too dense to understand, she said with simple directness, "Sam, I just want you to know that you can have me anytime you want."

He started to say something but nothing came out. The thumb continued its gyrations.

"I ... we ... no," he said after a moment. "I would like to. Actually, I would love to. But ..."

"Think about it," she said, giving his hand a small squeeze. "Anytime, Sam," she repeated. "Anywhere. All you have to do is ask, and I promise you, it will be better than anything you've ever known."

"I am ... ah ... flattered," he stammered. "But it's not a good idea. Actually, it's a great idea, but ... as Mark Twain said, the surest protection against temptation is cowardice. So ..."

"As Oscar Wilde said, the only way to defeat temptation is to yield to it. Sam, we both want each other, and we both know it."

She withdrew her hand from his and got into her car, sliding into the front seat, the slit on her dress riding up, exposing a fine line of shaved pubic hair, glowing gold and red in the car's courtesy lamp. Truitt stood there, dumbstruck, staring into paradise. With the promise of untold pleasures hanging in the night air, she closed the door and left him there, silent but with a noticeable bulge in his gray trousers.

◈

Shank sat in a four-door gray Chrysler, the most nondescript of cars. A cop's car. He'd been sitting there in the dark all evening, drinking coffee from a thermos, pissing in a second thermos, taking care not to mix them up.

Despite the chill, he kept his window down, smoking cigarettes, tossing the butts into the street. It was a three-pack wait. He wasn't impressed with the judge's house, a little brick cracker box, and he figured the guy made less money than a smart detective working narcotics, at least the way Shank had worked narcotics.

He thought of his parents' row house in Brooklyn, indistinguishable from a thousand others. The neighbors all tried to make the places look decent, sweeping the sidewalks, planting seeds in the flower boxes in the spring. He pictured his old man sitting on the front stoop reading the *Wall Street Journal* like he was some capitalist baron, even though Cezar Shakanian didn't own a single share of stock. He sold used furniture, for Christ's sake, out of a storefront in Bensonhurst. A dreamer, a guy who never saw things the way they were.

He could hear his father's thick accent, lecturing him, telling him how great America was, land of opportunity. Meanwhile, the lazy bastard sat in the back of the store sipping tea with his cronies, thinking a ratty old sofa with busted springs would sell itself. He could see the back of his old man's head, hair trimmed short and bristly, still looking thirty years later like he just got off the boat. He remembered the lilac scent of the cheap cologne, his father smelling like a barber shop, waves of the shit hitting you before you ever saw him coming around a pile of used coffee tables stuffed into a corner of the dark store.

But if his father was weak, his mother more than made up for it with her anger and guile. A woman with a high, broad forehead, her black hair pulled back into a severe bun, she taught Theodore Shakanian lessons with stern lectures and the back of her hand. "You want something, you got to take it," she told him. "If you don't, someone else will take it first."

Many times, she belittled her husband, using him as an example of ineptitude and failure. "There's a word from the old country your father never learned," she told her son, derision in her voice. "Ycdbsoya."

The boy was puzzled. He'd never heard such a word.

"You Can't Do Business Sitting on Your Ass," she said.

Seldom did either parent talk of the old country. It was as if they sprouted, fully grown, in America, with central European accents. Shank picked up snatches of conversations that led him to believe he was descended from gypsies, but no one ever directly told him so. He had cousins in New Jersey who seemed to be roofing contractors one month, plumbers or electricians the next, the signs on their panel trucks changing even though their tools did not. There was an uncle who went to jail for burglary and another for mail fraud.

When Shank was eleven, his mother's nephew Stefan came to the house on a Sunday afternoon. He had become a policeman across the river in Jersey City but did not dress like a policeman. He wore a double-breasted brown suit with a silk handkerchief in the pocket and drove a shiny new Thunderbird.

"Go for a ride with your cousin," his mother commanded, "and he will teach you things you cannot learn in school."

As they drove into the Connecticut suburbs, Stefan asked, "What's better, Teddy, to steal a little or steal a lot?"

The boy thought it was a trick question so he answered, "Neither one. It's better not to steal."

"Just like your father," Stefan said. He cuffed the boy across the ear, bringing tears to his eyes. Stefan pointed to an English Tudor house set back from the street. "How do you think these people got their money? By selling used furniture? By working in a factory?"

"I don't know," Teddy Shakanian boy said, his head ringing.

"Listen. A man with a gun can steal a little. A cop with a gun and a badge can steal even more. The people who live here use their brains." Stefan pointed at his forehead, where his hair was slicked back with oil, revealing a wavy widow's peak. "They're the ones who can steal the most. Use your brains, Teddy."

Shank remembered the advice, but like his cousin, he started by stealing small, using his badge and nightstick to shake down neighborhood hoods, taking a spare twenty from the till in after-hours clubs, ripping off drug dealers. It was only when he left the department and went to work for Katsushika Koshiro that Shank began to think big, steal big.

Earlier today, Shank had gotten a call from Osaka. One of Katsushika Koshiro's underlings wanted a progress report. Shank told him everything was fine; go to the *izakaya* and have some sake on me. But everything was not fine. Everything was a shit storm headed his way. Shank planned to fix it before word got back to Koshiro. The last time he counted, Shank still had all his digits intact. He had no desire to begin dialing the telephone with his elbows.

Now he watched as Lisa said good night to the judge, looking for any sign he might be slipping it to her when the old lady wasn't around. And there it was, a little hand-holding, just a bit too long. But something was wrong. Something in the judge's body language—stiff and awkward—told him they hadn't started playing hide the salami.

Lisa, honey, you're trying, I'll grant you that, but you need some help from your Uncle Shank.

"Tonight, I'm going to get you the *Atlantica* case," he said aloud. "You can thank me later."

She got into her car and took off. Two guys had already come out of the house and stood talking at the curb. The skinny one had to be Vazquez. The fat one, Klein, got into a white Toyota.

The same instant that Klein started his car, Shank turned over his ignition. Klein pulled out and headed toward Wisconsin Avenue. Shank did a U-turn and followed. By the time he reached the intersection of M Street, Shank was a comfortable two cars behind. The fat boy drove like an old lady, and Shank's mind wandered.

Yeah, Lisa, I'm doing you a big favor. I'm saving your life. So how you gonna show your appreciation?

⌀

Sam Truitt walked into the bedroom, having willed his erection into submission.

Jesus, I could not have been harder if her naked body was rubbing up against mine.

How long had it been since he'd reacted that way, how long since he had an overpowering physical need?

"How much is Uncle Sam paying law clerks these days?" Connie asked. She was sitting at her vanity, removing her makeup.

"What!" he said, seemingly surprised to see his wife in their bedroom. "I don't know, forty-three thousand, something like that."

"So how does Ms. Fremont afford designer dresses and custom-made jewelry?"

Figuring the question didn't require an answer and being disinterested in the cost of her clothing, as opposed to what was under it, Truitt kept quiet. He removed his jacket, still feeling the warmth of her thumb in the palm of his hand and the last vestiges of the tumescence in his shorts.

"Of course she saves money by going without underwear," Connie said.

"What?"

"Don't tell me you didn't notice."

"Well no."

"No panty lines and quite a nice view of the crack of her ass, didn't you think, Sam?"

"Like the Kohoutek comet, it passed without my noticing."

Truitt continued undressing, wishing it were Lisa in the bedroom with him.

"Does she have money in her family?" Connie asked, smoothing a green cream over her face.

"She has no family."

Connie laughed and turned around to look at him. "Mr. Associate Justice. *Everybody* has family. Only some people don't want to acknowledge theirs."

"All I know is her father was a commercial fisherman and her mother was a housewife, and they're both deceased."

He was down to his underwear now and wanted to think about Lisa and her offer and the sweet, slippery secrets unveiled beneath the slit dress. He did not want Connie intruding on his thoughts.

"Odd, isn't it?" Connie mused. "If she's really the daughter of a fisherman, and she's a year out of law school, she should have a ton of loans, not a wardrobe by Givenchy. If I had to guess, I'd say she was a kept woman, which means she has the morals of an alley cat."

"Come on, Connie. She's a refined, intelligent young woman."

"Spare me another recitation of her resume, Sam. I wasn't born yesterday. I'm surprised you didn't slip your toes up the front of her dress at the dinner table."

"I'm going to sleep, Con. I can't take this."

"Oh, please Sam. Humor me. What did the FBI check turn up? Any shady relationships, drug use, unexplained sources of money?"

"What background check? They do that for judicial appointees, not the clerks."

"You're kidding."

"We just get transcripts from the law schools, then check out their references."

Connie laughed, a hearty full laugh that nearly reminded him of the old days. Nantucket, blankets, a full moon.

"What's so funny?

"Isn't it ironic?" she asked, "that it's easier to get a job on the Supreme Court than to coach junior high football?"

CHAPTER 14

No Rough Stuff

SHANK WATCHED AS THE WHITE TOYOTA pulled into a downtown parking lot in a crummy neighborhood of hookers, gangbangers, and crack dealers all open for business—just like Denny's—twenty-four hours a day.

"What gives, fat boy?" Shank said aloud, slowing down but going past the lot. Even a civilian like Jerry Dumbshit Klein might notice if the car that had been behind him since he left Georgetown followed him into a parking lot.

Shank had been surprised when the kid came this way, thinking maybe the loser was going to pick up some scummy black whore in platform heels and platinum wig, a little walk on the wild side. A guy like Klein, how else would he get laid? Not that there's anything wrong with a little commercial transaction. Shank had wheedled oral sex from dozens of hookers in return for not busting them on trumped-up drug charges. What he called a *quid pro blow*.

But now, stopped halfway down the block, Shank saw Klein in the rearview mirror, standing on the sidewalk. Hoofing it, not the way to pick up a working girl.

And in this neighborhood, someone will carve up his fat ass, send him to that big law library in the sky.

Shank pulled into the last parking spot on the street, one reserved for the handicapped. He took a permit from the glove compartment—he'd earlier slim-jimmed the car door of a truly handicapped person. You never know when you'll need certain paraphernalia—a lab coat and stethoscope, a hard hat and ID badge, or even a handicap sticker—just to get into places you're not supposed to be.

Shank waited a moment, then followed Klein down the sidewalk past pawnshops, liquor stores, and sleazebag bars. Skinny black guys slouched in doorways, drinking from bottles wrapped in paper bags. A hard-eyed bald guy with a gold earring—ex-con written all over him—muttered something to Shank as he walked by. Shit, this neighborhood gave him the creeps. What was Klein doing here?

Halfway down the block, the kid stopped and turned around, shooting glances both ways, then ducked into a movie theater. Thirty seconds later, so did Shank.

ALL STUDS SHOW, according to the marquee. In the lobby, a poster advertised "Salt and Pepper Peckers," showing a black guy in tight jeans hugging a bare-chested white guy from behind. The few patrons coming in and out were racially mixed. A few black perverts, a couple of white pedophiles, he figured.

What we got here is your equal opportunity, affirmative action cornhole festival. Let my people come.

Once inside, the kid walked down the aisle, scanning the mostly empty rows of seats. Shank stood waiting just inside the door, letting his eyes adjust to the darkness. The air was stale with musty carpeting and what Shank thought smelled like jizz, some of the daisies buttering their popcorn with their pal's cream gravy.

On the screen, a white motorcycle cop pulled over a motorist, a black guy with a shaved head and a muscle T-shirt.

The kid walked slowly, passing a few couples, two guys leaning close, head on shoulder, and what Shank presumed to be hands in each other's pants. A couple of loners were hunched over, spanking their own monkeys. Klein went all the way to the front, crossed to the right, and began coming up that aisle. Shank walked through the top row and took the last seat on the right. Unless the kid found an accomplice, he'd pass Shank on his way up the aisle.

Shank turned his attention to the screen, where the black guy was looking into his rearview mirror, licking his lips as he watched the motorcycle cop, sitting astride his big cock of a chopper, making a call on the radio, long legs sheathed in leather boots, bleached blond hair sticking out from under his helmet.

The kid was a few feet away when Shank gave him a gruff "Hi," refusing to put any swish into his voice.

Klein stopped and gave Shank the once over. "You're kind of butch, aren't you?"

"Butch? I'm a mushroom-cloud-laying motherfucker."

"Are you alone?"

"Aren't we all?" Shank replied. "I mean, metaphysically speaking."

"You're funny."

"Hardy fuckin' har."

"May I sit down?"

Shank motioned the kid into the row, and he waddled into the next seat. They sat silently a moment, watching the screen. The cop dismounted his chopper, swinging his leg over like the Lone Ranger getting off Silver, you could see the wad in his tight motorcycle pants. The kid looked sideways at Shank, who was watching the black guy grin lasciviously at the cop.

"My name's Jim," Jerry Klein whispered into Shank's ear.

"I'm Mr. White," Shank said, thinking of Harvey Keitel in *Reservoir Dogs*, his all-time tough guy who said, "You shoot me in a dream, you'd better wake up and apologize."

"You really want me to call you mister?"

"I want you to call me Mr. White," Shank growled.

The kid melted, like he wanted to be bossed around. "Would you tie me up?"

"What? Here?"

"No, at my place."

"Sure. With Boy Scout knots if you want, truss you up, make you squeal like a pig." His mind off on a riff, thinking of Ned Beatty in *Deliverance*, taking it up the ass. Next to him, Jerry Klein sighed like he was getting his wiggle stick tickled.

"Let's go," Shank said.

"Later. Let's watch for a while. We can chat."

Chat? About what? Gerbil racing?

On the screen, the cop was writing the black guy a ticket. The cop's helmet was off, and he was wearing those dark reflective sunglasses, his hair down to his shoulders, pecs straining to pop the badge right off his shirt, the fairies loving guys in uniform, their movie cops looking like rejects from the Village People.

After a moment, the kid reached over and put his hand on Shank's thigh.

"You won't hurt me, will you, Mr. White?"

"Yeah, I'm gonna break your little heart."

"No, I mean when we go to my place, you won't do anything that hurts. I like to be scared, but—"

Shank wasn't sure what the fat boy wanted to hear. "No rough stuff, thrill seeker," he promised. "Okay?"

"Thanks," Jerry said, leaning over and brushing Shank's ear with his lips.

Shank grunted, thinking how much he'd like to bust the kid's face.

The cop took off his gun belt and shirt, revealing a nipple ring. Shank must have missed the plot development that led to this turning point in the story. The black guy had loosened his own pants and was unfurling his concealed weapon, a .44 Magnum cock, purple and flaring like the head of a cobra.

The kid began stroking Shank through his pants. Shank let him do it, figuring there was no way he'd go back to the kid's apartment. Step in a lighted elevator, you get made by a nosy neighbor when the cops come around the next day. Better take care of business right now in the darkened theater.

It didn't feel too bad, Jerry a/k/a Jim playing with him. Getting hard quick. A strange sensation, watching the cop and the black dude in the front seat of the car while Jerry Klein gave him a boner in the back row of the theater.

"Suck it," Shank ordered, grabbing the kid by the scruff of the neck and pushing him toward his lap.

Jerry clumsily dropped to his knees between Shank's legs and unzipped him. While the cop was eating some Negro knockwurst, Jerry Klein was sucking the Shankster, noisily lapping at him while simultaneously squeezing the base of his cock with his thumb and forefinger.

Chubby's done this before, and not half bad at it.

Shank guiding him now, keeping both hands on top of his head, fingers wound in his greasy hair, thinking about the weirdness of it all, knowing there was no way he'd ever tell anyone about this, they'd think he was a fag or something when really he was just doing his job, doing what it takes to get it done.

Still on his knees and without loosening his lip lock, the kid tried to say something, but all Shank heard was the hiss of escaping air.

"What?" Shank asked.

The kid backed off, and Shank could feel a cool draft of air on his wet cock. "Promise you won't come in my mouth?"

"Yeah, cross my heart and hope to die. Now, stick it in." Shank guided his cock back into the kid's mouth.

On the screen, the black guy was shooting his wad all over the cop's face, and within a few moments, Shank felt a surge building inside his balls. The kid was deep-throating him, really going at it like the boner queen he aspired to be.

Way to go, Jerry. Dean's list, Law Review, *summa cum cock.*

Shank slipped his hands from the kid's head down around his neck and began to press on his Adam's apple. Jerry coughed and pulled back, letting Shank's wet cock slip out.

"That's not the way it's done," Jerry sputtered. "You cut off the oxygen to the guy's who's coming to increase—"

"Shut up and keep sucking," Shank said, jamming himself into Jerry's open mouth and increasing pressure with his hands.

Jerry gagged and tried to draw away, but Shank held him there, pressing harder, his thumbs digging in deep. Jerry tried spitting him out, tried shaking free of Shank's grip, but he couldn't move and was running out of air.

"Eat me, Jerry."

Jerry Klein froze, his eyes opening wide as he looked at Shank from down under, terror stricken, tasting the fear along with Shank's cock.

"Oh, I'm sorry, Jerry," Shank said, sarcasm hanging on each word, pumping up his Samuel L. Jackson *Pulp Fiction* routine. "Did I break your concentration?"

Jerry tried to say something but only gurgled.

"Yeah, I know your name, Jerry Klein. Now, keep on suckin'."

Shank threw his hips into it now, jamming in his cock until it touched the back of the kid's throat. Tonsillectomy time.

The lava boiling up, the heat building, Shank closed his eyes and used all his strength to crush Jerry's neck. The kid struggled but couldn't move, and as his oxygen ran out, his body trembled. Pinpoint hemorrhages popped out on his eyelids and the cartilage of his larynx cracked liked a chicken's wishbone. Then, as Shank exploded into the slack mouth, the orgasm shaking him, his toes curling inside his shoes, he knew now and forever that he wasn't a fag. No fucking way, 'cause at that very moment, with his eyes squeezed shut, he didn't see the fat kid at all.

Jerry Klein wasn't even there. In his mind's eye, Shank saw someone else, the only one who could satisfy his needs. In that glorious flash of cataclysmic eruption, Shank was looking into the exquisitely terrified face of Lisa Fremont.

CHAPTER 15

Forbidden Fruit

SAM TRUITT WAS THE WORLD'S HIGHEST PAID DOORMAN.
He supposed this was true, but for all he knew, his $164,100 salary paled
in comparison to the pay of some red-uniformed, top-hatted fellow at a
fancy New York high-rise, once you took into account tips, Christmas
bonuses, and bribes from married men who sneak their mistresses up the
service elevator.

Mistresses being on Sam Truitt's mind, though he supposed that word
was as outdated as his narrow-lapelled three-piece suit. He couldn't stop
thinking about Lisa, and every time he thought about her, he became
aroused.

What was it she wanted? Just a quick tumble or something more?

*And what do I want? Why am I so excited? Why do I feel like a sixteen-
year-old with raging hormones?*

There was a knock at the conference room door, and Truitt rose
to answer it. One of the marshals was there with a casebook the Chief
Justice had requested. By tradition, the junior justice sat closest to the
door. His job—it hadn't been *her* job since Debora Kaplan was a rookie—
was to open the door if anyone had the temerity to knock. More likely,
the junior justice opened the door to hand notes to the messengers
stationed just outside. Often, too often for Truitt, Chief Justice Clifford
P. Whittington manifested an immediate and unquenchable desire for a
book, memorandum, or brief.

The Chief sat at the head of the table with the associate justices
arranged on either side in order of seniority. Whittington wore a tailored
black suit with wide chalk stripes, and his starched white shirt had cuff

links that looked like solid gold kumquats. A flashier look than most of his predecessors. With his flowing white mane, he looked like a riverboat gambler, Truitt thought. The Chief also had a personality at odds with what he wanted to project. He was more of an individual than the team player he pretended to be, despite the teamwork he demanded from the associate justices. He was supposed to be *primus inter pares*, first among equals, but he put all the emphasis on *primus*.

Surrounding the table were wooden carts, overflowing with briefs and official records of the cases in the lower courts. Truitt sat at the far end, staring at a portrait of John Marshall hanging over the fireplace, occasionally looking up at an ornate crystal chandelier that hung directly over his head. If it fell, the President would have an opportunity to appoint at least three new justices.

Truitt listened as the Chief presided, but his mind was elsewhere. To be precise, inside the slit of Lisa Fremont's leopard print dress. Tasting forbidden fruit.

"Anytime, Sam. Anywhere. All you have to do is ask."

Ask? I'd beg! But I can't. Too many eyes and ears, too many echoes, in this marble mausoleum. The media, the Family Values Foundation, the Chief Justice ... way too risky.

"Let's finish the housekeeping," the Chief growled, leafing through a leather notebook. He checked on the progress of several majority opinions that were in the works but not yet circulated, ran over some statistics on how many cases they'd considered and granted review, ran through the upcoming oral argument calendar, then cleared his throat with a *harrumph* and said, "Some of you may have been reading all the claptrap about the air crash case on the calendar. Seems the *New York Times* has already ruled against the airline, so I don't know why we should bother."

That drew some chuckles by a five to four vote, the Chief laughing at his own joke.

"I don't usually read the *Times*," the Chief continued, "but someone sent me the editorial, along with an article by one of our brethren who finds it necessary to expound in public." He shot a look down the table at Truitt.

"I'm glad you enjoyed it, Chief," Truitt said.

"Didn't say I enjoyed it, Sam. I was just glad you didn't give away our secrets."

I don't know any, except what a pompous windbag you are.

Several weeks earlier, a *Times* editor had called, soliciting an eight-hundred-word piece for the op-ed page, so Truitt wrote a chatty, pleasant account of seeing the Court from the other side of the bench. He'd done the article as much to remind people he was still alive as anything else. So far, the Chief had not assigned him any majority opinions, though he'd written several innocuous concurrences—what former Justice William O. Douglas called "little snappers." Little snappers from the long snapper, Sam Truitt. He was also working on a lone dissent.

"In the future, I'd appreciate knowing in advance if one of you plans to appear in the *mass media*," the Chief said, making mass media sound like a communicable disease.

"I've been waiting for the invitation to pose for the *Playboy* centerfold," Gwendolyn Robbins said, "but Hef never calls."

"If he read your opinions in the obscenity cases," the Chief said, "he'd probably send you champagne and caviar."

Gwendolyn Robbins cackled. She enjoyed her reputation as a crusty old bird and the Court's staunchest defender of freedom of expression. More than once, she opined that there were no dirty books, only dirty minds. Having just turned seventy, she always sat in the front row when the justices "went to the movies," viewing the exhibits in obscenity cases. While some of the male justices averted their eyes and coughed nervously, Gwen laughed uproariously, plumes of smoke from her Camels wafting into the projector beam.

"It seems the press has a burr under its saddle about this air crash case," the Chief said, scanning his notebook. "*Laubach versus Atlantica.* I've read my clerk's bench memo, and at first blush, I can't find a dang bit of negligence in the record. Besides that, it looks to me like Congress peed on its own leg when it took jurisdiction of airline cases. Not that I'm prejudging the case or attempting to influence my brethren."

More chuckles, and another five-to-four vote with Sam Truitt, Curtis Braxton, Debora Kaplan, and Gwendolyn Robbins dissenting.

"The argument is coming up right before Christmas break," Whittington continued. He consulted his pocket calendar. "In fact, it's the same day as the law clerks' party. Maybe the media will stop beating their drums by then. In the meantime, I'll resist my natural tendency to vote against any position taken by the *Times.*"

Atlantica. Truitt had skimmed the first draft of Jerry Klein's bench memo, a rather shrill call to arms. In his customarily overwrought prose, Jerry called the dismissal of the lawsuit "a cruel and heartless abomination that cannot be tolerated in a civilized society." Truitt would have to talk to him about toning down the rhetoric.

And where was Jerry? Usually, the first to arrive and the last to leave.

At the lunch break, Elly told him that Lisa had gone home. Not feeling well. Now Truitt remembered barking at everyone, Lisa included, at the 8 A.M. meeting—the meeting Jerry missed. One clerk AWOL, another claiming to be ill. He was not running what Justice Braxton would call a tight ship.

I might have upset her. She hung herself out there last night, and this morning I was churlish. Probably thought I'd rejected her. Doesn't she know I'm tormented? Stuck between a rock and a soft place.

Was she really sick or was she shattered that he did not respond to her extraordinary overtures? Jesus, what if she were in love with him in some immature, hero-worshiping way? If he bedded her down, then broke off the affair, would she become one of those *Fatal Attraction* types?

Too dangerous. I'm going to keep it in my briefs.

The Chief was running down the cases awaiting the Court's decision as to whether to grant review. The discussion proceeded in a traditional fashion that Truitt found tedious. First, the Chief summarized each case from the pool memo. The senior associate justice spoke next, with comments passing down the line to Truitt at the end, by which time there was little left to say. What did keep Truitt busy was the other job assigned the junior justice—keeping the scorecard. With dozens of cases being considered in a single conference, he had to pay attention so he didn't deliver the wrong message to the clerk's office and grant certiorari in a case in which it had been denied, or vice versa.

Doorman and note taker. Should have put that in the op-ed piece.

As the Chief was summarizing the latest death penalty case, indicating by his tone his disdain for the condemned, Truitt slipped Braxton a note: "Hey General, what was the verdict in the Leopold and Loeb trial?"

Curtis Braxton suppressed a smile and wrote his reply on an official Supreme Court memo pad. He slipped it to Truitt: "Are you stooping to trick questions, Scrap? There was no verdict."

Damn, it was hard to fool the General. He remembered there was no trial because Clarence Darrow pleaded the defendants guilty to murder and only argued the sentence, getting life, instead of death.

It was a game the two men played whenever the Chief became insufferably boring. Sort of a "famous trials" category on *Jeopardy* that they made up as they went along, frequently irritating Justice Victor Small, the dour ex-attorney general from Maine who sat next to Braxton.

The Chief was into a wearisome analysis of a case involving the constitutionality of a state tax exemption on natural gas used exclusively within Ohio when Truitt's mind began to wander again.

If Lisa is ill, I should call her. Or stop by her apartment. No! Would I stop by if Vic or Jerry had the flu?

Again, he vowed he would not put himself in a compromising position. His thoughts turned to Connie, whose cantankerous mood had carried over from last night's dinner to this morning's juice and coffee.

"You just love to surround yourself with those beautiful, brilliant creatures," she had said at the breakfast table, unwilling to let it go.

"Just for the record, Connie, I'm not screwing Lisa Fremont."

"I know that. I can tell when you're still in that infatuated, precoital mode. Afterward, you tend to lose interest."

"Connie, please."

"It's true! You did with me and with everyone else since."

A sadness swept over him, thinking of the years of friction between them.

"You're so easy to read, Sam. If you put fifty beautiful young women in a room, I can pick out the one you'll target, the one with the quick mind who's well traveled, well read, and well dressed, and soon will be well laid."

"Connie, I have no intention of—"

"You're bored with me. Hell, why shouldn't you be? So every time you meet one of these Wonder Women, you fantasize how exciting it'll be, and after you get your rocks off, *voilà*, you're bored again. So go ahead, Sam. Get it out of your system."

Ouch.

Does the truth always sting? Was he one of those pathetic men who kept searching for a mythical woman when, in fact, no woman could satisfy his infantile needs? No, damnit! He'd just never found the right woman.

Now, as the Chief droned on, Truitt kept thinking of Lisa, his mind working on a dozen fantasies, all involving their two naked bodies. Why had he been so brusque this morning?

Because I repressed what I was feeling. And what was I feeling, other than the sap rising in the tree?

He considered the question, and the answer startled him.

She might be the one! She might be the soul mate he'd never found. He might have the key that fit her lock, and every other damned corny cliché he'd never believed.

He imagined that perfect body slipping out of the front slit dress, the image interrupted by yet another knock at the conference room door.

Truitt, the good soldier, got up and opened it, the vision of an unclothed Lisa still sprawled across the king-size bed in his mind.

Chuck Olson, a young uniformed court policeman, stood there, ashen faced. He looked stricken, unable to speak.

"What is it, Chuck?" Truitt asked.

"I'm sorry, sir," Olson said. "It's so terrible. Your law clerk—"

Terror gripped him, and his voice broke. "Lisa! Has something happened to Lisa?"

"No, not her, Your Honor. It's Jerry Klein."

CHAPTER 16

Voice from the Grave

WEARING A WINTER LOUNGING OUTFIT—a long-sleeve brown tunic that came to mid-thigh with black leggings underneath—surrounded by stacks of casebooks, law review journals, and computer printouts, Lisa Fremont worked at the dining room table in her apartment. It was early evening and a cold rain pounded the window overlooking the nearby park. She was polishing her bench memo on the constitutionality of barring a Mississippi woman from appealing an order cutting off her parental rights when she was unable to afford a transcript of the trial. "A mother's rights to her children are as fundamental as the rights to liberty, for which we routinely provide counsel and waive fees for the indigent," she wrote.

The caseload was crushing, and everyone was falling behind. Sam Truitt had been a bear at the 8 A.M. case conference. Looking as if he hadn't slept, he snapped at Elly for not having the Danish ready, barked at both Vic and Lisa for imaginary shortcomings and demanded to know why Jerry hadn't shown up, as if it were their fault. Cases were pouring in—women's rights, gay rights, congressional redistricting, capital punishment, search and seizure—and everyone has to pull his weight or we'll fall behind, and damnit, where's Jerry and where's the coffee, and I've got judicial conference at 10 A.M.

Men were so transparent.

He had avoided her gaze, as if looking at her would bring back the memory of the slippery thumb in the palm of his hand. Then he retreated to the safety of his chambers behind a closed door.

He doesn't know what to do. He doesn't know whether to fire me or to fuck me. Please Sam! I want you, and I sure as hell need you.

She had dressed carefully that morning, putting on a single-button fuchsia jacket over a straight black skirt that was too short. Her lipstick was a shade redder, her heels slightly higher, her eye shadow a touch darker. The changes were subtle and might not even be noticed. But she would get his attention. She would close the deal. She had to.

But he hadn't responded, hadn't leapt at the bait. He had stayed in his chambers with the door closed, then went to his conference without another word to her. She worked alone in her office, waiting for an invitation that never came. After lunch, she told Elly she wasn't feeling well and would take her work home. She hadn't been lying. She'd been terrified, thinking about Shank, wondering when he would call on her to find out if she had seduced the judge. She had told him that she would make her move at the dinner party.

"Brief me afterward," he said. Then, with an obnoxious smirk, "But de-brief the judge first."

Now she was trying to focus on the equal protection clause of the Fourteenth Amendment and the case of the impoverished Mississippi woman when the buzzer sounded. Someone was at the front door downstairs.

Lisa felt her body stiffen.

Shank. Who else could it be?

She forced herself to remain calm and think it through.

Or could it be Sam? I told him anytime, anywhere. It's now, and he's here!

The buzzer sounded again. She lifted a handset on the wall and said hello.

"Lisa," said the young man's voice. "It's Greg. I've got to talk to you."

ℝ

Joe Drayton was dead, he told her, and she felt sorry that the crash of Flight 640 had claimed another life but glad that Greg Kingston, amateur sleuth, had run out of clues. Jesus, it could have been Greg floating facedown in a tidal pool.

"It's awful about Drayton," she said, when he was through. "I guess you'll go back to school next semester."

He was pacing in the living room, dripping rainwater from his nylon windbreaker, his Giants cap turned backward on his head. If he hadn't stood over six feet tall and been in need of a shave, Greg might be mistaken for a hyperactive twelve-year-old.

"Huh? This doesn't change anything. It makes it harder, but we're not finished."

"We?"

"You and me, Lisa. Look, you're in a perfect position to—"

"There's nothing I can do. I'm an officer of the Court. I shouldn't even be talking about this."

He stopped pacing, turned toward her, and pulled a small tape recorder out of a gym bag. "I want you to listen to something," he said, "then tell me you still don't want to help."

"What is it?" she asked, suspiciously.

"Just listen."

"Greg, you've got to drop this. You've got to get on with your life. I swear, sometimes I feel like I'm your mother, and you're a stubborn little boy."

"You're my angel, not my mommy." He gave her a sly grin, and they silently shared a memory. When Greg was eight and Lisa twelve, he asked his grandmother if Lisa was his mommy. "No, darling," Mary Kingston replied, "but she's your angel."

Yeah, your guardian angel. If I can steer you clear of this, you'll be okay.

"All right," she said with a sigh. "Whatever it is, I'll listen to it but that's it."

Greg pushed a button on the recorder, and she heard the drone of jet engines, and then a male voice cracking with tension. "Tony, I can't keep the nose down. I'm having a real nose up moment here."

What the hell!

Then a voice she recognized. Tony's voice: "More power, Larry."

It was as if a jolt of electricity surged through her veins. She could hear her own heartbeat in her ears. His voice was steady, but knowing him, knowing every inflection, she could hear the strain.

Another man's voice then, ragged around the edges, "C'mon baby. Level, level, level!"

"You're gonna have to back off some more." Tony again, speaking to her from the grave.

Her eyes welled with tears. Her body felt numb. She had gotten over losing him. Hadn't she told herself so a thousand times? But in truth, she had repressed it. All the memories flooded back now, the bliss with Tony, two souls whose hearts beat in sync, the agony of his death.

She had read the transcript of the cockpit voice recording, which was part of the case record, but she'd never heard the tape.

"Where'd you get this?" she demanded.

Greg shrugged. "The NTSB. It's a public record. *Shh.*"

"We're going too fast." Tony's voice again. "Try not to overcorrect."

"Without flaps or slats, I can't slow it down without stalling," came the voice she figured was Larry Dozier, the flight engineer who handled the throttles while Tony and Jim Ryder struggled with the yokes.

"We have to try," Tony said. "We're over two hundred knots and we'll break up on impact."

A few seconds of silence, a muffled sound, then copilot Ryder's voice: "Oh, shit! Number one stalled."

She listened to the rapid exchanges as number three stalled, too, the background noise gone. They were without power, Tony fighting the controls of the doomed aircraft as it plunged toward the swamp with no hydraulics, no way to land.

Having read these same words, having listened in her mind to the terse commands, the heroic efforts, she thought she had already experienced the crash. But this was different. It was almost as if Tony were still alive. For a moment she thought crazily that this time he might make it. This time, he might slide the big plane into the sawgrass, get everyone down the chutes, and come home to her, crooked smile in place.

She heard Dozier reciting the Lord's Prayer. That hadn't been in the transcripts. She knew that the NTSB routinely excised personal remarks, and now her mind raced. What else had Tony said?

What were his last words, his last thoughts?

"Oh, God. Oh, God. Oh, God." It was Ryder, his voice choked with emotion.

Then Tony with more frustration than fear, "Joe told me! Joe told me about the damned ..." Static crackled, and the rest was lost. Silence again, and finally, "Lisa, I love you. I love you so very—"

An explosion cut off the rest, and then the tape went silent.

A shudder ran through her like a sudden gust across still water. It was too much to bear.

In that final moment, when he must have known what was to come, Tony thought of me.

Her eyes brimmed with tears, and her throat was so constricted she could barely breathe. She wanted to get up and run. She wanted to escape the memories as she had done the past three years, but she was paralyzed by the pain. Tony was the first and last man she had loved.

Hero, lover, friend. You always did what was right. You were the force of good that drew me away from Max ... and without you, look how far I've fallen. A Judas in the temple, a prostitute among priests.

Outside, a cold November rain was stripping the multi-hued leaves from the trees. Inside, it was warm, but Lisa felt chilled.

"Damnit, Greg," she cried, her voice barely audible. "Why do this to me?"

"To force you to see the truth."

"The truth is your dad is dead, and there's nothing we can do to bring him back. The plaintiffs can win or lose their lawsuit. Max Wanaker can be a billionaire or go to jail … it doesn't matter! Tony's dead. He'll never be here for either of us."

She was sobbing and Greg took her in his arms. "I'm sorry to do this to you," he said, "but I can't let it go. Whatever was wrong with Dad's plane, whatever the mechanical flaw or maintenance foul-up or fabricated records, Joe Drayton knew about it, and he told Dad. You heard it yourself on the tape."

"Your imagination is running away with you," she said, sniffling back the tears. "You take the fragment of a sentence. 'Joe told me …' And that's supposed to be evidence? Told him what? Why do you insist on chasing shadows?"

"Why do you resist the truth?" he demanded, angrily.

"Please, let's not argue." Emotionally drained, Lisa sank into the sofa. "Do you want a drink?"

"Are you sure I'm old enough?" he asked sarcastically.

"Greg …"

"I gotta pee," he said, just as he did when he was twelve.

He walked down the corridor into the second bathroom, and Lisa stayed seated, her eyes closed, one arm resting on her forehead.

The little bathroom smelled of cinnamon potpourri. Matching guest towels hung on a rack, and a jar of colorful soaps sat on the sink.

Why *does* she resist the truth? Greg couldn't figure it out. Sure, Lisa dealt with her loss differently. She moved on, tried not to think about it. His way was healthier, Greg believed. Besides, it was the only way he knew. Greg felt a kinship with all those families whose loved ones were killed under vague circumstances. Vietnam MIA's, Pan Am's disaster over Lockerbie, TWA Flight 800. Maybe it can't be explained to outsiders, but those who've lost someone understand: you must know the truth.

Lisa almost seemed as if she didn't want to know.

She's closing her eyes to it.

Greg used the toilet, flushed, and washed his hands. He opened the door to leave and inadvertently knocked a garment from the hook on the inside of the door. He picked up a black silk robe and replaced it on the hook. He let his hand linger on the luxurious fabric. The robe was lined with gold piping. On the left side of the chest, in the same gold thread, was a monogram in fancy script: *MLW*. Puzzled, Greg examined the label. It was a size large in what was clearly a man's lounging robe. An expensive one, at that. The tag read, LANES CLOTHING, SOUTH MIAMI.

MLW. Maxwell Lloyd Wanaker!

It couldn't be! Greg resisted what he knew must be true.

Just as Lisa resists the truth.

A dozen memories flooded back to him, Lisa bandaging his scraped knee after a fall from a bike; Lisa making him baked apples with cinnamon and raisins; Lisa's joy at falling in love with his father. This girl, this woman, was everything to him. She couldn't be the enemy!

Then another memory: Lisa and Max getting into the limo outside the Fairmont.

⁒

Lisa opened her eyes at the sound of his footsteps.

Greg held the robe in front of him, away from his body, as if it were some loathsome object. Lisa looked at it and gasped.

"I shall not lie," he said sarcastically, mocking her own words. "I shall not cheat. I shall not make promises that I can't keep."

"Greg, let me explain."

He seemed to be on the verge of crying. When he spoke, his voice was filled with anger and pain. "What! What can you say that won't break my heart?"

Her mind raced. A lie would be senseless. The truth would be damning.

Oh Greg, the one person in the world I would do anything to protect ...

"I've known Max Wanaker a long time, before your father even. He helped me when no one else would. I know what it must seem like, but—"

"It seems like you're Max Wanaker's whore! If you're not, just tell me."

"You don't understand. What you're involved in is dangerous. I want to help you, but if I do, we could both be killed."

"Now, whose imagination is running wild? Look, Lisa, just answer my question. If you're not sleeping with Max Wanaker, the man Dad hated, the man responsible for his death, just tell me. Just tell me this is all some big mistake, and we'll have a good laugh."

But she didn't say a word.

Greg threw the robe at her, and tears streaming down his face, ran for the door.

℘

Who are you? Not the kind of guy you'd figure Lisa would be screwing, Shank thought, sitting in his gray Chrysler at the curb across the street from her apartment building. He'd been there for two hours, had watched the kid in the ball cap go in, carrying a gym bag, looked for signs of a little fucky-sucky, lights turning out, but it hadn't happened. Now here was the kid, not looking at traffic as he rushed across the street, a cabbie hitting his horn and cursing.

Something was wrong. The kid was steamed.

What's the matter? Didn't get to play hide the salami?

Shank followed the kid's car to a Holiday Inn on Rhode Island Avenue. Fifty bucks to the desk clerk got him a name: Greg Kingston.

Kingston!

Sure, Tony Kingston had a son. It was in his personnel file. Kingston had been a pain in the ass, a whistle-blower with the regulators. So what the hell was his kid doing with Lisa?

CHAPTER 17

Veritas

THINK LIKE A LAWYER.

Be logical, not emotional.

Analyze, don't rationalize.

Lisa tried. After Greg left, she stayed up late, going through the boxes of documents Max had provided her. Perhaps somewhere buried in the files was the evidence she prayed for, something that would discredit Greg's theories, something she could show him, something to get him back. His bitterness, the look of utter disgust on his face, had cut her to the soul.

I've lost Tony. I can't lose Greg, too.

She wanted to run to Greg and scream: "You don't understand! They're making me do this."

Struggling to think it through, she sat at the kitchen table sipping herbal tea, which supposedly had medicinal properties. But of course, she did not have a fever, a cold, or the flu. The only pain was in her heart.

She tried to push back her sense of overwhelming loss as she thought about Greg, and for a while, she managed to do it. She pored through the files, becoming engrossed in the diagrams and the maintenance reports, all the time considering Joe Drayton's hints and clues.

Lisa knew about as much as the next young lawyer about jet engines, which was to say, very little. Tony had talked to her about his love of flying, but the conversation never got into mechanics or aerodynamics. Now she was reading the experts' reports, picking up the basic principles: that air is drawn in and compressed, then combined with burning fuel, which causes it to expand enormously before passing through a turbine and exhausting at tremendous speed. The expulsion of gases from the rear of the engine creates jet propulsion, or thrust, to move the plane forward. She remembered as a child learning Newton's third law: every force must have an equal and opposite reaction.

Isn't that the truth? And for every step forward I take, someone is there to push me back a step.

Like most people, the only part of a jet engine she had ever seen was the fan, the many-bladed propeller that sucks in the air. The blades were called rotors and were attached to and driven by a disk of machined titanium alloy. The fan rotor disk.

Traces of titanium alloy were found on the severed hydraulic lines. Metallurgists agreed that the disk suffered "catastrophic failure" and separated, hurling itself and the rotors like shrapnel into the wings and fuselage.

The Atlantica maintenance records showed that the disk passed a metal fatigue test eight months before the crash. The records were signed by Joe Drayton. But Drayton, in the drawings sent to Greg, apparently had disavowed the records.

First, a file cabinet with open drawers. "*Follow the paper but the paper lies.*"

Next, a snake coiled around a pencil with a huge eraser. No caption, but an unmistakable message: the records were pencil-whipped.

A broken propeller blade. "Where's the stage one rotor disk?"

And finally, a cartoon bomb with an X drawn through it. There was no bomb.

Drayton was trying to tell Greg that the twenty-four-year-old fan disk ruptured and severed the flight controls. She thought about Tony, who had told her they'd cut back on their maintenance crews and farmed out work to unlicensed subcontractors. Hadn't Tony and his crew been talking about just that moments before the crash?

Joe Drayton had to be telling the truth. Why would he lie? He was implicating himself with his accusations.

The pieces were fitting together with blood-chilling clarity.

The fan disk blew itself apart because of metal fatigue, because Max Wanaker cut back the maintenance staff, because the whole company was rotten from top to bottom, with dirty money and false records, and …

Max killed Tony!

No! Lisa refused to believe it. If she did, her life would be turned upside down.

If there was no bomb, if Atlantica had falsified records to cover up maintenance flaws, then Max killed Tony and is using me to cover up his own guilt.

It couldn't be true.

Max had his failings, but not this.

With my lover dead, have I crawled into the bed of the man who killed him?

Suddenly, her head throbbed. Her skull felt like it would explode. She was filled with a dread and an acute physical pain.

No! It's not true.

Fate couldn't be that cruel. This wasn't some biblical tragedy. This wasn't King David sending Uriah to his death in order to take Bathsheba as his own.

She resisted everything Greg had said, everything the drawings and the tape and her own common sense told her was true. She had to block it out just to keep her sanity. She raised a steaming cup of tea to her forehead, letting the heat work its way toward the pain.

Her mind racing, she forced herself to slow down. Aware of every motion, she carefully placed the cup on the table. She focused on her breathing and thought it through. Could it be possible?

Acceptance came slowly. She was helping the people who killed Tony.

I'm turning the last spade of soil on his grave.

She fought to control the rage within her that surged like flood waters behind a dam. What would Tony have done? If she'd been killed, and he had lived, what would he have done?

Easy. Tony, who flew terrifying combat missions, who risked his livelihood to stand on principle, who fought so desperately to save his plane and passengers … Tony would have battled them regardless of the risk.

But he was made of sterner stuff, she thought. A hero. I'm just …

Just what? A poor kid, a runaway, a victim, a stripper? No! I'm a woman, a lawyer, a law clerk on the Supreme Court of the United States. I'm smart as hell, and I can fight back. I'll prove what happened. I'll do it for Tony, for Greg, for all the others.

∽

Lisa was putting the cartons of Atlantica documents back into the closet when the buzzer sounded again. Someone was at the front door of the apartment. Had Greg come back? She hoped so. They were on the same team now.

She picked up the phone, and at first, she didn't recognize the anguished voice.

"Lisa, I have to talk to you," Sam Truitt said.

⟳

"Oh no. Oh no. Oh no."

Lisa repeated the words until they became a mournful chant.

Sam Truitt, looking exhausted, stood in her living room, saying that Jerry Klein was dead. Murdered. His wallet missing. Must have been a robbery by some sadistic thug who preyed on homosexuals, probably picked Jerry at random, an easy mark.

Jerry dead?

A horrible thought sent waves of fear through her, and she trembled like a wounded bird.

A sadistic thug all right, but there was nothing random about it.

The more Sam told her about it, the more she was certain that it wasn't a robbery at all. She cried, her tears at first for Jerry, but then after a moment, sobbing uncontrollably, she realized she also cried for herself.

She believed she knew who killed Jerry, but how could she reveal it? She felt a noose around her neck, and each hour, each moment it grew tighter. She felt weak, as if her legs might buckle, as if her bones were soft and decayed, like a clump of autumn leaves after a rain.

Shank was sending her a message. Oh, he would say he did it to get her the case, but that's not the real reason. What was it he had said that first day in her apartment, the day she was hired?

"Lisa, you're not fully aware of the situation here."

But now she knew. Now she realized the extent of his power and his willingness to use it. Which is precisely what he wanted, she was sure. Shank wanted her to know that killing was easy for him, and that no one was safe from him.

She felt the anger spread through her like a fever until her cheeks were aflame. The image of Shank loomed up from her subconscious like a creature exploding from the depths of the sea. She wanted to run onto the balcony and scream at him, wherever he was, *"You bastard! I'm scared, but I'll still fight you."*

"I didn't even know Jerry was gay," Truitt said, shaking his head. "It's about the only thing he left off his resume."

He laughed ruefully, then stared off into the distance, as if remembering his slain law clerk. "Jerry would have made a fine back-office lawyer, writing briefs, plotting strategy. He had an unquenchable curiosity and a fierce intellect. He didn't deserve to die. Damn! I hate people who victimize the weak."

He was pacing around her living room now, angrily pounding his right fist into the palm of his left hand, as if he'd like to pulverize whoever did this to Jerry Klein.

Oh Jerry. I'm so sorry.

Another emotion hit her then. Guilt. Jerry died because of her. For a moment, she thought she might become sick. She fought off a wave of nausea that swept over her.

Suddenly Lisa felt chilled. A shiver of dread ran through her. Just like Joe Drayton, she wanted to expiate her sins. She wanted to tell Truitt the truth. Veritas. That had been Jerry Klein's computer password.

Oh, the doors that word might open. Or close.

She wanted to confess what she'd been hired to do. She wanted to tell Sam everything about Tony and Max and Shank. She wanted to tell him what happened—what really happened—to Flight 640. But what could she say?

I was a spy for Atlantica. I was working for the people who killed Jerry. My job was to bed you down and get your vote, but now, I've changed. Now, I'm going to help the other side.

He would fire her, maybe have her arrested, disbarred ... or committed.

Instead, she simply whispered, "I'm sorry. I'm so sorry."

She began crying, and Truitt stopped his pacing and came to her. He put his arms around her, and she dropped her head to his shoulder and began to sob uncontrollably, her body quivering. She wrapped her arms around his neck and drew herself closer until their bodies were pressed together. She looked up at him and he used a thumb to wipe a tear from her cheekbones.

It was a gentle gesture, warm and sincere. She tightened her grip around his neck. She felt safe, protected in his strong arms, and a warmth began spreading through her. She desired Sam Truitt, wanted to feel the heat of his body, wanted him close to her, wanted him inside her.

Her emotions rubbed raw by the ghastly realization about the crash, by the shock and outrage of Jerry's murder, she no longer thought about the case. Her needs now came from a place deep inside, and she was drawn to Sam Truitt with a fervent desire she scarcely knew.

And then, because he wouldn't, she did. She kissed him full on the mouth, soft and slow, sad and sweet. She tasted her own tears and knew he tasted them, too.

He kissed her back, exhaling a sigh, a hungry kiss that lasted and grew, and she tightened her grip around his neck, climbing up his body, grinding her hips into him, feeling him growing inside his suit pants. There was an urgency to their kissing, and as they pressed together, she felt her body tremble, and he held her all the more tightly.

"Lisa," he whispered.

"Sam, Sam, Sam."

She was feverish with desire, their kisses inflaming a mutual hunger. He held her face, cradled in his hands, and she lost herself in the kisses that seemed to have no end.

Suddenly, he pulled back, firmly removing her arms from around his neck. He was breathing hard, his face flushed. "We have to talk. About last night. What you said. About us."

She waited.

"I want you desperately," he said. "You must know that."

But. I hear a but *coming.*

"But we can't, Lisa. *I* can't. Not just because I'm married, but because of the Court. It would jeopardize …"

She felt as if he had grabbed her heart in his hands and then dropped it.

Oh, Sam, sweet Sam. I yearn for you and thirst for you. I want to devour you and drink you up. Please, Sam … don't leave me like this.

"I have a sacred trust," he said, "and it would violate—"

"Shut up, Sam," she said, taking him by the hand, wending her fingers through his.

"What?"

"I said, 'shut up.' You're in my apartment, not the Court. You're not a god here. You're just a man."

She was guiding him toward the bedroom now, and he was following, though not without protest.

"Lisa, we shouldn't," he said hoarsely, the conviction fading from his voice.

Can't to shouldn't. The path to the bedroom was strewn with semantic rose petals.

"Come on, Sam."

"But …"

She kept leading, and he kept following.

Men think of themselves as direct and assertive, but the truth is, if a woman didn't jump-start them, most would never get it in gear.

"I want you," she said. "I need you, and you need me, too, Sam."

She reached up to kiss him, and this time he kissed her greedily, ravenously sucking her lower lip, the starving man's last meal. Then he scooped her up, tucked an arm under her, and carried her easily into the bedroom.

Through the blur, he vaguely saw a feminine bedroom, a dressing table lamp with a rose-colored shade, window curtains in a white frill, a flowered silk comforter, and two vaguely French Impressionist prints on the walls. But he wouldn't remember the room because all he really saw was her.

He saw her close the curtains, pausing just a moment to look out into the darkness. He saw her light a fat red candle on the bedside table, and in a moment, a fruity tang filled the room. Soon, the fragrance of the candle was mixed with her scents and tastes, the soapiness of her neck, and after she pulled off the long, brown tunic, the fragrant powder between her breasts. Colors spun around him, the world red and pink and purple from the rose-colored lamp shade. Her hair was coppery, her taut nipples a burnished cinnamon, her fair skin had become a caramelized brown sugar.

His hands and lips moved across her—kissing, licking, biting. Her mouth demanded more and their tongues entangled, their hands tearing at each other's clothes. With one hand, she tore the comforter off the bed, and in a moment, they locked into each other's arms, the world swirling around them.

He was dizzy with desire, crazy with lust, and at that moment, nothing in the world mattered except the heat that rose from this woman, enveloping him. Somehow, his clothing landed in three different corners of the room, and he was tumbling over her, caught in her leggings as she stripped them off. He tore the high-cut black panties off her and buried his face between her legs, her bush glowing crimson in the candlelight, a trimmed fine hedge, an objet d'art. He drank in the smells and tastes of her, inhaling the perfume of her body.

His tongue found her swollen cleft and went after it—darting, teasing, tasting—feasting on her, his feverish mind imagining he tasted an exotic fruit.

Forbidden fruit.

"Yes! Yes!" Lisa's words were breathless, at the same time exulting and insisting.

When at last he entered her, he was on top, her long legs locked around his hips. They moved together in a synchronized rhythm, Truitt gently sliding into her, slowly building momentum, Lisa rising off the bed to meet him, their bodies in total sync.

As if on a silent signal, he followed her lead, and they pivoted, her legs still gripping him as he landed on his back, and she sat astride him, rising and lowering, pressing a hand into his chest, keeping him still while she did the work, riding him while he lay there, feeling her wet heat, opening his eyes to see her toss her head back, mouth widened into a silent scream, sweat dripping from her breasts onto him, until he felt himself ready to burst, then exploding into her, and still she rode him, curling her fingers in his shaggy hair, then screaming his name—"Sam! Sam!"—as she responded with furious thrusts and a thunderous orgasm to match his own, then settled down onto his chest, still moving, but slower now, luxuriating in a series of aftershocks that brought a feathery purr from her throat.

෮

They slept in each other's arms until Sam Truitt woke up with a start. He looked at the clock. Nearly 1 A.M. He had to get home. Lisa stirred, and he kissed her gently on the lips.

"Mmm," she purred. "That was so wonderful. So delicious."

"I have to go."

"Sam, we do need to talk. There's a lot—"

"I know. Tomorrow." He kissed her again and was gone.

෮

Later that night, he lay on his half of the bed at home, Connie on the other, separated by a Maginot Line of history. His mind still focusing on the encounter in the rose-colored dusk of Lisa's bedroom, he tried to remember the details of those surroundings but could not. There was a stuffed animal on the bed that ended up in a corner of the room under a jumble of sheets, but was it a bear or a monkey? Were the walls painted or papered? Did the bathroom have a tub or a shower? He didn't know. All he could remember was the image of her, the taste and feel of her, the electrifying surge of white heat that rose from her, pouring over him like a crashing wave of fiery lava. And all he knew was that he wanted her now more than ever. Before drifting into a deep sleep, a question floated by on the last strands of consciousness: in the morning, in the hard light of day, will I still feel the same?

∽

Among the details Sam Truitt could not remember was one he never saw and one Lisa—her heart aflame—never knew was there.

Unseen and unknown, it nonetheless existed.

Peeking out through the frame of a Chagall print, aimed directly at Lisa's queen-size bed, was a tiny cyclops, the lens of a low-light, fiber-optic video camera.

CHAPTER 18

Devil's Advocate

SAM TRUITT COULDN'T HELP BUT LOOK AT THE EMPTY CHAIR.

Jerry Klein's chair.

He was caught in a firestorm of conflicting passions. The anger and loss at Jerry's death. The elation and excitement of Lisa in his life … followed by the guilt and the fear. He wanted to shout to the heavens, cursing God for not protecting Jerry, thanking that same God for bringing Lisa to him, praying they wouldn't be caught, asking for divine guidance.

Should I end it? Should I just tell her that it's too dangerous, that we can't …

Ending it now might be best. They could spare each other untold pain. He thought about Connie, pangs of guilt shooting through him. But the thought of never kissing Lisa again, never feeling her passion, eliminated any thoughts that he would sever the relationship. No. He'd just as soon cut off a hand.

For the past hour, Truitt had sat in chambers with Lisa and Vic, doing their mourning, telling Jerry tales, making each other laugh and cry. He wished Vic weren't there. He wished he could hold Lisa close and kiss her and comfort her. He wished they were a thousand miles away on a windswept beach. He shot glances at Lisa, who looked tired, nerves strung tight.

Does she have second thoughts? Regrets? Maybe she wants to end it.

"What about Jerry's family, Judge?" Vic asked, intruding on his thoughts.

Truitt replied that he had called Jerry's parents and said he'd like to come to the funeral, bring along his other two clerks. They thanked him but said it would be a private ceremony as soon as the medical examiner released the body.

He picked up a note card embossed with a gold seal and the illustration of an eagle, arrows clenched in one claw, olive branches in the other. "The Chief extends his condolences," he said, scanning the card. "He also suggests that the brethren discuss ways to ascertain the 'personal predilections' of our clerks before they're hired."

"Why not just put up a sign, 'No cocksuckers allowed'?" Victor Vazquez said, bitterly. "The Chief's a real dickwad, boss."

Sam Truitt didn't disagree.

The police had visited him early this morning, two homicide detectives tromping down the marble corridor in their well-worn shoes. Jerry died of asphyxiation due to manual strangulation, one cop said. Semen was found in his mouth.

Oh Jesus.

"Death by blow job," the other cop said.

Sam Truitt could imagine how the Family Values Foundation would react. With a gay marriage case coming onto the docket, they'd load their muskets on this one.

"I know I don't have to remind you two of this, but I'm going to anyway," Truitt said. "Jerry was guilty of extremely bad judgment in his personal life. I don't mean his sexual orientation. I don't care about that. I'm talking about the recklessness in the way he conducted his private life. Your actions reflect on me, and my actions reflect on this Court, which is our most revered institution. So, what I'm saying is—"

"Don't get caught with your pants down," Vic broke in, "'cause those right-wing assholes are gonna be all over you, right boss?"

"Be judicious," Truitt said. "Be discreet. Be aware that we live in a fishbowl."

"*No problema, Jefe*," Vazquez said. "We won't do anything you wouldn't do."

"Yeah."

What wouldn't I do to be with Lisa? What wouldn't I risk?

"Let's get onto the cases," Truitt said, picking up a copy of the docket. "There's no way to replace Jerry during the term. Anyone I would want already has a job, so it's going to be up to you two."

"Jeez, boss, the other justices have four clerks," Vic said. "You're gonna kill what's left of my social life."

"How about you, Lisa?" Truitt asked. "Think you can handle it?"

"I haven't had a date in months," she said wryly. "Bring on the work."

"Good," Truitt said, eyes crinkling, the secret code of clandestine lovers.

Early that morning, Lisa had called the Holiday Inn, but Greg had checked out. She wanted to tell him they were on the same side, but she didn't know where to find him.

What if he comes to see Sam, or even worse, the Chief Justice, and accuses me of a conflict of interest? Would he do that?

Now Lisa waited patiently as Truitt ran through the cases, dividing them fifty-fifty. Jerry had finished nearly all the bench memos on pending cases, so she was surprised when Truitt sighed and said, "Atlantica Airlines. Lisa, you want to take a crack at it?"

"I thought Jerry already finished it."

"Only the first draft, and with the workload, I hate to ask you to plow the same ground, but Jerry really went overboard. Completely intemperate, it reads like a newspaper editorial. If there's one thing judges must do, it's divorce ourselves from emotion. We can't rule for the party we like better. "We have to apply the law, even if we don't like the results."

What is he saying? He can't intend to rule for Atlantica!

"I agree with Jerry that the trial judge erred on the preemption issue," Truitt said. "There was absolutely no intent on the part of Congress to take aviation crash cases away from the state courts. But on the second issue, I've read the briefs twice and still can't find any proof of negligence. Just how is a jury supposed to find that the airline did anything wrong based on what's in that record?"

"I recall Jerry saying there were allegations of maintenance flaws," Lisa said. "Inspections that weren't performed, possibly falsified documents."

If Shank could hear me now, arguing against the airline. She pictured him as his namesake, a human knife, a cold steel blade, sharp and deadly.

"Allegations don't get you past a summary judgment," Truitt said, sternly.

Is Sam just bending over backward to be fair, fighting against his own predisposition, or is he really leaning toward Atlantica?

"I don't see how the courts can deprive those poor, grieving people of a trial," Lisa said.

Truitt was already looking at the next file when her words seemed to catch up with him. "Are you just playing devil's advocate, Lisa, because I remember you giving Jerry a hard time when he went off the deep end for the plaintiffs? Weren't you railing against the tort system, saying the airline wasn't responsible for a bomb?"

"Or a meteor," Vic Vazquez said, raising his eyebrows.

"I may have been too hasty," Lisa said. "It just seems to me that the plaintiffs are entitled to try the case, not have it decided on the paperwork."

"It *seems* the same to me," Truitt said, "but we don't rule on feelings here. Go over the record. Read the depos, the affidavits, any proof of negligence that's cognizable on a motion for summary judgment. Find me some evidence, anything I can hang my hat on, and I'll vote to reverse. Otherwise ..."

Otherwise, you'll let evil triumph. Oh, Sam, sometimes you just can't follow the rules.

Truitt returned to his notepad. In a moment, they were into a new batch of cases, but Lisa's mind stayed with this one.

The evidence is buried in the swamp. It isn't part of the official record of the case. Even if I found it, even if it came to the Court wrapped in a pink bow, it wouldn't be cognizable—to use Sam's word—in the case.

If she could only tell Sam what she knew. But without his ever saying it, he had drawn a line. Once inside the holy temple, he was a priest, untouchable and inviolate.

And me? What am I? Harlot had a nice biblical ring.

She thought about the irony of her dilemma. She wanted to tell Sam the truth, but the truth was that she wanted to ignore the law in the pursuit of justice. She wanted to help the victims win because she knew what had happened, regardless of whether the facts supporting that knowledge were in the case record. He would be appalled. He would fire her and recuse himself and write some law review article on ethics that nobody would ever read.

Sam Truitt was not from the streets. He wouldn't understand.

To achieve justice, she would have to lie to him. Sam had to believe she was treating the case fairly, and Max and Shank had to believe she was doing their handiwork. While pretending to do her job, she would create issues where there were none and fabricate evidence if she couldn't find it. She'd do whatever it took to win.

She felt desperately alone.

I'm walking a tightrope. One little slip ...

Her heart was as cold as a stone in a mountain stream. And there it was, one of those painful moments of realization, when our self-image bumps up against reality.

After all this time, Max was still right about her, wasn't he? She tried to remember his exact words.

"We take the cards we're dealt, and if it takes sliding an extra ace up the sleeve to win, then damnit, we do it. We don't play by somebody else's rules."

Damnit, Max, I'm going to take those rules and tie them into knots. I'm going to beat you and Shank at your own game.

CHAPTER 19

The Smoking Gun

LISA WAS A BUNDLE OF CONFLICTING EMOTIONS. She tried to put her growing feelings for Sam on hold. Too much was happening too quickly.

Tony spoke to her from the grave ... seemingly asking her help.

Jerry Klein was dead ... and she blamed herself.

Sam Truitt was her lover ... but for how long?

And Greg. Where was he? She'd called his grandmother in Bodega Bay, but Mary Kingston hadn't heard from him, either.

She felt an unspeakable grief whenever she thought of Tony, a sadness tinged with guilt about Jerry, and a tingling sense of expectation when she closed her eyes and thought of Sam.

Max Wanaker had called, hoping for good news. Yes, she told him, she'd gotten the case, and Truitt was already leaning toward Atlantica.

Amazingly that's true ... but when I'm through with him, he'll despise the very name Atlantica.

She felt that events were spinning around her out of control. Last night, she dreamed she was on a raft being swept down a vicious series of rapids, coming ever closer to deadly boulders with each drop into the surging water. She paddled furiously but could not steer. The other rafters wouldn't help, wouldn't lift their paddles. Then she realized the others were all dead. There was Tony in his pilot's uniform and Jerry Klein and Joe Drayton and others she knew only by name, the passengers on Flight 640, lifeless eyes staring at her. She grew dizzy and the raft hit a rock, tossing her into the icy water. She awoke, yelling and kicking, trying to tread water, frozen to the core.

The dream weighed on her as she dressed for work two days after Sam Truitt first left her bed, leaving a warm indentation in the sheets like a bear's lair in a cave. She opened the vertical blinds, and the early sun slanted through the window and crawled up the opposite wall.

A tiny glint of light caught her eye. She padded over to the wall facing the bed and saw it then, staring out at her from the frame of the Chagall print. It reflected the sunlight directly into her eyes, a pinprick of pain, a sledgehammer of realization.

Shank wired my bedroom!

With her fingers, she frantically dug into the soft plaster, extracting a small camera lens that was attached to a flexible cable. She broke a fingernail but finally got a hand around the cable, then tore at it. A burrow in the plaster appeared like the trail of a snake as she pulled the cable hand-over-hand, ripping it out of the wall, following its path through her apartment. It took her into the living room, where it disappeared under carpeting, then back up another wall, then outside the front door into a corridor, winding into an air-conditioning closet. Inside, taped to the wall behind some ductwork, she found a small VCR. She was about to hit the eject button when she noticed that the cassette slot was already open.

And empty!

Maybe there'd never been a tape. Or maybe Shank had already removed it. The thought of him watching their lovemaking on video made her skin crawl. She angrily picked up the phone and called Shank in Miami.

"You bastard!" she shouted when he answered. "Give me the tape."

"Good morning to you, too, sweet buns."

"I've got the assignment and I've got his vote," she said. "You don't need to blackmail him."

"Good, then I'll just add the video to my personal library. *Lisa Does the Judge.* I'll file it between *Lawrence of Arabia* and *The Little Mermaid*."

"Don't even think about using it against him. He'd fire me and vote against Atlantica."

"Whatever you say, Lisa. We'll just keep it between us." He snorted a laugh. "Besides, I like the way your ass moves in slo mo."

 co

Shank sat at the table, waiting impatiently, growing more aggravated by the moment as Max Wanaker made several detours on the way back from the buffet table. Like a politician running for election, Max stopped to greet every banker, lawyer, and CPA, flashing his corporate smile, cracking jokes about golf scores, inquiring about wives and kids and the seventy-foot Hatteras with the teak interior, and see you at the club Saturday, aren't the greens fast now that it's the dry season?

What bullshit. Country clubbers in their custom suits and gold Rolexes think they're playing hardball with their mergers and acquisitions. You want some hardball, I'll take a baseball bat like De Niro in The Untouchables, *crack open some skulls, mash your brains into your gazpacho.*

They were at the Flagler Club, high atop a Biscayne Boulevard skyscraper with its view of Bayfront Park, Government Cut, and the Atlantic Ocean beyond. Shank was finishing his sliced tenderloin, bloody rare, waiting for Max to make his rounds, his plate loaded with a second helping of stone crabs and fresh shrimp. Finally, Max sat down, signaled the waitress for a refill of mango iced tea and looked at Shank, insurance salesman's smile still plastered in place.

"Wipe that shit-eating grin off your face, and I'll give you some good news," Shank said.

The smile disappeared, and Max appeared hurt. "What?"

"Drayton's dead."

Max regarded him suspiciously. "You didn't ..."

"Relax, Maxie. Either he tried to swim to China or he committed suicide. There's no dirt under your nails."

Max appeared relieved. "Fine. I have some good news, too. I spoke to Lisa last night. She's been assigned the case, and she's very optimistic. Apparently, in the wake of the other law clerk's ..."

Shank waited, curious how Max would sugarcoat it. *Untimely demise?*

"Tragic incident," Max said, "she and the judge have become quite close."

Closer than you think. Like to see you smile after watching a symphonic fuckfest in color with digital sound, beats the shit out of hotel Spectravision.

"But I must tell you," Max said, using his cocktail fork to spear a chunk of meat from inside a crab claw, "just for the record, I do not condone what you did."

"What fucking record?" Shank said loud enough for a woman in a blue suit and frilly silk bow tie to glare at him over her Caesar salad. She'd already given him a dirty look for lighting a cigarette. "Unless you're wearing a wire, there ain't no record, and I don't give a shit what you condone."

Max glanced around him, embarrassed. "It's just that I was shocked to learn what happened to that young man."

"'I'm shocked … shocked to find that gambling is going on in here,'" Shank said in a pretty fair impression of Claude Rains.

"I question whether such a radical action was truly necessary," Max said, "and in any event, I shouldn't have to learn about it ex post facto."

"It's my call, Maxie," Shank said, stabbing his fork toward the buffet table overflowing with food. "You just eat your stoners and key lime pie, the crumbs you're being allowed to enjoy for the time being, and don't tell me what to do or expect me to seek your approval before, during, or ex-post-fucking-facto."

And with that, Shank stood, tossed his fork onto his plate with a *clang*, and headed for the elevator. He'd been in a lousy mood all morning. One of Katsushika Koshiro's underlings had been calling, asking for a progress report, and Shank was ducking him. Killing Jerry Klein had not been on the program and would not be well received. Spontaneity was seldom rewarded by his Japanese boss. Too untidy. Shank would wait until there was good news to share.

Twenty minutes later, back at his desk, Shank was thinking about Joe Drayton. He was always the wild card, the guy who knew too much. Shank tried to put himself in Drayton's place, overcome by guilt, just to see how it felt. But Shank couldn't get there, not even close.

The loser.

To Shank, guilt was as foreign an emotion as love. He could feel neither one. Love required caring for another person's needs as much as for your own, a concept so alien as to be unfathomable. Guilt resulted from breaching one's own moral code. If you have no moral code, you can have no guilt.

Life is simple when you reduce it to its basic components, Shank thought, pleased with himself. Everything makes sense when you know exactly who you are.

Shank was feeling at peace with himself when his private line rang. He barked a greeting into the phone, then bolted to attention when he heard the voice of Katsushika Koshiro.

CHAPTER 20

Lovemaking and Lawgiving

SAM TRUITT SHOOK THE HONORABLE Clifford Whittington's hand. The old buzzard had virtually ignored Truitt ever since he wrote a stinging dissent from the opinion favoring the tobacco companies. The junior justice then moved on to give a hearty handshake to his buddy, Curtis Braxton. Then Gwendolyn Robbins. And then he finished the rounds: Victor Small, William Hubbs, Guido Tarasi, Debora Kaplan, and Powell McLeod.

It was a round-robin of handshaking, a traditional display of collegiality that began every judicial conference. Sam Truitt enjoyed the moment, the reminder that for all their differences, they still maintained professional respect for one another.

Shake hands, go to your corners, and come out fighting at the hell. Are you ready to rummmm-ble?

Truitt's mind began to wander halfway through a discussion of whether a three-judge panel erred in rejecting a $1.3 billion settlement of class actions against the asbestos companies. It didn't wander far, just out the corridor and down the spiral marble staircase to the small office occupied by Lisa Fremont.

Lisa, Lisa, Lisa. Omigod! I'm losing it!

He had caught himself writing her name, over and over, on his yellow legal pad. Instead of taking notes on the common issues that permitted the asbestos cases to be treated as a class action, he was doodling her name, giving the L a little curlicue. If he hadn't caught himself, in another moment, he probably would have drawn hearts all over the page.

Jeez, all I need is a face full of pimples, and I'd be the prototype lovestruck teenager.

It was the second week of December, and a light snow was falling, melting as it hit the muddy ground, dissolving like sugar in a sauce. It had been two weeks of lovemaking and lawgiving, and Sam Truitt wasn't sure which had become more important to him.

He wondered if it showed. Elly seemed to give him an odd look after Lisa came out of his chambers yesterday. They hadn't done anything except discuss cases, their hands brushing against each other for a moment when they reviewed a court of appeals decision. The hands, as if possessed by minds of their own, paused long enough for a caress, an affectionate squeeze, but that was it. When Lisa left his chambers, books and files in hand, and Elly came in, what did his face reveal? Did Elly really cock her head and study him, or was it his imagination?

Then there was Connie, blessed with an intuitiveness that bordered on sorcery. Already, she had noticed his shorter, more stylish haircut. "It's about time you're getting into the nineties," she said, "just in time for the millennium."

But did she suspect anything?

He used a pen to slash through his doodling, hiding the evidence, obstructing justice. At the conference table, there was an ongoing debate between the Chief and Gwen Robbins over some detail in the asbestos litigation.

Lisa, Lisa, Lisa.

Thoughts of her crowded out everything else. The sweet scent of her, the smoothness of her inner thigh, the tremor that shuddered through her body when she climaxed.

He cherished their moments together, longed for her when they were apart. Their routine had become familiar. As many evenings as he could—usually Monday, Wednesday, Friday, like a three-credit law school course—he would stop at her apartment on the way home. He had his own key and would sometimes get there before she did. He had always had a healthy sexual appetite, but now he was ravenous. They would make love furiously with a hunger and intensity that he had never known.

He knew that the sensations—the physical pleasure, the psychic guilt, the fear of disclosure—were heightened by the clandestine nature of their coupling. He had been there before, but never like this. And, his heart told him, he never would be again. He wanted her now and forever, but how could that be?

They would lie in bed afterward talking in the precious moments before he would leave for home. He wanted to know all about her, yet found there was a wall he could not penetrate. She simply would not talk about her childhood. Other than the facts gleaned in the initial interview—her father was a fisherman, times were hard—her life seemed to begin with undergraduate school at Berkeley.

"What makes you tick?" he asked.

"You do, Sam. You wind my clock."

"No, come on. What do you want?"

"My goals are simple," she said with a mysterious smile. "I want it all."

She told him she dreamed of a successful career, a loving husband, bright children, and a golden retriever.

Children.

He let his mind leap another chasm. He had missed so much, but it wasn't too late. Maybe he could still become a father.

Jesus, Mary, and Joseph! Sam Truitt, what are you thinking? You're a Supreme Court justice, for Christ's sake. You're supposed to be immune from the turmoil of human emotions.

Yesterday, in the hurried moments when he dressed to go home, retying the new silk tie, they discussed her assignments. He asked how she was doing on the *Atlantica* case, which seemed to be occupying much of her time. She had scoured the record but still was unable to come up with any evidence of negligence.

Still, she was hammering at him. "Sometimes it's not possible to point to one specific piece of evidence to reach the conclusion that the plaintiffs were deprived of their day in court."

"Unless there's some act or omission in the record that amounts to negligence, they won't get ten minutes in my court," Truitt said.

"Don't you thing that's a little flippant, Sam, when nearly three hundred people were killed?" she replied, irritated.

Whoa! This case had struck a nerve with her, and now it seemed to have become a test of wills between them.

"We can't resolve cases with our gut feelings and sugary clichés," he said defensively.

"Is due process a sugary cliché?"

"This isn't about due process, and you know it."

"Fine, I just wanted to see where you stood."

He shook his head in confusion, noticing he had made too big a knot in the tie. Frustrated, he started again. He was late getting home and growing weary of Lisa's obsession with one damn case when so many demanded her attention. "I think my lectures and writings make it pretty clear where I stand."

"They do! You pontificate about understanding the human side of the law. You teach your students that statutes and judicial decisions affect real people with real problems, that you can't just blindly apply the law, notwithstanding the blindfold on the bronze lady."

"Right. I've written exactly that."

"Do you also believe that it's revolting to have no better reason for a rule of law than that it was laid down in the time of Henry IV?"

"Yes, Holmes said it, and I've quoted it. I've never believed in dogmatic adherence to precedent."

"Well then, Sam, I guess it's time to find out if you practice what you preach. Here's a hypothetical. What if you know which side should win a case? You absolutely know what happened, but the evidence is not in the record to support that knowledge."

"Your question is inherently inconsistent," he said. "We only *know* what's in the record."

"That's rather dogmatic," she said, using his own words against him. "Take off the blinders. Assume that the knowledge comes to you from outside the courthouse. Maybe you even unearth the evidence yourself. What do you do then?"

"I'd recuse myself. A judge has to be shielded from outside influences."

"Even if a great injustice would occur by your recusal."

"I'd have to follow procedures," Truitt said.

"I thought so," she said and walked away, her mouth pursed in disapproval.

Why is she busting my chops?

He was dumbfounded. She'd submitted her bench memo, and it was as if Jerry Klein had come back to life, right down to the inflammatory adjectives and pejorative rhetoric. It was an outstanding brief for the plaintiffs, but hardly an impartial analysis. Sifting through the record himself, Truitt found little to support Lisa's emotional pleas for reversal. He attributed her fixation on the case to a youthful sentimentality. Hell, he'd like to give the plaintiffs a chance at a trial, but he couldn't find a way to do it.

He was still thinking about Lisa when another woman's voice invaded his consciousness.

"What's your view, Sam?" Justice Gwendolyn Robbins had asked.

"Ah, my view," he mused, buying time. "Well, I'm opposed to trial courts clearing up their dockets by creating class actions where the legal issues are not sufficiently similar."

"Good Lord!" Chief Justice Whittington bellowed. "The sky must be ready to fall. The junior justice and I actually agree."

"Then maybe I should rethink my position, Chief," Truitt shot back. He had decided early on that Whittington aptly fit Oliver Wendell Holmes Jr.'s disparaging description of a colleague: "He has not wings and is not a thunderbolt."

Curtis Braxton gave Truitt a two-fingered V, as if the younger justice had just nailed a jump shot on the basketball court. Next to them, Gwen Robbins looked as if she wanted to spank both of them and send them to their rooms without supper.

Truitt forced himself to concentrate on the discussion. Another school prayer case was coming up, and he would need all his faculties to rebut the Chief's bible-thumping oratory. He would also need a thick skin to ignore the attacks by the Family Values Foundation. What would they do, he wondered, if his affair with his law clerk hit the gossip columns or tabloids? Would Kenneth Starr be appointed to begin dispensing subpoenas like supermarket coupons?

எ

Over and over, Lisa repeated it.

I'm only doing it for Tony.

But there were so many emotional threads and psychological strings intertwined that she couldn't figure out how she really felt about Sam Truitt, the man, as opposed to Justice Samuel Adams Truitt, the swing vote on the case that now obsessed her. Sitting in her office beneath the Tasmanian poster, she analyzed her feelings and her actions. That moment outside his townhouse, when she stroked his hand and spread her skirt, announcing her availability with all the subtlety of a hooker in a latex mini—okay, that was calculated. But when he came over to her apartment that first time, when he told her about Jerry's death and she led him to her bedroom, that wasn't planned. It didn't have anything to do with Atlantica. That was just between the two of them.

Then, she hadn't been thinking about the case, or Max, or Shank, or even Tony. She wasn't thinking at all. She was responding to the chemistry, to the snap and sizzle of the synapses, giving in to a passion so strong as to overcome any conscious thought or design. It was a passion she had never known with Max, one that did not arise from need or debt or gratitude. It was the same fire she had felt for Tony, consuming and total, free and unbridled, met with a flame of equal intensity.

With Tony, there had been no doubt. She was in love. For the first time, and the last. Until now ...

No! I will not let myself fall in love with Sam. Sure, he rocks my world. But he will not shatter my armor.

I'm here to do justice in a way Sam Truitt would neither understand nor condone.

It's a job, she told herself. And then, just so there was no mistake, she told herself again.

CHAPTER 21

One Man's Poison

THE MAN CALLING THE CHAMBERS OF Supreme Court Justice Samuel Truitt asked for Ms. Lisa Fremont. "Who's calling?" Elly inquired.

"Scott Berenger."

When she came on the line, Lisa was annoyed. "Who is this?"

"Granny said you were looking for me."

"Greg! That was very macabre."

"You know the name?"

"Scott Berenger was sitting in seat fourteen-C of Flight 640."

"So you're as obsessed with the crash as I am."

"We're on the same side. Greg, I want to help. We can do this together."

The only sound was the *buzz* of the long-distance line.

He doesn't know if he can trust me.

"Greg, someday I'll explain everything to you. I've known Max Wanaker since I was seventeen. I wouldn't be here today if it weren't for him."

"But you'll work against him?" he asked

"Yes. You've got to believe me."

Another pause, and then he said, "I do. If you tell me we're working for the same goal, I believe you."

Thank God.

"Now what?" she asked. "How can I help?"

"I have a terrific plan," Greg said.

❧

Shank didn't want to be here, but he had no choice. When Katsushika Koshiro summoned, you damn well appeared. It didn't matter if he was in Osaka, London, or here, on the Hawaiian island of Molokai.

He was called "The Kat"—though Shank would never have attempted such familiarity—both because of his name and because of his ability to tread safely through a minefield of illegal activities that would have seen a lesser man imprisoned or killed. With his hazel eyes and a nose that occasionally twitched, The Kat also reminded Shank of an overfed feline in a Savile Row suit.

Now, riding in the Humvee with the tinted windows over a gravel road that ran parallel to the sea cliffs, two silent thugs in the front, a third sitting next to him in back, Shank chain-smoked and tried not to show his concern. Why had he been summoned? What had he done wrong?

The road ended at a pile of volcanic boulders, and when the Humvee pulled to a stop, the driver motioned Shank toward the cliff where Koshiro and another man stood. They all got out and Shank walked toward the precipice while his three escorts waited, leaning against the Humvee. The sun had long since set in the Kaiwi Channel to the west, and the only illumination came from a three-quarter moon. A light breeze blew from the sea, and the air was sweet with jasmine and white ginger. Walking along the highest sea cliff in the world, his mind raced.

It can't happen to me.

For a man as fearless as Shank, an unsettling feeling crept over him. Just the sight of the placid little man silhouetted against the night sky by the moonlight filled Shank with dread. He pictured himself floating face down in the angry ocean just like Joe Drayton.

What the hell does The Kat want?

Katsushika Koshiro stood at the edge of the cliff looking out over the peninsula and the Pacific Ocean. He was a short, plump man in his sixties whose expensive tailoring hid his paunch and disguised his rounded shoulders. In a custom navy suit with a thick chalk stripe, a Jermyn Street white-collared shirt with vertical blue stripes and sapphire stud cufflinks, he needed only an umbrella to look like a London banker instead of the head of Osaka's most powerful Yakuza family. Koshiro was a man both respected and feared, and Shank knew he could order a man killed on a whim.

As Shank approached, Koshiro carefully removed his suitcoat and handed it to a younger man who then knelt at the boss' feet. Suddenly Koshiro seemed to pivot in place, bringing his arms back. He was holding something, what the hell was it? These bastards loved to play with samurai swords. Shank froze in place. Then Koshiro swiveled forward, and Shank heard a *whoosh* of moving air followed by a solid *thwack*. He looked up and saw a golf ball disappearing into the night sky over the cliff.

The younger man, a crew-cut thug with a bluish tattoo of a lotus flower creeping up his neck, teed up another ball. Koshiro kept his head down, used a compact backswing, then let his hips lead the club face. His Big Bertha crushed the ball, and his follow-through was smooth. The ball soared straight, gaining altitude, defying gravity, glinting in the moonlight before fading into the dark sky.

"Nine hundred yards," Koshiro said, his English spoken with a British twist, legacy of a London-born tutor.

"Uh-huh," Shank replied, unwilling to call the man a liar.

"Two hundred yards out and seven hundred yards down," Koshiro chuckled.

The thug teed up another ball, and again Koshiro smacked a solid drive into the night.

"You got yourself a helluva driving range here, Mr. Koshiro," Shank said, letting the boss set the pace of the conversation.

"The air is different here," Koshiro said, still looking out to sea. "Lighter and cleaner. And the flowers!" He inhaled the scent of the night, his nose twitching. "How would you describe the bouquet, Mr. Shakanian?"

"I don't know. Real nice, I guess," Shank said.

Koshiro handed the heavy club to his killer caddy and motioned Shank to walk with him. "They say that smells evoke memories even more sharply than our conscious thoughts. What does a night sky laced with such a rich liqueur bring to your mind?"

Brenda, a whore whose cheap perfume made me gag in an elevator so bad I wished someone would fart.

"In Brooklyn we didn't have a lot of flowers," Shank said. He felt the eyes of the tattooed punk on his back, thought about the driver coming at him from behind, crushing his skull. Shank had been stripped of his handgun in the Humvee. He thought about the guys back at the Humvee and pictured a night-scoped rifle being raised, a shot crackling in the night, his body tumbling through space.

"I had forgotten you do not have the soul of a poet," Koshiro said, the moonlight flashing off a diamond pinky ring, the head of the family still possessing all his digits. "But then, in your work, it is not required, I suppose."

"No, I guess not."

They walked along the cliff, the thug following several paces behind, golf club in hand. In a melodious baritone, Koshiro recited:

"Now the swinging bridge
Is quieted with creepers
Like our tendrilled lives."

"Uh-huh," Shank said.

"It's haiku," Koshiro said, "the poet Basho creating both mood and emotion from the contrast of images. And what of your tendrilled life, Mr. Shakanian?"

"I don't know what you mean."

"Step closer," Koshiro said, stopping and turning toward the sea cliff. "I want you to appreciate where you are, the unique place in the world you occupy."

Shank stopped and cautiously approached the precipice. A dozen feet away, the tattooed thug also halted. Below them, in the darkness, waves crashed against the shore, but from this height, there was only the distant rumble of muffled thunder.

Koshiro continued, "The Kalaupapa Peninsula is the perfect prison. A desolate finger of hardened lava surrounded on three sides by a raging ocean and on the fourth by sheer cliffs two thousand feet high. It was here that they dumped the lepers more than one hundred years ago. A place of astounding beauty but total isolation."

Shank didn't think a reply was required, so he remained silent.

"I am beginning to feel like a leper," Koshiro said. "Unlike your Mafia, the Yakuza have been regarded as a legitimate profession, though one that carries out activities that, strictly speaking, are illegal."

Yeah, murder, strictly speaking, being a crime.

"We have had Yakuza who are mayors and government officials. We have had mutually beneficial contracts with major corporations. We proudly display our business cards, and our offices have our names engraved on brass plates. But that is changing. The new laws are forcing businesses to sever their ties with us. The National Police are cracking down on drug importation. There may come a time when I need to leave Japan and make my life somewhere else—but I hope not as a leper on a volcanic peninsula." He paused, as if thinking about a bleak future. "That makes our investments in the States all the more crucial."

"I understand," Shank said. "Everything is under control."

"Is it?" he asked, his tone implying that nothing was under control, that Shank was a lying *gaijin* who should have his tongue cut out and his

worthless body thrown to the sharks. He looked at Shank head-on for the
first time. "Is everything under *my* control?" The eyes were bottomless.
Shank felt himself stiffen, and despite the sea breeze, he began to sweat.

"Okay, I've had to do some things that weren't part of the plan," Shank
said, wondering how much Koshiro knew. "I didn't want to bother you
with details."

"You did not want to admit your failings. That is always a mistake."

"The girl will deliver. It's a done deal." Trying to show no doubts.

"I am concerned," Koshiro said.

*Concerned. Such a polite word. But Koshiro's concern could slash a man's
throat.*

"Your reports have not been entirely frank," Koshiro said. "You did
not tell me that the woman failed to get the case. So you took matters into
your own hands. Am I correct in assuming you are the one who killed the
other law clerk?"

"It had to be done," Shank said, defensively, the beginning of fear
creeping into his voice. He hated the way he felt. *He* was the one who
struck panic into men's souls, yet his hands were cold and clammy in the
presence of this little man in the London-tailored suit.

"Perhaps so, but had you informed me, it would have been assigned
to someone else. If you were to be arrested, the authorities would wish to
make a deal with you in order to get at me. You have jeopardized all our
operations in the States by acting independently like some"—he searched
for a phrase—"American cowboy."

"I would never, ever drop the dime on anybody, much less *you*, Mr.
Koshiro," Shank said, nervously, thinking he'd heard that line before. But
who and where?

*Jesus. One of the guys I'd dumped in the New Jersey swamps. "Shank, you
gotta know I'd never drop the dime on anybody, much less you."*

"I mean, Jesus. I swear," Shank babbled. "You gotta know that I'd
never—"

Koshiro silenced him with a wave of the hand. "This was intended to
be a simple matter of securing a just result in your highest Court. Now, I
want your guarantee that this is, as you say, a done deal. If it isn't, if you
have any doubt, tell me now so that we might make alternative plans."

"I have no doubts. Trust me."

"Then I have your guarantee."

"Of course."

"Say it," Koshiro instructed.

"You have my word. Atlantica will win the case. I guarantee it."

Koshiro smiled his catlike smile, and Shank relaxed. He wouldn't be killed. Not tonight anyway. They'd just made a contract. Shank promised to perform a service, and the collateral, the guarantee, was his life.

"Good," Koshiro said. "Now, please join me for a late supper."

∽

Shank had shared enough meals with Koshiro's boys to know their late-night snacks all looked like squid guts. During his stay in Osaka, he'd figured out quickly that he'd rather eat broken glass than sea urchin.

"It would be my pleasure," Shank said, with a slight bow.

Shank knew that Koshiro owned mansions in a number of countries so he expected something larger and more grand. But this was Koshiro's country cottage set back from the cliffs on the north shore of Molokai. It had a pointed roof with blue glazed tiles, a broad veranda, and an interior made entirely of wood. The walls were cedar, the ceilings combed spruce, the doors cherry, and the floors maple.

A stuffed white polar bear stood just inside the front door, raised up menacingly on its hind legs. Nearby was a wooden statue of a cobra, coiled and ready to strike, a gold sake cup in its mouth as some sort of charm. There were porcelain vases and glazed earthenware and lacquer boxes and paintings of cherry blossoms.

Shank didn't want to eat. He wanted to get back to the airport at Hoolehua and fly the hell home. There was work to do, a guarantee to be filled. But he could not insult his host, so he sat cross-legged on a tatami mat, his back stiffening, knees flaring with pain, as a servant brought sake and plates of food that appeared both mysterious and dangerous. It took only a moment for Shank to work through the logic of the late-night meal.

I hate sushi. Koshiro knows I hate sushi. Therefore, I am doing penance.

Still, it was better than sacrificing his little finger.

Koshiro gave him a short speech about each of the raw dishes that began the meal—giant clams, shrimp with flying fish roe, sea urchin, and eel. To Shank, everything looked as if it had just crawled out of a Flatbush sewer. Then they moved to the entrees, a cold mock duck made with tofu and warm pork belly cooked in soy and ginger. Shank was already fighting nausea when a servant brought him a tall ornamental glass in which the fin of a small fish peered at him from above the rim.

"*Hirezake*," Koshiro said. "Warm sake with the toasted fin of the *fugu*."

Toasted fish tail! What's next, the friggin' eyeballs?

"*Fugu?*" Shank said, suspiciously. "Never heard of it."

"What you might call the blowfish or puffer. It is the appetizer to the *fugusashi*, the blowfish itself."

Oh shit! Why not just strangle me and get it over with?

"*Chotto matte*," Shank said. "Wait a second, Mr. Koshiro. I know about blowfish. It kills people."

"It is perfectly safe, I assure you. My personal chef prepared the meal. He is an expert at removing the ovaries and liver, which contain the toxin." Koshiro smiled proudly as if having such a chef was one of his greatest accomplishments. "*Fugu* is considered a great delicacy in Japan."

Translation: I'd be offended if you refused my fugusashi, *you ugly American pig.*

Shank forced a smile and lifted the glass to his lips. Taking a sip, his tongue instantly went numb. He nearly dropped the glass. "What the hell!"

Koshiro smiled. "A tingling or numbness is quite natural. The fins contain a minute amount of the toxin, but hardly fatal. Do you not find that the drink heightens the anticipation of what is to come?"

Yeah, like putting on the blindfold as the firing squad loads its rifles.

"It is always a special event to eat *fugu*," Koshiro said. "At a dinner party, there is much nervous laughter. My guests always make jokes about dying. There is an undercurrent of anxiety, an uncertainty, that adds to the pleasure."

Only for you crazy Yakuza bastards.

"The toxin is two hundred times more powerful than curare," Koshiro continued. "If you are so unfortunate as to ingest it, you will collapse within twenty minutes. You will be wide awake, but your respiratory system will fail and you will watch yourself die as you asphyxiate." Koshiro smiled pleasantly and lifted his own glass with an identical fin sticking above the rim. "Come now. Drink to our success."

Shank weighed his options. If he didn't finish the drink, it would be a showing of both cowardice and disloyalty, a suicidal combination. The three thugs sat in an adjacent room, behind a sliding paper partition. Again, Shank didn't have a choice.

"And let us hope," Koshiro continued, "that your Supreme Court will be more equitable than its predecessor many years ago that permitted the internment of Japanese Americans."

You got it backward, Tojo. That old Court had the right idea.

"Cheers," Shank said, draining his sake, the fin tickling his nose. Immediately, a Japanese man in a white kitchen outfit and a chef's hat brought out two platters of thinly sliced *fugusashi*, served raw and arranged in a floral pattern with chopped onion and radish. Koshiro said something in Japanese; the man chattered something in return, bowed, and departed.

Shank picked up his chopsticks, then hesitated, and Koshiro said, "I would not dream of starting before my guest."

If he could get his legs uncrossed, Shank was reasonably certain he could kill Koshiro by jamming one of the chopsticks through his eye, straight into his brain. Of course, if he did, the thugs would burst through the paper wall and make sushi out of him, minus the onion and radish.

"Go ahead," Koshiro said. "I assure you that you will remember this meal for the rest of your life."

No matter how long or short that may be.

Beads of sweat appeared on Shank's upper lip. He sat rigidly upright, the tendons in his neck strung tight. He picked up a slice of the fish with the chopsticks and dipped it into a brown sauce, then raised it to his mouth. He let it rest on his tongue a moment, waiting for a seizure or a lacerating pain.

Clearly enjoying Shank's discomfort, Koshiro picked up his own chopsticks and began eating. "Wonderful, is it not?"

Shank didn't answer. He was still waiting, but nothing happened. No pain, no convulsions. His heart and lungs seemed to be in good working order. Now he relaxed and let himself taste the tender flesh. The fish was delicate and sweet and unlike anything he'd ever eaten.

Christ, it's delicious!

"Yeah, it's good. Damn good. A helluva lot better than the sea urchin."

Koshiro's laugh crackled like logs on a fire. "Now you are one of us."

"But don't you worry about it?" Shank asked. "Isn't eating this stuff like playing Russian roulette? Sooner or later …" Shank made a motion of pulling a trigger at his temple.

"Nothing of the sort," Koshiro said. "I told you it takes twenty minutes for the toxin to operate. Once my chef has prepared the fish, he is required to eat several slices. If he is still standing, he serves us thirty minutes later."

CHAPTER 22

Life with Max

LISA RANG THE BELL TO MAX'S SUITE, a nice homey touch, electric chimes on the penthouse door at the Four Seasons Hotel on Pennsylvania Avenue. One of Max's flunkies, someone from Finance, let her in, making a point of not staring down the front of her shimmering, black Calvin Klein strapless fishtail dress.

The Great Man was in the adjoining conference room of the suite with the boys from Legal and Government Compliance. Through a sliding partition door, she heard Max railing against the FAA, the bastards were trying to bankrupt him, they'd never put Delta or United through the wringer like this.

She was tense, her stomach knotted. She would have to relax or Max would sense something. Earlier that day, after getting instructions from Greg, she'd bought the necessary equipment at a shop, "I Spy," in a Virginia mall. The clerk, a paunchy middle-aged guy, was delighted to help her put on the wire, concealing the microphone in her bra, taping the battery pack and recorder to the small of her back. She'd told him she intended to trap her husband into admitting his infidelities, and the clerk asked her if maybe she'd like to have a drink sometime.

The battery was cold against her skin and sent a shiver through her. Now she trembled again, but this time with apprehension.

She tried to decipher her feelings about Max. Her life had become a war against her past. Whatever she had once felt for Max—affection, trust, gratitude—had been incinerated in the crash. But the hatred upon learning the truth gave way to something else. Max was weak and corrupt and could rationalize anything, but now she felt more pity than malice toward him. She would set him up and bring him down, but it was grim determination, a desire to achieve justice, not a thirst for vengeance that fueled her.

The flunky rejoined the meeting, leaving the sliding door slightly ajar. Lisa sidled up and looked inside. Through a haze of cigar smoke, she saw Max at the head of a long table, Peter Flaherty, his general counsel, at his side, plus half a dozen others, huddled over documents, preparing for a hearing before the FAA.

"The first charge is that we're using gray-market spare parts not approved by the Agency," Flaherty said. He was a tall, gray-haired lawyer in his early sixties whom Max had hired away from a lucrative partnership in a Miami law firm. His specialty was circumventing FAA regulations without actually violating them. "Second, they allege we violated 14 CFR 121 regarding records of airman training."

"This is bullshit!" Max thundered.

"Our position is that we did not receive reasonable notification of the approved manufacturer's list," Flaherty said, "and that in any event, the Taiwanese parts are built to the same tolerances."

"Yeah, for Manchurian Airlines," somebody at the table sniggered.

"As for the pilot training," Flaherty continued, not amused, "it's a just record-keeping snafu."

"Let's bury them in paper on that one, Pete," Max instructed.

Right. You're good at that. I've seen your paperwork.

"What about the maintenance issues?" Max asked.

"They say we haven't fully responded to the notice of probable violations from the surprise inspections," another voice said.

"The records are all here," Flaherty said. "We'll cobble together our response tomorrow."

Lisa crept closer to the door and caught sight of dozens of file cartons stacked next to the table. She wondered if any of the records related to the *Laubach* case.

What's in the files that you've kept from me?

"What else is on the agenda?" Max asked.

"The 640 crash is set for oral argument next week," Flaherty said.

"Are you ready, Pete?"

"Hell, Max, I could write the majority opinion." Flaherty dropped his voice into a basso profundo impression of a Supreme Court justice: "Try as we might, we cannot find any negligence of record on the part of Atlantica Airlines. For purposes of this litigation, this tragic crash was a misadventure in every sense of the word, a mishap with no villain, at least not one before the Court."

A smattering of chuckles ran around the table.

Bastards! If I can get Sam's vote, you won't be laughing.

"Music to my ears, Pete," someone said.

"Good," Max said. "That just about does it."

Lisa backed away from the door and into the living room. The ubiquitous fruit basket sat on the bar. The window overlooked a park, Max always insisting on seeing trees in the morning. The suite had textured white walls hung with flowery prints. There was a writing desk in a vaguely Early American style, richly upholstered chairs with hassocks, home-away-from-home for the harried executive. When she was younger, hotel suites impressed her. Champagne, caviar, and limos. Life with Max.

How could I have fallen for that?

The dining table was set for two with a bouquet of yellow roses as a centerpiece. The meeting would be over soon, and dinner would be brought up from the Seasons restaurant, where the executive chef personally handled Max's order. She thought of all the hotel suites she had shared with Max, all the late suppers served by white-gloved waiters. She was sure this would be their last meal together.

When Max had told her he'd be in town for the FAA hearings, she had asked if Shank was going to be there, telling him, truthfully, that the man terrified her.

"He's out of town on business," Max said.

Thank God.

Before hanging up, he had asked, "Is your judge on the team?"

"He's the captain. He thinks the preemption order is dead wrong, but he's going to vote to affirm on the ground of no negligence."

"Great! That's even better than winning on a technicality. Much better headlines."

It was what he wanted to hear and had the additional benefit of also being the truth. At the moment, Sam Truitt was leaning toward Atlantica, no thanks to her. Lisa had just a few days to change his mind. The case was scheduled for oral argument next Monday, and the justices would vote in a conference on Tuesday morning, just before their Christmas break. With time running out, tonight was crucial.

"I knew we could depend on you," Max said, "and I'm dying to see you."

Lisa heard chairs being backed away from the table, and the perfunctory good-nights-and-see-you-tomorrows. The men left through a separate door to the corridor, and Max came into the living room of the suite, his tie undone, looking haggard and exhausted.

"Hello, darling," he said, putting a little bounce into his voice.

"Hello, Max."

He placed a hand on each of her bare shoulders and kissed her gently. "My God, you're so beautiful. When we're apart, I actually forget how incredibly stunning you are."

"I've never seen you look so pale," she said, remembering their weekends on his yacht … mimosas in the morning, nude sunbathing at midday, lovemaking at night. "No more weekends at Ocean Reef?"

"All I'm doing these days is trying to save the company and my own hide. No boats, no tennis, damn little sleep, and the last time I was inside a woman, it was the Statue of Liberty."

He was playing for sympathy, she knew. "Things not going well at home?"

"Home," he said, shrugging, "is a deep freeze, and not just because Jill keeps the thermostat at sixty."

"She learned it from you, Max. You never liked to sweat."

"Jill's having an affair with her personal trainer," he said with resignation.

"Oh, Max. I'm sorry. But it is poetic justice, isn't it?"

"Yeah, Jill says it's my karma. My aura's all yellow and murky. My wife's getting planked by a guy who looks like Tarzan and wears an earring. My daughter's in drug rehab, Max Jr. is flunking out of Choate, and I owe two hundred million dollars to some Asian assassins. Is it any damn wonder I need you? I love you, Lisa."

"Max, don't. Please."

"I miss you, Rumpleteazer."

"We can't bring those days back, Max." But saying it with a wistful note in her voice, like maybe we can, or at least maybe we should try. Preying on his weakness, luring him at his lowest moment.

I'm sorry, Max. I really am, but I'm doing what I know is right.

He walked to the bar where a silver ice bucket cradled a chilled bottle of Dom Pérignon. Max examined the label as he always did, then popped the cork. "Remember our first date, our first champagne, our first lovemaking?"

"Max, please don't go off on one of your nostalgia riffs."

He poured the champagne and gave a simple toast. "To us and a new beginning."

She frowned at him.

"I'm sorry," he said after polishing off the first glass and pouring himself another while she barely sipped at hers. "It's just that I've been such a fool. You're the most important person to me, and I lost you. I blew it. I want another chance."

The doorbell rang, and two uniformed waiters brought in the food. One served while the other, a high-rise sommelier, Lisa supposed, uncorked a bottle of Haut Brion 1959. Max had ordered a case, which was kept at precisely fifty-eight degrees in the wine cellar. Lisa was still seventeen when Max first told her he was an oenophile, prompting her to ask if he'd ever been caught.

After the sommelier did the obligatory routine with the bottle, displaying the label, deftly working the corkscrew with manicured fingers, then handling the cork as if it were a family heirloom, Max sniffed at the wine and took a sip, proclaiming it gravelly and earthy, a bit cedary but not too spicy. Lisa tasted it and thought it was swell.

They were into the appetizers of raw tuna medallions in a spicy pocket of smoked salmon on a julienne of snow peas and Japanese seaweed when Lisa spoke. "Max, I want you to tell me the truth."

"What?"

"About the crash. About what really happened."

He drained his wine and refilled his glass. Lisa hadn't yet finished her first one. "You know the truth," he said. "Some crazy Cubans bombed the plane."

"Why didn't they bomb a Cubana airliner?"

"Hey, don't ask me. Terrorists aren't known for their logic."

It's not working. He hasn't told the truth so far. Why should he now?

She waited until they were into their entrees, crisp-fried sea bass on a bed of Oriental vegetables for her, rack of lamb encrusted with Indian spices for him.

"Don't you trust me, Max?" she asked.

"Of course I do."

"Then why can't you tell me the truth?"

"Lisa, darling. I have."

They had finished two bottles of the Haut Brion with Max doing most of the heavy lifting when the doorbell rang again. This time, a third waiter rolled in a cart with two steaming hot Grand Marnier soufflés. Close behind was the sommelier with after-dinner drinks. Max indulged in the brandy, while Lisa had coffee.

They finished the soufflés with Max making purring sounds—
"Mmmm, succulent, just like you"—then carried their drinks to the sofa.
Max settled back and propped his feet on the cocktail table. He looked
woozy.

It's now or never. C'mon Max.

"I've read the appellate record time and again," she said. "Even though
the plaintiffs couldn't prove it, I know you're covering up something with
maintenance."

"Oh, Lisa, darling. Let's not talk business."

"Okay, Max. Just tell me this one thing, and we can talk about
whatever you want. We can *do* whatever you want." She leaned over and
kissed him gently on the lips.

"Succulent," he repeated, as if she were the soufflé. He looked at her
through sleepy eyes. "You sure we have your guy's vote?"

"Signed, sealed, and delivered."

"Maybe, we cut some corners," he said with a sigh, "but we're not the
only ones. If you go into the kitchens of some fancy restaurants, you'll
never want to eat their food. Same thing if you go into the maintenance
shops at the airlines. We're no better or worse than the others."

"What corners, Max?"

"It doesn't matter now, does it?"

"I just need to know."

I need facts, specifics, proof! I need it on tape.

He groaned and closed his eyes. She ran her fingers through his hair.
In another minute, he'd be asleep. She had hoped that Max, like Joe
Drayton, needed to expiate his sins by confessing. But guilt did not burn
a hole inside Max Wanaker. He was trying to save his ass, not his soul.

"Let's get naked and go to bed," he said, slurring his words, his eyes
still closed. "God, you were good in bed."

"All right," she said, stroking his cheek with the back of her hand.
"But talk to me, Max. You can trust me."

Just like I trusted you.

"We stopped doing some routine maintenance," he said absently,
making it sound insignificant.

Her heart stood still. *Keep him talking!*

"What do you mean, 'stopped'?"

"Oh, we'd do a little and check off the rest. Like the FPI test on that
fan disk."

"What fan disk, Max?"

He was quiet a moment, drifting off.

"Max. What fan disk are you talking about?"

"The number two engine on 640, for Christ's sake! Ship 102 in the proud Atlantica fleet. Hell, the engine was twenty-four years old, flew twenty thousand cycles. We worked those old planes like they were plow horses. Didn't do the FPI test in '93 or in '95. No damn wonder it blew itself apart. Not that it's our fault, you understand."

"Whose fault was it?"

"The manufacturer got some nitrogen in the molten titanium when they cast the disk. At least that's what Drayton said. Imagine that. They've got a pot of boiling titanium, and a teeny-weeny bubble of nitrogen gets in. Nothing happens for twenty-four years, then ... ka-boom!"

"You could have found it?" Lisa said, making it a question.

"Sure. The test would have shown it, loud and clear. But we didn't do it, and who could know the damn think would rupture? That disk had been spinning like a son of a bitch for fifty thousand hours without a problem." He paused a moment and seemed to think about it. "Just like me. I spun for fifty thousand hours with no problems. It suffers metal fatigue and I burn out ... I'm just a burned-out old fan disk."

"How did he figure it out?" she asked.

"Who he?"

"Drayton. How did he figure out what happened?"

Max pitched sideways, and she wrapped her arms around him. He came to rest with his head between her breasts, his nose peeking down the front of the low-cut black dress, inches from the hidden microphone. "He found the disk," Max whispered, "or at least part of it."

"Where is it?"

"It sleeps with the fishes. Just like Drayton. Just like me if we lose the case."

"What are you talking about?"

"Drayton paid some Cracker to crisscross the crash site in an airboat as soon as it was light. The guy was an old rummy, smelled like rotten snapper, according to Joe, and his boat was filled with alligator hides, if you can picture that. They found a piece of the disk with a fatigue crack. Shank had Drayton deep-six it. Drayton was worried as hell that another piece would pop up out of the muck, but it never did."

"Did anyone ever look for it?"

Max didn't answer. His eyelids fluttered, and he began to snore. She eased him onto the sofa, placing his head on a pillow, taking off his shoes, and covering him with a blanket she found in the closet.

He looked as if he would be out for hours.

She had done it! She had the proof! Earlier, imagining this moment, she thought she would feel triumphant. But looking down at the pathetic, broken man who had once been the center of her universe, she felt no pleasure in her victory.

She had what she needed and should just leave. She would play the tape for Sam Truitt. Even if the confession couldn't get into the Supreme Court record, it would be branded into Sam's brain. She knew the man. He'd have to vote for the plaintiffs. His devotion to what was right would overcome a blind adherence to procedural rules.

Then, when the case was reversed, the tape would be admissible at trial as an admission by a party. The only flaw in the plan was that she had just sacrificed herself. She would have to go public and authenticate the tape to introduce it into evidence. She had just stepped out of her role as law clerk and into the role as plaintiffs' advocate. She surely would lose her job on the Court.

But Tony would have done the same for me.

Even with the tape, even with the proof of maintenance fraud, she knew there was still a missing link. The plaintiffs still must prove that the failure to inspect the disk was the proximate cause of the accident.

If we only had the disk ...

She turned toward the partition and the adjoining conference room. It was a long shot, but maybe there was something there, some scrap of paper in the cartons, some file that had never been sanitized, something to get them one step closer.

ϾϿ

Lisa spent twenty nervous minutes going through the boxes as Max snored on the couch. She found pilots' training files, check flight records, incident reports of wake vortex turbulence, fire prevention programs, but nothing tied to the crash of Flight 640. Finally, she concluded that it was hopeless.

She was replacing a sheaf of papers when she heard a noise. The soft *click* sounded like a door opening. Then a second *click*. Metal latching onto metal. She flicked off the light in the conference room. There was no sound except Max's peaceful snoring, audible through the sliding door. She stood there in the dark, a folder in her hand, afraid to move. It could be a waiter, quietly returning to remove the remains of their meal. It could have been a sound from the corridor.

God, let it be anything, but …

She heard footsteps coming from the tile foyer. Then nothing, the carpeting muffling all sound. Who was it?

An invisible hand pushed back the sliding door and reached inside. The lights came on, and she was staring into the angry face of Theodore Shakanian. He wore his trademark charcoal gray suit, his large-boned wrists sticking out of sleeves that had been cut too short. He needed a shave, his acne scars sprouting a three-day beard. He was a nightmare come to life, and Lisa struggled to remain calm.

"I knew it," Shank said. "First thing when I get off the plane, I check out your apartment, but you're not there. I know shit-for-brains Max is in town, so where would Little Lisa be on a Monday night? You could be in the library. You could be fucking the judge. Hell, you could be at the stadium, watching the 'Skins, but no, my instincts tell me you'd be here." His mouth twisted into a sneer. "So what's going on Lisa? You the new file clerk?"

She dropped the papers onto the conference room table. Inside, every organ seemed to clench into a tight ball. Her windpipe felt constricted. She struggled to appear calm. "Max asked me to look for something."

"I'll bet he did. He couldn't find his own dick with two hands."

The length of the table was between them. The door to the corridor was within reach. She fought the urge to run for it, to go screaming down the corridor. He would catch her, drag her back inside. She decided to tough it out though her heart threatened to beat itself to death. She forced her voice not to betray the panic rising inside her.

"It's not what you think," she said, putting some bravado into her voice. She walked straight toward him, intending to go through the open door to the living room, her legs trembling like a newborn foal.

"Maybe not. Maybe it's even worse than I think."

She forced herself to look at him as she approached. His gray eyes were as cold as a glacial lake. When she got close, he suddenly grabbed her by the shoulders and viciously ripped her dress down, tearing the fabric, exposing her bra and pinning her arms to her side. Startled and panicked, she fell backward, bracing herself against the conference table.

"You maniac! Leave me alone."

He reached for her lacy black bra, cupping his hands around her breasts, and she pulled away, simultaneously screaming and slamming down a high-heeled shoe hard on his instep.

"Fucking bitch!" Shank shouted, prancing on one foot.

Max awoke, startled, and yelled something incomprehensible.

"Max!" Lisa shouted. "Stop him. He's trying to rape me."

"You lying bitch!" Shank was rubbing the top of his foot, his face flushed.

Max stumbled to his feet, disoriented. "What the hell ..."

"Max, he's crazy!" Lisa shouted, covering her bra with both hands. "He wants to hurt me!"

Lisa felt her body twitching like a fish on a line. She tried to push away the terror. She had to get out of there. If Shank found the wire, he'd kill her right there and enjoy doing it.

Max, I need your help. Rescue me!

"Jesus Christ, Shank, what are you doing?" Max demanded, fully awake and furious.

"She was going through the FAA files," he said. "It looks like the little princess is working for someone else now."

"No!" Lisa protested. "He's lying!"

"You're wrong, Shank," Max said. "Lisa told me we've got Truitt's vote."

"Yeah? What did you tell her?"

Max waited a moment before answering, his eyes flicking toward Lisa. "Nothing. What would I ..."

"I don't believe either one of you," Shank said. He walked over to Lisa, who tried to back away. "I gotta pat you down."

"Go pat yourself down," she said, now clutching the torn fabric of her dress, trying to cover herself. "Maybe you'll enjoy it."

Please God, make him back off. Don't let him find it.

Shank laughed and turned toward Max. "She's a woman with spunk," he said with a toothless smile. "I gotta hand her that." Without warning, he wheeled around and threw a short right hook, his fist digging into Lisa's stomach. She pitched forward gagging.

"I hate women with spunk," Shank said, smirking.

"Jesus Christ!" Max yelled. "Are you out of your mind?" He came up to Shank, stopping just out of punching range. "I've known Lisa since she was a kid. She'd never—"

"You don't know shit!"

Lisa was on all fours, trying to catch her breath when Shank hoisted her up by a hand in each of her armpits. She was wobbling, fighting off the nausea, her dress open to her waist. With one hand, Shank yanked the bra straight down, exposing her perfect breasts and a small microphone attached to a wire that ran around her back.

"What do we have here?" Shank asked, his tone implying that he knew exactly what they had.

She was huddled on the floor, clutching her midsection, breathing hard, fighting the pain. Her worst fears realized! There was nothing she could say, nothing she could do.

Max moved closer. His face fell, his features melting like wax under a flame. "What is that? That's not ..."

"It sure is, and I can't wait to listen to it," Shank said. "Max, I'm getting real tired cleaning up your shit."

Shank leaned over Lisa and angrily pulled out the mike, ripping the wire and miniature recorder from her back. She screamed as the adhesive tape tore off patches of skin.

"Lisa!" Max gasped, tears in his eyes. "How could you do this to me? After all I've done for you."

She accepted it then, what she knew was coming. She would never walk out of here. She had tried everything she could to fight them, but it wasn't enough.

Oh God, Tony! I'm sorry. I've let you down.

"Lisa!" Max demanded. "Why?"

"You killed Tony!" she spat at him. "Do I need more reasons? You want two hundred eighty-seven more?"

"Tony? Who the hell ..." For a moment, he seemed genuinely puzzled. "Tony Kingston?"

"Yes."

"What's he have to do with it?"

"Figure it out, Max!" she said, sitting on her haunches, covering her breasts with her hands.

Max seemed incredulous. "You and Kingston! After we broke up, he's the one? You were fucking my chief pilot, a guy who hated my guts."

"No, Max. I was in love with him. You're the one I fucked."

"Tony Kingston," Max said in wonderment, still not quite able to comprehend it. "That son of a bitch brought the FAA down on us with all his goddamn memos."

Coiling the wire around one fist, Shank said, "The only bright spot in this whole shit storm was that Kingston went down with plane."

"You bastard!" Lisa fumed. "You monster!"

Shank was rubbing his knuckles across his forehead, as if coaxing out a thought. "So that's what Kingston's kid was doing in your place. The two of you were conspiring against us."

"No! Leave him out of this," Lisa yelled back.

"What kid?" Max asked. "What the hell is going on?"

"Why don't you ask her about banging the judge?" Shank prompted. "Jesus, figure it out. She's leading Truitt around by the dick to vote against us."

"Lisa, you told me the judge was voting our way."

"It's true," she said. "I wish to God it weren't, but it's true."

"Bullshit!" Shank said, whipping the trailing end of the wire at her. It struck her bare shoulder and left a stinging red mark.

"Don't touch her!" Max ordered. He got between them and knelt down next to Lisa. "Tell me the truth. How's the judge going to vote?"

She burst into tears but turned away when Max tried to comfort her. She wrapped her hands around her midsection and bent forward at the waist, staring at the floor, refusing to look at either of them.

"Lisa, tell me," Max said softly.

"I told you the truth," she said, sobbing. "He's leaning toward Atlantica on the negligence issue, just like I said. I can't find any evidence in the record that Atlantica was liable. God knows, I've looked for it."

"I believe her," Max said.

Shank shook his head. "I don't." He stuffed the coiled wire, the mike, and the recorder into a suit pocket. "Even if she's telling you the truth, we got a real problem here. I'd throw her out the window right now, except that would tie her to you, so we gotta figure out where to do it and where to dump the body."

Max appeared shocked. "What are you talking about? You can't kill Lisa."

"Sure I can."

"Don't be stupid," Max said, in a tone Lisa had never heard him use with Shank. "You think you can kill two of Truitt's law clerks and no one will notice. Anything happens to Lisa, who do you think would be a suspect?"

Max was coming to life, and Lisa was stunned. *He's trying to save my life.*

"You'll have the whole federal government coming down on us," Max continued. "Christ, Shank, I've got a paper trail with Lisa that goes back ten years. Our people get hit with grand jury subpoenas, we're through."

"We can't let her go," Shank said. "She'll tell her boss everything."

"Tell him what? That she's been working for Atlantica Airlines, but now she's changed her mind and working for the opposition? He'll fire her, get her disbarred."

It was the old Max, or at least some semblance of the strong man she once knew.

"Shank, you're not going to hurt her," Max commanded. "I won't stand for that. I'll call Osaka and—"

"Shut up," Shank said, but there was no anger in his voice. He was subdued, deep in thought.

✑

Max was right, Shank knew. He couldn't kill Lisa. Not without contacting Katsushika Koshiro. And that would be an admission of another failure. There are times you need brute power and other times you need finesse. Given the choice, Shank would rather knock down a door than fiddle with a lock, but this situation clearly called for delicate maneuvering. His ass was on the line, and he was determined to slow everything down, to fight his natural impulse to kill the bitch right there.

"Maybe you're right for once," Shank said. "If two law clerks working on the same case take a dirt nap ..." He let his voice trail off. "But we can't let her stay on the Court either. We got to get her away from the judge."

Lisa glared back at him. "I'm not quitting," she said, defiantly.

Shank was quiet a moment. Then the shadow of a thought crossed his face and his small teeth gleamed with a barracuda's smile.

"You won't have to," he said.

CHAPTER 23

The Plaintiff's Spy ... The Defendants' Whore

"YOU MUST THINK I'M A TOTAL LOSER," Max said, slumped onto the sofa.

"No. You're the man who saved my life," Lisa said. "Twice."

"Ten years ago and then tonight." She sat talking to him, holding his hand, her adrenaline rush replaced by exhaustion.

Shank had left minutes before, saying, "You lovebirds deserve each other."

Max seemed lost in his memories, his act of heroism fueling his sentimentality. "I've always loved you, Lisa. From that first night in San Francisco when we sat in the car watching the fog roll in over the bridge. Isn't that pitiful?"

"No," she said, tears rolling down her cheeks. "It's beautiful, and I know you mean it."

"I wish I could turn back the clock," he said, "not just with you, but with everything. I look around and see my whole world crumbling, and I wonder how I got here. What was the first misstep?"

She was caught in a tornado of emotions. Max had rescued her even after she had betrayed him. She was thankful but still intent on fighting him. Even now, with the pain of her raw flesh where Shank tore the tape loose, with the dull ache in her abdomen, with the fear still gripping her, she wasn't giving up.

"I wish there was something I could do for you, Max. You've been so many things to me. Lover, teacher, friend, even the father I always wanted but never had. I'm afraid for you, Max. I don't want anything to happen to you."

He smiled ruefully and kissed her gently on the forehead. "You're still going to try and get the case reversed, aren't you?"

"I can't give up."

"You're not afraid of Shank?"

"He terrifies me!"

"He'll stop you. He isn't stupid. Brutal, sadistic, and cruel … but not stupid."

"Will you be all right, Max?"

"You can't have it both ways, Lisa. If you succeed, Shank will kill both of us. Even if you fail, you'll destroy your career. You've worked so hard to get where you are. You said yourself Atlantica's going to win. Why not just go along? Let it happen."

"I can't."

He squeezed her hand gently and said, "I know." Then he walked into the suite's bedroom, where he closed the door behind him.

⌘

Lisa opened her mouth, but no words came out. Her apartment had been tossed. For a long moment, she stood just inside the door, unable to move. Then she cautiously surveyed the damage. The prints on the walls were either hanging akimbo or knocked to the floor. In the kitchen, a dozen plates lay smashed on the tile floor. In the bedroom, drawers were turned upside down, contents scattered.

Her best lingerie, a satin merry widow, a black lace body stocking, a white ruffled chemise, all torn to shreds. The cup of a dismembered floral lace bra hung over a sculptured table lamp, looking vaguely like a yarmulke on a rabbi's head. A pair of pink string-bikini panties floated in the toilet bowl.

She pictured Shank tearing through her apartment, cursing, destroying. Trembling with rage, feeling violated a second time on this horrible night, finally she screamed at her unseen intruder. "You can't scare me off! You'll have to kill me!"

Then she heard the voice and froze. Her stomach pitched, as if on a boat in rough seas.

Someone's here!

It seemed to be coming from behind the closed door to the second bedroom, which she had converted into her study. With her heart pounding, she approached the door and listened to a man's voice, the words so soft she could not make out what he was saying. Then murmurs, a moan and another voice, a woman whispering. It seemed, crazily, that she was listening to herself.

Omigod!

She threw the door open. Inside the darkened study, her television was on, the VCR running. On the screen, she and Sam were naked on her bed. Her legs were wrapped around his hips and his thrusting was growing more frenzied. Their first night together. Frantically, she turned on the lights. The walls were plastered with eight-by-ten photos of their coupling, grainy prints obviously taken from the video. The anger leaping from her like sparks of electricity, she tore down the photos.

Shank had been here. But what was the message?

She replayed the events of the evening.

"I'm not quitting," she had told him.

"You won't have to," he had replied.

Then she knew. She just hoped she wasn't too late.

℘

Constance Truitt answered on the fifth ring.

"Mrs. Truitt, this is Lisa Fremont. I'm sorry to bother you so late, but I need to speak to the judge."

"At eleven P.M. on a Monday night?" Connie said, sounding amused. "Is some poor innocent wretch about to be executed, or do you simply miss the sound of your master's voice?"

She's been drinking. Jesus, I don't have time for this.

"It's an emergency," Lisa said.

"Really? I wonder how they ever drafted the Magna Carta without his help. Do you need help with some pithy footnote the world anxiously awaits, or have you simply misplaced your panties?"

Stunned into silence, Lisa caught her breath. Mustering a professional tone, fighting the urge to strangle the woman with one of her Hawaiian leis, Lisa said, "Please Mrs. Truitt. May I speak to him?"

"You *may*, but you *cannot*. I was an English major, you know. At Bryn Mawr, the girls all spoke like Professor Henry Higgins. As for Mr. Associate Justice Truitt, my favorite sperm donor, he is at the stadium, drinking beer and bonding with other overgrown boys. Tell me, Ms. Fremont. Do you resent them their testosterone? Perhaps not. Perhaps you have ample doses of it yourself."

"He's at the Redskins' game?"

"Yes, sitting in Senator Gordon's box, just as I told the gentleman. High above the fray, far from the madding crowd, just as Sam likes it."

"What gentleman?" Lisa asked, her voice straining for control.

"An Asian man, I believe. Mr. Hankisana from the clerk's office. He said he needed to know the judge's whereabouts."

"Are you sure about the name?"

"Yes, dear. He spelled it for me. *H-A-N-K-I-S-A-N-A.*"

Oh no. God no!

Lisa worked out the anagram in her head.

There is no Hankisana. There is only Shakanian.

Of course. Frustrated that he couldn't kill her, unwilling to let her maintain contact with Sam Truitt, Shank had hatched a scheme to drive them apart. Unless she moved quickly, she would lose Sam.

She glanced at her watch. Eleven-ten. The game would last until midnight, perhaps a little longer. She thanked Connie Truitt and hung up while the woman was questioning whether men really were from Mars, or a more distant planet ... perhaps Uranus.

℮℈

She made one more call, this one from her cellular in the cab on the ride to the new stadium in Landover. She gave Greg an update, downplaying her own jeopardy, telling him about Drayton and a drunken old Cracker who piloted an airboat filled with alligator hides the morning after the crash.

"You've got to find him and hope he can remember where he found the disk," she said. "It's a long shot, but maybe the missing piece is nearby."

"I'll do it," Greg said, excited. "I'll come up with it."

As if it would be easy finding something missed by a hundred investigators who looked for a year. The glorious naiveté of youth.

"Be careful, Greg," she said, feeling old and maternal, then clicking off.

The cabbie shot a look at her in the rearview mirror. "I hate to tell you, Miss, but the game's damn near over."

She told him to step on it, and if he ran a few red lights, the tip would be double the fare. He complied, and she handed him a fistful of bills as she leapt out. The gate attendants saw her coming at double time, her businesslike pumps *clacking* on the pavement. She had hurriedly changed into a wool checked jacket and matching pleated trousers and carried a briefcase.

Look purposeful, dignified, confident.

Lisa flashed her Supreme Court employee badge to the attendant, a young African-American woman in a blue uniform, and said, "Official business. It's quite urgent."

"Here? Now?" the woman asked.

"I'm the death clerk," Lisa said. "Please direct me to Senator Gordon's box. I must find Justice Truitt. It's a matter of life and death."

She actually carried a petition for a stay of execution of a Texas prisoner. Unfortunately for the prisoner, the stay had been denied a week earlier, and as of midnight last Tuesday, his case became—to use the legal term—moot.

Above them, the crowd roared its approval at some play, and the PA announcer blared the news of a Redskins' first down inside the Giants' ten-yard line.

The woman spoke into a walkie-talkie, and in a moment, a uniformed man in his sixties rolled up in a golf cart and told Lisa to hop aboard. "Have you upstairs in a jiffy, the elevator's right over there," he said, looking at her briefcase as if it might contain enriched plutonium. "When I worked at RFK, I used to bring President Nixon communiqués from Saigon. He wouldn't read them if the game was close."

They zipped along to the nearest elevator, then left the golf cart behind. The door opened, and the uniformed elevator attendant waved them inside, his portable radio informing them of a Redskins' touchdown.

၏

Shank was wearing a waiter's white tunic whose sleeves were too short. He had used a phony detective shield to get into the stadium, then gave the waiter three hundred-dollar bills for the jacket, another two for his ID badge.

Shank walked into a service area, picked up a tray of chocolate chip cookies, pretzels, and a fruit platter, and headed for Senator Gordon's box on the mezzanine level.

So far, it had been easy. He started with a simple phone call to Truitt's house, where the judge's wife had answered, sounding on the far side of several gin and tonics. He'd seen her picture in the paper. Tall and skinny like a lot of those upper-crust WASPs. Not bad if you like that Blythe

Danner bet-you-can't-make-me-come look: Shank preferred his women with more meat on their bones.

He did the bit about an urgent message for the judge, where can I find him, and she gave it up, sounding as if she didn't care whether he made it home before dawn.

On the way to the stadium, he had listened to the tape, Slapsie Maxie spilling his guts, the sorry son of a bitch. When this was over, win or lose, Max was a dead man. But tonight belonged to Lisa, and that thought excited and aroused him nearly as much as the video he had watched so many times.

෫ා

The elevator door opened, and Lisa raced out. Jim Saxton—the uniformed guy had introduced himself—didn't seem to appreciate the urgency. If body counts from 'Nam could wait, so could some death row inmate's sniveling plea. He toddled behind Lisa, pointing toward the closed sky box door. Lisa burst inside without knocking. Looking around, she saw a dozen people on two levels. Some were watching the game through the open window, while others studied an instant replay on a wall-mounted TV set, and a few ignored the game altogether and sat at the bar, drinking. She did not see Sam Truitt.

"Has Justice Truitt been here?" she asked, loudly.

No one answered.

From the row of seats at the glass window overlooking the field, someone shouted, "How 'bout them Redskins!"

"Is this Senator Gordon's box?" Lisa yelled. Demanding now.

An overweight man with a flushed face gestured toward a buffet table. "No, ma'am," he said with a southern accent. "This is the American Tobacco Institute. But c'mon, stay and have a drink."

She turned and bolted. Outside the door, Jim Saxton was looking confused and sounding apologetic. "Oh, Jeez. Senator Gordon's got the matching box on the far side of the field. You could look out the window and see right into the senator's. I'm sorry, but I got mixed up, what with the new stadium and all. Back at RFK, I never—"

"What's the fastest way to get there?" she asked, hurriedly.

"We've got to walk all the way around," he said gesturing.

Lisa took off running down the concourse that connected the sky boxes to the concession area. Fans were already beginning to pour down the ramps. There were still three minutes left, and according to the scoreboard, the Redskins were leading the Giants, 35-17.

ᔐ

"Could we get some more popcorn?" asked a young man in a white shirt, burgundy tie, and suspenders. "And this time, could you hold the salt?"

Shank would like to tell this Yuppie scum where he could hold the salt. The kid had congressional aide written all over him.

"I'll see what I can do," Shank said, forcing an undertaker's smile. He put down the tray of cookies and fruits and scanned the sky box. He recognized Senator Bert Gordon, a Florida Democrat, Truitt's sponsor for the Supreme Court nomination. Gordon sat at the bar, ignoring the game, jawing with several suits equally disinterested in what was going on below them.

Sam Truitt sat in the first row, watching the field through a pair of binoculars. As far as Shank could tell, the judge was the only one who gave a rat's ass about the game.

"Would you like a cookie, sir?" Shank asked the aide, who was still waiting for his popcorn.

"Yeah, sure," the kid said.

Shank handed him the plate with the cookies, then reached inside his tunic and drew out a manila envelope. "I wonder if you could do a favor for me," he said. "While I get the popcorn, could you give this to Justice Truitt? A messenger just brought it by."

"Sure thing," the kid said, half a chocolate chip cookie sticking out of his mouth.

The kid walked down the three stairs to the first row of the box and handed Truitt the envelope. He turned around and pointed toward the waiter who had given it to him, but the man was gone.

Back on the club-level concourse, Shank smiled to himself. Lisa Fremont was out of the picture. He'd pulled it off without spilling blood. They would win the case. Koshiro would be pleased, and with Christmas coming, Shank figured there'd be a helluva bonus in his stocking.

ᔐ

Lisa burst through the door to the sky box, her eyes frantically scanning the small enclosure. At first, she didn't see him. But there he was, sitting alone in the front row, a pair of binoculars slung around his neck like some bird-watcher. He was opening a manila envelope and pulling something out. By the time she yelled "Sam!", he was staring intently at a photograph.

She called his name again, but he was thumbing through the contents of the envelope, a series of eight-by-ten black-and-white photos, duplicates of what had been taped to the walls of her study. Then Sam turned around and looked up at her. Bewildered, confused, hurt.

She started down the steps toward his seat, but he was already on his feet, moving her way, the envelope clutched in one hand. With the other hand, he dragged her by the arm toward the door. They brushed past the startled congressional aide, who was still waiting for his popcorn.

"Oh Sam, I'm so sorry. It's all my fault. Please let me explain," she pleaded, but he wasn't listening. Once on the concourse, now filled with fans streaming toward the exits, he pulled her toward a door marked, EMPLOYEES ONLY, and pushed her inside. They were in an overheated kitchen filled with service personnel and steaming ovens.

ↇ

A fire was building in Sam Truitt's stomach and moving up through his chest. He wanted to hit someone. His first thought, the instantaneous reaction when he saw the photos, was that someone from one of the tabloids had gotten into Lisa's apartment. Those pricks would stop at nothing. Or those wackos from the Family Values Foundation may have been behind it. Or maybe it was someone else altogether, someone engaged in a seamy blackmail scheme. But that didn't make any sense. He didn't have any money, not real money anyway.

One thing was sure. His career was in jeopardy if the photos got to the Chief Justice.

Can I be impeached for conduct unbecoming a monk?

Then he heard Lisa calling his name and turned around to see her stricken face. That look, a spring wound too tight, and her voice, dripping guilt like melted butter, gave it away.

"Oh Sam, I'm so sorry. It's all my fault. Please let me explain."

The realization hit him hard. The photos were taken in her apartment! She must have known.

The door swung open, and a worker hustled in, pushing a chrome cart loaded with dirty dishes. Truitt led Lisa deeper into the kitchen and opened a steel door. They stepped inside, entering a walk-in cooler loaded with trays of hamburger patties.

"All right, explain," he said, his voice hoarse and reedy.

Lisa looked as if she didn't know where to begin. "Oh, Sam ..."

"What do you know about this?"

"I was part of something I'm ashamed of, Sam, but we can fight it. We can fight it together."

"Fight what? What the hell are you talking about?"

"In legal terms," Lisa said, "it was a conspiracy ..."

"What was it in human terms? What was it between you and me?"

She shivered, both from the frigid temperature of the cooler and her anxiety. "I have so much to tell you. I should have done it before, but I was afraid you wouldn't understand."

"Understand what? Talk to me, damnit!"

"They wanted your vote on the *Atlantica* case. I was coerced into setting you up, but Sam, I've changed so much. I love you. I really—"

"You slept with me to blackmail me?" His mouth had gone dry, and his body seemed filled with lead.

"No. I didn't know about the video, I swear!"

"You didn't think you needed it," he said bitterly. The truth hammered at him, cleaved him open. "You knew your talents. One taste of the apple, and you'd have my vote, right?"

"Sam, please ..."

Suddenly, he was very tired. The fire in his chest had burned itself out, and now he had a dull ache in his skull. He was gaining the most precious commodity, knowledge of self, in the only way possible, through a cracked mirror of agonizing pain. He looked at himself and saw a fool.

Those bedroom whispers. All lies!

"I trusted you," he said. "I thought I loved you, but was it really you? I must have been crazy. I mistook your youth for innocence, your beauty for purity. I never saw the real Lisa Fremont."

"I'm not innocent or pure, but I'm on the right side of the case."

"The right side? You shouldn't be on either side! What the hell's so righteous about being an agent for a bunch of PI lawyers?"

"No. In the beginning, I was helping Atlantica. They're the ones who made the video."

Now a maelstrom of confusion swirled over him. "Atlantica? For the last three weeks, all you've done is tell me what a travesty it would be if we let the summary judgment stand."

"I learned the truth. I'm helping the plaintiffs."

This cannot be happening, he thought. His law clerk, his lover, was a wayward spy, flipping sides like some double-crossing CIA agent. "What happened? Did you get a higher bid for your services?"

"Sam! Listen to me. Atlantica hid evidence and corrupted discovery."

"I don't care! I don't care about the case. I care about us."

"Sam, please listen. Atlantica's entire defense is a fraud."

"Our relationship is a fraud! You're a fraud!"

"I know you're angry, and I know you're hurt. But please try and understand."

I'm not hurt. I'm mortally wounded.

He felt like a bull impaled by the toreador's sword, his blood draining from a dozen wounds. He had been deceived and the pain filled him, smoldering inside like a relentless fire. "What is there to understand?" he asked, his eyes welling with tears. "What is there that makes sense?"

"I love you, Sam," she said.

℃

He walked her back into the empty sky box, holding her arm above the elbow, as if she might try to flee. Through the window, they looked down at the green field, shimmering under the lights. Sam Truitt poured himself a vodka over ice and listened as Lisa told him the story of her life.

Her voice anguished, she began with her father, who lurched into her bedroom in the middle of the night. She could hear his breathing, could see the orange tip of his cigarette, could smell the smoke and the booze on his breath. For years, the sight of a glowing cigarette in the dark would paralyze her with fear. She told Truitt about the Tiki Club and Crockett, her abusive boyfriend, and how Max Wanaker came along and rescued her. "Max isn't a good man, Sam, not by your standards. He's weak and corrupt, but he only wanted the best for me, and he let me grow, even if it meant leaving him behind."

She told him about Tony Kingston and his son, Greg, how the crash crushed her. "Tony was the first man I ever really loved. I was devastated when he died."

Tony. She'd never mentioned Tony or his son. Or Max. Or the Tiki Club. My God, I don't know her at all.

"I don't get it," he said. "If you loved Tony, why didn't you blame Max after the crash?"

"I thought Max was a victim, too. I thought he'd lose everything because of some crazy terrorists."

She told him about Joe Drayton and the phony maintenance records and the fan disk with the fatigue crack, and Truitt shook his head and closed his eyes, as if he shouldn't be listening. Finally she told him about Shank and his threats, and how she believed he was capable of anything.

"I'm sure he killed Jerry," Lisa said, barely above a whisper.

"What!" Truitt was shaken. "He killed Jerry Klein?"

Truitt finished his drink and poured himself another. He was spinning in a new direction. Jerry Klein had been little more than a boy, someone Truitt felt responsibility for. What kind of an animal would brutally kill a helpless kid?

Truitt's head was reeling, his world crumbling. He lived by a code of conduct and expected others to do the same. Only respect for the law allowed society to function. Perhaps he was naïve. For too long, he'd been strolling along marble corridors behind ivy-covered walls. He could barely comprehend that someone would commit murder to win a court case.

Truitt fought a losing battle to control his emotions and the rising tide of anger from within. He wanted to strike out at Lisa, to hurt her as much as she'd hurt him. "See if I have this right. Before you were old enough to vote, you were a stripper who conned guys into buying carbonated champagne. Then you left your G-string behind and became this airline executive's mistress for ten years, except for the year you were with the pilot who went down on Flight 640, after which you hustled back to Sugar Daddy. The only reason you applied for the clerking job was to corrupt the judicial process in the crash case, because of some perceived obligation to the guy who wrote all the checks. Sort of like repaying your school loans. To that end, you came to my house for a luau, but I'm the stuffed pig. You flashed me a slice of the merchandise, whetting my appetite with a tawdry but delicious view of your—"

"Sam, that's hateful!"

"Never interrupt the judge, counselor," he said, regarding her with an icy stare. "You seduced me to get my vote for the airline, but having had a falling-out with Sugar Daddy, you began illegally working with the plaintiffs, and now your most fervent desire is to subvert the judicial process in their favor."

"No!" She looked hurt. "That's unfair! You make it sound so dirty. The plaintiffs deserve to win."

"Not on the facts in the record, only by your extrajudicial contacts."

"What difference does it make?"

He laughed, but it was a hollow sound. "How could someone who graduated with high honors from Stanford Law ask that question?"

"*Fiatjustitia et ruant coeli.* 'Let justice be done though the heavens should fall.' Isn't that what you always preached at Harvard?"

"That's a distortion. I taught that technical niceties shouldn't be allowed to frustrate justice, but I don't recall advocating illegal means to accomplish a desired end, and I'm quite sure I never suggested that a Supreme Court law clerk surreptitiously become a double agent while simultaneously screwing her judge."

She recoiled as if struck in the face. "You're contemptible."

"And you're lying. Or in the words of every two-bit cross-examiner, 'Were you lying then, or are you lying now?' Which side are you really on? Which side will you be on tomorrow? It's hard to keep up with you."

"I'm telling you the truth. I had Max Wanaker on tape admitting to the maintenance fraud."

He shook the envelope of photos in her face. "Your story would be more believable if you'd told me before I had these glorious Kodak moments."

"I was going to tell you. Before the oral argument, I was going to tell you everything."

"Really?" he said, disbelief in his voice. "And who's talking now? The plaintiffs' spy or the defendant's whore?"

ℰℐ

Tears came to her eyes, and she turned away from him. She had lost everything. Her heart ached, and an overwhelming emptiness enveloped her. Outside the windows, half the stadium lights were shut down, and the field turned a grayish green. "I just revealed everything about myself— the most painful moments of my life—and that's how you respond?"

"Spare me your wounded feelings, Lisa. And spare me your protestations of love." He opened the envelope and pulled out a photo. "This isn't love. It isn't tender. It isn't what I thought it was at the time. Jesus, I thought you were this brilliant, caring, giving woman, not some undercover agent for the Japanese mob, or whoever the hell you say is behind Atlantica."

"Forget about me. Try not to take this personally. Atlantica's going to steal the case. They killed all those people and they're going to get away with it unless you stop them."

"That's not my job. I'm a judge. I evaluate the record the way it is, not the way a hysterical woman with blatant conflicts of interest tells me it ought to be."

"I'm just trying to achieve justice."

"Regardless of the means? We're still a government of laws, not of men or women."

"That's so damn self-righteous, so pious."

"It's the law!" he thundered.

"You sound like Inspector Javert. Would you imprison a man for stealing bread for his starving family?"

"I'm not ashamed of playing by the rules. Christ, it's all I have. I can only decide cases on the facts properly in front of me. And in this case, I can't rule at all. I'll recuse myself tomorrow."

"No! You can't!"

Recuse me from your life, Sam, if you must, but not that.

"I have no choice. You've given me extrajudicial information, and I've been tainted."

"Coward!"

"You' re right. I'm afraid. I fear vigilante justice because the next time some judge decides to break the rules, it won't be me. It'll be the Chief Justice or some clown on a trial court with his own unique ideas of right and wrong."

It was hopeless, she thought. He couldn't see past the rules. He couldn't see that justice needed a helping hand. He couldn't even see that she loved him.

"I'm just doing it by the book," Truitt said softly, running out of steam. "That's why we have a book. I'll send a memo to the Chief in the morning informing him of my recusal." He started for the door to the concourse.

"No, Sam! Please."

Her voice beseeched him, and the sound of his name on her lips stopped him. "What?"

"What about us?" she asked.

"Us? There is no us. Us was a lie."

"Then what about me?"

"You're fired," he said.

☙

A tumbler filled with cranberry vodka gave Lisa a headache but didn't help her sleep. A second dose, spiking her chamomile tea, made her sweat but still didn't put her under. She had cleaned up the mess in her apartment as best she could while virtually in a trance, numb from the events of the endless night. Now, she lay in bed, turning from one side to the other, shooting glances at the LCD display on the dock, watching the numbers magically dissolve from 3:15 to 3:16.

Her life was a shambles.

She'd lost Sam. And her job. And the case.

Not since she was seventeen, hitching a ride south from Bodega Bay, had she felt so alone, so lost. These last few weeks, when she wasn't preoccupied with the case, her thoughts had been of Sam ... the two of them together.

Sam. Why didn't I tell you how I really felt? Tonight was too late. Tonight, you weren't listening.

Outside, a cold rain pelted the bedroom window. An ambulance siren wailed, and the wind slapped the branches of an oak tree against the building. Her dream was dead, but still she replayed the fantasy—Sam wasn't happy with Connie. Fifteen minutes into the dinner party, Lisa knew it was a barren relationship, a marriage bonded not by love but by inertia. Sam would divorce Connie and marry her. Talk about a power couple, the international lawyer and the Supreme Court justice.

The big Chicago law firm had a Washington office. She could be based here but still travel to Europe, doing deals. International banking, telecommunications, government contracts. Her potential was infinite; her future was bright as the stars.

Just how far can you get from the Tiki Club?

Not very far, because it can never be. No Sam, no job with a deep-carpet firm. How stupid she'd been. As if he would ever leave his wife and jeopardize his career for her.

"The Justice and the Stripper," a musical comedy in three acts.

The numbers on the clock smoothly flowed into 3:21. She was plunged into a dark cloud of despair. She would be lucky not to be disbarred. She faced a life filled with loneliness and pain.

I should have told him. I could have prepared him. Should have ... could have. I'm such a loser.

Angry that she was wallowing in self-pity, she thought of the victims' families, anxiously awaiting their day in Court. Oral argument was next Monday.

It was over. Shank had won.

She had discreetly done her head count last week, polling the other law clerks in the cafeteria, the gym, and finally at the rehearsal for the annual Christmas party. Just after she had run through her skit, a wacky send-up of Gwendolyn Robbins, she'd totaled up the votes. The conservative faction—Chief Justice Whittington, Victor Small, William Hubbs, and the elegant Guido Tarasi—would likely affirm Atlantica's victory. The two women justices—Gwendolyn Robbins and Debora Kaplan—would vote to reverse. The moderates—Curtis Braxton and Powell McLeod—were sitting on the fence, awaiting oral argument.

But it wouldn't matter. With four solid votes to affirm, Atlantica had won the case once Truitt recused himself. Even if both Braxton and McLeod went with the women justices, it would be four-four, and the summary judgment would be upheld. More likely, in order to achieve a clear majority, one or both of them would side with the Chief Justice. Without Sam Truitt to vote for the plaintiffs and to persuade the moderates, the case was over. Max's lawyers had been right all along. Sam Truitt was the swing vote. He was the key, and she had lost him ... she had lost everything.

Outside, a car door slammed. Inside, the apartment felt warm and stuffy. Her mind was racing. What would she do tomorrow? Which, of course, is today. Go to the Court early, clean out her desk. Pack her Tasmania poster, come home and pack everything else. Head west, maybe back to California. Then what?

She heard a metallic noise that sounded like the latch on her front door. She held her breath, listening. Another metallic *click-ing*, as if the door closed.

No, it couldn't be. Please, no!

Shank had won. What did he want now? She lay there in bed under the sheet. Nude, defenseless, paralyzed with fear.

Maybe she was wrong. Sounds from the corridor sometimes seemed ...

The *squeak* of a shoe on the tile floor.

She sat up in bed, her mind racing. She needed a weapon but didn't have anything more lethal than a feather pillow with a crocheted cover. She reached for the phone, which she had taken off the hook when she climbed into bed. She got a dial tone and began dialing 9-1-1, when her bedroom door pushed open.

"Lisa," he whispered.

Omigod!

"Are you awake?"

"Sam! What are you doing here?"

"I'm sorry," Sam Truitt said as he walked to the bed.

For a moment, she thought she really had fallen asleep, and this was just a cruel dream. She sat up, clutching a sheet to her, though she'd never been modest with him before. But was this him or some cruel apparition?

Truitt sat on the edge of the bed and wrapped his arms around her. She began crying, great gushing tears that ran down her face as her body was wracked with sobs. Her head was on his shoulder, but she cried so hard she almost missed what he whispered into her ear.

"I was thinking only of myself," he said. "I was thinking of my career, my life, my principles. It took a while to sink in, how much you risked for something you believed in. Whatever danger you're in, you're not going to face it alone. I'll be there with you."

She couldn't believe his words. "You will?"

"I don't have a choice," he said. "I love you, too."

℘

Passions unleashed, emotions raw, they made love with a fury. An hour before, she thought she would never see him again. A moment before, she thought she would be killed.

Lost love, lost life.

And now this. The wide expanse of his shoulders, the deeply defined chest, the line of soft, sandy hair that traced down his belly toward what now had become a sword that sought her out. She kissed him, drawing his tongue into her mouth, clamping down with her teeth, hurting him. His hands cradled her head, holding her motionless, a prisoner of his desire. It was love tinged with fear and anger, but dwarfing every other emotion was a burning lust.

She grabbed his hair and yanked hard, at the same time releasing his tongue from her mouth. He kissed her harder, their teeth grinding into each other's lips. She could barely breathe.

She was wet with desire, ravenous in her passion, voracious to devour him. His hands swept over her, his tongue now tracing a line down her midsection. Her nipples tingled, and below, she throbbed with damp heat, pulsating as she lifted her hips, longing to take him inside her.

With his weight supported by his arms, he loomed above her. When he entered her, she opened herself to him, and he rammed homeward, each thrusting toward the other with a frenzied delirium, an unconscious rage that seemed to reflect all that they faced, apart and together. It was as if their bodies knew that their lovemaking was threatened. Their world was a jagged mountain peak, their handhold so fragile that they could lose each other—they could lose their very lives—with one slip.

She screamed when she climaxed but never stopped her crazed movements, drawing him deeper inside her, willing herself to swallow him into her womb. Her head tossed back, she locked her ankles behind his buttocks, and he gasped, then shouted her name, again and again as he exploded into her. They lay there, drenched in sweat, and when she began to cry, he kissed away the tears.

The second time, it was soft and tender, and they were unhurried, luxuriating in each other's closeness. It was as if they had made a silent pact, a conspiracy consecrated with a thousand kisses and infinite caresses. Then they slept, the tangled sheets and blankets tossed into a heap in the corner of the bedroom, their naked bodies entwined like vines.

CHAPTER 24

Eye of the Gator

IN THE MORNING, SAM TRUITT RECOUNTED the events of the past twelve hours, a nanosecond of time that would change his life forever.

What have I done? Where will it lead?

He didn't know. All he knew was that, uncharacteristically, he did it for love. He had always been a man of books and words and lofty ideals. He led a life dictated by logic and reason, but now—clichés be damned!—he had followed his heart.

In his chambers the morning after, he retraced it all, step by step. Hours earlier, photos in hand, feeling empty and betrayed, he had left the stadium and headed straight home where he sat and brooded. He had fought to hold back the emotions, forcing himself to be analytical, drawing a line down the middle of a yellow legal pad. On the left side were the debits: Lisa had lied to him and acted unethically, perhaps feloniously. On the right side was only one credit: he was crazy about her. Which only magnified his loss. He was furious with her for having deceived him.

But what about her passion? I felt the heat of her. That wasn't fake.

It was more real than anything he'd ever known. And there at the stadium, hadn't she said she loved him?

Yes, and damnit, I love her, too.

Admitting it to himself made the rest easy. Balancing the Scales of Justice—their love on one side, her unethical conduct on the other—the love carried more weight.

How much weight? Love is an eight-hundred-pound gorilla.

Just before 3 A.M., he had poked his head into the bedroom. Connie was sleeping heavily, taking up the center of the bed. She'd been to the

OB-GYN during the day but, as usual, said nothing about it when they spoke earlier on the phone. He padded over to her, and when she stirred, he told her he had to go to the Court.

"Death watch," he lied. But what could he have said? "I need to see the woman I love. I'm going to risk everything for her."

"I know," she mumbled. "They were looking for you earlier."

He was about to bend over and kiss her on the forehead, thought better of it, and backed toward the door.

"Fry the bastard," Connie muttered, before turning over and tumbling back into sleep.

Truitt drove to Lisa's apartment where they made love with a fury, then again with tenderness. He returned home for a quick shower just after dawn.

જી

The sun was shining in Tasmania. At least, it looked that way on the poster above Lisa's desk. She was humming a song, Vanessa Williams' "Save the Best for Last." She was feeling goofy, silly … in love.

Before Sam had left the apartment, he asked her to run through it all again. She did, beginning with Max at the Tiki Club, ending with Greg heading to the Everglades. Sam sat there in his boxers, nodding, thinking it over.

"An affidavit from Drayton would have overturned the summary judgment," he said when she had finished. "But to win at trial, not even his eyeball examination of the disk would have been enough. The plaintiffs still would need metallurgical tests. They need the missing piece of the fan disk."

"Greg is looking for it, but it seems like an impossible task."

"Get me the evidence, Lisa. Get me something I can see and touch, and I'll get you five votes."

"'Five votes can do anything around here," she said, smiling, showing off.

"Justice Brennan was right about that," he said, acknowledging one of the classic quotations about the Court.

"Even if Greg finds something, it won't be in the record," Lisa said. "How can you get your colleagues to consider evidence that doesn't have a page number and citation?"

"Don't underestimate my persuasive ability," he said.

She kissed him lightly on the lips. "I don't."

Now, in her office with her door closed, sitting at her desk under the Tasmania poster, she heard the buzzer ring, signifying 9:55 A.M. Sam should be headed for the robing room for the 10 A.M. oral arguments. Her mind buzzed with possibilities. Sam was on her side. He loved her and believed in her. There was new hope.

But reality closed in on her. She pictured Greg tromping through the vast swamp. Had she sent him on a fool's mission? How could he possibly find that precious slab, the key that would unlock the door to justice?

∾

Greg Kingston stared into the menacing slit of an eye. Alligator mississipiensis, not to be confused with Crocodylus acutus, according to the ponytailed Miccosukee guide in the tribal jacket of multicolored stripes. Greg had just parked his rental car in the lot and joined the tourists at the Miccosukee Village, a dusty collection of open-sided chickee huts with roofs of thatched palm fronds on the edge of the Everglades forty miles west of Miami.

He was looking for an airboat pilot, the smelly Cracker who, three years ago, chauffeured Drayton through the sawgrass with the stench of scorched flesh and aviation fuel in the morning air. On the flight to Miami and on the drive west on Tamiami Trail, Greg pictured that horrific day. In his mind's eye, he saw Drayton finding the chunk of fan disk and tried to imagine how it must have felt to lay his hands on proof of his own dishonor.

Now, Greg swatted mosquitoes from his ears and listened to the bored guide do a show-and-tell as the tangy aroma of cooked boar came from an open pit in one of the chickees.

"The alligator has a broad, rounded snout," the guide said, pointing to a ten-foot bull sunning himself on the muddy bank of a canal. "The crocodile's head is tapered to a narrow snout."

Greg had already taken a half-day airboat ride into the Glades, his Giants cap blowing off in the draft of the propeller, the pilot fishing it from a cluster of swamp lilies with a tarpon gaff. Greg pretended to study the birds and the flora, but at each opportunity, he asked every fisherman, bait shop clerk, airboat pilot, and anyone who looked like a local where he could find the drunken Cracker who took Joe Drayton around the day after the Atlantica crash. They all remembered the crash—who could forget it?—but no one recognized the photograph of Joe Drayton he showed them; no one knew who took him into the swamp. And why should they? It had been chaos, with helicopters landing, police cars and ambulances careening along the dirt roads that cut into the slough, TV cameras everywhere.

"Stay away from both gators and crocs," the guide said, in what seemed to Greg to be a statement of the obvious. "They eat turtles, garfish, and birds, but *filet de Homo sapiens* is quite tasty, too."

Standing on a boardwalk above the canal bank, several sunburned tourists giggled. A slight motion caught Greg's attention, and he shielded his eyes against the hard Florida sun. A snake slithered along the bank, choosing a route several feet behind the lounging gator, out of its field of view.

"Cottonmouth," the guide said. "Poisonous as hell."

Suddenly, without moving its head, the gator whipped its huge tail, flipping the snake into the grass, away from the water, and just a few feet from the tourists, who reflexively leapt backward. The gator lunged so quickly that, one second it was sunbathing, the next, it was a dozen feet away, chomping on the snake, swallowing it while its narrow gator eyes focused on the tourists, now edging away on the boardwalk.

Later, Greg ate fried Indian bread and broiled frogs' legs at the village restaurant, then walked into the general store, a dingy place filled with rubber alligators, miniature orange trees, Indian drums made in Taiwan, and peace pipes from Honduras. He approached the man behind the counter. A plastic sign on the wall read: ON DUTY—JIM TIGER.

Tiger wore a Miami Dolphins T-shirt, dirty blue jeans, and dusty cowboy boots. He was swarthy and thick-necked with a sour expression. His long black hair fell nearly to his shoulders, and his fingers were decorated with several silver rings, his wrists with jade bracelets. He was smoking a cigarette as he stacked cellophane-wrapped sausages into a display counter.

"I'm looking for someone," Greg said, retrieving the photo of Joe Drayton from a folder and respectfully removing his ball cap. "Were you here three years ago this month?"

"I been here my whole stinking life."

"This guy rented an airboat the morning after the plane went down," Greg said. "The pilot was a local, a Cracker, heavy drinker, maybe sixty, needed a bath. I'm looking for him."

Tiger laughed, exhaling a plume of cigarette smoke. "That don't narrow it down much. Sound like just about every white man out here." Ashes fell from the tip of his cigarette as Tiger seemed to be remembering the crash. "Jesus, what a day that was. Lots of people, lots of boats. My cousin rented his out to Channel Seven. Two thousand for the day. Can you believe that? But he could have gotten five thousand. Of course, if Indians was smart, we'd be living in Palm Beach, and the white man would be out here with the gators and skeeters."

"So you don't know who it could have been?"

"Those guys don't have names, at least none they drop. No telephones, no social security numbers, 'cause they ain't exactly what you'd call social. They live in shacks out on the high ground, just fishing and trapping. Only come down to the Trail for gas and provisions."

A cockroach scampered across the concrete floor and disappeared under a rack hung with potato chips and pork rinds. "Thanks anyway," Greg said.

Tiger dropped his cigarette onto the concrete floor and ground it out with the toe of his boot. "I could ask around, though."

"Thanks."

"If you're going to be around awhile, I'm a pretty good fishing guide," Tiger said.

Greg shook his head. "This trip is all business."

"Where can I reach you if I learn anything?"

"The Holiday Inn in Everglades City. My name's Kingston."

"I better write that down," Tiger said.

Greg thanked him again and walked out, the door chime ringing as he left. Tiger moved to the window and watched him get into the rental Escort. With his pencil still in hand, Tiger waited until Greg backed out and pulled onto the highway. Then he wrote down the license number and went back to the counter. Opening his wallet, he pulled out another business card. It had been there three years and was creased and discolored. He dialed the phone, and when a young woman answered, "Atlantica Airlines, how may I direct your call," he said, "Lemme speak to Mr. Shakanian."

CHAPTER 25

A God in Ruins

SAM TRUITT HELPED GWENDOLYN ROBBINS into her black robes before putting on his own. They were just minutes away from one of the small ceremonies of the Court, the grand entrance through the parted red velvet drapes that separated the robing room from the courtroom. One moment the great mahogany bench was empty, and the next the nine justices swooped in from behind the bench and settled into their high-backed chairs as the crier sang out "Oyez, oyez, oyez."

"Thank you, Sam," Gwen Robbins said, with a slight curtsy. "At least the South still produces gentlemen."

"He's just currying your favor," Curtis Braxton said. "Sam wants your vote on the Maine case taxing charitable trusts that benefit out-of-staters."

"Oh, he does not," Gwen said. "Sam hasn't even read the briefs. Not sexy enough for him."

"Why are you two busting my chops?" Truitt asked.

"Comes with the territory, Junior," Braxton said, laughing.

Truitt smiled. "Maybe I can talk someone into retiring so there'll be a new kid on the block."

"I wonder who Sam would like to put out to pasture," Gwen said, winking.

"I don't know," Braxton said, "but now that you mention it I don't see His Holiness."

Truitt looked around. Five other justices were slipping into their robes, making small talk about golf scores, Christmas plans, grandchildren, everything except the cases they were about to hear. But where was the Chief, the biggest, blackest robe of all with its four gold stripes like some pompous magistrate in a Gilbert and Sullivan musical? Missing, just moments before the buzzer would sound again, signifying the start of the session and the nine scorpions would magically appear in the majestic courtroom, ready to dispense wisdom and justice. They were never late.

Just then, the door to the robing room opened and Chief Justice Whittington swept in, back straight, chin high, cheeks flushed, white mane flowing, regal as a potentate, divine as Zeus. But, defying tradition, he was not alone. Accompanying him into the sanctuary were two Court marshals in blue sport coats and ties and two uniformed Court policemen. The other justices stopped their chitchat and froze.

Truitt sensed trouble, intuitively knowing it involved him.

"Good heavens!" Victor Small said, annoyed at the intrusion into the inner sanctum. "This is quite unprecedented, Chief."

"So it is, Vic," the Chief acknowledged, obviously pleased to be the center of attention. "But these are dangerous times, and dangerous times require resolute, even radical measures."

Gwen Robbins nudged Curtis Braxton in the ribs. "Either we're under a missile attack, or the strawberries are missing from the Chief's pantry."

Whittington turned to Truitt and with excessive formality said, "Justice Truitt I must request that you accompany me to my chambers."

"Now? What's going on?"

"A matter that strikes at the core of the Court. Now, please remove your robes and accompany me." He nodded toward his phalanx of troops, as if they should be ready to subdue any resistance. The marshals and policemen studied the tops of their shoes.

"What the hell is it?" Truitt insisted, "Skip the theatrics."

"Justice Truitt, I shall explain everything in my chambers. Trust me that I am protecting your interests by not speaking freely here. Now will you accompany me?"

Or what? You'll march me there at gunpoint? Would someone please tell the Chief I don't work for him?

Feeling like a sheriff turning in his badge and gun, Truitt peeled off his robes, and with a brooding sense of foreboding, silently followed the Chief Justice to his chambers.

છ્જ

"Where did you get those?" Sam angrily demanded, staring at the grainy eight-by-tens neatly arranged on the Chief's mahogany desk. The chambers were decorated in antiques dating from the colonial period plus a smattering of Frederic Remington cowboy sculptures, but at the moment, Truitt was oblivious to the artwork. He was watching the Chief peer at *The Best of Sam Screwing Lisa.*

"So you admit that you are the man in the photos?" the Chief said accusingly, sounding like a small town prosecutor.

"Of course it's me!" Truitt boomed, his face reddening, dreading what was to come. He had no doubt that the Chief was delighted to have caught him with his pants down.

How much does the old bastard know?

The Chief stood and locked his hands behind his back as he paced past the mahogany Regency table, the Hepplewhite sideboard of inlaid satinwood, the bookcase that had once belonged to Abraham Lincoln. He stopped at the window. A light, feathery snow was falling. "And the young woman," he said, looking toward the Capitol, "the woman who is naked as a jaybird, that is your law clerk, Lisa Fremont, is it not?"

Christ, is he recording this, or does the Chief always talk this way?

"Yes, it's Lisa."

"Have the pictures been doctored or altered in any way?"

Feeling like a witness before the grand jury, Truitt examined the photos. There he was on his back, Lisa astride him, eyes closed, mouth open in apparent ecstasy. There he was again, this time on top, her legs wrapped around him. On another, his face was obscured, buried between Lisa's thighs. Then, indignity piled upon embarrassment, in the final one, his full erection was pointed at the camera in a priapic salute.

"No, nothing's been altered, though something's been engorged. Good thing they were using a wide-angle lens."

The Chief approached the sitting Truitt, towering over him. "Do you think this is funny, Sam?"

"No, I think it's humiliating, demeaning, and none of your goddamn business!"

"We'll see about that. Would you agree that the photos are all true and accurate representations of what they depict, i.e., that you and your law clerk are having sexual relations?"

He's rehearsing his testimony for the impeachment trial: "I then asked Justice Truitt to authenticate the photos ..."

"Look, Chief. This is a personal matter. It's got nothing to do with the Court."

"We'll damn well find out. I warned you, Sam. You've got a first-rate mind, but what good are you if you think with your cock?"

"It's not like that. You don't understand."

"I understand that if this gets out, you'll bring disgrace on the Court. Hell, what happens if the girl cries sexual harassment? Did you ever think of that? Here we are ruling on employment rights cases every day, and one of the brethren uses his office to take advantage of a young woman."

"That's not the way it is. And she's not going to sue."

The Chief sat down behind his desk. "What if she's like that Anita Hill woman, a little nutty, a little slutty? I'm just trying to protect you and my Court."

"I hate to break it to you, Chief, but it's not *your* Court."

"You have a problem with authority, Sam. Do you know that?"

Truitt wanted to tear up the photos and stuff them into Whittington's craw. "I have a right to know where you got these."

"They were delivered to me anonymously, along with this." The Chief handed Truitt a single sheet of paper. Two pictures had been photocopied onto it: a head shot of Lisa Fremont and a photo of a ruggedly handsome man in an airline pilot's uniform. Typed below the photos was a single sentence: "If the Justice of Love doesn't tell you who the Flyboy is, I will." The note was signed simply, "Amicus Curiae."

Bull! He's no friend of the Court and sure as hell no friend of mine.

I'm being torpedoed, Truitt thought. He felt his world crashing down around him. He had underestimated the opposition, a fatal flaw on the football field, in the courtroom, or on the streets. Lisa had told him that Shank was a thug, probably a sociopath. Truitt hadn't figured he also possessed Machiavellian cunning.

Shank and Wanaker had counted on him firing Lisa, turning on her when he learned the truth, Truitt figured. When he didn't, they went after him. And they just nailed him. Now, it was no longer just a fling with his law clerk, which maybe the old goat could forgive after a stern lecture about morality and women who cry wolf. Now there was a conflict of interest involving a pending case.

"What about it Sam? Who's the man?"

"I've never seen him before," Truitt said, "but I assume it's Tony Kingston, the pilot of the Atlantica flight that crashed in the Everglades."

"What's he have to do with this? What's his connection to your law clerk?"

I could lie, but he may already know. There could be a second envelope with photos of Kingston and Lisa.

A good lawyer should always know the facts, and Truitt didn't. He decided to stick with the truth. "Tony Kingston was Lisa's lover."

"Jesus H. Christ! And you knew this?"

"Not until recently."

"Once you learned of your clerk's conflict of interest, is it safe to assume you built a Chinese wall between the girl and the case?"

"No. She'd already written the bench memo."

"Did you destroy it and assign your other clerk to redo it?"

"No."

Whittington seemed to consider these damning facts. He opened a cedar box on his desk and drew out a briarwood pipe, which he began tamping full of cherry-scented tobacco. He clamped the unlit pipe in his teeth and leaned back in his chair. There was no sound in the elegant chambers except the ticking of a grandfather's clock, which stood sentinel in one corner.

"Until further notice, you're off the bench," Whittington said.

"You have no authority to suspend me."

"That's true, but I'm not suspending you. You're taking voluntary leave. Some medical problem—stress, hypertension, herpes for all I care—you come up with it. You'll have to fire the Fremont girl *instanter*. Your remaining clerk will be reassigned to do pool memos."

"I won't do it. I won't let you run me off."

"Think about the consequences if this comes out."

"It doesn't have to come out," Truitt said, realizing he was groveling in front of the Chief, beseeching the bastard, and hating himself for it.

"You set yourself up above the rules, Sam. You tried to play God."

The bitter truth was that the Chief was right. He had been guilty of hubris, and the deities were about to make him pay. "'A man is a god in ruins,'" Truitt said softly.

The Chief wrinkled his broad forehead, then laughed. "Ralph Waldo Emerson. It's no damn wonder what you've done if you believe all that transcendental freedom bunk."

"I never did," Truitt said. "I considered myself bound by the artificial restraints of the law. Now, I'm thinking Emerson was right. Man ought to look into his own heart for guidance."

"Anarchy!" The Chief was shaking his head, a querulous teacher facing an argumentative student. "Sam, I need an answer. If you insist on staying on the bench, it's my duty to take action. I'm a straight shooter, so let me tell you how it is. Either you agree to sit out the rest of the term, after which we'll revisit your status, or I walk over to Capitol Hill and have lunch with a senator or two who'd love to file impeachment papers first thing tomorrow."

You son of a bitch. You've been lying in wait for this moment.

"Take your best shot, Chief. I'll fight you every step of the way."

"I knew that would be your first reaction. But damn it, Sam, just because you played football looking between your legs doesn't mean you have to stick your head up your ass. If you don't care about destroying your own career, consider the effect on your wife, and think what this would do to Senator and Mrs. Parham. Think about the President, who put his faith in you and stuck by you during the confirmation hearings."

Truitt seethed with anger. The Chief was trying to manipulate him, and it was working. Truitt fought to control his emotions. He hated to let the old buzzard chase him off the Court, but by stepping aside now, he could marshal his forces and counterattack. He would live to fight another day.

"I have been under a lot of stress," Truitt conceded.

"Good. I knew you'd come around. You're too damn smart not to. The media would make a great deal of mischief with this. I'll prepare a press release. You might want to check into Walter Reed, get a doctor to say you need some rest, that sort of thing. Or, you may just want to get away for a while. Go somewhere warm."

"I might do that," Sam Truitt said. "Florida is real nice this time of year."

℘

A court marshal sealed Lisa's office with yellow crime scene tape and escorted her home. He wouldn't let her remove any files or even her personal belongings, and when she tried to take down the Tasmania poster, he stopped her with a firm, "I've got my orders, ma'am. Nothing goes."

Feeling like a criminal, filled with shame, she was drowning in a sea of guilt.

I'm sorry, Sam. Oh God, don't let them destroy him.

The phone was ringing when she stepped into her apartment. "Sam, I'm so sorry," she said when she heard his voice. "It's all my fault. I should never have involved you."

"It's all right," he said.

"No, it's not. For me, it doesn't matter. But you've worked your whole life to get here, and I've destroyed it. I've ruined everything for you."

"It's not over yet," he said, with an almost eerie tranquility. "In a way, it's liberating. I'm away from the marble walls and bronze statues. I can act like a man again, not some demigod. It's time to take off the robes and put on the spikes again."

At first she thought he just didn't want her to know how badly he was hurting. But that wasn't it at all. He wasn't covering up his feelings. He was determined, strong, and focused. Solid, like Tony. If there was a problem, here was the man to handle it.

"Do you have any mosquito repellant?" he asked.

"What?"

"Where we're going, we'll need it."

It took a moment to sink in. "The Everglades?"

"Your young friend doesn't know the territory or the people like I do. We'll give him some help. Hell, I built my own airboat when I was sixteen. From the time I was a kid, I walked the trails and explored the hammocks and inland islands."

Oh Sam, sweet Sam. The Eagle Scout wants to blaze a trail through the woods.

"Sam, are you sure you want to—"

"I'll be at your place in fifteen minutes. Pack a bag. Jeans, sneakers, windbreaker, and mosquito repellant, if you have any."

She could hardly believe it. Just weeks ago, he would have closed his eyes to any evidence not officially stamped, spindled, and paginated. He had changed.

Jesus, I've changed him!

She loved the way he had taken charge. Sam Truitt may not have been a god, but he was surely a divine specimen of a man.

CHAPTER 26

Roadkill

GREG KINGSTON WAS SQUINTING into the fireball of a setting sun as he headed west on a gravel road that ran alongside a canal overgrown with water lilies. The map said he was near Chokoloskee, but in truth, he was lost.

Jim Tiger had called the motel and told him that an old Cracker named Thigpen might be his man, giving complicated directions that took Greg south of Tamiami Trail and then west on a gravel road between a canal and a swampy marsh. His rental Ford Escort kicked up a cloud of dust and scattered blue-eyed, long-legged white ibises as he looked for the cottage Tiger said would be right next to a pumping station.

So far, no cottage, no pumping station.

Twenty minutes earlier, he'd seen a few fishermen on the bank of the canal, and a couple more in an outboard puttering down the waterway, but since then, nothing. Green lilies floated in the dark water, and the bank was swarming with wildflowers, swamp rose vines climbing six feet high, their flowers pink, their saw-toothed leaves a bright green. He passed Brazilian pepper trees and a leafless strangler fig, two vultures perched on a barren limb, watching him pass.

The blazing sun, sitting just above the horizon, was giving him a headache, and he pulled at the bill of his baseball cap to shield his eyes. He swerved on the narrow road to avoid a raccoon, then spotted something in his rearview mirror. Coming out of the plume of dust behind him was a pickup truck.

The truck closed the distance between them and rode his rear bumper.

"Hey fellow, I'm going as fast as I can," Greg said into his rearview mirror.

He picked up speed, but at forty, the little Ford was bouncing in the potholes, shocks screeching, and he slowed down again. A horn blast from behind jarred him. The asshole wanted to pass, but there was no room.

Suddenly, the pickup hit his bumper with a *clunk* that whipped Greg's head forward and backward.

Shit! What's wrong with this guy?

Greg inched to the right but the truck was on his tail, and he couldn't slow down. Then the pickup pulled alongside on the left, forcing him even closer to the canal. Greg shot a look at it, a black Dodge 4x4. Hoping to see the driver, he saw instead only the terrified face of a young man in a baseball cap, his own reflection in the heavily tinted passenger window.

Greg fought the urge to shoot a bird at this backwoods bozo.

Maybe it's some of those shotgun-toting retards you see in the movies.

Suddenly, the pickup slammed his left side, knocking him sideways in the seat and sending the car up the embankment toward the canal. He fought the wheel, yanking it back to the left, when he was hit again, metal shrieking against metal. The Escort shot up and over the embankment, tore through a tangle of ten-foot-high punk trees, ripping cream-colored flowers from their branches, then rolled over once before plunging into the water.

Greg was belted in but still managed to bang his head on the ceiling as the car rolled, then sank, into fifteen feet of water. The car was on its right side, and for several seconds, nothing happened. Silence except for the sound of water bubbling. He looked around frantically in the murky darkness, dangling inside the shoulder harness, unable to reach the release button. His left arm felt numb, and a sharp pain shot from his shoulder to his elbow, stunning him with its ferocity. The right side of his torso flared with white heat, and he knew he'd broken several ribs, then saw that he'd fallen into the parking brake lever, breaking it off cleanly.

Water began pouring into the car. He pivoted inside the harness and with a hand twisted behind his back, painfully managed to hit the release button. He slid down toward the passenger door, fighting off the panic, fighting the urge to take great gulps of air, fighting the knowledge that he was running out of time.

A vision of his father came to him then, in the last seconds of his final flight. He heard his dad's voice, the calm voice of a man doing everything possible to save his passengers, his crew, himself. Dad was so strong, so competent.

I've failed you, Dad. I've let you down.

For a moment, Greg couldn't tell which way was up. Then, getting his bearings, bracing his feet against the passenger door, he tried to open the driver's door, but it was sealed shut by the water pressure. The electric windows were dead. Water was waist deep and growing higher. He tried pounding on the driver's window with his fist, but it wouldn't give. He tried kicking it out, but the window held, and his broken ribs burned with pain.

He thought of Lisa, who had loved his father and loved him. Lisa, who had trusted him to do this job, who had warned him to be careful.

I've let you down, too.

A metallic creak came from somewhere below him as the car shifted position, settling into the muddy bottom, water pouring in faster, neck deep now. Reaching out to steady himself, his hand inadvertently wrapped around something metallic, the parking brake lever he had broken off. As much out of anger as a sense of survival, he swung it like a cop's nightstick, hitting the driver's window squarely, shattering it. Water gushed in, bathing him in a shower of exploding glass. He took a breath and launched himself against the surging tide, pulling through the opening and kicking hard, propelling himself upward, breaking the surface of the water, gasping for air.

Opening his eyes, he was staring into the blazing orange sun, which seemed to sit on the surface of the canal itself. He heard a *pop* which seemed distant and hollow.

Damn, that almost sounds like …

Treading water, he whirled toward the canal and saw the silhouette of a man standing on the bank, two arms raised in front of him.

Another *pop*. The second gunshot tore into him, and he sank into the dark water.

ço

Driving west out of Miami on Tamiami Trail, heading into the orange glow of a setting sun, Sam Truitt kept the speedometer at eighty. With Lisa at his side, he roared past overloaded rec-vees and pickups hauling fishing boats. He was on a journey into his past.

Even here, on this tourist-trapped road of novelty shops, reptile farms, and alligator-wrestling sideshows, there was still a hint of the beauty ahead. The roadside utility poles were topped with egret nests. The wet prairie flanked each side of the Trail, and overhead, herons soared across the sky.

For years, he thought he had come a long way from Everglades City, a town of fishermen, crabbers, and froggers.

But how far have I come? Apparently, 360 degrees.

As they sped farther into the Glades past wet marshes and sawgrass, he indulged in a little fantasy. To hell with the Chief Justice and the Supreme Court. When this was over, he'd come back home and hang out a shingle. He'd write wills and research tides and take the occasional case where a used Mercury outboard goes kaput the day after it's sold. When clients are sparse and cases slow, which would be often, he'd tack a gone fishin' sign to the door.

Okay, okay, maybe I'm rationalizing this just a bit, preparing myself in case I don't get back on the Court.

But that didn't put an end to the fantasy. He'd divorce Connie, or vice versa, and marry Lisa, and they'd have three children, two boys and a girl, and his bride would make hush puppies and swamp cabbage. It all sounded wonderful and ridiculous at the same time.

But why not dream of a different life? What is there to go back to? Maybe not the Court. Certainly not Connie.

Before picking up Lisa, he went home to pack his bag and confess to his wife. After all these years, she deserved the truth.

The house was empty, a squeezed lime and an empty vodka bottle standing on the kitchen counter. Spread out nearby were duplicates of the black-and-white photos that seemed to follow him everywhere. First the stadium, then the Chief's chambers, and now in his own home.

That son of a bitch Shank!

One photo was turned facedown. Scrawled on the rear in Connie's handwriting: "You are such a predictable bastard."

No, it's not like that! Lisa's not just a willing coed with a nice ass and an inflated GPA. Christ, I love her!

He flipped the photo over, and there he was, on top of Lisa, his face contorted in a grimace of excruciating pleasure. He felt an ache in his heart for Connie, trying to imagine how she felt when she opened the package. Damn! It didn't have to be this way. He could have spoken to her. She didn't have to be hit in the face with it.

Now where the hell was she? They could still talk this out like adults.

He called her name, thinking she might be upstairs. No answer.

She could be at her sister's. He picked up the kitchen wall phone, then spotted the notepad with a handwritten Virginia telephone number and nothing else. He dialed the number, and the receptionist answered, "Women's Medical Center, please hold."

The name meant nothing to him. As he waited for the receptionist to return, a recorded message began playing. "For eighteen years, Women's Medical Center has provided compassionate, gentle, and discreet health services at our modern, comfortable offices in Virginia, Maryland, and the District."

What the hell is this?

"We offer board certified gynecologists, free pregnancy testing, safe and painless pregnancy termination, and ..."

Oh no! God no!

"May I help you?" the receptionist said.

Stunned, he didn't answer until she asked a second time. "I'm calling for Mrs. Truitt. Constance Truitt. Is she there?"

"I'm sorry, sir. We have a policy of confidentiality. However, if you leave your name and number, and if there is such a person here, which I'm not at liberty to either confirm or deny ..."

Christ, she's reading from a script.

"Your message will be delivered. In such event, you may receive a return call in the discretion of the person who—"

"Goddamnn it! Let me talk to her. I'm her husband!"

"I'm sorry sir, but our policy ..."

He slammed down the phone and bolted for the door.

ల

Connie was in a bed in the recovery room by the time he found the clinic, having called directory assistance from the car for the address. She was pale and heavy lidded but nodded to him with a smile that stopped just short of a smirk. "I remember you. You're the bastard who knocked me up back on the island. Déjà vu all over again, Sam."

"Why, Connie? Is it to punish me?"

"No, you egocentric prick! It's to get rid of you. So go! Go to your little clerk or whoever next year's blonde will be. Get out of my life!"

ల

They were an hour out of Miami when Truitt began telling Lisa tales of his adolescence that she considered exaggerated, if not downright apocryphal.

"You didn't really eat roadkill?" Lisa asked in disbelief.

"Sure I did," Sam Truitt said. "You haven't lived till you've had pavement possum or crushed 'coon."

She smiled and watched the road signs fly by as they drove deeper into the Glades. She thought Sam looked more at home in his jeans and polo shirt than in his black robes. Lisa wore indigo blue leggings with drawstrings and a snug short-sleeved white cropped Lycra tank top that revealed her flat stomach.

They passed a ramshackle restaurant advertising fried catfish and frogs' legs. "Don't sell roadkill short," he said. "Muskrat ragout was a rite of passage for the boys in the Ten Thousand Islands."

"That's disgusting."

"You wouldn't say that if you'd ever eaten asphalt armadillo ... on the half shell."

"Sam, I know you're into your country boy *shtick*."

"Country boys don't say shtick."

For a moment, Lisa stared toward the towering sawgrass, then turned to him. "What's Whittington going to do?"

"Try to force me to resign. The Senate Republicans will pressure the President for a more conservative appointment. After all, the Harvard liberal choked."

"On his pavement possum," she said. They passed a faded billboard advertising a half-hour airboat ride and pulled around a pickup truck hauling a skiff on a trailer. "Sam, you've got to get back on the Court."

"Let's not worry about it. We have work to do here. Then maybe I'll get my seat back. If I don't, there's still a lot of mullet I haven't caught."

"What does that mean? Would you step down?"

"Let's just say I'm realigning my priorities, and right now, being with you is more important than sitting in Oliver Wendell Holmes' chair."

He said it casually, but the words moved her nearly to tears. Would he really give it all up for her? She wanted to scream at him, "*I'm not worth it! Save yourself.*"

"Sam, I love you, but I don't want you to sacrifice everything for me."

"My job isn't everything."

She leaned over and buried her head on his shoulder, wrapping an arm around his chest and hugging him tightly.

They passed the Miccosukee Village and the entrance to Shark Valley, heading west. When they were just outside Ochopee, less than ten miles from where Sam grew up, he pulled the rental Pontiac off the Trail and into the ranger station parking lot.

They walked up to the counter and were met by a young man in a U.S. Park Service uniform with a name tag that read, D. REED. He was tall and lanky, and his dark brown hair was creased where his ranger hat had left its impression.

"We'd like to see the records of all gator poachers in the last five years," Sam said. "Everyone convicted of hunting gators without a license or exceeding the kill limit, hunting out of season, possession of illegal hides, that sort of thing."

"Why?"

Because the old Cracker had gator hides in his airboat, Lisa thought. Why didn't I think of it?

"They're public records, aren't they?"

"I don't know," D. Reed said. "No one ever asked before." He looked suspiciously at Sam. "You folks with the TV?"

"No," Sam said.

"'Cause if you're with *60 Minutes* or something, I'll have to get my supervisor."

"Actually," Sam said, "I'm a justice on the Supreme Court of the United States."

The ranger coughed out a laugh. "No shit. I'm Dick Tracy." He turned around and called out, "Lieutenant!"

A ranger name-tagged J. SANDERS moseyed up from an office behind the counter. He was a big man in his mid-forties with a sunburned face and a pink scalp where his hair had deserted him. A bulging belly fell over his belt buckle. "What's up, Danny?"

"Got a fellow here who says he's a judge. Supreme Court variety."

The older ranger looked at Sam Truitt and grinned a gap-toothed smile. "Impersonating a judge gotta be a crime, doncha think?"

"No more than shooting a white ibis and barbecuing it on a mound of oyster shells," Truitt said.

"Criminy, Scrap! We were fifteen then."

"And we called it Chokoloskee chicken."

Truitt laughed, and Sanders walked through a swinging gate to bear hug him, lifting him a foot off the floor. Then they separated and appraised each other's bodies.

"You haven't been missing many meals, Jimbo," Truitt said.

"And you're looking like you could use some swamp cabbage with ham hocks."

"You're making my mouth water. Does Flora still make that key lime pie?

"Do gators shit in the swamp?" Sanders shot an apologetic look at Lisa, his face turning even pinker. "Oops, sorry, Miss."

Miss? I'm stuck in a time warp.

Sanders elbowed Sam in the ribs while keeping his eyes on Lisa's bare midriff. "Did you tell the little lady about how we used to wrassle gators at Lostman's Creek?"

Little lady? Get off it, Barney Fife.

"I didn't want to brag on myself," Truitt said, sounding as southern as fried catfish.

"It ain't bragging if you done it," Sanders said. "Sam here used to crawl into gator holes and pull out some bulls that could break your leg with a flick of their tail."

"Uh-huh," Lisa said.

"Hell, Sam. The little honey don't believe you ever wrapped your bare hands around a bull gator's snout," Sanders said.

"All in the technique," Truitt said. "An alligator can crush a big old boar's skull with one bite, crunch through it like it was a marshmallow. But the muscles to open the jaw aren't that strong, so you can clamp his mouth shut if you're quick about it."

"Sam had the quickest hands in the Glades," Sanders said.

"Don't I know it?" Lisa said with a smile. "By the way, my name's Lisa."

"Oh, I'm sorry," Truitt said. "My momma taught me better than that. Lisa, say hello to Jimbo Sanders, the best linebacker to come out of the Ten Thousand Islands. Jimbo, this is Lisa Fremont, my law clerk."

Jimbo Sanders examined her from head to toe, stopping a few places in between. "I'll bet," he said.

They were sitting in Jimbo Sanders' small office, warming up the computer, when the call came in. A couple of fishermen in a small boat spotted a car at the bottom of the Strangler Fig Canal. Fresh tire tracks on the bank, no sign of survivors, just a ball cap floating like a lily pad.

"A what?" Lisa asked.

"Baseball cap," Sanders repeated.

It could be anyone. Everyone wears ball caps.

"What color?" Lisa asked, and Sanders looked puzzled, but he got back on the radio and found out.

"Black and orange. San Francisco Giants cap. Why?"

Omigod.

She tried calling the motel. No answer in his room. She called her own answering machine. Greg was supposed to check in every day at 6

P.M., just to let her know he was okay. It was after seven, and there was no message from him.

"Sam!" she cried out, and from the look on his face, he knew.

℘

Two Collier County sheriff's cars were pulled up alongside the canal, black and foreboding on this moonless night. Portable lights on metal stands played across the dark water. An ambulance sat nearby, its red light turning endless circles, reflecting off the scrubby trees. A scuba diver was surfacing as Jimbo Sanders, Sam, and Lisa got out of the U.S. Park Service Ford Explorer. The diver was shaking his head.

No one inside.

Lisa felt her knees buckle, and Sam gripped her by an elbow to keep her from falling.

It's my fault. I sent him here.

Lisa fought to keep her composure. As long as there was no body, there was still hope. No one knew Greg the way she did. If only she could figure out what had happened, she might know what he would have done.

"Is there a current?" she asked suddenly, a thought coming to her.

"Yeah, it's a tidal canal," Sanders replied. "Tide's running out, west toward the Gulf."

"He would swim that way," she said. "He's a great swimmer, could do miles a day."

Sanders looked at her skeptically. "Why wouldn't he just swim to shore?"

"Because he had to get away from whoever was here."

"Jeez, that sounds screwy. This ain't—"

"C'mon Jimbo," Sam said, "Let's look."

They took off through the undergrowth, the three of them plus a paramedic in a blue jumpsuit. The paramedic, a young man about Greg's age, carried a black medical bag like a doctor on a house call. Walking west, Sanders shining a three-foot-long Kel-Lite in front of them, they pushed through the trees and shrubs, scraping their arms on thorns. They listened for human sounds but heard only the croak of frogs, the buzz of insects, the splash of unseen fish.

Finally, unable to bear it, Lisa shouted, "Greg! Greg!"

Still no reply.

They had gone half a mile when Sam yelled out, "There!"

They had almost missed him. He had pulled himself up the bank and hidden in the undergrowth. He was semiconscious but managed a feeble smile when Lisa bent over him, wiping wet strands of hair from his eyes. "Hi, Mom," he whispered.

The paramedic took over. He examined Greg quickly, asking him questions, announcing he had a broken left humerus and two or three broken ribs on the right side and was going into shock.

"Jesus! And what looks like a gunshot wound in the right deltoid. Through and through."

He took Greg's blood pressure, ninety over sixty and falling. He injected Greg with ephedrine to stabilize him, gave him another injection of antibiotics, placed pressure bandages on the entry and exit wounds, put his arm in a temporary splint, and inserted an IV of Ringer's lactate. He called for the ambulance on a walkie-talkie, and within minutes, Greg was inside and stabilized.

"I'll go with you to the hospital," Lisa said to him.

"I'm okay," he said. "But you gotta finish the job."

ↄ

It was 1 A.M. when they got back to the ranger station. The doctors had pronounced Greg in stable condition and told Lisa to go home for the night. The police took a statement from Greg, but he never saw the man's face, never got a license number.

It was Shank, Lisa was sure, but there was no way to prove it. The rage was boiling up inside her.

You won't scare me off, you bastard. I'll fight you, but not your way. I'll hang you with the proof of what you've done.

Lisa was exhausted and famished. They had missed dinner, though at the time she hadn't noticed. Now they sat in Jimbo Sanders' office, munching stone crabs he had confiscated the prior night from a boat running with no lights and no license. Sanders apologized for the lack of mustard sauce, but they had fresh limes from a tree out back.

She had insisted they work through the night, that they continue the job, just as Greg had requested. Truitt told Sanders they were looking for a swamp rat who would have been piloting an airboat on the day of the Atlantica crash.

"It's a long shot," Truitt said, "but he had a bunch of gator hides on the boat, so I figured there's a chance he'd have a record. Maybe, if we worked with the database of all poaching arrests, we could narrow it down, find the guy."

Sanders shrugged. "Let's give it a try."

Jimbo Sanders worked at his computer while Truitt expertly cracked the stone crab claws with a wooden mallet. Lisa sliced the limes, and they ate while the computer separated gator poachers from drug runners, canal polluters, bird molesters, turtle egg thieves, and other Everglades miscreants.

"You know what that mallet reminds me of?" Sanders asked, looking over his shoulder at his old high school buddy pounding the crabs.

Truitt appeared baffled for a moment. Then a smile crept across his face. "My elbow!"

Lisa sat there, waiting for an explanation.

"We were both juniors in high school when it happened," Sanders said, digging meat from a claw with the tip of a U.S. Marine survival knife.

"Barbecuing endangered waterbirds," Lisa added, helpfully.

"Not then. We were playing football, and old Scrap here busted up his elbow. 'Course he didn't go to the doctor, and in a couple weeks, there was all this bleeding and calcification, so he couldn't straighten it out. I mean, it was bent at ninety degrees by the time he went to the hospital."

"The doctor wanted to operate," Truitt said. "Told me there'd be so much nerve damage, I'd never play football again. Hell, he didn't think I'd ever hold a fishing pole again."

"So, Scrap and me figure we can do it without surgery. Sort of a home remedy."

As he spoke, the printer was spitting out a list of gator poachers along with their photos, addresses, and Social Security numbers.

"First we tried scalding water," Truitt said. "The doctor said the elbow was frozen …"

"So you tried to defrost it," Lisa said, thinking it's a long way from Everglades City to Harvard Square.

"We stopped when he blistered up," Sanders said. "Then we went to the wood shop at the high school and put the arm in a vise. I grabbed a big old wooden mallet we used to pound dow rods, and I whacked his elbow a dozen times, aiming to smash the bone, trying to break up the calcification. Had to stop when Scrap passed out from the pain."

"Finally, I just did it myself," Truitt said. "Spent a week doing curls with dumbbells, listening to the bone crunching till the swelling went down, and I could move my arm."

"Sam's got a pretty high threshold for pain," Sanders said.

Lisa was shaking her head in disbelief but thinking the story told more about Sam Truitt than even he knew. She was gaining confidence in him. He wasn't always a Latin-spouting legal scholar.

If we have to face Shank, Sam will stand and fight, not cut and run.

Jimbo Sanders tore off the printout and said, "Let's have a look-see."

They eliminated the poachers who were too young, or were jailed at the time of the crash, or were Miccosukees or Seminoles, or who clearly didn't fit the physical description, or—in two cases—were women. They were left with three suspects, or in Jimbo Sanders' words, "three of the meanest redneck bastards what's ever been hatched."

Sanders studied the printout and read aloud. "Abel Postlethwaite, age sixty-one, arrested twenty-nine times, convicted of illegal possession of alligator hides four times, once with sixty hides on his dock."

"He's good at his work," Truitt said, studying the mug shot of a tough-looking man with a scruffy beard and steel-hard eyes. "It could be him."

"Doubt it," Sanders said. "Never known old Abel to use an airboat. Does his poaching in a canoe, can put a slug from a 30 Weatherby through a gator's eye at two hundred feet. Uses a twenty-one-foot outboard to get around the islands, but never saw him in no airboat."

Truitt thumbed to the next page. "Sylvan Pettigrew. Sixty-eight years old. Killed and skinned eighty-nine gators in one night, did eighteen months at Avon Park."

"Forget him," Sanders said. "Sylvan bought the farm about a month ago. Was siphoning gas from some tourist's car at Monroe Station when a semi slipped off the berm, made an omelet out of his skull with the big rearview mirror."

Roadkill, Lisa thought.

"But it could have been him," she said. "I mean, he could have been the one Joe Drayton hired."

"You just have to hope he wasn't," Sanders said. "Who's left?"

Truitt scanned the last page of the printout. "B.G. McClintock, age sixty-four, five feet eleven, one hundred eighty pounds. Charged with alligator poaching fourteen times, never convicted. Indicted by a federal grand jury for conspiracy to import marijuana, acquitted."

"On an airboat?" Lisa asked.

"He worked a shrimp boat for a while," Sanders said. "Would meet mother ships coming up from Colombia, off-load into his pals' boats, then bring the stuff into the islands where the Coast Guard couldn't find them."

Truitt kept reading. "Theft of sea turtle eggs?"

"They're considered an aphrodisiac by some of your Caribbean types over in Mia-muh," Sanders explained.

"Trespassing on federal property," Truitt went on, "and theft of water spider orchids."

"From the Fakahatchee Strand Preserve," Sanders said.

"Assaulting a federal officer, resisting arrest with violence, arson of public property ..."

"He stuffed rags down a police car's gas tank and lit up a cigar," Sanders explained.

"Crab pot theft, possession of undersize lobsters, manufacture and possession of untaxed spirits, all not guilty," Truitt said. "Finally convicted of income tax evasion, and did twelve months at FCI in Miami." Truitt put down the printout and looked at his old friend, who was picking a shred of crab from his front teeth. "Who the hell is this guy, Jimbo?"

"B.G. McClintock," Sanders said, "a fellow who owns a mighty fine airboat."

"So he could be our man."

"I was sort of hoping he wasn't."

"Why?"

"'Cause ole B.G. is a coon-hunting, gator-poaching, fish-scaling, crab-stealing, moonshining son of a bitch who'll probably shoot you the second you set foot on his dock."

CHAPTER 27

City Folk

"DO YOU KNOW HOW TO DRIVE THIS THING?" Lisa screamed over the roar of the engine.

Sam Truitt couldn't hear her. They were both wearing ear protectors, so he simply nodded and gave her the thumbs-up sign. She looked at him skeptically, and he blew a kiss into the wind.

She had called Greg in the hospital, telling him she would stop by, but he said no, go do what you came for. Besides, a pretty nursing student was about to take his vital signs, which he assured Lisa were vital indeed.

Now, Lisa and Sam were skimming over the sawgrass prairie and lily-covered sloughs in an airboat. They passed oyster bars and Indian mounds and mangroves rich with purple pickerelweed and yellow bladderwort flowers. They flew by pinelands and palms, flushing herons and egrets out of the shallows.

Jimbo Sanders had told them it would be a mistake for him to go along. Old B.G. would either skedaddle deeper into the islands or would pepper their boat with buckshot at the first sight of a uniform. So he gave them a chart, a compass, a metal detector, and an airboat confiscated from a drug runner—a twenty-foot screamer that thankfully lacked the U.S. government insignia of Sanders' own boat.

Sitting high on a bucket seat Truitt worked the throttle pedal with his right foot and the rudder with his left hand. Behind him in a metal cage was the seven-foot wooden airplane propeller driven by a hellaciously noisy 472-cubic-inch engine from a 1968 Cadillac.

Truitt enjoyed the sensation of power in the growling engine. He liked the freedom that came with setting out on a mission into uncharted waters. Nothing he had learned from law books in the past twenty-five years could help him here. Now, he was going back to lessons learned as a boy. It made him think of his father, who could navigate a boat at night with a glance at the stars.

It took a while to get the hang of the overly sensitive rudder. At first he'd give it too much, and they'd fishtail like a car on ice. After a few hairy turns, he got the knack of small, smooth movements. It had been a long time. You don't see many airboats on the Potomac or the Charles. Some sculls maybe, but not these howling machines that scoot up on a plane and skip across the water at eighty miles an hour.

They were looking for a tiny spot called Buzzard Island. B.G. McClintock lived there when he wasn't camping out on any one of thousands of other hardwood hammocks and spits of sand and limestone that rose out of the water in the wilderness. "There are two thousand square miles of waterways and islands," Sanders had told them. "If he don't want to be found, you ain't gonna find him."

Truitt eased off the throttle, and the roar subsided. He was looking at an almost invisible creek, its mouth hidden by moss-draped oak and cypress trees. Air plants and wild coffee made the place look like a jungle. He studied Sanders' chart, checked the position of the afternoon sun dipping to the southwest, and looked at the compass. "I think this is it," he said to Lisa, who had removed her ear protectors.

She peered into the darkened tunnel of the creek, the water stained the color of a richly brewed tea by the tannin from the trees. "It's spooky, Sam."

But to Truitt, it was adrenalizing. He felt his pulse quicken. They were about to enter the unknown, and it was a feeling that could not be duplicated in the marble palace. For too many years, he'd either been sitting atop a pedestal or piloting a desk from a cushioned chair where every move had been programmed by the rule book. Now, there were no rules. They entered the mouth of the creek just as an airboat came out of it laden with alligator hides. Two swarthy men wearing colorful, striped Miccosukee tribal jackets stared hard at them as the boat passed off their port side.

The air was cooler in the shadows of the narrow creek, overhung with green moss flowing from the trees. Occasionally, a fish leapt from the water, and they saw the snouts of several alligators poking above the water line.

"Do you get the feeling we're chasing Br'er Rabbit into the briar patch?" Lisa asked.

Truitt had never faced physical danger and wondered how he would react if the time came. For a moment, he questioned what he was doing here. Had his love for Lisa turned his brain to Jell-o?

No, he'd made a conscious decision, and despite his uncertainty about what they faced, he would plunge ahead into the darkness.

They glided up the waterway for half an hour, then following the chart, took a fork to the left, and kept going. In another twenty minutes, their branch joined another and formed a wider river as they continued upstream.

"Sam! What's that?"

Lisa pointed toward the riverbank. Lodged on top of a wooden stake was a human skull.

"A NO TRESSPASSING sign," he said. "I have a feeling we're going the right way."

"Sam, it's like something out of 'Heart of Darkness.'"

"'Mistah Kurtz—he dead,'" Truitt said.

"Maybe not."

They were quiet for several minutes as they cruised slowly up the river, the engine purring contentedly. Finally, Lisa said, "This is too creepy, Sam. McClintock could be just as dangerous as Shank."

"It'll be okay," he said, trying to sound as if he believed it.

An unseen animal splashed in the dark water, startling Lisa. "I'm scared. We're really out of our element here."

"Actually," he said, putting on a brave front "I'm in my element."

But, staring into the gathering dusk, he wondered if it were true. Did he really know how to survive in the wild? Oh, he knew how to make a meal from the sprouts of wild bulrushes and how to drink fresh rainwater from the cones of pine air plants. But as darkness fell, as he watched a diamondback rattlesnake slither through the inky water, he could not help but wonder just how prepared he was for what lay ahead.

∽

It was three hours after nightfall, and Truitt was navigating with the aid of two powerful headlights mounted on the deck. They were nearly alongside a small island, really nothing more than a spit of limestone and topsoil in the middle of the river, when he saw it an unnatural shape rising from inside a strand of mahogany trees. He killed the engine and turned the lights into the small forest. There it was, a ramshackle two-story house on stilts, dark and sinister, with no sign of life.

"That's it," Truitt said. "At least that's where Jimbo's chart says it should be."

"Jesus, Sam, it looks like a haunted house." Despite the warm, muggy night, she felt chilled.

Truitt played the spotlights across the structure, which seemed to have been built in different stages. Some of the wood was pine, some mahogany. A porch bordered two sides, then abruptly stopped as if the carpenter had grown tired or had run out of materials. The house seemed out of plumb, sagging on its stilts, like a drunk against a lamppost. The steep roof was made of shiny, corrugated metal in some spots, plain black tar paper in others. Drain spouts emptied into a cistern. A number of hubcaps were nailed to the walls, apparently plugging water leaks. An airboat and a skiff were tied up at a dock, and a canoe sat, upside down, on the shore. A few feet away, a bowed set of stairs led up to the front door, some twenty feet off the ground.

"Robinson Crusoe wouldn't have slept here," Lisa said.

They were silent a moment, studying the place. The only sound was a symphony of jamming frogs and the relentless sawing, clicking, clacking noises of insects. Lisa swatted a mosquito, squishing it against her arm.

"No one's home," Lisa said softly.

"Why are you whispering?"

"I'm scared."

He poled the airboat to the dock and tied up. Once he killed the lights, they were in almost total darkness, the trees above them cutting off any starlight on a moonless night. He handed her a flashlight, which she flicked on as she stepped onto the dock. He was in midstep, right behind her, when Lisa screamed.

"Sam! Sam!" She leapt backward, nearly knocking him into the water.

"What?"

"There!" She aimed the flashlight beam into the darkness, and they both stared into the face of a dead deer, lashed at the neck to a cypress tree barely six feet from where they stood. It was a scrawny doe, its tongue sticking out. Blood dripped from its midsection—where it had been gutted—into a wet, black puddle on the ground. Truitt scrambled onto the dock and stuck his hand into the open carcass.

"Sam! What are you—"

"Still warm. He's not far away."

Lisa took several uneasy steps toward the house. "Omigod!"

"Now what?" he asked.

"Look!"

She had nearly walked into the slack jaws of an alligator. Or at least the remnants of one. Eight hides hung on a line strung from a piling to one of the house stilts. "What's next?" she asked. "A pit filled with rattlesnakes?"

"Next," came a chilling voice from the darkness, "you two city folk can explain what the hell you're doing on my property."

"Oh shit!" Lisa jumped again.

She swung the flashlight toward the voice, finally stopping on a rough-hewn picnic table. Sitting at the table was a wiry, shirtless man who could have been sixty or eighty, there was no way to tell. Every sinew, tendon, and muscle seemed to be visible under his leathery skin. Sam's and Lisa's attention was not on the man, however, but on what he held. A double-barreled shotgun was cradled in his heavily veined arms. The sight froze both of them in their tracks.

"Turn off the goddamn light," the man commanded, his eyes squeezed shut.

Lisa obeyed. They could no longer see the man but knew the man saw them. To preserve his night vision, he had kept his eyes closed, not allowing his pupils to dilate in the light. All Lisa could see were dark splotches racing across her eyes.

"I asked a question," said the voice in the darkness. "What the hell are you doing on my property, fussing and screeching like a couple of bobcats in heat?"

Truitt said, "We're looking for B.G. McClintock."

"What for? You tin canners want a guided tour of the Devil's watering hole?"

"We're not tourists. No tin trailers, no tin boats, no tin cans to spoil your Glades."

"Least you know whose damn Glades it is, or was, till they diked it, drained it, poisoned it, and polluted it. What do you want with old B.G.?"

"We want to ask him some questions about the day the Atlantica plane crashed," Lisa broke in. "Are you Mr. McClintock?"

In the darkness, the shotgun's pump action *ker-clacked*, and a voice snarled, "I'm asking the questions, girlie."

At the sound of the pump, Lisa stiffened. Sam put a calming hand on her shoulder.

"My name's Sam Truitt. I grew up around here."

Suddenly, a flickering light appeared, the man adjusting the wick of a kerosene lamp that sat on the table. The man coughed out a laugh. "You look like a city boy to me."

"I was born and raised in Everglades City."

The man studied him. "Are you kin to Charlie Truitt, ran a shrimp and mullet boat?"

"He was my dad." Truitt's eyes were beginning to adjust to the light.

"Your pa was a holier-than-thou bastard, wasn't he?"

"No, sir. He wasn't that way at all."

"I'll tell you a little story, Sam Truitt, son of Charlie," said the man they now recognized from the mug shot. Around his neck he wore a necklace of shark's teeth. His face was creased and tanned the color of cedar. His hair had gone white and was tied back in a ponytail by a rope of rattlesnake skin. But it was the same face with one addition: an ugly purple scar ran from behind one ear to the corner of his milky white left eye. On the way here, Truitt had told Lisa that gator hunters often lose an eye to a whipping tail.

"One day back in the early eighties, your pa came into the Crab Pot where me and some of the boys was drinking," McClintock continued. "Everybody knew Charlie Truitt had the best chart ever made of the Ten Thousand Islands."

"He drew it himself," Truitt said, proudly. "Every sandbar, every snag, every island, creek, and river, every pass and fishing hole."

"So I heard. Anyway, I thought I'd do your pa a favor, so I offered him more money for one night's work off-loading square grouper than he made all year mullet fishing."

Lisa's look shot a question, and Truitt said, "Marijuana bales. He wanted Dad to become a smuggler. Help him navigate through the islands, unload bales of pot."

"I wanted him to have some fun. Son, until you've seen a Coast Guard boat run aground in Nightmare Inlet, you haven't lived."

"I can figure out the rest," Truitt said. "Dad turned you down, probably dressed you down, too."

"Got real self-righteous with me," McClintock said, "called me the scum of the earth. Hell, I was just trying to put food on the table. The feds weren't letting me frog, crab, or net mullet. Pretty soon, we'll need a permit just to breathe. I had half a mind to put your pa through the wall of the saloon, drop his ass into Dead Man's Bay."

"You would've needed all your friends to do it," Truitt said, steel in his voice.

"You think so, city boy?"

"Sam," Lisa said, her voice pleading, her eyes on the cradled shotgun.

"I know so. Dad was tough, smart, and honest, and you wouldn't have scared him any with your backwater bullshit."

"Sam!" Lisa punched him in the side. "It's really not necessary for you two country boys to wag your dicks. I'm not impressed."

This time, the man's laugh showed two missing front teeth. "Your girlie's got a dirty mouth, don't she? Comes from watching the TV, I'll bet."

"You weren't the only one to ask Dad to haul pot," Truitt said. "He never did it, even when the fishing was lousy. He never compromised."

"No, he didn't. And he didn't testify, neither, when the DEA slapped him with a subpoena to come tell what he knew about his neighbors."

"Actually, he chased the process server off his property with a tarpon gaff," Truitt said.

"I got respect for that," McClintock said, nodding. "So I guess old Charlie Truitt was okay with me, even if he was a little pucker-assed when it came to breaking the law. Now, what I want to know is, do you take after your pa?"

"I'd like to think so," Truitt said, "but he was the better man."

CHAPTER 28

The Sea Is So Vast

"SURE, I REMEMBER IT," B.G. MCCLINTOCK SAID. "Ain't every day a goddamn plane drops out of the sky."

And he remembered Joe Drayton, too. "Fellow wanted to go east, back where the explosion happened. Took him thirty miles that way. Weren't much wreckage there, some cables, some piping, what looked like little propellers …"

Sam and Lisa sat at a wooden table in McClintock's kitchen. The house consisted of one open room with a small kitchen at one end, a bathroom without any walls, a bare desk, and a single bed placed beneath a window along one wall. The furniture was wood and appeared homemade. The walls were decorated with the heads of various animals, including a boar and a fourteen-point buck whose antlers were utilized as a rack for numerous caps. A stuffed bobcat, its mouth open in a snarl, stood just inside the door.

McClintock had started up a gas generator, and the room was now illuminated with two bare bulbs hanging from the ceiling. He stood at the kitchen counter, which was, in a former life, the stump of an oak tree. He was chopping Florida lobster tails with a sawtooth diver's knife, tossing the white morsels into a frying pan with slices of onion and some swamp peppers. The cooking oil sizzled and filled the house with pungent aromas. Sam had carried a Styrofoam cooler from the airboat and offered McClintock a housewarming gift: a case of Samuel Adams beer on ice. The gift was enthusiastically received, and McClintock was currently working on bottle number three as he simultaneously cooked and answered questions.

Truitt was enjoying his role. He was a lawyer again, out in the field, not a passive jurist in black robes ensconced on a throne.

Maybe I'd convinced myself that I belonged in that Athenian temple, but crazy as it sounds, I'm starting to feel at home here.

"What all did you find?" Truitt asked.

"Some curios, mostly," McClintock said, "what you might call artifacts. Stuff nobody else would want."

Truitt wanted to ask, *What artifacts?*, but stopped short when he saw the blur of movement from the corner of his eye. McClintock held a machete in both hands and with a *whoosh*, swung the blade in a downward arc toward him.

"Hey!" Truitt yelled, leaping backward.

The machete sliced cleanly through a coconut that rested on the tree stump in front of him. McClintock gave Truitt a sly grin. "If you can stand still long enough to grate some coconut meat for me, I'll finish the lobster."

"Sure," Truitt said, shaken from the samurai chef routine. He chose not to mention that trapping lobster out of season subjected the poacher to forfeiture of his boat.

"Is there anything I can do to help?" Lisa asked.

"How 'bout stirring the chowder?" McClintock suggested.

Lisa approached the boiling pot filled with pieces of redfish and snook, chunks of potatoes, squares of salt pork, and slices of onions in a tomato broth. She searched for a spoon without finding one, then McClintock handed her what looked like an animal bone perhaps three feet long and the circumference of a baseball bat. She began stirring, studying the knobs at either end. "This almost looks like ..."

And then she stopped stirring.

"Yep, a thigh bone," McClintock said.

"A femur, a human femur!" she cried, a look of horror freezing her face.

"The thigh bone's connected to the hip bone," he sang out, his milky eye looking off in a distant direction. "And the hip bone's—"

"Shit!" Lisa shouted, dropping the femur into the pot and splashing chowder over the stove.

"It's an artifact," McClintock said, "just like my paperweight. He gestured toward the desk and what looked like a grayish white rock which sat on a messy pile of papers. "I figure it's a kneecap."

"Oh Jesus!" Lisa turned frantically to Truitt. "Sam, let's get out of here."

"A couple of the skulls I mounted on stakes down by the mouth of the creek," McClintock said. "Keeps out the tin canners."

"Sam!" Lisa motioned toward the door.

"Woulda had me some more curios," McClintock said, "but the gators had themselves a feast 'fore I got there." Unperturbed, he poured some wine from a jug into the frying pan with the lobster and began dumping in pinches of the shredded coconut as fast as Truitt could cut them. Then he added some tomato paste and curry powder. "Hope you folks are hungry."

"We sure are," Truitt said, polishing off one of the beers.

"Are *not!*" Lisa was tugging at his sleeve.

"Relax, Lisa. That's just B.G.'s way of drawing boundaries, telling us who he is and warning us not to try to get too close. It's a country thing."

McClintock stopped stirring to appraise his two visitors. "You're pretty smart for a city boy. Now, what exactly do you want from old B.G.?"

"When you were with Joe Drayton, you found something else, a piece of the fan disk," Truitt said.

McClintock nodded. "Don't know what it was, but we fished out a chunk of metal, heavy as hell, only about yay big." He held his hands eighteen inches apart.

"That's it," Lisa said. "It's made of titanium alloy."

"Fellow just hoisted it onto the boat and ran his finger along a crack, oh, less than an inch wide," McClintock continued. "He was crying like a baby, said something like, 'for the want of a nail, the shoe is lost.' You know that old saying?"

"The shoe, the horse, the rider," Truitt said. "Two hundred eighty-eight lives. What happened to it?"

"He paid me one thousand dollars cash to dump it in the deep water of the Gulf."

"Shit!" Truitt's jaw muscles worked as he thought about it. "Any chance you can remember where?"

"It's a mighty big Gulf."

"What about where you found it?" Lisa asked. "Could you take us there? Another piece of it could be nearby."

McClintock scratched his head, trying to dig up a memory. "It was a mile or so east of where Lostman's Creek empties into Sandy Bay ... or was it west? I was hitting the bottle pretty hard back then."

"Did you give a statement to the NTSB?" Truitt asked. "Ever tell them about this?"

McClintock used a wooden spoon to taste the fish chowder, then smacked his lips in approval. "Nope. Just like your pa, I don't talk to the feds."

Truitt cursed under his breath. A dead end.

"Just 'spose for a second I could find what you wanted," McClintock asked, "What's in it for old B.G.?"

"You'd help us prove what really happened," Truitt said.

"And the people who caused the crash would be brought to justice," Lisa added.

"Uh-huh," he said, chewing it over along with a morsel of lobster he speared from the frying pan.

"And I'll throw in the best chart anyone's ever made of the Ten Thousand Islands," Truitt said. He pictured his father's steady hand drawing the rivers and creeks, filling in the blues and greens, and with a fine-tipped fountain pen, neatly printing the names BUZZARD KEY, UNKNOWN BAY, FROG PASS.

"Your pa give it to you?"

"Just before he died," Truitt said, remembering the slogan his father inked at the bottom of every chart he ever drew: "*Oh Lord, Thy sea is so vast, and my boat is so small.*"

McClintock cleared his throat with a disapproving sound. "What kind of a man would take it from you? Not B.G. McClintock." He turned to Lisa. "What'd you mean when you said someone caused the crash?"

"To save money, the airline didn't do the required inspections on the plane, then after the crash, the executives covered it up and lied about it. They cut corners to save money, then destroyed the evidence. With a piece of the disk, we can prove it."

McClintock nodded, taking it all in, then said, "You may think I'm cold-blooded, what with the bones and all. But they're just bones. They're not the people, not their spirits. I wouldn't tamper with no Miccosukee burial ground and I respect the Calusas' customs that go back a thousand years. Now you're telling me that some lousy sons of bitches in suits caused that crash. I seen people cut in two. I seen feet lying all by themselves, without shoes or legs attached, sliced clean off by the seats in front of them. I seen heads cleaved down the middle." He focused his one good eye on Sam Truitt. "You don't have to give me your pa's chart or one red cent. A simple 'thank you' will do just fine."

"Then you'll help us look for another piece of it," Lisa said, her voice rising with excitement.

"Hell, no! We'd never find it. God's watering hole takes, but it don't give back."

Lisa appeared puzzled. "Then …"

"I said the fellow paid me to dump the durn thing. Never said I did what he wanted. What you're looking for is setting down in my shed."

"You've got it!" Lisa exclaimed. "You've got the disk here?"

"Was gonna make an anchor out of it for the little runabout. Waste not, want not, my pappy taught me. Patched my roof with some of the skin of the fuselage, saved some tubing and wiring for boat repairs, even got a full row of three seats I mounted in the cockpit of my fishing boat."

Lisa rushed over to B.G. McClintock, threw her arms around his neck, and kissed him on the cheek. He could not have looked more startled than if a bull gator had latched onto his privates.

"I guess that oughta do for the thank you," B.G. McClintock said, blushing.

CHAPTER 29

Jingle Bells

SHANK HATED CHRISTMAS.

Christmas meant sappy jingles playing in the stores, endless traffic jams on Collins Avenue, and nobody doing any work for the better part of December. Right now, most of the Atlantica employees were up to their asses planning the office party, buying gifts, and exchanging recipes for ginger snaps. Even Max Wanaker was caught up in the insanity, spending several thousand dollars of their employers' money on a blowout at the trendy Delano Hotel.

It's a good thing somebody paid attention to business. Morikawa, one of Koshiro's underlings, a guy with a crew cut that made his head look like a cinder block, had paid Shank an unexpected visit, demanding a progress report. The guy was missing two digits on his left pinky and wore a turtleneck to hide a tattoo that crept up the front of his neck to his chin.

Shank told him it was in the bag. The judge who might have been trouble was off the bench; his law clerk had been fired; there was nothing to worry about. Shank showed him the story he'd clipped from the *New York Times*, a measly three paragraphs under the headline, "Justice Takes Leave." Samuel Truitt was undergoing medical tests for an irregular heartbeat.

I'll give him an irregular heartbeat. I'll flat line the bastard.

Morikawa looked at him suspiciously but Shank took him to dinner at Joe's, and after a double portion of stone crabs and hash browns, sent him to a place in Surfside where the hookers were all blonde Amazons.

What Shank refused to tell Sushi Breath was that he didn't have any idea where Lisa Fremont was, and it was bugging the hell out of him. He'd called the apartment dozens of times, but there was no trace of her. The judge either. Shank always demanded that everything be under control, and this loose end was tormenting him like a headache that throbbed with every heartbeat.

Not only that. In the past few weeks, Max Wanaker was getting cocky, as if he were off the hook, as if Shank fixing the case had somehow saved his sorry ass. Like there'd be no punishment for having screwed up in the first place, putting them into this spot where they'd bet two hundred million dollars on a crapshoot lawsuit.

How could Max not realize that he was dead either way?

Now, as the sound of "Jingle Bells" wafted in from the outer office, irritating him, Shank was engrossed in the company's financial details. When the time came, he wanted to show the bosses he knew more about the business than Max. Sitting at his desk, chain-smoking, he studied the computer printout showing load factors for the two weeks following Thanksgiving. They were flying at 91 percent of capacity with solid bookings through the first of the year. The airline was making money on a cash basis, and once they won the court case, the stock market would react favorably, and with the good publicity, Atlantica should be a healthy business in the new year.

Thanks to me.

After the crash of Flight 640, as Atlantica's stock plummeted, the Japanese consortium had increased its holdings through dozens of agents and now had effective control of the company. Max could be forced out at any time, either legally or with a .38 Smith & Wesson jammed in his teeth. Win the case, show some black ink on the books, and Shank had plans. Screw the security job at the casino. Let some burned-out cop with flat feet keep the card counters away from the blackjack tables. He wanted to run the airline.

Not that they would make me the president, no way. Hire some flunky accountant or CFO type for that. Just give me the office next to his, call me executive vice president, and I'll call the shots. Jingle all the way … to the bank.

He could salt away big bucks for the place in Costa Rica. Already, Shank thought he knew more about the business than that lightweight Max, who had the attention span of a sixteen-year-old boy with raging hormones. Max spent half his time whining about how he'd lost Lisa and the other half banging Loretta Franklin, the head of the flight attendants' union, a broad with as many miles on her ass as the oldest ship in the fleet.

If Shank didn't keep an eye on him, Max would be promising the flight attendants full-pay sabbaticals in the south of France.

Shank walked to the window and peered out over Bayfront Park, the Port of Miami, and Miami Beach. The cruise ships were lined up, like ducks in a row, reminding him of Pearl Harbor. On the street below, silvery Christmas decorations were draped over the towering palm trees, and workers were installing bleachers for the upcoming Orange Bowl parade.

Unburdened by the holiday spirit, Shank focused on the problem.

Everything is resolved, isn't it?

He knew his enemies regarded him as hired muscle, and that was okay by him. No one ever gave him credit for his preparation, how hard he worked figuring all the options. Some of them may have even thought he was stupid.

They don't think it anymore. They don't think nothing.

The Kingston kid was unresolved. That morning, Shank had read the two-paragraph story in the *Miami Herald*. A motorist had been run off the road into a canal and shot. The victim couldn't identify his assailant. Shank figured there'd be police guards at the hospital. No reason to risk that, the kid was out of action anyway.

Now he asked himself two questions: What have I forgotten? What's undone?

He ran through everything again. According to the lawyers, the worst case scenario was a four-four vote, which would affirm the victory for Atlantica. More likely, without Lisa or her pussy-whipped judge there to muck up the others, it would be six-two, the only dissenters the pair who piss sitting down. Nothing to worry about.

But Shank still worried. He could feel Koshiro breathing down his neck. He had guaranteed the victory, just like Namath at the Super Bowl. But all Joe Willie would have lost was a game.

His thoughts turned back to Lisa Fremont.

Where the hell was she, anyway?

Again, he dialed Lisa's number. No answer, just the damned machine: "Please leave a message at the tone."

I got a message for you, sweetie pie, and I'll deliver it right between your legs.

Just for the hell of it, he called the judge's home number. There'd been no answer yesterday. This morning, the cleaning woman picked up the phone.

"Oh, the missus is visiting her parents," the woman said.

"And the judge?" he asked. "This is Mr. Hankisana down at the Court. We have to deliver some of his things."

"I don't know," the woman said. "The missus just said he was out of town."

Shank sat there thinking about it, rubbing his knuckles across his forehead. Always know where all the players are.

If a snitch tells you there are three scumbags inside an apartment and you bust down the door, and two of them are sitting in the living room drinking beer and eating Slim Jims, your asshole tightens up looking for third guy, some whacked-out crack freak who's likely to come out of a bedroom firing an Uzi.

What did it mean, he wondered, that he couldn't find either Lisa or the judge? Maybe nothing. But if they're together, maybe …

Shank used his computer to access Atlantica's reservation records. He plugged in the names Fremont and Truitt. Nothing. He switched to a program that accessed all the other domestic air carriers. In thirty seconds, up popped the information: L. Fremont and S. Truitt had booked an American flight from National to Miami yesterday. Open-ended return.

Miami! Either they're coming to visit me, which ain't likely, or they're heading down to the Keys for some F&F, fishing and fucking, or …

Shank suddenly realized he'd made a mistake. He should have gotten rid of Lisa when he had the chance. Now he had to do it anyway.

CHAPTER 30

Gator Hole

JUST AS JOE DRAYTON HAD DONE THREE YEARS EARLIER, Sam Truitt traced a finger along the crack that ran through the roughly triangular piece of titanium and disappeared at its edge. He'd wanted evidence, and here it was. Cool to the touch, hard and heavy ... and cracked.

Their Holy Grail. Lisa gasped when she saw it, and together they laid their hands on it, exchanging looks of wonderment. Now, all they had to do was haul it to Washington, find a metallurgist to test it over the weekend, then somehow convince Truitt's brethren to consider it, even though it wasn't part of the court record. They had scaled Everest but still had to figure a way to get down.

Oh, and one more thing. Sam Truitt needed to get himself back on the Court. What he intended to do—vote on a case in which he possessed extrajudicial knowledge, hell in which he'd dug up that knowledge with his bare hands—was blatantly unethical but, in his mind, morally right. He would never do anything that was *malum in se*, inherently evil, such as take a bribe. Rather, he was acting in a way that was *malum prohibitum*, wrong only because the law makes it so. Wouldn't John Calvin have given him the right to resist the positive law when it conflicts with the natural law? Or was that just a blatant rationalization? Was it the truth that he would do anything Lisa asked because he was crazy about her and she was more important to him than the rules in any book?

After a breakfast of biscuits with tomato gravy and coffee filled with grinds, Truitt lugged the heavy chunk of titanium on board. Lisa gave B.G. McClintock a second hug—a brave act, considering that he hadn't bathed since the rainy season—then joined Sam on the deck.

"C'mon back when the mullet are running," B.G. told them, standing on the dock and untying the bow line. "I wouldn't mind taking a gander at that chart of your pa's. Not to keep it or anything, just to see it."

"Why don't you come to Washington for a visit?" Truitt suggested.

McClintock's laugh hacked up some phlegm as he tossed them their line. "Sure thing, if you'll introduce me to President Truman."

Truitt guided the boat back down the creek, past moss-draped oak trees looking like stooped widows wearing shawls. It was a bright, clear morning with hardly a trace of wind, and for the moment, he thought he had it all.

I have the evidence. I have Lisa. All that matters now is turning titanium into gold—forging justice from molten metal—and making a new life with the woman I love.

But would that be enough? What if forcing his way onto the bench for the *Atlantica* case—in which the Chief knew he was tainted—would lead to his impeachment? Had he just bought himself a one-way ticket out of town?

He had gone where his gut and his heart had led him, and he wasn't sorry. He was still on a path of exploration that made him question everything that had seemed important. When he was teaching at Harvard, he'd dreamed of an appointment to the Court, but he never thought it would happen. One million lawyers in the country, and only nine justices of the Supreme Court, only 108 since the founding of the Republic. He had been, for the briefest time, one of the elite, a lawgiver from on high, an adjudicator of the most complex issues, a man whose words would be etched into history.

He wanted back on the Court, but just how important was his job, anyway? Strangely enough, despite all the pressures and the doubts about the future, he was happy here. So close to his roots. His senses, so long dormant, had come alive with a tingling clarity. He felt strong and capable of doing anything that needed to be done.

Now as the airboat moved down the creek toward open water, he listened to the *caw* of an unseen bird and took stock of his life. Last night, just before they fell asleep on a mat of woven palm fronds in McClintock's house, Truitt had asked Lisa, "Could you be happy here?"

"Here, in Buzzard's Bay or Nightmare Inlet, or whatever it is?"

"In a little town on the edge of the wetlands, a place with a town square and a barber shop with a red and white pole, and men tip their hats and say, 'Yes, ma'am'?"

"That's a fantasy, Sam. I don't know if I believe in places like that."

"What about that poster in your office?"

"Tasmania's a place of refuge, but only in my mind. I don't think any of us can escape by running away."

"What about our starting a family where we could hear the birds sing and see the stars at night? Would you be happy with life in the no-passing lane?"

"Would *you* be happy, Sam?"

"I don't know. Part of me belongs here. Part of me on the Court. Maybe I'll figure it out after we've righted this terrible wrong."

"You'll never leave the Court. Not willingly."

"What makes you so sure?"

"There'll be other wrongs, Sam. There'll always be other wrongs."

◌

Immortality was on Shank's mind, specifically the question, do you gain everlasting fame by doing something that's never been done—if no one learns you're the one who did it?

He was deep in this thought because he couldn't very well talk to Jim Tiger above the noise of the engine that was sending them skimming across the wet prairie, mowing down sawgrass in their path. Shank was sitting on the bow of Tiger's airboat, his daydreaming assisted by the engine's somnolent drone. They were headed toward Buzzard Island because two of Tiger's friends, the Osceola brothers, were poaching gators yesterday when they saw a man and a woman on an airboat going that way. He couldn't be sure it was them, but the description was right. Big guy with a short-haired, hot-looking blonde.

A part of Shank wanted the fame, and a part of him knew his thirst for recognition was foolish. But shit, it was great back when he was a cop and the Knapp Commission was looking up his asshole with a flashlight. He remembered walking into the precinct house and hearing the whispers: "*That's Shakanian. They say he killed two guys.*" He'd leave the diner to find two DEA agents sitting in their Chrysler, the same guys who'd been his tail for months, and he'd piss on their tires. He was *somebody*, and everybody knew it. Now, the stakes were bigger, but nobody knew his name.

Shank was aching to do something no one had ever done. Kill a justice of the Supreme Court. He almost wished Truitt would get back on the Court. Then he'd do it up close and personal, let the judge look into his eyes.

Not like that chinless weasel Oswald, sitting up there in the window as the motorcade goes by.

He'd be the stuff of legends. They've killed presidents and preachers, congressmen, and mayors, but never a Supreme Court justice.

So even if Ted Koppel didn't know my name, I'd still be famous.

The airboat had skimmed over open water for the past hour. Now, Tiger slowed and turned into a creek lined with moss-covered oaks and green leafy marsh plants.

"It ain't far," Tiger yelled.

Shank had his .38 in a shoulder holster, but he picked up Tiger's 12-gauge shotgun, better for wide open spaces. The varnish was worn off the butt and the fore-end wood was splintered. The damn thing looked like it had been used to drive posts into the ground. He opened Tiger's knapsack and grabbed a handful of shotgun shells, immediately noticing that the star crimping on most of them was not completely sealed.

"What's with these shells?" Shank asked. "They look homemade." He hefted them, one at a time. "And they're heavy as hell."

"I emptied the buckshot," Tiger said, "took solid pieces of lead from some fishing nets, packed 'em in and resealed the shells. Like shooting little cannonballs."

"If one of these blows up in my face, I'm gonna bust this piece-of-shit gun over your head!"

"Relax. It'll work fine. Enjoy the scenery." He reached down and handed Shank a pair of binoculars.

The scenery?

To Shank, born in Brooklyn, the ibis flying overhead, the lilies floating in the water, the towering sawgrass in the open prairie, were about as interesting as the Jersey swamps. In fact, there was one distinct similarity: both were fine places to bury a couple of bodies.

❧

Heading down the creek toward open water, perched in the skipper's chair, Sam Truitt saw the airboat heading toward them. It was too far away to make out the faces, but he saw there were two men aboard. The pilot wore the colorful jacket of the Miccosukees, and oddly, the man on the deck seemed to be wearing a dark suit. Truitt eased up on the throttle. The man in the suit lifted something to his face with both hands. Binoculars ... the sun glinting off the lenses. He turned and said something to the pilot, and the airboat picked up speed, coming up the creek toward them. The man put down the binoculars and lifted something in both hands. Though Truitt could not make out what he held, he recognized the position of the man's hands, left hand higher than the right. The man was cradling a rifle or shotgun!

It had to be Shank!

He had found them, just as he had found Jerry Klein and Greg Kingston.

"Hold on, Lisa!" Truitt shouted.

He turned the rudder hard, wheeling the boat 180 degrees in little more than its own length, the flat bottom sliding across the water. He stepped hard on the throttle, and the airboat picked up speed, planing over the shallow water at more than fifty miles an hour, scattering half a dozen birds, purple gallinules that had been lazing in the creek.

Truitt could not hear the blast of the shotgun or the whistle of the shell over the noise of the Caddy engine, but he saw the effect of the lead plug as it skipped past the boat, kicking up water like a skipping stone, before disappearing. Instinctively, he hunched over in the chair. "Get down!" he yelled at Lisa. "Flat on the deck!"

The next blast was wide, and the third thudded into an overhanging branch of an oak tree, severing it cleanly like a cleaver through a spare rib.

Jesus, what are they firing? We gotta get out of this creek! We need room to maneuver.

There was an opening at a bend just ahead. He didn't know if it was a fork leading somewhere or just some wet ground, a one-way street that led nowhere. But it bent to the east, and he knew from Sanders' chart that there was an open bay in that direction. It was their only chance.

He headed for the opening, which was half hidden by the overgrowth. Without slowing down, he turned hard left, and the airboat slid into a narrow canal overhung with low branches. Truitt leapt down from the chair and ducked, branches thwacking the empty skipper's perch. Crouching on his haunches, he leaned on the throttle with one hand and kept the other on the rudder. Branches and vines tore at his flesh. They were slowing down, though he had the throttle full out.

"Sam! Where's the water?" Lisa yelled.

They were bouncing over hard ground, skimming mud flats, the aluminum hull scraping rocks and logs, the boat careening side to side, feeling as if it might flip over. The blast of a shotgun reverberated through the morning air. Shank's boat was following them through the mud. Another blast, and a shell clinked off the fan cage.

In a moment, the mud gave way to a thin layer of water, and they picked up speed, but there was still no opening to a bay. They were trapped in this narrow gauntlet surrounded by choking vegetation and barren, ghostly gray trees whose branches reached toward them like skeletal hands.

Truitt squinted and peered ahead into the shadows. Shafts of sunlight cut through the trees, creating a glare, and he couldn't see clearly. It almost looked as if this muddy ditch ended in a mountain, but there weren't any mountains out here. There was only flat land and the slow, sure current of the River of Grass. What the hell was that in front of them?

Another close blast, and Truitt glanced back toward the stern. The other airboat was gaining ground. Lisa's shout turned him around.

"Sam!" She was pointing off the bow, gesturing wildly.

Oh shit!

Rising in front of them out of the muck was a levee, an earthen dam, thirty feet high. They were being chased down a blind alley with a dead end, a solid wall ahead of them. There was nowhere to go but … up! Truitt climbed back into the skipper's chair and stomped on the throttle. The Caddy engine roared, and the airboat began planing, with only its stern in the shallow water.

"Hang on!" he screamed at Lisa, pointing at the bow line. She grabbed the rope, but instead of simply holding on, she began wrapping coils around the titanium disk, securing it to the deck. Then she gripped the taut line, bracing for what was to come.

Sam watched her lashing herself to the disk, saw the determination in her face.

That piece of metal is her anchor, and I can't let it drag her to the bottom.

The noise was deafening, the speed surreal—sixty, seventy, eighty miles per hour—as the boat skipped across the water. The scooped bow hit the slant of the levee, which like a ramp, catapulted them toward the sky. In a fraction of a second they were airborne—sailing, flying, soaring above the levee—passing over a dirt road, then down the far side of the decline, bouncing once, twice in clear blue water, jolting each of them hard. The fan disk slid across the deck, dragging Lisa with it.

"Are you all right?" Truitt yelled. He wanted to get down from the skipper's chair, but she waved him off. Looking shaken, she gave him a thumbs-up sign.

Truitt glanced behind them, hoping. No sign of them.

Great! They must have stopped short of the levee.

But in a second, the pursuing boat was vaulting into the air, sailing across the road, and splashing into their wake, following them.

Damn! Whoever was driving knew what he was doing.

They were both in an open bay now, skimming over short needle grass and royal ferns, shearing the tops off yellow bulbs sticking out of lily pads, cruising past tangled banyan and Brazilian pepper trees. Startled by the noise, several white herons were flushed from the taller sawgrass toward the middle of the open bay. With room to maneuver, Truitt was putting the airboat into motion, doing wide sweeping arcs left and right, then hard turns, sliding across the water, running Z-patterns to confuse the shooter.

∾

On Tiger's airboat, Shank could barely stand up, much less brace himself for a clear shot. His leather-soled loafers were sliding on the wet metal deck, and the damn boat kept skidding across the water, seemingly out of control.

"Straighten it out!" he yelled at Tiger.

The Indian made a wavy motion with his hand.

"I know what the son of a bitch is doing!" Shank shouted. "But you go straight. It's the only way I can steady the gun."

As the airboat in front of them swerved from the short needle grass into a forest of razor-sharp sawgrass fifteen feet high, Tiger kept his boat on a line in the open water, just as Shank had ordered. Shank got off a shot, firing too low now as Truitt's boat used the sawgrass as a magic carpet to lift itself several feet above the water.

Suddenly, Tiger yanked the rudder hard, throwing the boat into a skid. Shank tumbled to the deck, cursing. "Son of a bitch!"

He looked off the port side and saw a small outboard with a local yokel fishing. They had nearly collided. There was just time to see the startled look on the old guy's face as the airboat flew by.

Tiger was slowing down now, the engine roar subsiding. "What the hell!" Shank yelled, jamming the barrel of the shotgun in the direction of the fleeing airboat. "Follow them!"

"A witness," Tiger said, pointing at the small fishing boat.

"Who gives a shit? Get going!"

"I'll need more money. Ten grand."

"Fine! Just go!"

If I didn't need you, I'd send you to the happy hunting ground right now.

Tiger hit the throttle. He turned the rudder hard right and in a few moments, the airboat was riding the crests of the sawgrass. But then he slowed again. "Now what?" Shank demanded. Tiger shrugged, and Shank scanned the horizon. *Shit!* Nothing but birds and blue sky.

෫ఞ

Truitt killed the engine and let the airboat sink down into the tall sawgrass. They were deep in the middle of the bay, hidden from view. The path they had carved had disappeared within seconds, the deep grass springing back, ten thousand millennia of nature engulfing man's feeble tracks within seconds.

Truitt climbed down from the skipper's chair and embraced Lisa. "Are you okay?" he asked.

She put her head on his shoulder and held him tightly. He felt her tremble in his arms. For a moment, they listened to the sound of the other airboat. The engine grew louder, then softer, as their pursuers searched fruitlessly.

"Sam, I'm so sorry," Lisa said, burying her cheek against the side of his neck.

"Sorry? For what?"

"For getting you into this. For getting Greg shot. For ruining your life."

He was dumbfounded. "Hey, Greg's gonna be okay, and I've never felt more alive. Do you know how much I love you?"

They kissed a salty kiss, slick with perspiration, made all the more passionate by the danger of their surroundings.

The noise of the other airboat died altogether. "They've stopped," Truitt said, wrapping his arms tightly around her. He pictured the driver of the other boat standing atop his chair with binoculars, searching for movement, some sight of them. "We'll wait until dark and make a run for it."

"Oh Sam, look at that."

"What?" He turned around. A bird with the intense bluish purple of a peacock sat perched atop the skipper's chair. It had a bright red beak with a yellow tip and a turquoise shield on its forehead. "Damn! A purple gallinule."

"Why? What's wrong?"

In a moment, three other birds were sitting on the boat, and another dozen were gripping the top of sawgrass fronds with their large yellow feet, swaying back and forth. One squealed a high-pitched squawk, and then another. Then another ten or twelve birds joined in, an orchestra of hovering, cawing purple birds.

"They're used to being fed by the fishermen around here," Truitt said, "and now they're telling all their buddies to join them for lunch."

In a moment there were fifty birds, then perhaps eighty, all singing off key, all wanting to be fed.

"Welcome to Bodega Bay," Lisa said, dazed by the sight.

"Yeah, these guys look like they're auditioning for Alfred Hitchcock."

Truitt listened a moment, and above the noise of the birds, he heard the other airboat, the roar growing louder. "It's like we sent up flares."

He fired up the engine but kept it idling. The roar of the oncoming airboat grew louder.

They can't see us yet, but they know we're here, and they expect us to run.

"Sam, aren't we going to get out of here?" Lisa asked, her voice tight.

He waited until the last possible moment, then engaged the gears and hit the throttle hard. The noise scattered the gallinules. "Hang on, darling!"

The airboat shot out of the sawgrass onto a plane.

Four hundred yards away, the other airboat screamed toward them.

Truitt aimed directly for the oncoming boat.

∞

Shank got off one shot, but the wind resistance pulled at his barrel and he missed badly. He watched as Truitt's airboat headed right at them, right at *him* actually, as he stood in the bow. He'd be the one decapitated when the bow of the other airboat flew up over their own. He wheeled toward Tiger in his high chair. "Hey, what gives?" Shank screamed.

"He's playing airboat chicken, but he's a pussy!" Tiger screamed back. "He'll wimp out."

Shank watched as the airboat closed the distance. It would only be a matter of seconds.

"Screw this!" he yelled at Tiger, who kept the same course. "You crazy fucking Indian! Turn this—"

"No!"

But Shank saw the look on Tiger's face. The beginning of fear.

Shank turned back toward the oncoming boat. It seemed to be flying at them. The crazy bastard was going to kill them all.

At the last second, Tiger wheeled to the right, lifting the port side out of the water, nearly turning the boat over. Shank fell to the deck and gripped the gunwale as the boat slowed. The other airboat roared past them, no more than six feet away, and Shank, sprawled on the deck, got a good look at Sam Truitt. In that frozen moment of time, Shank realized several things about the man who had aimed the boat right for them and never wavered, the man he ached to kill.

Truitt doesn't look like a judge. In New York, the judges were old farts, political hacks who grew fat and lazy sitting on their asses. This guy's square-jawed and broad-shouldered and tough as nails. It's going to be a real hunt.

෨

Truitt had hoped the sudden movement would spill the other airboat, and they'd have a clean getaway. It didn't work. Within seconds, Shank's boat had turned and was on their tail. Truitt steeled himself for what was to come. He had seen Shank on the bow, so close he could have clobbered him with a gaff. He had seen the look of blazing hatred in the man's eyes. He had to protect Lisa from this monster.

To avoid the gunshots, Truitt cut a serpentine path across the bay. He tossed the rudder hard left, and they glided that direction. Once he had picked up speed, he tried another hard turn, but in the deep sawgrass the airboat felt unsteady, and he was afraid of tipping over or sending them into a cartwheel.

The gunshot seemed to whistle by his ear, and he ducked. The next shot made a hellacious shriek as it crushed the exterior of their steel gas tank. Truitt looked toward the stern and saw gas pouring into the water from a gaping hole in the drum.

He fought back against a wave of panic. He felt like a wounded rabbit in front of a pack of rabid hounds.

They'll catch us as soon as we run out of gas. We're trapped. Defenseless.

From the high chair, he saw a string of hardwood hammocks, small islands, each just a few acres in size, heavily wooded, on the far side of the bay.

Gas continued to pour into the water. The fuel gauge was dropping, second by second. With the gushing leak and the monstrous Cadillac engine sucking the tank dry, they had a few minutes at best.

"Lisa!" he shouted. "Do you have a match, a lighter, anything?"

She looked at him as if it were a peculiar request and shook her head.

"Open that compartment," he told her.

She flipped the top on a plastic storage compartment, and he saw what he wanted. "Toss me that flare gun."

She did, just as a shotgun blast ripped through the fan cage barely missing the propeller. A lead slug ricocheted and spun across the aluminum deck.

They were out of the sawgrass now and in clearer water. Truitt turned right, away from the hammocks, and their pursuers did the same.

We need some misdirection. Have the linemen pull right, and I'll naked bootleg left.

He aimed the flare gun off the stern and pulled the trigger, launching a missile into his wake. An explosion of orange flames shot across the water, chasing their trail of spilled fuel. The flames turned black, and thick choking smoke rose behind them.

With the cover of curling smoke, Truitt turned hard left, sliding across the water, then straightening out. They were half a mile from the hammock. He skidded past an oyster mound, the bow scraping over the hard shells, then tipping on one edge, threatening to turn over. He locked both hands on the rudder and fought for control, bringing the boat back down. They cleared the mound and were headed straight for the hammock, a small spit of limestone and mud overgrown with vegetation and red mangrove trees. The engine sputtered and died just as the boat pulled up to the shoreline. Truitt hopped out into knee-deep muck.

"They're going the other way!" Lisa said, looking back at their pursuers, emerging from the smoke.

But then the boat took a wide, arcing turn and headed right for them.

"They've seen us," Truitt said. He leaned over the short gunwale and struggled to haul out the fan disk, which he figured weighed at least 150 pounds.

"We can't get far with that," Lisa said.

"Just around that strand of trees," Truitt replied.

Splashing through the shallow water, breathing heavily, he carried the wedge of titanium past the outcropping of red mangrove trees, their roots propped three feet above the ground. In a moment, they were out of sight of the approaching boat.. Truitt looked at the shore and lined himself up between a pond apple and Florida oak tree, memorizing the position. Then he dropped the disk into three feet of water and hurriedly buried it in the mud.

"C'mon," he said. "Let's find some cover."

He looked at the tangle of vines and trees on the little island. How long did they have? Where could they go? They had no weapons, no boat, no nothing. No place to run, no place to hide. Maybe they could scramble up a tree or bury themselves in the overgrowth, but a methodical search would find them. Then he saw it. A mound of dirt piled three feet above the ground, perhaps twenty feet from the shoreline.

"Wait!" he said. "There's a cave under the hammock. If we can find the opening, we'll be fine."

"A cave?" she asked. "It's flat here? Where—"

"Underwater," he said, choosing not to explain. "C'mon," he said, leading her toward the shoreline. "We used to do this all the time as kids."

Okay, maybe not all the time, but Jimbo Sanders once bet me I wouldn't swim into one. I won his Orvis fishing rod.

"Sam! Where are we going?"

"We're looking for the tunnel."

She seemed confused, but he wasn't about to practice full disclosure. After all, if he told the truth, she wouldn't go.

So it's not really a cave. It's a gator hole, and I'm just hoping the gator's not home taking a nap.

He guided Lisa through knee-deep water, trying to guess the spot where the alligator began digging under the shoreline. "It's got to be around here somewhere," he said, checking the position of the mound of dirt on shore.

The roar of the approaching airboat grew louder. It was just out of sight, around the outcropping of trees. They didn't have much time. And they didn't have a choice. Truitt took several steps before his footing gave way. He took a step and suddenly, the water was chest deep.

"Here it is," he said. "C'mon. We're going to swim under the island."

"Sam, this seems crazy."

"Just trust me," he said. But inside, he was filled with doubt. The tunnel could be blocked. If Lisa panicked and turned the wrong way or became stuck, she could drown. If they had to come back out Shank would likely just be pulling up to the shore. If the gator were there, they'd be the animal kingdom's equivalent of home delivery pizza.

He reached up and broke off a small limb from an overhanging tree. It was about three feet long and no more than two inches around.

Shank's airboat appeared in the distance.

"Let's go," he said. "No time to argue."

 es

Lisa was frightened. She was only a fair swimmer. The Pacific Ocean was too cold where she grew up, and she never had the benefit of a country club swimming pool. She'd taken little Greg to the YMCA pool where he did his laps as she timed him, but the water smelled of chemicals and was uninviting. With Max, there'd been hotel Jacuzzis, but nothing ever like this. Sam Truitt was dragging her into chin-high water, telling her to take a deep breath.

He dived and she followed. The water was clear and clean, ferns waving at them from the sandy bottom. Truitt headed for what looked like a black hole, which she realized was the opening of a tunnel. He extended the tree branch in front of him like a divining rod.

Total darkness. She swam behind Sam, grabbing one of his legs, letting him carry her along. Her shoulder scraped against the side of the tunnel, dug from rough limestone, and she wondered how much farther they had to go. The mound she saw on the shore seemed so close to the waterline, but the tunnel wasn't a straight path, and she was running out of breath.

Sam! Sam! I'm going to drown.

Suddenly, she was being pulled. Sam's hands grabbed her by the elbows and dragged her straight up. Lisa's head broke through the surface. There was no light, but there was air. She drank in several breaths before even trying to speak.

"Are you okay?" Truitt asked.

"I think so," she gasped. "I didn't think I was going to make it."

"You did great" he said. "We're under the mound."

They were treading water together now in a small cavern perhaps five feet across. Truitt reached above their heads with the stick and jammed it into the earthen roof. When he brought it back down, a clod of dirt fell into the water, and a shaft of sunlight peered through the opening. Fresh air streamed through the hole. "We may have a long wait," he explained.

ↄ

Shank stepped out of Tiger's boat, ruining his loafers when he sank into soft mud. He looked at the beached airboat with the hole in the gas tank, studying it like a homicide detective looking for clues. Then he hopped aboard and crouched down. The deck was scarred with fresh scratches. Little shards of bright aluminum floated in an inch of dirty water. The deck had been gouged by a stronger metal.

Like titanium ... The bastards have the disk!

He looked around. At least they weren't going to get far.

He considered the possibilities. They could have jettisoned it a mile from shore or buried it two feet from where he was standing. Either way, he'd never find it. But it wouldn't matter. If he killed them both, *no one* would ever find it. Cradling the shotgun, he stepped ashore in his squishy loafers and said to Tiger, "Let's find the bastards and finish this."

❦

Lisa and Sam heard every word. Shank and a man he called Tiger were standing somewhere near the mound arguing whether they should split up or stick together, and if they split up would one of them accidentally shoot the other in the dense undergrowth?

It went on for a few minutes until it grew quiet as the men took off, apparently in different directions. Truitt had his arms around Lisa, helping her tread water, both of them anxious and growing weary.

Lisa looked at this man she loved. His hair was matted into thick curls from the water. His face was smudged with dirt. A drop of water clung precariously to his eyelashes and he blinked it away. He was, she thought, the most deliciously handsome man she had ever seen.

"We're going to make a break for it," Truitt said, after several minutes.

"Why? Aren't we safe here?"

"They can wait us out, and we can't stay here after dark."

"Why not?"

He took a deep breath, sighed, and said, "Because Al's coming back."

"Who?"

"Mr. Al E. Gator. This is his condo, and we're in sort of a Goldilocks scenario. He's likely to be pissed that somebody's been sleeping in his bed."

"What!"

He was trying to make light of it, but she wasn't buying it. Suddenly, she felt claustrophobic in the dark cavern. Was that a splash or her imagination? She was tired and cold and fighting off panic. She wanted to get the hell out of there and she was angry—wildly and irrationally, she knew—at Sam. "Damnit, Sam, I'm not leaving. Shank scares me more than any alligator."

❦

Shank clomped through the dense tangle of mangrove roots, entwined like snakes. He was sweating and mosquitoes were dive-bombing his ears, sucking at his neck. He'd just twisted his ankle stepping into a crab hole, and he tore his suit pants on a jagged root, so by his third orbit of the small island, his anger tasted like rusted iron on his tongue. He cursed Sam Truitt. He cursed Lisa Fremont. He cursed Max Wanaker, and he cursed Jim Tiger, too.

Then he emerged from the underbrush along the muddy shoreline, near the outcropping of trees where Truitt's airboat was beached. That's when he saw two sets of footprints in the muck. He'd missed them first time, but now he followed them into the shallow water where they disappeared, then picked up again on the island.

When they got off the airboat, why didn't they head straight to shore?

Tiger emerged from the underbrush and walked to the shoreline behind him. "I searched every square foot of this stinking place," he said. "They're not here."

Shank scanned the water in front of him.

"What are you looking for?" Tiger asked.

Shank ignored him. The guy was useless. Shank shielded his eyes from the sun and squinted into the clear water that came up to mid-thigh. He almost missed it, but right there, in knee-deep water, peeking out of the mud, was the glint of shiny metal.

"It's here!" he yelled.

"What is?" Tiger asked.

"The stuff dreams are made of," Shank said with a smile like the blade of a knife.

&c&

They heard the airboat's engine start up. "They're leaving," Lisa said.

Truitt was suspicious. Why would they leave without finishing them off? It could be a trap. Tiger could have taken the boat; Shank could be waiting behind a tree. They should wait it out, but the alligator could be coming back at any time.

"Okay, let's get going," Truitt said. "Just inhale and exhale a few times, then take a big breath."

Again she followed him out, heading, quite literally, toward a light at the end of the tunnel. They came up for air in the shallow water just outside the opening, the winter sun shining brightly, the sky never before looking quite so blue. Keeping low with just his head above water, Truitt surveyed the horizon. The roar of the airboat was diminishing, but it was clearly visible, moving back toward the open bay. Two figures were on board.

"They've gone!" Truitt said excitedly, standing up in the shallow water. "All we have to do is get the disk and hitch a ride home."

"How?"

"I think I can still make a fire with some dried twigs, leaves, and sunlight."

"If this keeps up, Sam, you're going to earn your Eagle Scout badge before sundown."

"Already got it," he said, tromping through the water toward the spot at equal angles to the pond apple and Florida oak trees.

Still carrying the broken tree branch, he prodded into the mud, searching for the fan disk. Nothing.

He used his foot to poke around but managed only to become tangled in some swaying ferns. He stuck his head under the surface and skimmed the bottom with an outstretched hand, disturbing some hermit crabs and pomacea snails ... but no disk. He held his breath and dived under, his face inches from the bottom. Still, nothing.

"It's gone!" he yelled as he broke the surface. "The disk is gone!"

"Are you sure you're in the right spot? Maybe you're turned around or—"

"I know exactly where it was," he said, brusquely.

"Fine," she said.

"I'm sorry. It's just that, after all we went through ..."

"That's why Shank left," she said, turning toward the horizon. "He didn't have to kill us to stop us. If he has the disk, he's won."

Truitt was still looking, dragging his feet, hoping to stub his toe on the hard metal. Lisa was walking behind him, trying to help.

"Damnit!" he grumbled. "I just can't believe it."

We came so close.

Sam Truitt was beyond despair. He had let Lisa down. They'd come all this way. They'd held the evidence in their hands, and now it was gone. He should have been happy to be alive, but all he could think about was that he had blown it. He turned the anger inward, cursing himself. What made him think he could save the world? Probably the same conceit that made him think he could live by his own rules. Maybe he didn't deserve to be on the Court. Maybe he didn't deserve to have the love of a wonderful woman.

He was walking in a circle now, knowing it was hopeless, but refusing to give up.

"Stop splashing," he said. He was furious with himself, but taking it out on Lisa.

"I'm not, Sam."

Another soft splash sprayed water on him. "Damnit, Lisa!"

He heard her gasp. "Sam! Look out!"

At the sound of the terror in her voice, he wheeled around.

There was another splash … and an undulating tail.

There was the rounded snout and the two piercing black eyes.

A ten-foot bull gator stood between them and the shore.

Truitt positioned himself between the gator and Lisa in the waist-deep water.

"Are you gonna wrestle him, Sam?"

"Wrestle him! Are you nuts?"

The gator seemed to sink a little with only its snout and eyes visible. Truitt feared it would go under and attack his legs.

"But Jimbo said you used to drag gators out of their holes at Lostman's Creek," she said, sounding confused and scared.

"He wasn't under oath when he told you that," Truitt said. "The only alligator I've ever touched was a pair of size twelve Bally loafers."

"What do we do?"

"Slowly, very slowly, circle around him toward shore. No sudden movements." He wasn't sure this was the correct advice but it was all he could think of.

Jesus, I don't belong here! What have I gotten us into?

They began sidling along the shoreline, getting space between themselves and the gator, taking care not to splash, Truitt lingering just enough to let Lisa get out of the water first. The gator opened its mouth in a wide yawn.

"We're boring him," Lisa said.

Truitt didn't reply. To him, the gator looked hungry.

They were two steps onto the beach when the gator thrashed its huge tail, and with a powerful surge of its webbed feet, launched itself toward the beach.

"Run!" Truitt shouted.

ல

When he first heard the two airboats ninety minutes earlier, B.G. McClintock knew several things. He knew from the sound that the airboat heading into the deep sawgrass was the same one that left his dock this morning with the Truitt boy and the pretty girl aboard. The roar of a 472-cubic-inch Caddy engine can't be mistaken for anything else. He also knew the pilot of the second airboat was a horse's ass because the man was watching Truitt's boat instead of where he was going, which was straight at old B.G., who was minding his own business, fishing for bass or whatever might jump into his nineteen-foot outboard. He recognized the pilot as Jim Tiger, a petty thief and ne'er do well. He didn't know the fellow wearing the dark suit and shooting a shotgun at Charlie Truitt's son, but he was sure as hell a city boy.

McClintock couldn't keep up with the two airboats in his little outboard, but he followed them at a distance, then eased into the seclusion of a red mangrove hammock half a mile off the island where they both had beached. He sat there, cursing himself for having gone fishing without a firearm. There had been a day when he didn't leave the house without a sidearm, a shotgun, and a rifle, but he had mellowed. He was also on probation and prohibited from carrying guns, though that wouldn't have stopped him in the old days.

I'm getting too civilized.

Didn't it figure, the day you leave your gun home is the day you'll need it?

He waited patiently, hidden by the spreading branches and propped roots of the mangrove trees, and he listened as the engine kicked up on one of the airboats. From the sound, he knew it was Jim Tiger's, and within moments, he saw the boat rounding an outcropping of trees on the island, heading back into the open bay.

McClintock kept perfectly still as the airboat seemed to head straight for him, then quickly realized that Tiger was searching for the creek that would get them out of the bay. When the airboat neared the mangrove, it slowed to a near stop, and the man in the suit struggled to lift something from the deck. As he hoisted it over the gunwale, McClintock saw the shiny chunk of metal that had been in his shed for three years.

It sank into five feet of water with a soft splash, and then the airboat headed for the creek and disappeared.

A few minutes later, McClintock guided his outboard to the spot where the man in the suit had deep-sixed the metal. McClintock jammed a fishing rod into the shallow bottom to mark the spot. It would take two men to get that damn thing into his boat. Then he headed to the small island. As he approached the shore, he saw a ten-foot bull gator slither into the water and disappear, probably headed for its hole. Killing the engine, B.G. coasted to a stop in the shallow water and looked around for the judge and his lady friend.

He didn't see them but heard a feminine voice. "Is it gone?"

Now where the hell?

He looked around, and there they were, a couple of city folk perched on the lower limbs of a pond apple tree, looking as if they sprouted there, just like the bromeliads.

"What the Sam Hill!" B.G. exclaimed.

"The gator treed us," Truitt said. "Your engine scared him off."

The two of them scrambled down and the girl came running to him. "Thanks B.G.," she said, throwing her arms around his neck and hugging him for the second time today.

Whoa doggy! When I tell 'em what's buried in the bay, I reckon I'll get an old-fashioned smooch on the lips.

PART THREE

"Five votes can do anything around here."
—William J. Brennan, Jr. Associate Justice, Supreme Court of the
United States, 1956-1990.

CHAPTER 31

A Man Without Fear

SAM TRUITT WALKED INTO THE ROBING ROOM AT 9:55
A.M., PAUSING A MOMENT TO OBSERVE HIS BRETHREN.
*Nothing has changed. My world is upside down, but nothing here has
changed for two hundred years. Maybe that's the beauty of it. I could slip into
my robes and turn around, and there would be Chief Justice John Marshall
expectorating into a brass spittoon.*

He was torn. In Florida, on the run, Truitt thought he might have
wanted out. But now, listening to the hushed whispers of history in the
marble corridors, with the adrenaline flow of the chase stanched, he wasn't
sure. Not that it would be entirely his choice. Nobody had invited him
back. He simply planned to claim his seat. Just like B.G. McClintock
declaring the Everglades to be his, Sam Truitt would occupy the bench
and dare anyone to remove him.

He tried to sort through the conflicting feelings. Part of him wanted
to spend the next thirty years in the temple of justice. He thought of
Justice Story's classic line: "The law is a jealous mistress and requires a long
and constant courtship." Part of him wanted to be with Lisa, wherever she
might go.

Lisa. Everything comes back to you.

She would make a cameo appearance today, sitting in the law clerk's
section, but then tomorrow, if all went according to plan, she would be
the star.

"We're either going to win the case or both get arrested," she had told
him that morning.

Now, before anyone caught sight of him, Truitt watched his brethren
going about their rituals. The atmosphere was subdued, voices muted, and

Truitt thought of Justice Holmes' famous description of the Court as "the quiet of a storm center."

Oh, you bet Ollie. It's gonna be a Force 5 hurricane at the judicial conference.

Victor Small was fiddling with a cuff link that had become snagged in the sleeve of his robes. He looked up, startled. Guido Tarasi and William Hubbs were in one corner of the room discussing tulips—both were amateur gardeners—when they spotted the junior justice, freezing their conversation in mid-blossom. Gwendolyn Robbins and Debora Kaplan sat at the table, thumbing through the briefs of the day's arguments, neither noticing the black sheep of the family. Powell McLeod stood talking with Chief Justice Whittington. The Chief's back was to Truitt.

"Hey Junior!" It was Curtis Braxton, slugging Truitt's shoulder. "How's the old ticker?"

"Still beating," Truitt said.

The Chief turned around and was clearly shocked.

Braxton leaned close and whispered, "Rumor is you're in fine health, but you ran off to Las Vegas with your law clerk. Best scandal around here since Abe Fortas was having tete-à-tetes with Lyndon Johnson, even better than Thurgood Marshall being an FBI mole."

The Chief Justice strode over to them, his gold-braided robes rusting, color rushing to his cheeks. "Mister Truitt!"

"Whatever happened to Sam?" Truitt demanded. "Or judge? I'm still a justice of the Supreme Court."

"You're on medical leave! What are you doing here?"

"I've had a remarkable recovery." He turned his back on the Chief and opened his closet, removing the black robes. "I'm here for the Atlantica Airlines argument."

"You're not sitting!" the Chief thundered, spraying spittle on the back of Truitt's neck.

Truitt spun around to face him. "No? And who's going to stop me? I took a voluntary leave, and now I'm back. You have no authority to suspend me. If your fellow storm troopers in Congress want to draw up impeachment papers, I'll respond at the appropriate time."

"You may just have to," the Chief sneered, leaning close to Truitt until their faces were just inches apart. "If you attempt to hear a case in which you've been tainted by outside influences, I'll personally see to it that you're impeached, disbarred, and—"

"Tarred and feathered?" Truitt added, helpfully. "I appreciate your concern for both my health and my ethics, but I'm still a justice, and right now, we have a jurisdictional dispute."

"What the hell's that supposed to mean?"

"If you don't get out of my space, I'm going to put you on your lard-filled ass."

From somewhere behind them, Victor Small gasped.

"Just you try it," the Chief said, jaw muscles quivering.

"You first, old man. Take your best shot."

The room was deadly quiet. Planted like trees, holding their ground, Truitt and Whittington glared at each other, daring each other to blink. The spigot was wide open, and Truitt's adrenaline flowed.

"You two better stop pawing the earth like a couple of angry stags," Braxton said, pushing between the men, "'Cause one of you is gonna do something you'll regret. Now, we're supposed to be the one body in the world that resolves disputes with reason, so wouldn't it be better if—"

"Stay the hell out of this, Braxton. This is between Truitt and me," the Chief said, never taking his eyes off the junior justice.

"A justice hasn't been impeached since Samuel Chase in 1805," Braxton went on, "and he was acquitted. So, Chief, unless you've got something you want to share with the rest of us, I've got to assume this is just a personal feud between two pigheaded ex-jocks trying to prove who's got the biggest balls."

The buzzer sounded, a discordant mechanical grinding.

"It's the bell for round one, Chief," Truitt said. "Weren't you the intercollegiate boxing champion? You beat Teddy Roosevelt for the title, didn't you? Or was it Martha Washington?"

Truitt hoped the Chief would slug him. He'd counterpunch and rattle the old buzzard's fillings. But Whittington just stood there, scowling, his face growing redder.

"There'll be a reckoning of this day," the Chief said through clenched teeth. He took a step back and smoothed the wrinkles in his flowing robes. "But now, we have an argument to hear."

He turned on his heel and headed for the courtroom. Like black-feathered geese, the other justices followed, for the first time in memory foregoing the traditional handshake.

Truitt exhaled a long breath and unclenched his fists. So far, the plan was working. He was back on the Court, at least for now. But there was much more to be done.

"Jesus Christ, Sam!" Braxton said as they walked through the red velvet curtain to their seats on the left side of the bench. "You want to tell me what this is all about?"

"Nope. Not yet."

"Be careful, Sam. That old scorpion's still got a stinger."

They settled into their cushioned chairs, Truitt at the far left side, next to the American flag with the eagle atop the pole.

"Oyez, oyez, oyez," the Court crier called out. "All persons having business before the Honorable, the Supreme Court of the United States, are admonished to draw near and give their attention, for the Court is now sitting. God save the United States and this Honorable Court."

God save us all, Sam Truitt thought.

☙

Albert Goldman stood at the lectern, shuffling his feet, running through his canned argument, speaking too quickly in a New York accent, jerking his head nervously, pleading for the victims, all the time keeping his eyes on the Chief Justice. To Sam Truitt, the plaintiffs' lawyer looked like a sinner standing before St. Peter, begging for a place inside the pearly gates. Goldman had the short lawyer's disadvantage of looking even shorter at the lectern. His suit coat was too tight around his bulging middle, and an overhead light turned his bald spot into a shimmering white mirage. Truitt listened, silently rooting for the woebegone mouthpiece, all the time knowing that Goldman couldn't win.

Only I can win, and not out here on the bench, but later, in conference. And I can't do it without Lisa's help.

Truitt made eye contact with her in the law clerks' section. He couldn't wait to see her at the end of the day and wondered how long those overpowering feelings could last. Forever? Why not? Now, like a schoolboy, he calculated the number of hours until she would be in his arms. She would meet him back at their hotel. Truitt hadn't returned home, and Lisa hadn't returned to her apartment. They were staying in a small suite at a residential hotel near Dupont Circle and drove circuitous routes to get from there to the Court and back. Even though Shank could not know they had found the disk, they were taking precautions.

Losing the disk then recovering it turned out to be a blessing, Truitt thought. As far as Shank knew, they were no longer a risk. Still, Truitt had learned not to underestimate the man. They had briefly considered going to the Collier County sheriff's department, trying to get Shank arrested, but there was no physical evidence. It was their word against his, maybe even enough to get him indicted. Besides, going public would reveal their mission and virtually assure that Truitt would never get back on the bench.

As Goldman droned on, Truitt shot a look at Peter Flaherty, taking notes at the respondent's table, waiting his turn. But the man next to the Atlantica lawyer interested Truitt even more. Max Wanaker. He wore a tailored pinstriped suit and sat quietly with his hands folded on the table in front of him. A handsome man pushing fifty with some weathering around the eyes, dark hair turning gray. Wanaker looked up and their eyes met, Truitt's jaw tightening as he stared the man down.

I know what you've done, you bastard.

He wondered if some of his rancor came, not from Wanaker's actions, but from the fact that both of them loved the same woman. Lisa had made excuses for the man. Max wasn't always corrupt, she told him. Maybe not. Maybe he tried to walk a tightrope across Niagara Falls, never intending to get wet. All Truitt knew was that Wanaker was responsible for the deaths of 288 people and had put Lisa directly in the line of fire. He deserved what was coming ... if only they could bring it off.

Thinking about the judicial conference tomorrow, Truitt smiled to himself. What they planned was something that had never been done in more than two hundred years of the Court's existence.

We'll either win or be run out of town.

Though tense and worried, he was at peace with himself. When he came to the Court just two months ago, Truitt feared a thousand ghosts. He was afraid he wouldn't measure up. He was afraid of his enemies, who yearned to run him off the Court, of scandal should his wife ever leave him. He was a prisoner in his chambers and in his home. But now ...

I left my fear behind in the Glades, and a man without fear is all-powerful.

So much had changed in his life in such a short time. He now questioned nearly all his prior beliefs.

I thought I'd devoted my life to justice. But it was the process I worshiped, the tortuous journey through rules and regulations. Lisa's the one who made me see real justice.

Truitt looked toward the rear of the courtroom at the marble frieze above the main entrance. The powers of Evil—Corruption and Deceit—were offset by the powers of Good—Security, Charity, and Peace. A figure representing Justice was flanked by Wisdom and Truth.

The architects and artisans knew what they were doing, he thought. A sitting justice cannot help but focus on the metaphorical figures that stare him in the face. The triumph of justice over the power of Evil. Fancy words, high falutin' theories. But is there justice in a courtroom? You'll find a masquerade ball of great pretenders. You'll find mendacity and fabrication. You'll find sleazy lawyers, inept judges, lying witnesses, and lazy jurors. You'll find a contest to determine which side has the better hired gun and the more appealing client.

But justice, that idealized concept, has to be dragged—kicking and screaming—into this gilded palace. Justice tracks mud across the marble floors.

He listened now as Goldman argued that the summary judgment should be reversed for two reasons. "First, the trial court erred in ruling that the 1978 Airline Deregulation Act bars state claims resulting from air crashes. And second, there is sufficient evidence of Atlantica's negligence to preclude the entry of summary judgment. Therefore a jury—"

"But if you fail on point one, that's the ball game, isn't it?" the Chief asked, seemingly pleased the case might be disposed of so readily.

"Yes, of course," Goldman said, "but our argument hinges on the fact that Congress clearly did not intend to abolish the state remedy for wrongful death when it took jurisdiction of airline safety and regulatory matters. It would not have done so without providing a substitute federal remedy."

"What if you're half right?" Guido Tarasi broke in, professorially scratching at his neat beard with a pencil. "What if Congress didn't *intend* to abolish the state remedy but, by using overly broad language, it accomplished just that? Wouldn't your clients be left without a remedy?"

"It is abhorrent to the law that a tortfeasor be immune from liability," Goldman said, a bit pompously. "In law school, we're taught that, for every wrong, there is a remedy."

Resorting to clichés, Truitt thought. This was not Daniel Webster imploring John Marshall in the Dartmouth College case: *"It is, sir, a small college, and yet there are those who love it."* This was not the aging but elegant former president, John Quincy Adams, arguing cases before Chief Justice Taney. This was not Henry Clay borrowing a pinch from the justices' snuffbox, then waxing eloquent.

"As a former professor," Tarasi said with his gotcha smirk, "I assure you there is much balderdash dispensed in law school." Tarasi waited a moment as the gallery tittered, keeping its chuckling to a respectably low volume. At the respondent's table, Flaherty and Wanaker exchanged little smiles. "Regardless of the harshness of the decision, if Congress abolished the remedy, even inadvertently, would we not be bound to follow the clear dictates of the statute?"

"Yes, but—"

"Let's talk about negligence," Justice Small piped up in his squeaky Ross Perot voice. "Where is it? Where can you point to a single instance in which a breach of the duty of care on the part of the airline contributed to this aircraft being blown out of the sky?"

"It's our contention that flawed maintenance, not a bomb, caused the crash," Goldman said feebly.

"That's your allegation!" the Chief Justice proclaimed loudly, "but where's the evidence? Try as I might, I can't find any negligence of record. Unless you can point to something specific, this tragic crash looks to be a misadventure in every sense of the word, a mishap with no villain, at least not one before the Court."

In the clerk's gallery, Lisa seemed to stir, Truitt thought. She was leaning forward in her chair, shaking her head. From that distance, he couldn't tell, but it seemed she was staring hard at the Chief.

℘

Lisa was stunned, not quite sure she had heard the Chief correctly. Certain words were reverberating in her mind.

"Tragic crash."

"Misadventure."

"Mishap."

"Villain."

Where had she heard those before? Now she was barely listening as the argument continued.

"Perhaps there is no direct evidence, no smoking gun," Goldman said, "but it may be inferred from the sum total of the evidence regarding maintenance defects, FAA inspections, and the like."

FAA inspections! I remember!

"Isn't that a bridge too far?" Hubbs asked. "General complaints about maintenance cannot be tied to this specific crash."

Goldman stood there mutely, his shoulders slumping. After a moment, he said, softly, "We think that's a jury question, Your Honor."

It all came back to her. She had been standing with her ear to the door in Max's hotel suite. Peter Flaherty was boasting about the case, predicting how the opinion would be written.

"Try as we might, we cannot find any negligence of record on the part of Atlantica Airlines. For purposes of this litigation, this tragic crash was a

misadventure in every sense of the word, a mishap with no villain, at least not one before the Court."

How could the Chief Justice use the same words as Atlantica's lawyer? Flaherty hadn't yet gotten to his feet for oral argument. Lisa had virtually memorized the Atlantica brief and knew that the phrases did not appear there, so the Chief couldn't have picked up the words that way.

Unless ...

Unless Flaherty and Whittington had already spoken. Oh sweet Jesus!

The red light came on, and Goldman looked at it with resignation, thanked the justices, and sat down.

Peter Flaherty, general counsel of Atlantica Airlines, staked out an aggressive position. A handsome, tall man in his early sixties, he had worked in the Justice Department as a young lawyer, collecting three goose quill pens for arguing before the Supreme Court.

છ

"First, we believe the trial court ruled correctly on the thorny preemption question," Flaherty said confidently, "but even if it did not, there is simply no evidence of negligence in the record. Nothing! Not a whit!"

Sam Truitt looked into the gallery and saw Lisa, who seemed agitated. Whatever was bothering her would have to wait.

"But the record is replete with the plaintiffs' complaints about insufficient discovery," Gwendolyn Robbins said. "They were thwarted in their attempts to depose the head of maintenance, a Mr. Drayton."

"The company provided a spokesman who had the same access to the records," Flaherty said, without missing a beat. "Mr. Drayton had retired and made himself unavailable to both plaintiffs and defendants. Indeed, Atlantica believed his testimony could have helped its case and desperately tried to find him."

Indeed? Truitt marveled at the man's oily ease in mixing fact and fiction.

No artist ever interpreted nature as freely as a lawyer interprets the truth.

"This plane crashed because of an explosion in the number two engine, correct?" Curtis Braxton asked in his no-nonsense tone.

The former army general might be the only one on the panel to really understand how a jet engine worked, Truitt thought.

"Yes, the terrorists' explosives apparently were planted inside the nacelle. I say 'apparently' because the NTSB never conclusively established the cause of the crash and the plaintiffs have been unable to produce any evidence indicating that the explosion was the result of anything other than the unforeseen criminal act of a third party."

Truitt broke his silence. "If there was no bomb and the plane nonetheless crashed, wouldn't that have been indicative of negligence?"

Flaherty paused before answering. Good lawyers are wary of hypothetical questions, knowing that one often leads to another, and at the end of the road may be a pit of quicksand. "Not by itself," Flaherty said, unwilling to concede the point.

"But isn't it true that we don't expect engines to explode without someone having done something careless or negligent?" Truitt asked.

"There could be design defects that are the manufacturer's responsibility, not the airline's," Flaherty said, employing the lawyer's trump card of shifting the blame.

"But this engine was more than twenty years old," Truitt said. "At this point, shouldn't any defects have been discovered in the maintenance and inspection process, and if they hadn't been, wouldn't that be evidence of negligence by the airline?"

Flaherty smiled, as if he had led the young justice into his trap. "Precisely! But the engine was inspected just eight months before. Neither the fan disk nor anything else revealed any defects or excessive wear. Hence, there can be no negligence, regardless whether there was a bomb or not." He was on a roll, obviously using his prepared argument to answer a specific question. "The airline did all it could. The only wrongdoers are the vicious terrorists. Atlantica is as much a victim as any of the plaintiffs. There is simply no liability here. Now, if I may turn to the issue of—"

"If the disk had been recovered," Truitt broke in, "and metallurgical tests showed indisputably that it wasn't inspected when it was certified to have been, and if tests further showed that the disk ruptured, not from a bomb, but from metal fatigue, would you concede—"

"That's a lot of 'ifs'," the Chief Justice interrupted.

Truitt glared at the Chief, and the other justices shot surprised looks toward the center of the mahogany bench, appraising the Chief's breach of protocol, mocking one of the brethren's questions.

"Nonetheless," Truitt carried on, turning his attention to Atlantica's in-house lawyer, "in such a case, would you concede that the plaintiffs should get to the jury on the question of negligence?"

"*If* those were the facts, Justice Truitt," Flaherty said, smiling confidently, a poker player unveiling four aces, "I'd love to swap places with Mr. Goldman. I'd argue the plaintiff's case."

☙

Lisa began talking even before Truitt had removed his coat. She came out of the suite's small kitchen holding a freshly made martini in a chilled glass. "You're going to need two," she said, handing him the glass. "They've got the Chief in their pocket, Sam."

He took a sip and winced from the searing heat of the icy gin. "Of course they do. He's never met a corporate defendant he didn't like."

"That's not what I mean. They've gotten to him."

"What?"

She told him how the Chief repeated almost verbatim the statement Flaherty made in the meeting with Max. "Flaherty bragged to Max that he could predict how the case would turn out. He even said something like, 'I could write the majority opinion.' That's just what he's done! He must have fed the Chief a proposed opinion, and the Chief parrots it as a question from the bench. 'Misadventure.' 'Mishap.' Blah, blah, blah."

"I can't believe it."

"It's true, Sam. They bought the Chief as insurance."

For a moment, Truitt was speechless. It had never occurred to him. It was unthinkable. In the history of the Republic, no Supreme Court justice was ever known to have taken a bribe.

"I knew he was a prick," Truitt said, shaking his head. "Pompous, vain, egotistical, all of that. But I never figured him for a crook. Never."

"But think about it, Sam. Maybe the photos didn't come to him anonymously. Maybe Shank or Flaherty delivered them. Once the Chief was told you weren't on the team, Atlantica needed him to bounce you off the bench. The photos gave him the ammunition."

Sam drained the martini. It was almost too much to comprehend. Compared to the other branches of government, the Supreme Court was virtually untouched by scandal.

"What are we going to do?" Lisa asked. "He'll fight us with everything he has. We'll never get Tarasi, Hubbs, or Small. McLeod should be on the fence, but if the going gets tough, don't count on him. Even if you can get Braxton and the two women, you've got four votes tops. You've got to concentrate on McLeod."

"We'll never win that way," he said, seeming to think it over.

"What way?"

"Vote by vote. Whittington will call in all his favors. I have to discredit him, knock him off the bench."

"In the next eighteen hours! How?"

"Isn't the Christmas party tonight?"

"Yes, but you can't possibly be thinking about going."

"Not until five minutes ago. Aren't you in some of the skits?"

"I was supposed to do my impression of Gwendolyn Robbins, but that was before I got fired."

"You're rehired. I need you to assure me that the Chief won't get up and sneak back to his chambers to use the phone or take a pee. Can you do it?"

She thought a moment before answering. "If he's a man," Lisa Fremont said, "I'm your woman."

❧

Shank looked out the window of his hotel suite into a blur of snow flurries dusting the trees in the park. He had been listening to Max Wanaker blubber for the past hour. "Are you crazy, trying to kill a Supreme Court justice? They'll have federal marshals and the goddamnn Secret Service crawling all over me."

You spineless piece of shit.

"Forget about that," Shank said. "The bastard got away. Now, just tell me what the hell Sam Truitt was doing on the bench today? What the hell are we paying that blowhard Whittington for?"

"Flaherty says not to worry. It's in the bag."

In the douche bag. Same old Max, same old grease job.

"It better be."

Shank was in an even worse mood than usual today, even though he considered the Everglades escapade to have been a qualified success. He'd dumped the fan disk. But the sight of Sam Truitt in his high-backed chair today had shocked him. Shank had worn tinted glasses and a salt-and-pepper wig and sat in the last row of the gallery. He'd even put on a brown suit instead of his customary gray. He watched Lisa Fremont come into the courtroom a few minutes before ten and take a seat between two marble pillars in the clerks' section.

What the hell is she doing here?

When he saw Sam Truitt come through the parted red velvet curtains, Shank growled, "Well, do me up the ass," and a schoolteacher from Georgia moved her junior high students away from him. The Chief had promised Flaherty that Truitt would be off the Court, but there he was, sitting confidently at the end of the bench, giving Lisa little looks, ain't that touching?

Shank replayed the old fantasy, taking a shot at Truitt, putting one right in his chest, blood spurting like a geyser over his black robes. One for the history books.

His mind drifted a moment, all the way across the Pacific. Katsushika Koshiro wanted to know the minute the case was decided. Shank felt his testicles shrivel just thinking about the Japanese crime boss.

Now it was up to the lawyers and the judges, and if Shank knew anything, it was that strange shit comes down when those bastards get together.

Max was dispensing his chicken-shit advice about balancing the risk against the potential gain. "You should never have gone after Truitt," he said. "We've already got the case won. We've got the Chief Justice, for Christ's sake! He's got the authority, the seniority, the clout."

"He didn't have the clout to keep Truitt off the Court today. I nearly shit my pants when I saw that son of a bitch up there."

Seeing Truitt now in his mind's eye, bullets peppering him.

"I could ace him tomorrow when he pulls into the parking garage," Shank said, shaping a gun out of his right hand. "Bang-bida-boom! And justice for fucking all."

"No!" Max poured himself another Scotch. It was growing dark outside. "Flaherty spoke to Whittington after the argument today." Max looked around, as if someone were listening. "The old guy told Flaherty not to worry. He promised to steamroll Truitt when they have their little conference tomorrow."

"For the two million bucks he's making, he ought to give Truitt a blow job," Shank said.

"Just stop worrying, and don't do anything stupid. Flaherty said this Truitt's a lightweight. Three months ago, he was a lousy professor for Christ's sake. The Chief's been on the Court for twenty-five years. He's holding IOUs from everyone there, and he's calling them in. He says it'll be six-three, just Truitt and the two old broads for the plaintiffs."

"Flaherty's pissing on your leg," Shank said.

"What's that supposed to mean?"

"I've looked into Truitt's eyes, and he's no lightweight."

CHAPTER 32

The Cat Burglar and the Torch Singer

ASSOCIATE JUSTICE VICTOR SMALL WAS SITTING on Chief Justice Clifford Whittington's lap, his head bobbing, his mouth squeaking, "I agree with the Chief! I agree with the Chief!"

Okay, so it wasn't really Small and Whittington. Small was Danny Grossbard, a diminutive law clerk who had been a gymnast at Penn State and law review editor at Virginia. He was the ventriloquist's dummy, and Bill Tanner, a prematurely graying law clerk, wearing an oversize suit with a stuffed shirt—literally stuffed with packing material—was the Chief Justice.

The two clerks, fueled with bourbon-spiked eggnog, were running through a series of inside jokes, the theme being that Small always voted with the Chief, who pulled his strings this way and that. The crowd of law clerks, secretaries, administrative clerks, and marshals roared. In the front row, the justices, by a five-four vote, concurred, Gwen Robbins' hacking smoker's laugh speaking for the majority.

"There are too many lawsuits, too many lawyers," boomed the ventriloquist Chief Justice. "Lawyers as thick as locusts in a biblical plague."

"Lawyers! Locusts! Plagues!" squealed the dummy in agreement, his head bouncing furiously.

Lisa shot a look at Chief Justice Clifford Whittington, the real one, sitting in a high-backed chair. He seemed to be forcing a smile, his ego not allowing him to show that the satire stung. Whittington had come in late, apparently cleaning up paperwork at his desk, letting his brethren know just how taxing it was to be the Chief. He had missed the skit where

Aaron Pitts, one of Braxton's law clerks, portrayed his boss in a Boy Scout uniform loaded with medals, strutting around the makeshift stage, spine straight, chest out, chin tucked in, acting as if he had a steel rod up his ass.

The Chief arrived just in time to see Vic Vazquez doing a pretty good Sam Truitt, wearing shoulder pads and a Wake Forest jersey, bent over a football with Bill Tanner, the Chief, several yards behind, calling out, "Hut one, hut two, hut, hut, hut!" Vic snapped the ball, but instead of rocketing a spiral to the Chief, he slammed it into his own groin. While Vic rolled on the ground in mock pain, Bill admonished him, "No playing with yourself, Sam! It's teamwork that gets the job done."

Whittington laughed at that one.

The law clerks' skits were better suited for the basement of a beer-soaked fraternity house, but they were in the East Conference Room, a stately place with rose-colored carpeting, plush curtains, a coffered ceiling, and a fireplace with the Rembrandt Peale portrait of John Marshall.

Lisa was getting ready for the first of her two skits. Earlier she had called Greg at the hospital in Miami. He sounded strong and said he'd be released in a few days. He was thrilled when she told him they had the disk, and he wished her luck. She would need it.

Lisa glanced at Sam, who was seated next to Gwen Robbins, then at the Chief. Whittington was known to have an exceptionally short attention span. Her job was to make sure he didn't suddenly decide to stroll to his chambers.

Now she joined several other law clerks on the stage, converted into a unisex rest room with nine urinals, a spoof of the plumbing in the old building, which had not been designed for women justices. With one clerk standing at each urinal, back to the audience, Bill Tanner the Chief bellowed, "Short arm inspection! Time to see what the brethren have in their briefs."

Tanner went down the row, apparently examining each justice's equipment, emitting "oohs" and "aaahs" and "tut-tut-tuts." When he came to Lisa, portraying Gwen Robbins, he stopped and did an exaggerated double take.

"Gwendolyn! You're the kind of judge I want on my Court."

"Why's that, Chief?" Lisa cooed, slowly turning to face the audience. "Is it because I speak softly and carry a big ...."

Laughter erupted as the crowd caught sight of a three-foot dildo sticking out of Lisa's suit pants. The loudest roar came from Gwen Robbins, who turned toward Sam Truitt's chair and said, "Damn right." Then she looked into the empty seat and asked, "Where's Sam?"

જ

Sam Truitt leaned his elbows on the open Dutch door of the marshal's office. The deputy on duty would be one of the new ones, he knew, because the others were at the Christmas party.

"Excuse me," he said pleasantly, startling the young woman at the desk, whose head was buried in a *Prison Life* magazine.

"Oh, hello, sir!" It was obvious she recognized him as a justice but couldn't quite remember his name.

"I've done it again," he said, sounding helpless.

"Again?"

"Locked myself out of chambers."

"Oh. I'll let you in then."

"No need," Truitt said. He opened the bottom half of the door by reaching inside and turning the knob, then walked to a wooden cabinet on the wall. The deputy marshal was still in her seat, and Truitt's back blocked her view as he opened the cabinet. I'll just borrow the key, then return it. Wouldn't want you to leave the office unattended."

"Yes, sir."

"Be back in a few minutes."

"You're missing the party," she said.

"Aw, you know Christmas parties," Truitt said. "If you've seen one ..."

જ

Even with the gray wig and the black-and-white bird's-eye wool suit with braiding and black velvet trim, Lisa did not look like Gwendolyn Robbins. The skirt came below the knee. The white silk bow tie was trademark Robbins, but nothing else was quite right. Of course, Gwen Robbins was forty years older, had yellow-stained teeth from a lifetime of smoking, droopy eyelids, a lined face, and stood a petite five feet two. She was beloved by the law clerks for her ability to laugh at herself and her habit of cracking wise about the other justices. Already, as Lisa took the stage, she heard Robbins' raucous laughter.

Okay, Sam, please be careful, and don't make me stay up here all night.

Looking straight at Chief Justice Clifford Whittington, smiling coyly and putting some gravel into her voice to simulate Gwen's whiskey and tobacco contralto, Lisa said, "Some of you may wonder what goes on behind closed doors. Well, just the other day, the Chief invited me to his chambers and asked if there was anything he could do to make my tenure on the Court more fulfilling."

Lisa nodded to Vic Vazquez at the foot of the stage who turned on a boom box, and the music began. "'Well, Cliff,' I said, 'there is one thing.'" With an alluring smile, she sashayed directly toward the Chief and softly crooned to him in a breathless voice that she could use a lover with a slow hand and an easy touch, in her best Pointer Sisters come-get-me voice.

The Chief fidgeted in his chair and a hush fell over the crowd. All eyes were on Lisa as she moved across the stage with writhing, snakelike movements.

"I want somebody who will spend some time.
Not come and go in a heated rush."

Lisa danced with a seductive grace, eyes closed, body in tune to the music. Some of the clerks let loose with wolf whistles.

"A party's a party," the Chief growled unhappily, "but this is still the Supreme Court."

∽

Sam Truitt's hands shook as he pulled on the surgical gloves.

Some cat burglar. If I did this for a living, I'd be one of those guys who drops his driver's license at the scene of the crime.

Leaving the lights off, he worked with a small flashlight, first trying the drawers of the Chief's mahogany desk. They were unlocked.

What am I looking for? The Chief is no fool. If he's on the take, there won't be any numbered Swiss bank accounts lying around.

No. But there might be something. Truitt just didn't know what. Unfortunately, the desk held no surprises so he turned to a file cabinet. Again, unlocked. He opened it and thumbed through hanging folders of memos, docket sheets, calendars—the odds and ends of administering the Court's mundane business.

He looked around, the room spooky in the shadows created by the flashlight. On the wall, a portrait of Oliver Wendell Holmes Jr. seemed to glare at him.

Sorry, Ollie, I know you wouldn't have done this ... but you did say that "life, not the parson, teaches conduct."

Truitt scanned the polished Regency table, the Abraham Lincoln bookcase, his eyes finally coming to rest on the Hepplewhite sideboard.

It was filled with antique plates and pitchers, pewter mugs, and a gravy boat the Chief claimed was used by Dolly Madison, though for all Truitt cared, it could have been Dolly Parton. In the drawers were some knives and forks that looked as if they'd been used to dig foxholes at Valley Forge. Truitt closed a drawer too quickly and two utensils clanged into each other. Then, he heard another sound, something from outside the chambers that froze him.

He stood still and listened. Footsteps echoed down the corridor. If the Chief popped through the door, he was finished. He pictured himself in handcuffs being placed into a police cruiser, the Chief gloating. In addition to numerous violations of the Judicial Canons, his rap sheet would list several felonies: obstruction of justice, evidence tampering, breaking and entering.

He flicked off the flashlight. The footsteps came closer. Someone was approaching but at a leisurely pace. The sound stopped, then started again. After several more steps, silence. Then he figured it out.

One of the court police. Checking the doors.

Did I remember to lock the door when I came in?

The footsteps moved even closer then stopped. He heard the doorknob turning and the squeak of the door as it opened. Damn! The lights came on in the outer chambers and a man called out, "Anyone in there?"

He recognized the voice of Chuck Olson, one of the young Court policemen.

ɔ

Lisa's body undulated to the music, her hips moving fluidly. The other female law clerks and the women on the support staff were on their feet, joining in. Lisa wondered if this was what the Chief had in mind when he suggested a Christmas carol sing-along.

The Chief looked as if he might hold her in contempt at any second.

Where was Sam?

Suddenly, the door to the conference room opened.

Thank God. I'm willing to do almost anything to achieve justice, but I never thought I'd have to die of embarrassment.

In walked Chuck Olson, one of the uniformed court policemen. He looked harried, a man on a mission, not a partygoer. He was in his early twenties, the son of a Baltimore cop, a handsome, polite, shy kid. He scanned the audience, obviously looking for someone. She watched him as he made a slight gesture, trying to get the Chief's attention in the front row, but the Chief didn't notice.

Olson monitors the justices' chambers. Oh shit!

It was time to improvise. She bounded off the stage just as Olson headed toward the oblivious Clifford Whittington. In one nimble motion, Lisa managed to keep gyrating, step gracefully to the floor, and simultaneously peel off her suit jacket and hurl it toward the hooting law clerks. Underneath, her white silk blouse was slick with sweat and clung to her body. She wore no bra, and her nipples were outlined against the thin fabric.

She stood over the Chief now. The only way he could leave the room would be to carry her with him.

She untied the white silk bow tie, drew it from her collar with a slow, exaggerated gesture, then wrapped it around the Chief's neck. It was a sight, Lisa thought, quite likely never envisioned by the Founding Fathers. John Kennedy, maybe; John Jay, probably not.

Suddenly the Chief rose halfway out of his chair, and Lisa nearly panicked, taking a quick backward step. For a moment, Whittington just stood there, as if he intended to take action but didn't know what to do. "Never in the history of—"

"Sit down, Cliff," Gwen Robbins said. "If I had moves like that, I'd be a torch singer, too, but I'd make you horny old bastards pay for it."

☙

Sam Truitt had seen something from his position on all fours under the Chief Justice's desk. But what was it?

Truitt had ducked under the desk just as Chuck Olson came into the chambers and turned on the lights. He heard Olson pacing around the room, checking to make sure nothing looked amiss. Then he heard the crackle of the young cop's walkie-talkie. Olson called in the incident, making it sound as serious as a Brink's million-dollar heist.

"Lock the office," came the scratchy reply on the walkie-talkie, "and inform the Chief Justice of the breach in security."

It was just before Olson turned off the lights that Truitt saw it. Peering out from under the desk's modesty panel, he caught a glimpse of a narrow slit in the satinwood sideboard. The opening was about one foot off the floor and eighteen inches wide, running straight as a carpenter's rule.

It was the right size and shape. It just might be …

A drawer without a handle! A hidden compartment.

Truitt waited until the lights went out and he heard the key turning in the lock, then crawled from his hiding place. He tried opening the hidden drawer with his hands, scratching at the slit with his fingernails, but he couldn't get any purchase. He squeezed his hand behind the sideboard and tried pushing, but the drawer didn't go all the way through, and there was nothing to push.

If it's a drawer at all. And even if it is, what's inside? George Washington's false teeth?

Frustrated, angry, feeling out of control, Truitt wondered what he was even doing there. So stupid. So desperate. The odds were stacked against them from the start. They were outnumbered and always a step behind. So damned aggravating to know the truth but not be able to prove it. Atlantica had bought the Chief. But where's the evidence?

I can't point at the Chief and shout, "J'accuse!" I need the proof. I was hoping for a miracle, but ...

Defeated, Truitt pounded the front of the sideboard with his fist, just above the crack. With a *boing*, the drawer slid open, pushed by a rusty spring.

ↄ

"That's just about enough!"

The Chief Justice's enraged voice drowned out the music. "Turn off that infernal noise!"

Vic Vazquez hurried to the boom box and hit the switch.

"And put your jacket back on!" the Chief bellowed at Lisa. "This is not a burlesque hall." He turned to Olson, "Officer ..."

For a moment, Lisa thought he might say, *"Arrest that woman."*

"What is it you want?" the Chief demanded.

"There's been a security breach, sir."

The Chief wheeled around and stormed out of the room.

ↄ

Truitt had already replaced the key in the marshal's office and was sitting in the passenger seat of Lisa's car when she opened the driver's door and slid inside. Reading in the light of the courtesy lamp, fiercely concentrating on what was in front of him, he barely noticed her.

She leaned over to kiss him. "Thank God that's over. What happened?"

"You won't believe this," he said, kissing her quickly, but getting back to a thick typewritten document. "You just won't believe it!"

"What?"

"It's the Star of India, the Northwest Passage, the Ark of the Covenant. You name it, this is it!" He laughed heartily, waving the document toward the heavens.

"So tell me!"

"You remember the Blue Cross case?"

"Of course. Five to four against requiring the tobacco companies to reveal their secret formulas. Whittington wrote the majority opinion."

"No, he didn't. The tobacco company lawyers did. I have their draft. The lazy bastard didn't rewrite it, even kept the footnotes about tobacco being an honorable American tradition dating back to colonial times."

She started the engine and drove out of the garage, heading back to their hotel. As he read, she glanced at the document. "How do you know where it came from? Is it on their letterhead?"

"Of course not."

"Is there a cover note?"

"No. They're not stupid."

"Then, Sam, how can you tie it to the tobacco company? The Chief will say it's just a draft he was working on, and we can't disprove it."

"As usual, you're one hundred percent right," Truitt said, his voice filled with enthusiasm, "which is why the second opinion is so important."

She stopped at a traffic light on Independence Avenue. Outside, a light snow was falling on the Mall. "What second opinion?"

"Atlantica!" He turned to another document. "It's already written! It affirms the summary judgment on the ground that there's no evidence of negligence, just like Flaherty argued, with a lot of the same language. How will the Chief explain that one—signed, sealed and delivered even before we vote on the case?

"He'll say he was just putting his thoughts on paper," Lisa said, unwilling to share Truitt's excitement. "It's just a coincidence that Flaherty used some of the same terms. It's like the defense of *scenes a faire* in copyright law where similarities are expected in two stories with similar plots. The Chief will say that he and Flaherty think alike, and that's no crime. You're still lacking proof of contact between Atlantica and—"

"It's here!" he yelled, pointing to the document. "Flaherty faxed it to him, but he wasn't careful about it."

In the red-tinged light from the traffic signal, she looked at the tiny type at the top of the page, the sender information automatically affixed by the fax machine: "Atlantica Airlines, Office of General Counsel."

"Omigod, Sam, you did it! It's the smoking gun. You've got him."

"Yeah, I do," he said, "and I'm gonna shake the marble pillars of that old man's courthouse."

"Like Samson," she said.

"What?"

"The first day I saw you on the bench, you seemed so strong and vital, well, it didn't seem like such a stretch from Sam to Samson. If you remember your bible, he was a judge, too."

Truitt thought about it a moment. "And you were Delilah!"

"Right. My job was to shear your locks and sap your strength. But look what's happened. Just like in the bible, Sam, you recovered your powers and you're about to destroy the Philistine temple."

"If I remember my Sunday school lessons," Truitt said somberly, "when Samson brought down the pillars, he was killed, too."

CHAPTER 33

One Scorpion

CHIEF JUSTICE CLIFFORD WHITTINGTON SHOOK HANDS
with each of the associate justices, and they shook one another's in the
round-robin, time-honored ritual. When Truitt approached, the Chief
stiffened but extended his hand. Truitt grabbed it eagerly and wouldn't
let go. Leaning close, he whispered, "It's okay, Chief. We're betting on the
same pony today."

Whittington recoiled. "What?"

Lowering his voice even more, Truitt gave him a conspiratorial wink.
"Atlantica. It's in the bag."

The Chief pulled his hand away, his ruddy complexion going pale.

*Make him think about it. Confuse him. Instead of trash talking, sweet-
talk him.*

He remembered a game against Duke where the nose guard facing him
softly said, *"Ira furor brevis est,"* and as Truitt figured out the translation—
"Anger is brief madness"—he forgot the snap count. Now Truitt imagined
the Chief wondering, "What does that SOB know?"

The justices took their positions in the high-backed chairs at the
green-felt-covered table, with the Chief at the head, and Sam Truitt at the
far end, nearest the door.

"Before we begin our case discussion, let's do some housecleaning,"
the Chief said, "and I mean that quite literally. The less said about the
Christmas party last night, the better, but you'll be pleased to know that
I've taken corrective measures."

"He's overruled Santa Claus," Gwen Robbins whispered.

"I've circulated a memo this morning informing the clerks that henceforth all skits are to be submitted to me in advance for approval," the Chief continued.

Henceforth, Truitt thought, you'll be on the High Court in hell.

"Censorship," Curtis Braxton said.

"A prior restraint, Chief," Gwen Robbins added. "I thought we disposed of that in the Pentagon Papers case in 1971."

"Absolutely right," Debora Kaplan chimed in. "As set forth in *Near versus Minnesota*, there can't be a prior restraint in the absence of a threat to national security."

"I don't think the Chief is saying that the clerks are prohibited from exercising their free speech rights," Guido Tarasi said. "It's a matter of time and place. They could gather for drinks at a neighborhood tavern and criticize us with impunity. But within the confines of this sacred building, the Court has the authority to prohibit crude and offensive expression."

Then let's put a muzzle on the Chief.

"I agree with the Chief," Truitt said, and eight heads turned his way in disbelief. "Let's have a sense of decorum at our festive occasions. Whatever happened to 'Silent Night, Holy Night'?"

For a moment, no one said anything. The brethren appeared stupefied. The last time Truitt concurred with the Chief was when the majority voted for roast beef over ham and cheese for lunch. Truitt smiled guilelessly.

"Thank you for your support, Sam," the Chief said, warily. Then he cleared his throat and moved a stack of briefs from a wooden cart to the table. "First case is *Laubach versus Atlantica Airlines.* As is our custom, I shall begin the discussion. We granted cert because of the preemption issue. I fear that the trial court may have misapplied the Airline Deregulation Act but nonetheless reached the correct result on the summary judgment. First, there can be no doubt that this was a tragic incident that resulted in a horrific loss of life."

Truitt knew the script, having studied Flaherty's fax into the early morning hours: *In such circumstances, there is a natural tendency to attempt to attach blame.*

"In such cases, there is a natural tendency to attempt to attach blame," the Chief said, shaking his head, mournfully. "In difficult cases like this, I never know if I'm Caesar crossing the Rubicon ..."

Or Captain Queeg cutting my own towline, Truitt scribbled on a notepad.

"Or Captain Queeg cutting my own towline," the Chief said with a rehearsed chuckle.

Flaherty does have a way with words, you've got to give him that.

The Chief rumbled on, "Jurors are often carried away when confronted with these situations. They find liability where there is none. They award millions when thousands would do. In this case, the trial judge took a courageous and quite unpopular stand. He just said no. He said there was *no* evidence of negligence, so you get *no* trial by jury."

Just say no. No more Whittington.

"I have scoured the record for any evidence or even the inference of evidence that would contradict that finding," the Chief continued, "but there is none. Therefore, even drawing all favorable inferences in favor of the nonmoving parties, the summary judgment was properly granted because there was no genuine issue as to any material fact."

"I agree!" Sam Truitt said, happily.

"Wait your turn," the Chief snapped. "We go by seniority here. Justice Hubbs speaks next. We're not about to change two hundred years of tradition just because you—" He abruptly halted. "What did you say, Sam?"

"I said I agree with you, Chief. The precise cause of the crash has never been determined, and unfortunately for the plaintiffs, it's their burden to prove causation."

The other justices looked astonished; the Chief was utterly baffled; Sam Truitt was beaming like the village idiot.

The words sound familiar, don't they, Whittington? Now you're rattled. You're wondering why Flaherty didn't tell you I was on board, and you're mad as hell that he must have told me you were along for the ride. Which means I know more than you do. Just how much more, you've got to be wondering.

"Do my ears deceive me," the Chief said, forcing a nervous laugh, "but did the junior justice just agree with me?"

"Are you drunk?" Curtis Braxton hissed at Truitt.

"Sam, I'm disappointed in you," Gwen Robins said.

"I'm with you on this one, Chief," Truitt said, sounding as obsequious as possible. "Without a showing that any tortious act of commission or omission has been committed by Atlantica, this Court has no choice but to affirm."

Yeah, Chief, another of Flaherty's bon mots. Now, you're looking a little flustered. What's the matter, worried you'll have to split the bribe with me?

"If Justice Truitt and I are on the same side," the Chief said, trying to mask his confusion, "I dare say this one could be a unanimous opinion. Do we really need much discussion?"

"Yes, we do," Gwen Robbins said, firmly.

"Gwen, you're just a bleeding heart," Truitt said, reaching into his coat pocket and pulling out a pack of Marlboros. He slipped one into his mouth, turned to Braxton, and said, "Got a light, General?"

"You can't smoke in here," Guido Tarasi said. "Surely you know that."

"Sam, what the hell are you doing?" Braxton demanded. "You don't even smoke."

Truitt felt eight sets of eyes staring at him in total bewilderment.

Good! Keep looking at me as if I'm a madman.

"But isn't that a bit hypocritical of us?" Truitt asked, digging a pack of matches from his pocket. "Chief, you oughta agree. You wrote the majority opinion in favor of the tobacco companies in the Blue Cross case."

"What are you talking about?" Curtis Braxton asked. "Sam, you're losing me."

Truitt lit his cigarette, inhaled deeply, then exhaled a long plume of white smoke. "Where there's smoke, there's fire," he said, cryptically.

"What the hell does that mean?" Gwen Robbins demanded.

"I'm just trying to demonstrate what happens when the Court has been corrupted. And it only takes one. Only one ..." Truitt stood up, another violation of protocol. Pointing a finger as if it were a dagger at the Chief Justice, he calmly said, "There aren't nine scorpions on this Court. There's only one, and that's him. Clifford Whittington has taken bribes from the tobacco companies and Atlantica Airlines, and God knows who else."

"Oh Jesus Christ," Powell McLeod muttered under his breath.

"Mother of mercy," Gwen Robbins said. "Give me one of those cigarettes, Sam,"

"Damn it, Sam," Braxton declared. "You don't accuse a superior officer without indisputable proof."

"Oh, dear," said Victor Small, who looked as if he might faint.

Whittington came to life, pounding the table with his fist. "Lies! Damnable lies! This man is mentally unstable. You all know it. He took a voluntary leave to get himself straightened out, and he never should have come back. You heard me warn him not to take the bench yesterday. I've tried to help him, and this is the thanks I get."

"Sam, if you need psychological counseling, we can get it for you," Guido Tarasi said, sounding concerned.

"He's out of his mind!" Whittington continued, his face reddening. "I have proof he's having an affair with his law clerk. I'll show you the pictures. You can't trust him. He's insane."

"Having an affair with Lisa Fremont seems pretty damn sane to me," Braxton said. "But what about the rest of it, Sam? Are you having delusions? What the hell's going on?"

"My first day here," Truitt said calmly, "the Chief started lobbying me on the tobacco case. We hadn't even read the briefs yet, and he was lining up the votes. I didn't think much of it at the time, but now it's all clear. Everyone always knew the Chief was cozy with corporate litigants, but it's a helluva lot worse than that. He's up for sale!"

"You'd better have proof of that, Sam," Braxton said, shaking his head in astonishment.

"Whittington's questions from the bench yesterday came right out of a draft opinion slipped to him by Atlantica's lawyers. So did his comments at the beginning of conference today. But it gets even worse. The Chief Justice of the United States is in bed with the people who murdered Jerry Klein."

"What!" Braxton bolted upright in his cushioned chair. There was a collective gasp from the others. They couldn't have looked more startled if the crystal chandelier had crashed to the floor.

"Maybe he didn't know they'd actually kill Jerry," Truitt said, "but he's still responsible. He told the henchmen for Atlantica which of my clerks was assigned the bench memo. When it wasn't the one they wanted, they killed Jerry so the assignment would be switched."

"This is an outrage!" Whittington fumed. "You all know me. Who is this man, this ... this fornicator who seeks to divide us?"

"Shut up, Whittington!" Truitt ordered. "I'm not finished yet." He paced alongside the conference table, stopping in front of the fireplace, just beneath the portrait of John Marshall. All eyes followed him. "Deciding these cases is damn difficult, isn't it? All of you have spent sleepless nights worrying whether you're doing the right thing. Whether it's an inmate's last appeal, a deadly dull patent case, or a constitutional issue that harkens back to the Founding Fathers, the answer isn't always clear. Hell, it's seldom clear. I came to this Court with respect for each and every one of you. I knew that Guido Tarasi and I would seldom agree, but damn it I respect his mind and his integrity. We strive for excellence, for true justice. We take the imperfect law administered by imperfect people and try to attain that most elusive of commodities, *veritas*, the truth. We are doomed to fail as often as we succeed, but we still do our damndest, bringing to the table our different backgrounds, our prejudices and preconceptions. We all try to do our best. All except Clifford Whittington. He doesn't care!"

He takes his marching orders from the highest bidder and goes full speed ahead. He's a disgrace to the great jurists who have come before him, and he debases the work that each of you do."

Truitt came back to the table, reached into his briefcase, and slid eight photocopied documents down the table toward the other justices. "Here's what I found yesterday in Whittington's chambers."

"What!" Whittington looked as if might have a stroke. "I'll have the marshals arrest you."

"It's the opinion in *Atlantica*, as scripted by the airline's lawyers, to be carried out by our Chief. In addition to being corrupt, shallow, and weak, Clifford Whittington is also a plagiarist." Glaring at the Chief Justice, Truitt said triumphantly, "It's all over, Whittington. You just cut your own towline."

&

The shouting lasted an hour.

Whittington denied and denied and denied. Guido Tarasi, who was once a U.S. attorney, cross-examined, demanding an explanation for the documents, asking about the sender identification imprint on the fax. "What about it, Cliff? It appears the fax originated in the office of the airline's general counsel."

"An obvious forgery!" the Chief, thundered. "You can reprogram a fax machine to say a document came from heaven itself. Can't you see this is a conspiracy of the plaintiffs' lawyers and Sam Truitt to chase me off the bench?"

"Then you've never seen this document before?"

"Never!"

Tarasi studied the document. "What about your questions from the bench, your statements at the beginning of conference today? They're direct quotes."

"Pure coincidence!" claimed the Chief, whose eyes flicked from one justice to another, soliciting support. Most avoided his gaze; some appeared horror stricken. Frantically trying to turn the tide, he began sputtering, "How do we know Truitt didn't write these himself? Perhaps he and I talked about the cases. He picked up my speech patterns. I'm known to use certain phrases. I'm considered quite eloquent, am I not? He insidiously took my words, twisted them to his own liking, and put them into these counterfeit documents, these forgeries, these fabrications."

The other justices murmured among themselves in disbelief.

The Chief paused and withdrew a monogrammed handkerchief from his coat pocket. He wiped beads of sweat from his forehead, and like a filibustering senator, continued the attack on his accuser. "Why even listen to this man who admits breaking into my chambers, this criminal? What has he done? He purloined documents. He invaded my privacy. He conducted an illegal search and seizure, did he not? Under *Mapp versus Ohio*, you can't consider the evidence. It must be excluded."

"For somebody who'd like to overturn the exclusionary rule," Truitt said, "you've suddenly become quite fond of the Fourth Amendment."

"You bastard!" the Chief wailed, his face crimson.

Tarasi looked sadly toward his old friend. "Cliff, a moment ago you said the documents were fabricated. You denied ever seeing them. Now you accuse Sam of stealing them. You can't have it both ways."

"It's called pleading in the alternative," Whittington stammered. "It's a wise practice, really. Maybe he stole them, and then again, maybe he didn't."

Maybe the mess boys stole the strawberries, and then again ...

They were all silent then, watching with horror as Whittington tried to stand, then sank back into his chair, shrunken and defeated, deserted by his brethren.

"What do we do now?" William Hubbs asked.

"I don't know," Guido Tarasi said. "It's never happened before. I suppose we contact the attorney general and—"

"No," Truitt said. "Let's preserve one tradition today. Nothing said in this room will ever be repeated outside."

"What?" Gwen Robbins asked. "You're not suggesting we cover this up."

"No. But for the sake of the Court, we should resolve it ourselves. We must not do anything to tarnish the institution." Again, Truitt reached into his briefcase. "I've taken the liberty of preparing a letter of resignation for the Chief, effective today." He handed the paper to Gwen Robbins, who passed it on down the table until Tarasi gave it to the Chief. Whittington stared at the document but made no move to sign it.

"No," he muttered, his voice barely audible.

"Cliff, it would shake the foundation of the Republic if you insist on fighting this," Tarasi said. "What you've done makes Watergate look like a fraternity prank. Resigning will spare you untold humiliation and will preserve the integrity of the Court."

His face slack and turning gray, Whittington looked as if he'd aged fifteen years in the past hour. He turned to Guido Tarasi, his eyes pleading.

"Trust me, Cliff," Tarasi said. "It's for the best."

His hand trembling, Whittington picked up his fountain pen and, with all the dignity he could muster, said in a weak voice, "As a matter of fact, I have been contemplating retirement for some time. The President will understand." With that he scrawled his name on the signature line, stood up, bowed stiffly to the others, and left the conference room for the final time.

"Now what?" Victor Small asked.

"We have three cases to resolve," Guido Tarasi said, "beginning with *Atlantica*."

A moment later, there was a knock at the door. In keeping with the custom of the Court, the junior justice answered it.

CHAPTER 34

A Court of Law...Not of Justice

SHE CAN'T COME IN HERE!" GUIDO TARASI SAID, raising his voice for the first time Truitt could remember. "Sam, if you want to talk to your law clerk, go outside, but she can't ..."

His voice trailed off as Truitt stepped into the foyer, leaving Lisa standing in the doorway, holding a briefcase, looking both demure and professional in an Anne Klein dark gray suit.

With Lisa a step behind, Truitt came back inside, lugging a heavy wooden carton.

We're halfway home. Now, with the brethren babbling, with confusion reigning, we have to strike quickly.

"Sam, would you please tell me what's going on here." It was Tarasi again, having taken over from the Chief. "The sanctity of the conference has never been breached. Never! Now, we've just had a traumatic event, perhaps the most traumatic in the history of the Court. Let's not add anarchy to the chaos."

Lisa watched as Truitt opened the carton with a clunk, dropped a heavy triangular piece of machined titanium onto the felt-covered table.

"What's that?" Victor Small asked, moving away from the object as if it were a bomb.

A look of recognition spread across Curtis Braxton's face. "It's a piece of a jet engine fan disk. Sam, how the hell did you—"

"Atlantica's maintenance chief found it the morning after the crash," Truitt said. "The company tanked it before the NTSB got there, but Lisa and I recovered it."

"Evidence!" Tarasi cried out. "Evidence that's not part of the record. Sam, we've got to follow procedures. We've got to follow rules."

"We've got to do justice," Truitt said.

"Not this way," Powell McLeod said. "We're judges, not detectives. We sit here with blinders on. We're duty bound to exclude from view everything not properly before us."

"Then we're going to perpetuate a horrible injustice," Truitt said. "Atlantica Airlines killed two hundred eighty-eight people, covered it up, then corrupted this Court by trying to steal the case."

"By God, Truitt, this isn't a debating society," William Hubbs brayed. "You can't do this!"

"Yes we can, Bill. Someone has to."

Gwen Robbins was shaking her head. "Sam, you're fond of quoting Holmes. Well, he once said, 'This is a court of law, young man, not of justice.' We don't like to think of it that way, but Holmes was right. We follow the law. We follow rules and procedures even if injustice sometimes results."

"Then it's time to change the way we do business," Truitt said, his heart sinking.

If we don't have Gwen, we can't win.

Braxton sat stiffly in his chair, shaking his head. "Sam, you know I'd love to help you, but I've spent half my life following orders and the other half giving them, and always by the book. You've gone way outside the chain of command on this one."

And without the General, we're doomed.

"What you're asking is quite extraordinary," Debora Kaplan agreed.

"Unheard of," Powell McLeod said.

With the rumble of voices growing against him, Truitt looked toward Lisa for help.

They're so caught up in rules and traditions that they won't hear the truth. We've come so far. We can't fail now.

Lisa pointed to the fan disk. "You can all see the fracture line. It was caused by metal fatigue."

"This is outrageous!" ranted William Hubbs. "We're listening to ex-parte argument in conference. Guido, we must adjourn at once before we're tainted by this."

Tarasi nodded his assent. "Ms. Fremont, I must ask you to leave."

"We're judges," Truitt protested, "not automatons. Have the guts to hear her out. Then disregard all of it if you want. Tell her you care only about the rules, not the truth."

"Just a second, Guido," Gwen Robbins said. "We're not an impressionable jury. We can always reject what she says, but I want to hear what Sam thinks is so damned important."

ℝ

Shank was in his Washington hotel suite when the call came from Peter Flaherty in Miami. CNN had just reported that the Chief Justice of the United States had suddenly resigned. A messenger had delivered a one-page letter to the White House, and the Chief was unavailable for comment.

"What the hell's going on up there?" Flaherty asked.

"Truitt!" Shank spat. "It's got to be him."

The Chief was supposed to bounce Truitt off the bench, not the other way around!

"What? How?"

"I don't know," Shank said, "but I'm gonna find out."

He took a cab to the Supreme Court, his adrenaline surging, his mood darkening. He measured his rising tide of emotions, trying to distill his jumbled feelings. Disgust for Max, this whole thing was his goddamn fault. Hatred of Lisa and that swamp rat judge. And fear, too. A knot formed in his gut thinking about Katsushika Koshiro. Shank knew the price of failure. He'd given his guarantee. He'd bet it all, not just his little finger. Flaherty had told him that the Court was supposed to vote on the *Atlantica* case that morning. The case could already have been lost. If so, he was a dead man.

But I won't lay down for them ... and I'll take out the judge and his little whore first.

The cab ride took only ten minutes. Reporters jammed the press office and spilled out into the corridor. Wearing a badge that identified him as an Associated Press employee, Shank spent five minutes at the edge of the throng, listening to the yelled questions and the subdued answers from the press officer. He learned that the Chief Justice gave no reasons for his sudden resignation and was in seclusion with his family. The other justices were still in conference and would answer no questions.

Someone's sure as hell gonna answer my questions.

Shank waited until a uniformed Court policeman looked the other way. Then he took a staircase up to the second floor and entered the office immediately adjacent to Sam Truitt's chambers. There was no one there, so Shank sat down and propped his feet on the desk, looking up at a poster of the rocky coastline of Tasmania.

∽

They were giving her a chance. With Sam smiling at her, nodding his approval as she spoke, giving her confidence, Lisa went through the story from the beginning. She told the justices how Atlantica had falsified its records, how the mechanics never did the tests, and how the disk ruptured from metal fatigue.

Lisa reached into her briefcase and began handing documents to the justices. "Here are the drawings made by Joe Drayton, the maintenance chief. His account of pencil-whipped records was corroborated to me personally by Max Wanaker, president of the airline."

All eyes were on the chunk of titanium. Lisa felt a sense of excitement building inside her. They were listening intently. "These people will stop at nothing. They corrupted the Court and they killed Jerry Klein. One of you could be next."

The justices murmured among themselves.

"Let's get to proximate cause," Braxton said, practical as ever. "How do you know the disk caused the crash?"

"We had a lab perform a Fluorescent Penetration Inspection over the weekend," Lisa said. "Technicians shined ultraviolet light on the metal, which had been coated with a dye. It showed a tiny defect under the crack, no larger than a grain of sand, what they call a hard alpha inclusion. It caused the disk to break up. Had Atlantica performed the test, the defect would have shown up, the disk would have been replaced, and no one would have been killed."

"How do you know the inspection wasn't performed?" Tarasi asked, becoming involved for the first time. "All you have is the word of this former mechanic. He could have had a grudge against the company."

Lisa handed out a second set of documents. "The lab did a mass spectroscopy test, too. If the FPI had been done, there would have been traces of triphenyl phosphate on the disk, but as you can see, there wasn't any."

"What about 2-ethylhexyl diphenyl phosphate?" Curtis Braxton asked, and the other justices shot him astonished looks.

"No trace," Lisa said. "You'll find that on page three of the report."

"Then they didn't do the test," Braxton said. Looking at the others, he stifled a smile and explained, "I studied chemical engineering before the army sent me to law school."

"What do you think, Curtis?" McLeod asked. It was a rare question from the most imperturbable of the justices.

"It makes sense," Braxton said. "With the disk and the tests, the plaintiffs could prove negligence and causation. At the very least, they've got themselves a jury question."

Turning to Lisa, Tarasi asked, "What is it you're asking us to do?"

"Just make it a fair fight. Let the plaintiffs try the case now that they'll have the evidence."

"That's cutting to the heart of it," Gwen Robbins said. "The victims' families never even had a trial. Let's give 'em their day in court. I vote to reverse. Now who's with me?"

"The voice in my head tells me we cannot rule this way," Braxton said. But …"

The others waited. With his military bearing and adherence to honor and duty, Curtis Braxton was a figure of towering integrity. "My heart tells me that this young lady is right. We cannot foist a terrible injustice on the families of nearly three hundred people, and we cannot exonerate those who have been so callous toward human life. I vote to reverse."

"I concur," Debora Kaplan joined in.

"With me, it's four," Truitt said.

One more, Lisa thought. All we need is one more!

"Have you all lost your minds?" Tarasi pleaded. "How will you write the opinion? Surely you can't refer to this so-called evidence."

"If I may make a suggestion, Lisa said, "you could—"

"You may not!" Tarasi interrupted. "And since we are apparently voting on this matter, I must now insist that you leave. We've destroyed quite enough traditions for one day."

છ૭

Lisa shot a look at Truitt, who winked and gave her a warm, loving smile. She'd done all she could. Now, Sam would have to corral another vote. She picked up her briefcase and left the room, passing a marshal and court policeman in the corridor and saying a brief prayer on the way back to her office.

Lisa opened the door and found the lights off and the blinds drawn. She reached for the switch and flicked on the lights. Her Tasmania poster no longer hung on the wall. It lay across her chair, nearly sliced in two.

Oh no! Not here!

She heard a click behind her and wheeled around to see Shank turning the lock on her door. Then he leaned against the door and began idly cleaning his fingernails with a black knife. "Glass-filled nylon," he said, gesturing with the blade. "Doesn't set off the metal detector downstairs, cuts paper cleanly, and will carve my initials on your belly before you can say your Hail Marys."

She was numb with fear. Before she could scream, before she could move, his left hand shot out, grabbed her by the wrist and pulled her close. He pressed the knife to her neck. She started to cry out, but the pressure of the blade on her throat petrified her. The scream died before it reached her lips. Her mind raced.

If he's going to kill me, please God ... let it be quick.

⁇

Guido Tarasi paced around the conference table, looking exhausted. The chaotic events of the day had drained him. "What is it you're looking for, Sam?" he asked, exasperated.

"Unanimous reversal would be best," Truitt said.

"What!" Tarasi appeared stunned.

"I agree," Gwen Robbins said, nodding, seeing the wisdom of it. "We overturn the cockamamie preemption holding, cite one case for the proposition that summary judgment should be cautiously applied in negligence cases, then hold that the plaintiffs were deprived of sufficient time for discovery. Nothing earth-shattering, no violation of precedent."

"We can't do that," Tarasi said. "It's intellectually dishonest."

"Guido, we can do anything," she replied. "We're not the Supreme Court because we're infallible. We're infallible because we're the Supreme Court."

Victor Small cleared his throat. "If we do what you say, Gwen, we must never breathe a word of what happened today outside this room."

"We never do, Vic," Tarasi said, irritated. "That's not the point."

William Hubbs said, "If Vic votes to reverse and it will help resolve this crisis, I'll go along."

"If Bill's in, so am I," Powell McLeod said.

Sam Truitt forced himself not to smile, not to shout. He wished Lisa were here to share the moment and couldn't wait to tell her what a fabulous job she'd done. God, he was so proud of her, so lucky to have her. He let his mind wander just a moment, imagining their life together. She was going to be a great lawyer and wonderful wife.

"That leaves only you, Guido," Gwen Robbins said. "Do you want to write a dissent?"

"And air this dirty linen for the *New York Times?*" he asked. "The integrity of this Court is the paramount concern. If the public loses faith in this institution, the Republic may not fall, but it will be sorely wounded." He frowned and lowered his eyes, as if he couldn't bear to say the words. "For the sake of the nation, I reluctantly concur. It's unanimous for reversal."

Lisa, darling, we've done it. Justice against overwhelming odds.

We're a helluva team, he thought, which made him ponder all the other things they could do together over all the coming years. For the first time in ages—he couldn't remember how long—Sam Truitt was a truly happy man.

೮೧

Shank ran his free hand down over Lisa's body, following the contours of her jacket. Then, he took the knife and inserted it under the top button and sliced the threads. The silver button popped off, and he went after the next one, and then the third. When the buttons were scattered on the floor, he yanked the jacket open by the lapels and inserted the knife at the neck of her gray silk blouse.

Lisa held her breath and instinctively moved backward, but Shank's free hand gripped the back of her neck. "You ain't goin' nowhere, Lisa, so just relax. You might as well enjoy it."

With a downward thrust of the knife, he sliced the blouse open from her neck to her waist. She gasped and again reflexively moved backward, but he increased the pressure on her neck and jammed her head forward. This time the tip of the knife dug into the skin between her breasts, pricking her, drawing blood. With a quick motion, he cut the bra in two, then roughly pulled it off. He held her jacket open by one of the lapels, and she shivered with terror.

"I wonder," he said, "if anyone's ever gotten screwed in this building, besides getting fucked up the ass by the judges."

"I'll scream," she said.

"And I'll cut out your heart."

She fought against the fear, which threatened to paralyze her.

Stay calm. Reason with him.

"Does Max know you're here?" she asked, forcing a tone of normalcy into her voice.

Shank laid a calloused hand on her right breast and squeezed hard. She winced as his thumb and forefinger closed over her nipple.

"Max can't help you now. You've ridden that old horse straight to the glue factory." He pinched her breast, then laughed. "Look at that. Your nipples are as hard as little jujubes. You must like me."

"Please ..."

"Please what? Please don't kill me. Please fuck me. Please *what?*"

"Horror gripped her.

She braced against a wave of nausea.

Don't let him see your fear.

"Why, are you too good for the old Shankster, you skinny bitch!" He squeezed her breast so hard Lisa gasped and her knees buckled as the pain shot through her. Then he let go and propped her up with one hand, raising the knife with the other to the tip of her nose. "You're afraid of the knife, aren't you, Lisa? It's that sound of tearing flesh that puckers up the old asshole."

Panic rose in her throat, choking her. She felt as if she couldn't get enough air.

"I could put the blade up your nose like Polanski did to Nicholson in *Chinatown*, unless you got a better idea where it could go."

She was too terrified to respond.

"Maybe where the judge puts his? I watched you on the video, Lisa. I listened to the noise you make. Over and over, a hundred times I watched you when I was alone. Only I'd change the ending. I'd make it a snuff flick. It'd be me there instead of the judge, and I'd fuck you to death."

Shank waited for a reaction, and when he didn't get one, he pressed his lips to her neck, brushing back her hair, flicking inside her ear with his tongue.

The cold, wet feel of his tongue made her stomach heave. She'd rather be licked by a snake.

"No earrings today, Lisa. What a pity." He was sucking at her earlobe, making a slurping sound.

"Please stop," she cried, fighting for control, her mind urging her body to summon strength. "What do you want?"

"Ain't it clear?" he asked. "I want you, Lisa, but I also want some information. Whittington got caught, didn't he?"

She didn't hesitate. She wanted to keep him talking. "Yes."

"And the case? Are they hearing it without him?"

I need to buy time. If he thinks the case is over, one way or the other, he'll kill me now.

"No."

"What then? Tell me!"

"They've deferred ruling on all cases Whittington heard," she said, making it up as she went along.

He grabbed a fistful of her hair and pulled her tight against him. "Bullshit!"

"It's true. Whittington was tainted, and the justices wanted to put some time and space between themselves and the cases. *Atlantica* will be scheduled for reargument after a new justice is confirmed."

Shank seemed to think it over, some of the sadistic anger draining out of him. "So the fat lady hasn't sung. There still won't be any grounds for reversal, especially if you're not around to cause trouble." Again, he pressed the knife to her neck. "How do you want it, Lisa? Fast and easy, or slow and hard."

Buy time, keep him talking.

"We have the disk," she blurted out.

His face froze. Then he seemed to think it over and growled a humorless laugh. "Like hell you do!"

"You were seen dropping it. We fished it out of the bay in the Glades. It's under lock and key in Miami."

He let go and backed off. Her legs felt rubbery. He'd been propping her up, and now, she had to concentrate just to stand.

"Miami? Why Miami?" he demanded.

Because if I said it was here and couldn't get it, you'd kill me. Miami gives me time.

"It's in a lab for testing."

"Name, address! Where is it?"

"In an industrial section near the airport, but that won't do you any good. It'll only be released to Sam or to me, and if one of us doesn't show up to claim it, they're under instructions to deliver it to the plaintiffs' lawyer."

"You're lying," he said, but there was uncertainty in his voice.

"Then kill me. Kill Sam, too. Kill the whole damn Court." She fought the tears that were welling in her eyes as she thought of Sam.

Sam, I love you and I need you.

Shank grabbed her by the neck and shoved her across the room. She banged into the wall and grabbed onto a bookshelf to keep from falling.

Shank picked up the phone on her desk and called a number. When someone answered, he gave a suite number. After a moment, he said, "Max, tell them to saddle up the corporate jet. We're going home, and we've got a hitchhiker."

CHAPTER 35

Test Cell

INCREDIBLE, TRUITT THOUGHT. Wait till Lisa hears who's writing the opinion.

Hurrying back to Lisa's office to tell her the news, he marveled at her courage and competence, at how she came through when he needed her, and how they had accomplished the impossible. He'd never known anyone like her. Hell, there *wasn't* anyone else like her.

Now, they could be together. They should plan the rest of their lives, but where should they start? He couldn't get over the events of the morning.

Amazing! I'm on the Court and the Chief is off. He opened the door to Lisa's office, and for one moment, nothing made sense.

The Tasmania poster was draped across her chair, sliced in two. Lisa's bra lay on the floor, the fabric cut cleanly between the cups. He spotted a large button on the floor near the bookcase, then two more.

Then it all made horrifying sense, and he dashed into the corridor. He raced down the stairs to the marshal's office, and stunned everyone by demanding to know if anyone had seen Lisa. No one had. He tore down another corridor, nearly knocking over Chuck Olson, the young Court policeman, as he entered an open elevator. He hadn't seen her either.

"You're in a hurry, too," came the scratchy voice from inside the ornate, brass-doored elevator. It was Harold Franklin, the octogenarian elevator operator who, legend had it, came with the building. "That fellow with your law clerk was in a hell-fired hurry."

"When? Where?"

"Just took them down to the garage a minute or so ago."

Truitt shot a look into the elevator, decided against it, ran down the stairs, then out the rear entrance of the building. It was cold and sunny, the street gutters packed with blackened snow. Truitt could see his breath as he bolted toward the opening of the underground garage at the rear of the building. He reached the ramp just as two cars approached. Lisa's gray Toyota was stopped on the exit ramp, waiting for the mechanical arm to lift. Vic Vazquez, in his ancient Olds Cutlass, was stopped at the entrance gate, trying to slide his access card into the slot while jamming a slice of pizza into his mouth with his free hand. Truitt ran toward Lisa's car, which shot forward just as the arm lifted. He saw her terrified face and the shape of a man in the backseat, an arm wrapped around her throat. The man was looking to the right as if checking the oncoming traffic.

"Out!" Truitt yelled at Vazquez, who mumbled something incomprehensible.

Truitt yanked the door open and grabbed his shocked law clerk, pulling him out of the car. The pizza slice fell to the ground. Truitt leapt in and threw the car into reverse. "Do you have a cellular in here?" he demanded.

"On my salary?"

Truitt was already pulling out when he yelled, "Call the police!"

"And tell them what?" Vazquez asked, but Truitt was gone.

Truitt caught sight of the Toyota turning right onto Independence Avenue. He floored the Cutlass, waited as the engine backed off then fired up, and went after them, shooting past a tourist bus made to look like a trolley. By the time he turned onto Independence, heading west, he'd lost sight of the Toyota. He prayed they hadn't turned onto a side street.

He passed the Capitol on his right, then the museums along the National Mall. Finally, he saw the Toyota stopped at a traffic light at Sixth Street. He was half a block behind, looking around frantically, hoping for a policeman, a friend, anyone who could help. He thought about getting out of the car and running up to the Toyota, but if the light changed ...

The light flashed to green, and the Toyota shot through the intersection.

✄

"It could have been so easy," Shank was saying. "All you had to do was play along, and none of this shit would have come down."

They were on the bridge, crossing the Potomac, heading into Virginia. Lisa wore a trench coat over her torn clothing, and with the car's heater on high, was beginning to perspire.

"Play along?" she said. "With you. With Max, with the people who killed Tony."

"I got news for you, Lisa. You and Tony are gonna be together again real soon."

In the rearview mirror, she saw the white Cutlass with the rusted hood. She'd seen it behind them on Independence Avenue, and she'd stopped at the traffic light at Sixth Street even though it was still yellow and Shank was yelling at her to run it.

"If you want a policeman to stop us, it's fine with me," she had said, and he quieted down.

She still had a chance. Sam was coming for her.

&

Sam Truitt followed the Toyota across the bridge and onto the Washington Memorial Parkway. He considered coming alongside and forcing them off the road, but what would that accomplish? He could end up injuring Lisa. Or Shank might kill her right there in front of his eyes.

He was still trying to figure out what to do when the Toyota pulled off at the exit to National Airport, and Truitt cut across two lanes in pursuit.

A few minutes later, he nearly lost them again. Headed toward the terminal, the Toyota suddenly turned onto a perimeter road. Stuck in the wrong lane, unable to turn, Truitt went through the intersection, did a U-turn in front of oncoming traffic, eliciting a blaring of horns. He doubled back, but by the time he made the turn, the Toyota was out of sight.

Cursing, he pounded his steering wheel. He was desperate. Where were they?

&

Shank pointed toward a ten-foot-high fence topped with razor wire, and Lisa turned into an access lane. Inside the gate, an industrial building seemed to stretch for a mile. A sign with the company logo, an A with wings, read: ATLANTICA AIRLINES HANGAR AND ENGINE SHOP—AUTHORIZED PERSONNEL ONLY.

They stopped at a security kiosk where a bored security guard sat on a high stool. Shank waved at the man, who recognized him and pushed a button opening the gate. They drove into the parking lot, stopping next to the massive building near the door.

A worker in a hard hat drove by on one of the small, open trucks they call tugs. Lisa thought about screaming, running, doing anything to get away, but in a moment, he was gone, and they were inside the hangar. Shank had clipped his ID badge to his suitcoat and they walked across a solid concrete floor deeper into the structure.

On one side were several aircraft, some with parts removed. On the other side, huge jet engines hung from the ceiling on heavy steel trolleys and hoists, like mechanical sides of beef.

Workers on forklifts moved crates of parts through the massive building, and there was the drone and hum of machines echoing off the rock hard floors.

I could run, but how far would I get? I could scream, but would they even hear me?

"Try anything, and you're dead," Shank said, as if reading her mind.

They passed what looked like a five-story concrete building inside the hangar and heard a muffled roar from the other side of the walls. A sign read DANGER—TEST CELL, and a red light flashed, warning that a jet engine was being run at full power.

Just past an employees' cafeteria, they stopped at a door marked EXECUTIVE ENTRY ONLY. Shank used a key on the lock, and they stepped into an incongruously plush waiting room, similar to a VIP lounge at an airport. There were leather chairs, a large-screen TV, a bar … and Max Wanaker.

∽

Truitt nearly missed it. He was looking for the Toyota, so he almost missed the sign. It was an industrial street of warehouses, machine shops, and businesses servicing the airport. Caterers, engine repair, freight forwarders, and finally there it was: Atlantica's logo.

Truitt pulled up at a security kiosk where a uniformed guard appeared, armed with a clipboard.

"I'm with Mr. Shakanian," Truitt said, rolling down his window.

The guard looked puzzled.

"Didn't Shank just come through here?" Truitt asked, as if they were old friends. "Shank and a woman in a gray Toyota?"

"Yeah, few minutes ago, but he didn't say anything about another visitor."

"I was supposed to be right on his tail, but I got caught in traffic."

"Uh-huh. I'll just call it in."

The guard returned to the kiosk and picked up the phone. Truitt floored the accelerator, waited a second for the old engine to gather its strength, then tore out, splintering the gate arm.

༼

Max had a drink in his hand and it wasn't his first of the day.

"Lisa! What …" He turned to Shank. "What's she doing here? What's going on? I thought we were going to leave her out of this. Didn't I tell you—"

"Max, you are one sorry sack of shit," Shank said. "She's the one who won't let us out of it. She's got the fan disk!"

"I don't care," Max said, sounding both exhausted and defeated. "I just don't care anymore."

Shank laughed. "What's the matter, Maxie? Having a little burnout? A midlife crisis … or end-of-life crisis 'cause if we lose the case, you're—"

"We lost! We already lost."

"What are you talking about?"

Lisa looked toward Max, her eyes pleading.

Please, Max! Whatever you know, keep quiet.

"They voted this morning," Max said. "Eight to zero. Truitt's going to write the opinion."

"How the hell do you know that?" Shank demanded.

"One of Whittington's clerks heard, then the clerk told Whittington, who called Flaherty to tell him he was sorry."

"Eight zip?" Shank said, incredulously, wheeling toward Lisa. "You lying bitch!" He backhanded her across the face. She stutter-stepped backward from the force of the blow and tears welled in her eyes. Red marks rose across her cheekbone where Shank's knuckles had struck her.

"Don't touch her!" Max yelled.

Shank wrapped his forearm around Lisa's neck and tightened his grip until she gasped.

"Let her go!" Max insisted.

"No way."

The gunshot tore into a leather chair. Shank froze a moment, then turned around and released Lisa. Max was shakily pointing a nine-millimeter Glock at him.

"If you hurt her, I'll kill you," Max said, his voice quavering.

Shank barked out a laugh. "You stupid bastard. What do you think Koshiro's gonna do? We're both dead men."

"I'll reason with him," Max said.

"You can't talk your way out of it, Max. You can only buy your way out, and you don't have two hundred million dollars."

"Then there's no reason to threaten Lisa. Let her go."

"Screw that! She's the one who did it. I'm taking her down."

"I'll shoot you," Max said, pointing the gun at Shank, hand trembling.

Shank curled a lip in a nasty smile. "You ain't a killer, Max. If you were, you wouldn't have needed me." He advanced on Max, who took a step backward.

"Shoot him, Max," Lisa pleaded. "Shoot him or he'll kill us both."

"For some people, it's easy," Shank said, looking Max hard in the eyes. "For others, it's damn near impossible. Some people can't put down a flea-bitten dog or a horse with a bum leg, much less a human being."

"That leaves you out," Lisa said. "Shoot him, Max!"

"Stop right there," Max said, the gun doing little circles in his hand.

"Nah. You stop," Shank replied. "Give me the gun, Max."

"I'll shoot! I'll do it."

"No you won't."

Shank closed the distance. They were four feet apart. Max tried to steady the gun with both hands, his finger tightening on the trigger. Suddenly, a discordant ringing startled Max. The gun jumped in his hands and fired, putting a hole in the wall. Before Max could get off another shot, Shank grabbed the gun and twisted it from his grip, then slammed the butt into his temple. Max fell backward over a hassock and lay on the floor moaning.

A telephone rang a second time. Finally, Shank pulled a cellular from his inside suit pocket and answered the third ring with a gruff "yeah." Then he shot a look at Lisa, who had gone to Max's side and was holding his head in her hands. "Here?" Shank said. "He's here?"

Shank clicked off the phone. "You got another guardian angel, Lisa. You better hope he's not a fallen one like old Max here."

He pulled Lisa away from Max who struggled to get to his feet, holding his head. Blood seeped from between his fingers.

"He's hurt," Lisa said. "He needs help."

Shank aimed the gun at Max's chest and pulled the trigger. The gunshot knocked Max backward into the wall. Blood sprayed over Lisa, who screamed, and Max crumpled to the floor.

"Not anymore," Shank said.

☙

Truitt was crouched behind an orange steel rack laden with engine parts. Uniformed security guards scurried through the huge building looking for him, speaking into their cell phones and walkie-talkies, poking under tarps, climbing onto wooden cartons, chattering among themselves. Truitt imagined the hunt for an intruder was an exhilarating break from the tedium of the job.

He had to find Lisa, and to find her, he had to figure out where Shank was. But how? The hangar and shop were larger than a city block. There were vast open spaces and a myriad of rooms, plus a maze of corridors and what seemed like smaller buildings inside the massive structure. They could be anywhere.

From his hiding spot, he watched a heavyset man in a security uniform giving orders to several guards who quickly dispersed. The heavyset man dialed a number on a cell phone, then began talking while he walked briskly past a row of jet engines propped on platforms, out of their nacelles, their fan disks, turbines, and compressors exposed like the bones of cadavers. Truitt followed the man from an adjacent row of parts, keeping his head down, ducking between racks of piping and tubes.

The guard stopped and knocked on a door with a sign reading: EXECUTIVE ENTRY ONLY. The door opened and a man's face appeared in the shadowy light.

Shank!

The man was nodding as if he were being given instructions and *yes sir*, he'd follow them. Then the door closed and he departed.

☙

"The way I see it," Shank said, "it was a lover's quarrel." He snapped the clip out of the nine-millimeter Glock, wiped his prints off the gun, then tossed it to Lisa. She fumbled it, then caught it.

Shit! Realizing what she had just done, she dropped the gun. Shank picked it up and, holding the clip in a handkerchief, reinserted it.

"Maybe you were tired of all of Max's physical abuse," Shank said. "Hell, you're gonna have a bruised face tomorrow ... if there is a tomorrow. So you shot old Max and left your prints all over the gun. Which leaves only one question. What am I gonna do with you?"

The hellacious crash of steel against concrete startled both of them.

"What the hell was that?" Shank asked, heading toward the door.

℘

The shattered engine lay less than twenty feet from the door of the executive suite. Shank was the first one there.

Sam Truitt looked down from the steel bridge near the ceiling six stories above the concrete floor, then crawled onto the trolley cable. He had used the electric hoist to lift the engine fifty feet into the air, then released the catch and dropped it. Stunned workers were hurrying to the spot on the floor below. He waited until he saw Lisa's face appear in the doorway to the executive suite, then hit a switch on the bridge and let the steel cable unspool toward the floor. His feet were on the huge steel hook at the end of the cable that previously held the engine, and he used his weight to swing forward. As the cable swung toward the floor like a giant pendulum, he called out, "Lisa!"

All eyes looked up at him, and Lisa ran from the doorway. Shank lifted his gun toward the moving cable, but fifty workers were now watching. Cursing, he lowered the gun.

The cable and hook picked up speed as they came lower, sweeping near the floor. Holding on to the cable with one hand, Truitt reached out with the other and grabbed Lisa as she leapt toward him. She nearly slipped from his grasp but hung on as the cable kept moving in its track through the huge building. Shank and the startled security guards gave chase.

The cable began slowing down. "We gotta jump!" Truitt yelled. "Now!"

They leapt off, tumbling onto the hard floor, then scrambling to their feet. "C'mon!" Truitt grabbed her and they ran, ducking into a doorway under a flashing red light. It took Truitt both hands to open the door, which was made of steel and concrete. In a moment, they were inside a rectangular interior building, a test cell with poured concrete walls three feet thick and a five-story ceiling.

On a platform raised thirty feet in the air, a technician was adjusting a fuel line running into a mammoth DC-10 engine that hung suspended from a steel frame bolted to the ceiling. Behind him, an exhaust tube wide enough for a station wagon led from the rear of the engine to the exterior of the building.

"Hey!" the technician shouted. "For christsakes, we're gonna start the engine. You can't be in here."

The man waved toward the window of a control room that overlooked the platform from a catwalk. Inside two men sat at computer consoles.

"Up there!" Truitt yelled, leading Lisa toward a set of steel stairs that connected to the catwalk.

Behind them, the heavy door opened, and Shank burst in. "Freeze!" he yelled.

"Keep going," Truitt told Lisa, who was ahead of him on the stairs.

Truitt stopped and turned. Several steps below him, Shank steadied a handgun on the railing, aiming at Truitt's heart. "Don't move a muscle, asshole."

Truitt didn't move but Lisa ran across the catwalk and into the control room.

"What are you going to do, Shank?" Truitt asked, gesturing above him toward the catwalk. "Shoot a Supreme Court justice in front of witnesses?"

Three men, the two computer operators and the technician, stared down at them, mouths agape.

The door opened behind Shank, and two security guards appeared. "Get outta here!" Shank yelled. "I'm handling this myself." The men obeyed, closing the heavy door behind them.

Shank looked toward the control room. "You guys! Out of here, now!"

The men raced down the stairs and out of the test cell. Lisa stayed put in the control room. Truitt remained perched on the stairs, a dozen feet above Shank, who kept the gun trained on him.

"Now it's just the three of us," Shank said. "You first, Judge." He squeezed one eye shut to aim.

A man without fear is all-powerful.

Truitt vaulted the railing and launched himself toward Shank. The first gunshot ricocheted off the steel railing, barely missing him. Truitt plowed into Shank, knocking him to the floor but failing to dislodge the gun from his hand. They flipped over each other and rolled across the floor, grunting, cursing, flailing. When they came up, Truitt was on top, but Shank hit him with the gun, a stinging blow on the temple, just above the ear.

They rolled over each other once more. Truitt wrapped a hand around Shank's right wrist, keeping the gun pointed away. It was a battle of strength and leverage, Truitt whipping Shank's arm back and forth, slamming it against the concrete floor, then at the ceiling. Two more shots went off before the gun flew from Shank's hand, skidding across the floor into the center of the giant room, just in front of the platform that held the suspended engine.

The two men scrambled to their feet. Shank turned to run for the gun, but Truitt tackled him, a picture-perfect wrap-up, legs churning, head up, just the way the coaches taught. They crashed to the floor, arms and legs tangled, elbowing each other, throwing short, ineffective punches.

In a clinch, Shank gouged at Truitt's eyes, getting a thumb into one, momentarily blinding him as both eyes blinked furiously. Truitt broke the hold, and they struggled up again. Barely able to see, Truitt landed a punch that glanced off Shank's forehead and another that sideswiped his nose, then dug a short right into his gut.

One for Jerry, one for Greg, and one just for me.

Shank retaliated with two wild right-hand leads. Truitt warded off several blows with his forearms then missed with his own hook. Shank ducked underneath the punch and caught Truitt with an uppercut to the throat that gagged him, then kneed him in the groin. Truitt collapsed in a heap.

Shank kicked him in the ribs, once, twice, three times and twice more in the head. The world was turning gray and Truitt had the impression he was underwater, moving in slow motion as he clung to the edge of consciousness. Shank reached into a pocket, pulled out a pair of handcuffs, and fastened Truitt's right wrist to the steel staircase banister.

છ

Lisa was frantic.

As Shank beat and kicked Sam, she used a phone in the control room to call the police. They were on their way but would be too late. Frenzied, she looked for weapons. Nothing.

At last, she scanned the control panel. There were gauges measuring exhaust gas temperature, fuel flow, air pressure, and there was a simplified version of what she had seen in the flight deck when she rode in Tony's jump seat: a starter and ignition switch. She'd watched him run through the checklist, and now her mind raced, trying to remember the steps he used to start the engine.

Tony! Help me. Help me now.

છ

Truitt was vaguely aware of a foggy presence swimming above him, but his mind retreated into the peacefulness of a deep ocean. Shank stood over him, breathing hard, his face flushed, blood dripping from his nose. He kicked Truitt one more time and snarled at him, "I'm gonna kill you, Judge. I'm gonna kill you and then I'll kill your little girlfriend." He looked up toward the control room and bellowed, "I'm coming for you, sweetie pie."

Limping, Shank walked into the middle of the test cell where the gun lay on the floor. The DC-10 engine hung above him.

❧

Lisa pictured Tony at the controls. She remembered him turning to her, smiling his crooked grin, and saying, "Easy as one, two, three. Fuel valve, starter, ignition. All there is to it."

She looked at the console. Everything was clearly marked. Her hands a blur of motion, Lisa opened the fuel valve switch, uncovered the red safety tab on the starter, hit the switch underneath, and then the ignition. Through the window, she saw Shank bending over, picking up the gun, looking toward the engine as it fired up.

Pinching his nostrils to stop the blood flow, squinting up at the engine, he seemed momentarily puzzled as the fan disk began rotating and the turbine whined.

Lisa turned off the starter and ignition and jammed the red throttle lever forward as far as it would go, powering the huge engine with fifty thousand pounds of thrust. Outside the window, the fuel line throbbed to life, the engine roared with the screams of an angry god, and on the floor, Shank hesitated just a second. Then, realizing what was happening, he pivoted and started for the door. He got two steps before his leather soles slipped on the concrete floor, and he fell to his knees, covering his ears against the unbearable noise.

A red line on the floor marked the danger area, a half-moon like the three-point arc on a basketball court, extending forty feet from the front of the engine.

Shank almost made it.

He was five feet inside the line, scrambling to get to his feet, when forty-thousand horsepower of suction lifted him from the floor. He clawed at the air. He yelled something that no one—not even Shank himself—could hear. He hung there a second, weightless as an astronaut in orbit.

On the floor at the staircase, Truitt cringed in pain as the noise ruptured his eardrums in two quick *pops*. The suction pulled at him, and he lost his footing, his legs beginning to rise off the floor, but he was anchored to the staircase by the handcuffs, and they held him there, his body parallel to the floor, his shoulder tendons stretched to the maximum.

Shank floated on his back above the concrete floor, slowly turning somersaults, arms flailing. As the engine reached full power, as the noise seemed to shake the building like a massive earthquake, he flew higher. The last sight he ever saw was the blue, cloudless December sky visible above him through the baffled ceiling that opened directly to the heavens. He was sucked into the rotating fan blades, whirling counterclockwise at blinding speed, and—like the fan disk—made of a fiercely hard titanium.

With his hands in front of him, Shank's fingers hit the blades first and were chopped into tiny slices, a hundred more than a Yakuza's self-mutilation. The powerful suction held his body to the rotating fan as its relentless revolutions ate his hands, then his wrists, then his arms, chewing away at one shoulder, and then his head, shaving his skull into smaller and smaller pieces, drawing him inexorably into its maw.

დ

Inside the control room, Lisa clutched the red-knobbed lever with both hands, refusing to let it go, consciously willing even more power from the mammoth engine, imploring the fan disk to turn faster than it ever had, each revolution striking back for Tony and all the rest.

დ

By the time Shank's head disappeared between the rotor blades, bits of his bones and tendons, ligaments and muscles, internal organs and connective tissues were blowing out the rear of the turbine. Superheated to fifteen hundred degrees, propelled by a turbine turning nine thousand revolutions per minute, the bits of matter that were once a man were reduced to gristle and grit and speck-size particles, and then finally, just a red mist expectorated at two hundred miles per hour into an exhaust tube that ran to the roof and the clear blue sky.

Moments later, when Lisa finally released the throttle and shut down the engine, there was not enough left of Theodore Shakanian to prove he had ever existed.

CHAPTER 36

One of the Brethren

IT WAS MID-MARCH, AND THE SNOW HAD MELTED, REPLACED BY SPORADIC chilly showers. The ground had softened. It was mud season, too late for winter, too early for spring.

It had been almost ninety days since Sam had seen Lisa. Or heard from her.

His last memory of her—as best he could recall through the haze of a concussion—she was leaning over him, her hands cradling his head, calling his name. The voice came deep from an underground well, echoing in his brain. He was semiconscious, and she was saying something else, but with his damaged eardrums, he couldn't make out the words.

He had his hearing back in two weeks. It took several more for the dizziness and blurred vision to subside and the broken ribs to mend.

How long would it take my heart?

He vaguely remembered two policemen standing over him and then the paramedics lifting him onto a stretcher.

Where was Lisa?

She should have been with him in the ambulance, but she wasn't. The policemen wanted to take her statement, but when they returned to the test cell, in all the commotion, with workers crowding around, with someone shouting that Max Wanaker's body was in the executive suite, she had slipped away.

No one had seen her since.

Greg Kingston had visited Truitt in the hospital, and they compared bandages and injuries, showing off their scars like army veterans. Now, Greg was back in college on the West Coast. Truitt called him several times, asking if he'd heard from Lisa.

"She's okay," he said, "but she doesn't want to be found."

"You've talked to her!"

But Greg wouldn't say.

Why was she doing this? Doesn't she care about me? Or the case?

Truitt began writing the *Atlantica* opinion while he was still in the hospital. He had become something of a celebrity, the TV networks getting the story partially right. They called it an assassination plot in which the assassin had been "eviscerated," as one of the tabloid shows described it, "as if he'd been tossed into a giant SaladShooter(tm)."

A mystery woman had saved Justice Truitt's life. One newspaper speculated that she was a pilot; another said she was a mechanic; a third described her as an undercover agent assigned to protect the justice. Feminists claimed her as one of their own, a Wonder Woman.

When he was interviewed by the police, Truitt claimed to have no recollection of the incident due to his concussion. Lisa was never identified, which must have been what she had wanted.

A week after the Court's unanimous opinion was released reversing the summary judgment and ordering a trial, Atlantica Airlines, Inc. declared bankruptcy. The company had little choice. With the plaintiffs' lawyers in possession of the fan disk, with publicity over the attempted killing of a justice all over the news, Atlantica faced certain defeat. The company was being liquidated, its aircraft were being sold, and the victims' families would be splitting the proceeds, a pot expected to reach nearly $500 million.

We achieved justice. We won the case …

But lost each other.

Now, sitting in the conference room, listening to his brethren debate the Mississippi indigents' rights case, Truitt found himself doodling her name across his yellow pad, just as he had done before. When was it?

God, it seems like a thousand years ago, but it's only been a few months.

Lisa, Lisa, Lisa, Lisa … he scribbled on the page.

"States cannot bolt the door to equal justice based on a person's financial status," Gwen Robbins said. She turned toward Truitt. "Sam's piece in the *Harvard Law Review* back in '94 should be the primer for the decision. Here we have a woman too poor to pay a court reporter for a transcript of a trial, so she has no way to appeal an order cutting off her parental rights."

Chief Justice Guido Tarasi looked down the table and nodded at Curtis Braxton.

"I concur," Braxton said. "There are few consequences of judicial action so grave as the severance of family ties."

Debora Kaplan cleared her throat and broke in: "The Mississippi law also gives the party with greater financial clout, usually the man, an unfair advantage. If the father had lost the case, he could have paid for a transcript and appealed. Why should the mother be barred from the appellate court because she is poor?"

"But where does it end?" asked Victor Small. "Who gets free transcripts? Homeowners sued in foreclosure? People whose property is taken in eminent domain? They consider their rights important too."

"They're not in the same ballpark," Truitt said, stirring himself out of his reverie, thumbing through Lisa's old bench memo on the case. "Severing the parent-child bond is irretrievably destructive of the family relationship. Having access to the courts is a fundamental right of constitutional significance."

"I don't find that right in the Constitution," Powell McLeod said.

"The Constitution means what we say it does," Truitt shot back.

"All right," Tarasi said, "we've been around the horn twice on this already. I don't think anyone's mind is going to be changed at this point. Let's vote."

In a moment, the Chief had placed the tally at five-four in favor of striking down the Mississippi law and ruling in favor of the indigent mother. "Sam, we're on the same side here," Tarasi said. "Do you want to take a crack at the majority opinion?"

"Sure," he said, without enthusiasm. He was getting his share of opinions. His words were being etched into history, but he was alone in life. He wanted something from this lifetime, something beyond respect for his judicial acumen.

Truitt lived in a rented apartment and ate his dinner from deli containers standing at the kitchen counter watching CNN. The divorce wasn't yet final, but the terms had been agreed. Connie would get the townhouse, the furniture, half their savings and half his pension. He got Sopchoppy and felt he'd come out ahead. But he was the loneliest he'd ever been because now he knew what it was to love and be loved ... and lose it all.

The justices were about to move onto a prisoners' rights case when there was a knock at the door. Out of habit, Truitt started to get up, then settled back down when Anton Capretto bounded out of his chair. Capretto, the former governor of New York, now occupied the junior justice's seat.

When Capretto came back to the conference table, he slipped a note to Truitt. It was from Eloise, his secretary. "Please come back to chambers before going to lunch."

❧

"What is it, Elly?" Truitt asked.

"I just thought you'd want to see this as soon as possible," she said, handing him an oversize envelope plastered with a colorful row of foreign stamps.

It was postmarked Launceston, Tasmania.

He retreated to his chambers, removed his suit coat, and closed the door. Taking a deep breath, he sliced open the envelope and removed a handwritten note.

Dear Sam,

It's even more beautiful here than I imagined, but I miss you terribly. Each day, I sit beside a waterfall, watching a rainbow play across the sky, thinking only of you. I'm sorry I left the way I did, but it's for the best. I didn't want to answer a grand jury's questions. I didn't want to go before an inquest to determine if it was justifiable homicide. I didn't want the tabloids to tell the story of a married Supreme Court justice who was having an affair with his law clerk. My past would have come out. The whole dirty business would have been on the front pages of all the papers. "The Justice and the Stripper." It would have ruined you, Sam.

So, if you're angry with me, if you hate me for leaving like that, please try to understand. I did it for you. I love you.

Lisa

Along with the note was a packet of airline tickets and a photograph of a waterfall. The tickets were issued to "Scrap Truitt."

Washington to Los Angeles to Sydney to Launceston.

One way.

He studied the tickets, read the note again, then looked at the photo of the falls. He wanted to race to the airport, not even pack a bag, just go! But there was so much to do here.

There was another tobacco case on next week's docket. Chronically ill flight attendants who had been subjected to years of smoke-filled cabins were suing the cigarette companies for fraudulently concealing the risks of secondhand smoke. Later in the term was a case involving a government contractor who was fired for speaking out on public issues. Then there was the Tennessee state judge who raped courthouse workers and claimed the federal civil rights laws couldn't be used to prosecute him.

What was it Lisa had said to him? "There'll always be other wrongs." *And somebody has to right them.*

He would have to wait until the summer recess. And even then … a one-way ticket? Surely Lisa didn't think that he would resign. He needed to talk to her.

Damn! Why didn't she just call me?

Then he realized the depth of his anger. He didn't hate her, as she had feared. He loved her, but she had left him achingly alone. At first, he'd felt betrayed. Now he was empty and numb.

How could she have left me like that?

Elly buzzed, and he picked up the phone. "Justice Tarasi would like you to join him in the justices' dining room," she said. "He wants to talk about how you're going to structure the equal protection analysis in the Mississippi fee case."

"Tell the Chief I don't work for him," Truitt said.

"Sam!"

"Okay, okay. Tell him I'll be right there."

Sam Truitt slipped the tickets and postcard back into the larger envelope and put them in his desk drawer. He closed the drawer, stood up, and headed for the door. Then, realizing he had forgotten something, he returned to his desk, picked up his suit coat, and slipped into it. Buttoning the top button, smoothing his lapels, he turned off the lights and headed for the dining room where his brethren waited.

CHAPTER 37

A Man and a Woman

THE AIR WAS WARM AND SWEET on the first Saturday in April, the cherry blossoms blooming along the Tidal Basin in Potomac Park. The Supreme Court law clerks, emerging from a winter of endless work and little play, had declared a holiday. Instead of putting in their usual half day, they had scheduled a picnic and softball game. Sam Truitt promised to be there as soon as he finished some work. He sat alone in his office, the window open, the spring breeze riffling papers on his desk.

Looking out the window, he spoke into a Dictaphone. "Elly, take a memo to Vic regarding the assisted suicide case. Vic, please update all the cases since *Cruzan versus Missouri* and give me your thoughts on the distinction between—"

"The constitutional right to withdraw life support in Cruzan," a woman's voice interrupted, "and the actual termination of life through suicide."

Jolted, he wheeled around to find Lisa standing in front of him, wearing jeans and a windbreaker, a green duffel bag slung over her shoulder. Her golden red hair had grown, and she had tied it back in a ponytail. Except for a light lipstick, she wore no makeup and she looked angelic as she gave him a soft, silken smile."

He could not have been more astonished if an apparition had appeared in his chambers. His heart seemed to swell up in his chest and tears came to his eyes. He couldn't speak, couldn't move from his spot.

"God, I've missed you, Sam," she said.

"I can't ..." he said, squeezing out the words. "I can't believe you're here."

"If the mountain—Olympus in this case—won't come to Lisa …"

Sam Truitt bounded out of his chair and they rushed toward each other. She wrapped her arms around his neck, and he hugged her back. Both of them cried. They kissed softly, and then she laughed and said, "I'm a mess. Thirty hours on airplanes, and—"

"You're beautiful. You're the most beautiful sight in all the world."

They kissed again. Then she looked around the chambers, as if taking it in for the first time. "I guess you've given up your plan to be a fishing guide and alligator wrestler."

"Don't exaggerate. Country lawyer."

"Right, you were going to hang your shingle from a gumbo limbo tree," she teased.

"I decided to stick around after the President appointed a new justice. I don't have to answer the door anymore."

Her laugh was silvery and melodious, like coins shaken in a silken pouch. "I guess that means we won't be moving to Possum Key. And I was looking forward to you sitting on the front porch whittling in your rocking chair while I was in the kitchen, barefoot, pregnant, and baking hush puppies."

"Actually," he said, "you *fry* hush puppies."

"You really believed that you wanted the quiet life, but I knew you were just reacting to the situation," she said. "At the time, everything seemed so futile to you. You went back to your roots because you didn't think you could achieve justice on the Court. But now you've done it."

"With some extrajudicial help from you."

"So here you are. Right where you belong. You're going to be a great justice, Sam. Your name will be carved into the history books."

"I'm not sure how important that is. I just want to do what you taught me, to balance the hard, written law with a sense of humanity."

"You'll do just that for a long, long time."

Truitt laughed. "On his ninetieth birthday, Holmes was still on the bench. A reporter asked him about the key to his life's work, and old Ollie said—"

"'Young man,'" Lisa said, beating him to the punch, "'the secret of my success is that at an early age, I discovered I was not God.'"

"You have a habit of finishing my sentences," he said.

"Your footnotes, too."

"Holmes was right, and so were you. I'm just a man."

"And I'm just the woman who loves you, but you didn't pick up my hint about finishing your footnotes."

"What do you mean?" he asked, puzzled.

"Do I get my old job back?"

"No way! Absolutely not."

"What!"

"The Court has rules against nepotism," he said. "How would it look for bench memos to be written by a justice's wife?"

"Oh, Sam. Do you really want—"

He silenced her with a kiss.

###

"BUM RAP" SNEAK PREVIEW

"Bum Rap," a Number One bestseller on Amazon, brings together Jake Lassiter with rivals Steve Solomon and Victoria Lord. Here's a sneak preview. For more information or to purchase, please visit the BUM RAP AMAZON PAGE.

-1-

The gunshot hit Nicolai Gorev squarely between the eyes. His head snapped back, then whipped forward, and he toppled face-first onto his desk.

There were two other people in the office of Club Anastasia.

Nadia Delova, the best Bar girl between Moscow and Miami, stared silently at Gorev as blood oozed from his ears. She had seen worse.

Steve Solomon, a South Beach lawyer with a shaky reputation, spoke over the echo still ringing off the walls. "I am in deep shit," he said.

-2-

ONE WEEK EARLIER...
Office of the United States Attorney for the Southern District of Florida
In Re: Investigation of South Beach Champagne Clubs and one "John Doe"
File No. 2014-73-B
Statement of Nadia Delova
July 7, 2014
(CONFIDENTIAL)

Q: My name is Deborah Scolino, assistant United States attorney. Please state your name.
A: Nadia Delova.
Q: How old are you?
A: Twenty-eight.

Q: Where were you born?

A: Saint Petersburg. Russia. Not Florida.

Q: What is your occupation?

A: What do I look like? Nuclear physicist?

Q: Ms. Delova, please . . .

A: Bar girl. I am Bar girl.

Q: What does that entail?

A: Entails my tail. [Witness laughs]. Is simple job. I get men to buy cheap champagne for expensive price.

Q: How do you do that?

A: We go to nice hotel. Fontainebleau or Delano. Me and Elena on hunting parties.

Q: Do you dress as you have today? For the record, a tight-banded mini in hot pink. I'm guessing Herve Leger.

A: Is knockoff. But shoes are real. Valentino slingbacks with four-inch heels. I dress good on hunting parties.

Q: And just what are you hunting for?

A: Tourists. Men with money. We look for expensive watches. Patek Philippe. Audemars Piguet. Rolex Submariner.

Q: So you approach the men?

A: At the hotel bar. We make small talk. "Oh, you are so handsome. Tell us about Nebraska." We say we know a private club with good music.

Q: What club is that?

A: Anastasia. On South Beach.

Q: What happens when you get there?

A: Bartender serves free vodka shots, except ours—mine and Elena's—are water. When the man is drunk, we order champagne. Nicolai buys it for twenty-five dollars at Walmart. Charges a couple thousand a bottle, but the man is so drunk, he signs credit card because Elena has her tongue in his ear, or my hand is in his crotch. Or both.

Q: Just who is Nicolai?

A: Nicolai Gorev. Owner of Club Anastasia.

Q: Ms. Delova, we need you to help the government's investigation of Nicolai Gorev.

A: Nyet.

Q: Ms. Delova . . .

A: I am not as stupid as you might think.

-3-

"I didn't shoot the bastard," Steve Solomon said.

"Tell me the truth, Steve."

"Jeez, Vic, I am." Sounding frustrated. Telling the story over and over. He spread his arms and held his palms upward, the gesture intended to show he wasn't hiding anything.

Victoria studied him. She'd been studying Solomon for several years now. He was her law partner and lover. Solomon & Lord.

Victoria Lord. Princeton undergrad, Yale Law.

Steve Solomon. University of Miami undergrad. Key West School of Law.

Victoria graduated summa cum laude. Steve graduated summa cum luck.

She practiced law by the book. He burned the book. But in court . . . well in court, they were a powerful team.

Solomon & Lord.

Steve had street smarts and was a master of persuasion. Victoria knew the law, which helped with judges. Plus, she was likable, a necessity with juries. Steve also had one talent Victoria lacked: he could lie with a calm certainty no polygraph could ever discover.

She loved Steve. And hated him. Sometimes they argued over "good morning." But life sizzled when they were together and fizzled when they were apart. Right now, one wrong move, and they could be apart forever.

"Tell me again," she said. "Everything."

"Why?"

"I want to see if you tell the same story two times in a row."

"Aw, c'mon, Vic."

They were sitting in a lawyers' visitation room at the Miami-Dade County jail. The metal desk and two chairs were bolted to the concrete floor. Victoria hated the place. It smelled of sweat and disinfectant and something vaguely like cat piss. Her ankle-strap Gucci pumps had slipped on something wet—and yellow—when she had walked down the corridor. She always felt nauseous visiting a client here. Now that the accused was Steve, she also felt a throat-constricting fear.

To get into the jail, she had shown her Florida Bar card. To get out, Steve would need a very good lawyer. She had tried—and won—several murder trials. But with all the emotional baggage, she felt incapable of representing Steve. A surgeon didn't operate on a loved one.

"If you didn't kill Gorev, who did?" she asked.

"Like I said, Nadia Delova, our client."

"Our client?"

"Okay, you were at a hearing in Broward. Nadia was a walk-in. She had five thousand in cash and said she just needed me for a one-hour meeting."

"Where's the money?"

"In an envelope in my desk drawer."

"When were you going to tell me about it?"

"That reminds me of a lawyer joke."

"Not now, Steve."

"A lawyer sends out a bill for five thousand dollars, and the client mistakenly sends him ten thousand dollars. What's the ethical question?"

"Obviously, should he return the money?"

"No! Should he tell his partner?"

Steve laughed at his own joke. He had a habit of doing that. A lot of his old habits were starting to irritate her. Accepting new clients without her approval was one. Straddling the border between ethical and sleazy conduct was another. Getting charged with murder was a new one.

"Where's Nadia now?"

"That's what I need to find out. Or you do."

"You understand your predicament?"

"The cops found me in a locked room with a dead man and a smoking gun. Yeah, I have a pretty good idea."

"Tell me everything from the top."

"Nadia was waiting when I unlocked the door to our office at about eight fifteen a.m. She said she was a Bar girl. Very up front about it."

"How admirable."

Steve ignored her sarcasm and plowed ahead. "She must have come straight from work, because she was all dolled up. Minidress. Heels. Jewelry. Gloves."

"Gloves in Miami. In July."

"Dressy black gloves. Up to the elbows. Like Holly Golightly in Breakfast at Tiffany's."

"Wasn't Holly a prostitute?"

"Only in the book. In the movie, she was more like a fun date."

Just outside the door, a baby wailed. It was a weirdly discordant sound in this dreadful place. The common visitation area, a dismal space with rows of benches for families, was adjacent to the lawyers' room. The baby's keening reached an impossibly high pitch, and Victoria felt a headache coming on.

"Physical description of this Nadia?" she asked.

"About your height. Nearly six feet. Without her heels."

"She took off her shoes?"

"In the office. For a minute. She rubbed her feet. Is that important?"

"I don't know. Had you ever met this Bar girl before?"

"Of course not."

"But she felt comfortable enough to take off her shoes and rub her feet in your presence?"

"Is that a lawyer's question or a girlfriend's question?"

"Just keep going. What else besides her height and her tired feet?"

"Dark hair. Nearly jet-black. Pale skin and blue eyes. Unusual combination. Very . . ."

"Striking?"

"Well . . ." He swallowed, and his Adam's apple bobbed. Victoria made a mental note that Steve—for all his bluster—might not hold up well under cross-examination.

"If you like that sort of thing," he said finally. "I always preferred blondes. Like you."

"Of course. What else about Nadia can you remember?"

"Her lips were very . . . What's the word?"

"I don't know, Steve. What is the word?"

"Big?"

"Pouty," Victoria said. "Bee-stung?"

"Yeah. Exactly."

"Unlike my very average, very WASPy lips?"

"C'mon, you have great lips. Anyway, she had a nice . . ." He made a flowing motion with both hands, the male pantomime for a curvaceous woman. Victoria figured that men had been communicating this way since they first emerged from caves. Not that today's men were that much different from those of the Paleolithic Era.

"Body?" she helped him out. "Curvy body?"

"Yeah, great body. I mean, no greater than yours, but . . ."

"Bigger boobs?"

He nodded, as if saying it aloud might shatter her fragile ego.

"Okay, so at eight fifteen a.m., this striking, long-legged, cantaloupe-breasted woman wearing gloves up to her elbows gives you five thousand in cash, and, like a puppy wagging its tail, you follow her to this South Beach club."

"Actually, I drove us both."

"And just why did she need a lawyer?"

"Her boss, Nicolai Gorev, was holding her passport. She wanted it back plus some money he owed her."

"And how exactly were you going to help her do this?"

Steve let out a long, slow breath. "Well, that's where it gets a little sticky."

"Doesn't it always?"

"I think it was maybe a language thing, her being Russian and all."

"Damn it, Steve. What aren't you telling me?"

He was quiet a moment, then gave her that twinkling smile. It was intended to distract her from whatever he needed to say but didn't want to. He was a handsome man with black hair and deep-brown eyes. Mischievous eyes, Victoria thought. Devilish eyes, her mother always said. She did not mean it as a compliment. He had an aquiline nose that reminded Victoria of George Washington, except that if Steve had chopped down a cherry tree, he would have lied about it.

At last, Steve said, "Well, you know how you always hated that TV commercial I did for the firm?"

"The blasphemous one? 'If you want the best lawyers in Miami, hire the wisdom of Solomon, the strength of the Lord.'"

"Nope. The one where I was a cowboy with the pearl-handled pistols?"

"How could I forget?" Victoria said. "The cease-and-desist letter from the Florida Bar is on my desk."

"Well, if you want to know exactly what happened . . ."

"I do! Word for word."

So before Victoria could begin pulling out his fingernails with pliers, Steve told her.

⁊

"Do you have one gun or two?" Nadia asks.

"What?" Steve answers. They are inside Club Anastasia, headed toward an office at the end of a corridor behind the bar. A heavyset woman in an apron is mopping the floor. Two thick-necked men in black suits are riffling through a stack of credit card receipts and using an old-fashioned, noisy adding machine with a paper scroll. The men glance at Nadia and return to their work.

"On the TV, you have two guns," Nadia says.

"You talking about my commercial?"

"I told you. I got your name from the television."

In the commercial, Steve was dressed in cowboy garb. Right down to the chaps, Stetson, and pair of six-shooters. He fired at a blowup doll—a man in a suit intended to resemble, well, The Man. The doll exploded, and Steve blew smoke from the gun barrel.

An actor's baritone voice intoned: "If you need a lawyer, why not hire a gunslinger? Steve Solomon. Have briefcase. Will travel."

On the screen, the logo of Solomon & Lord. And the phone number: 555-UBE-FREE.

"No guns," he tells Nadia as they approach Gorev's office. "I hate guns."

"Then what can you do to frighten Nicolai?"

"What I always do. Threaten to sue."

She exhales a little puff of displeasure, opens her purse, and shows Solomon what is inside. "Well, at least I have a gun," she says.

**

"Don't say it, Vic. I know I screwed up. That's why I need you so much now. Have you filed your notice of appearance?"

She shook her head, felt her gold hoop earrings swinging. They had been a present from Steve after they'd won their first murder trial. "I can be your lawyer or your lover, Steve, but not both."

"Jeez, Vic." His eyes went wide with surprise. "We're partners in everything."

Victoria could feel his disappointment. Didn't he realize you don't put this sort of burden on the person you love?

"You won't listen to me," she said. "As soon as you're indicted, you'll try to take over."

"No way. You'll be the boss."

"You'll push me to go over the line. Like that stupid saying of yours."

"'When the law doesn't work, you gotta work the law.' It's the truth, hon."

"Not the way I practice."

They were both quiet a moment. Somewhere inside this hellish place, a steel door clanged shut. Shouts of men could be heard on upper floors. The cat piss smell seemed to grow stronger.

"I need you, Vic."

"I already retained Jake Lassiter."

"Lassiter! I want a lawyer, not a linebacker."

"He's won some tough cases."

"He's a slab of meat. If you won't represent me, I want Roy Black."

"We can't afford Roy."

"Tell him it's me."

"Already did."

"And he didn't offer a courtesy discount?"

"He doubled his fee."

"What about Marcia Silvers? She's won some big cases."

"Marcia's in Washington, prepping for a Supreme Court argument."

"Damn! But why Lassiter?"

"Because he won't put up with your bullshit. And if you're innocent, he'll tear apart the courthouse to prove it."

"Says who?"

"He promised me. He'll be like Samson ripping down the pillars of the Temple of Dagon."

"If I recall my Old Testament," Steve said, with an air of resignation, "that's what killed old Samson."

-4-

I want an innocent client.

I need an innocent client.

I don't mean not guilty because the state can't meet its burden of proof. But innocent. "Factually innocent," as we mouthpieces call it.

I've been trying cases for twenty years after a short, unspectacular career as a second-string linebacker with the Miami Dolphins. I made a few memorable hits on the suicide squads—the kickoff and punt teams—but mostly I sat so far down Shula's bench, my ass was in Ocala. I went to night law school in the off-season, graduated in the top half of the bottom third of my class, and passed the bar exam on my fourth try. I've been bouncing from courtroom to courtroom in the so-called justice system ever since.

My name is Jake Lassiter, and I'm a grinder. I am not called to speak at fancy conventions in five-star hotels. The governor has not offered me black robes and elevated me to the bench. I am not interviewed by CNN to comment on the latest trial of the century. And I am not rich.

Here's what I do. Burglary. Robbery. Assault and battery. Con games. Stolen cars. Embezzlement. Drug possession. And, of course, murder. For whatever reason, I'm particularly good at murder. Maybe because the stakes are so high, my engine revs to the red line. Not that a murder trial is a sprint. It's a marathon where everyone along the road throws rocks at you as you chug along. You have to be able to take a hit.

It's a lot like the kickoff team in football. The fastest man is not necessarily the one who makes the tackle. More likely, the flier will be picked off by one of the blockers. The player who's not particularly fast but senses the blocker's angle can knock the bastard aside, keep rumbling along, and make the hit. That's what kept me on the Dolphins for three years, and it's my theory of trying a murder case. Play within yourself. Predict your opponent's move before it happens, and beat him to the punch. If you're not particularly swift or shifty—meaning if you're me—a forearm blast to the throat will do.

On the field or in the courtroom, try not to get knocked on your ass, but if you do, never let them see your pain. Bounce to your feet and head for the ball.

Here's what I won't do as a lawyer. I won't represent a man accused of violence against women or children because my granny taught me that such scum do not deserve my time or effort. Otherwise, it's pretty much anything goes.

I take a lot of cases other lawyers turn down. Either the money is short or the odds of winning are long. That's earned me the name "Last Chance Lassiter."

I pick up cases here and there. Sometimes I just stand by the elevator on the fourth floor of the Richard E. Gerstein Justice Building. Someone who's headed for an arraignment naked—without a lawyer—will spot me. I'm a big guy in a suit with a briefcase, and I don't look lost. Maybe they like my broken nose or my decent haircut, or maybe they're just scared.

"You a lawyer, dude?"

"Best one you can afford . . . dude."

Money is always a problem. My first question to a potential customer— yeah, I sometimes call them that—is not "Did you do it?" It's "How much money do you have?" And, yes, I take credit cards. But not a mortgage on a customer's house. Not because I'd feel lousy about foreclosing. Because I once got burned when the IRS leapfrogged the mortgage I was holding with a lien for unpaid taxes, leaving my client without a house and me without a fee.

Sometimes former customers refer their pals. This puzzles me, because those ex-customers are nearly always in prison. I guess they don't blame me for losing. After all, they were guilty, and they watched me work my ass off on their behalf.

That's a fact of the business. Most of my customers are guilty as hell. I only win when the state can't prove its case or otherwise screws the pooch. I'm a damn good cross-examiner, and I've won cases by catching cops in lies. That doesn't mean my customer wasn't technically guilty. But if I can eviscerate the state's witnesses and then work my magic in closing argument, I can get my customer off.

How else can I win? Sometimes the cops will conduct an unconstitutional search, or the prosecutors will fail to turn over exculpatory evidence, or the trial judge will err. On the occasions I win, I receive little gratitude. No Christmas cards or baskets of fruit. Maybe a grumbling complaint about the size of my fee.

The customer sees the stage play, not the work behind it. Writing the script, building the sets, painting the props, and learning the lines. The ingrate couldn't care less. I'll never hear from the victorious client again . . . until he's arrested for something else.

Mostly I lose. Or plead my guy guilty. It's a dirty little secret, but that's the deal with most criminal defense lawyers, even the big names who pontificate on the tube. If anyone knew our real winning percentage, they'd cop a quick plea or flee the jurisdiction.

We all want to be heroes to our paying customers. John D. MacDonald, my favorite Florida writer—yeah, I read a bit—once began a book: "There are no hundred percent heroes." If you ask my customers, they'd probably give me 51 percent. MacDonald also wrote, "If the cards are stacked against you, reshuffle the deck." Well, I'm tired of holding a pair of deuces or a busted flush. Tired of the grind. Tired of losing. Which is why on this sweaty July day with a sky as gray as an angry ocean, I needed an innocent client.

I was juggling these thoughts while driving north on Dixie Highway toward I-95 on my way to the jail. Victoria Lord had called this morning while I was slicing mangoes for my nephew Kip's smoothie. Victoria's law partner and live-in lover, Steve Solomon, had managed to get himself arrested in the shooting death of some Russian club owner on South Beach.

"I don't like Solomon," I told her on the phone.

I know. I know. My marketing skills could use work.

"Do you like most of your clients?" she asked.

"Practically none."

"But you bust your hump and break down doors to win."

"I hate losing more than I hate the clients."

"That's why I'm hiring you. Plus you have street smarts and won't fall for any of Steve's bullshit."

"Has he agreed to this?"

"Not yet."

"Tell him I've punched out clients who lied to me."

"You have no idea how many times I've wanted to smack him."

In front of me, a landscaper's overloaded Ford pickup was dropping palm fronds and dead ferns all over the highway. I goosed the gas pedal and pulled my ancient Eldorado convertible into the passing lane. "Victoria, do you ever get tired of representing guilty people?"

"Steve swears he's innocent."

"And the law presumes he is. But I'm not talking about him. Does it ever get you down? That nearly everyone is guilty."

She was silent on the phone a moment. Maybe wondering if she'd called the wrong guy. Then she said, "It comes with the territory, Jake. We force the state to meet its burden of proof. If they do it, we haven't really lost. The system has won."

"So you really believe the stuff they teach in law school?"

"If I didn't, how could I go on?"

Exactly, I thought. She hadn't practiced long enough to lose her religion, the belief in the holiness of the justice system. I didn't want to be a prick, so I didn't say, "Give it ten more years, Victoria; then get back to me."

Instead, I said, "See you and your presumably innocent partner in an hour."

I knew them both a bit. They lived together on Kumquat, and I'm on Poinciana in Coconut Grove, so we're practically neighbors. I'd recently seen Solomon tooling around the neighborhood in a jazzy new Corvette with a paint job they call "torch red." Not my style. I'm also too big to fit comfortably in the driver's seat. His personalized license plate was "I-OBJECT," a pretty good summation of his temperament.

Solomon was a herky-jerky guy, always in motion, always gabbing. About six feet tall with dark hair that usually needed trimming. He weighed about as much as one of my buttocks, but he had that wiry strength. I'd seen him jogging down Old Cutler Road, and he kept up an impressive pace. In court, he badgered witnesses, pestered lawyers, and interrupted judges. His files were always a mess, and, basically, he was a pain in the ass. Showy and over the top by my standards, and I'm not exactly the shy and retiring type.

One day, in the Justice Building cafeteria, I joined Solomon at a luncheon table with several other lawyers. He was spouting off about "Solomon's Laws," rules he makes up that flout the system.

"If the facts don't fit the law, bend the facts," Solomon said, stuffing his face with eggplant Parmesan.

Everybody laughed. Except me. When I was a young lawyer, I represented an old musician named Cadillac Johnson whose song had been stolen by a hot young hip-hop artist. The copyright claim was murky and documents had been destroyed, but I knew in my gut that my guy had written the song several decades earlier.

"It's a tough case, maybe impossible," Cadillac told me.

"If your cause is just, no case is impossible," I said.

Ever since, I've tried to live by those words. Problem is, just causes are hard to come by. And, oh yeah, I won a pile of cash for Cadillac's retirement without bending the facts, though I did punch a guy out.

The first time I saw Victoria Lord, she was in court, and what I noticed was her posture. A tall, slender blonde who stood very straight and spoke with quiet confidence and authority. Tailored business suits and patrician good looks. Her table was neatly arranged with color-coded files that I'm sure were alphabetized and cross-indexed. Highly organized. A real pro at a young age. Maybe overly earnest for my taste. I could be wrong, but she seemed to be one of those anti-gluten, pro-yoga, organic wine bar, Generation-Y echo boomers. A Gwyneth Paltrow type who would name her first daughter Persimmon or whatever.

They're really different, Solomon and Lord, but as people say, opposites attract. For whatever reason—maybe because they each bring different strengths to the courtroom—they've become a damn good trial team.

Traffic slowed to a halt between Seventeenth Avenue and the entrance to I-95. A mattress lay in the middle lane. Typical. At least it wasn't on fire. I was stuck behind a muddy old Chevy that belched oily smoke. The tag was expired, and I'd bet a hundred bucks the driver had neither a license nor insurance. I squeezed my oversize Eldo into the left lane, cutting off a young guy in a white Porsche. He banged his horn, and through the rearview, I saw him shoot me the bird.

Aw, screw you, Porsche Boy. And your designer sunglasses, too.

I'm tired of Miami. For a long time, I've felt out of place, a brew-and-burger guy in a pâté-and-chardonnay world.

I got a call a few weeks ago from Clarence Washington, an old Dolphins teammate. After retirement, he picked up a master's degree and then a doctorate in education. And this from a kid who grew up in the projects. I have a lot of respect for Clarence. Now, he's headmaster at a boy's prep school in the green hills of Vermont. And to think I knew him when he tossed a beer keg off a seventh-story balcony into a hotel swimming pool. With a Dolphins cheerleader riding that keg all the way down.

Anyway, Clarence said he needed a new football coach. The guy who had the job had retired after like a hundred years. Apparently, there's very little pressure coaching a bunch of pampered skinny white boys who play against others of their ilk. It doesn't really matter if you win, as long as the uniforms don't get too dirty and the parents' cocktails are chilled. And you get to wear a sweat suit to work with the crest of the school on the chest.

So Vermont was on my mind as I drove to the stinkhole county jail, stuck in traffic, horns blaring, and the thermometer closing in on ninety-six degrees.

Steve Solomon, you may not know it, but you're the tipping point. If you're a lying scumbag murderer, I'm hanging up my shingle and heading north.

Green hills. Autumn leaves. Ben & Jerry's.

Half an hour later, I pulled off the Dolphin Expressway onto Twelfth Avenue and parked my thirty-year-old convertible, canvas top up, in an open lot.

I walked to the jail, a hot rain falling, as it did practically every day in the summer. But as the fat drops pelted me, I could smell the dewy grass of a manicured playing field on a cool September morning.

#

PREVIEW: "CHEATER'S GAME"

"Cheater's Game" dives deep into the true-to-life college admissions scandal with an explosive federal trial that rocks the courthouse. With the odds stacked against him, Lassiter matches wits with the mastermind of the fraud in a longshot effort to keep nephew Kip out of prison.

For more information or to pre-order, visit the "Cheater's Game" Amazon Page. A Kindle Unlimited title.

PROLOGUE
Road Fury

With the recklessness of a 20-year-old who had not yet been scorched by life's wildfires, Kip Lassiter floored the Tesla X, which whooshed along the narrow road, splashing through potholes barely two feet from a murky Everglades canal.

Kip checked the satellite map on his touchscreen. Six miles to Tamiami Trail, then a straight shot east to Miami. He opened the windows, and a humid blast enveloped him. It had been a great morning. Twenty-five thousand in cash under the back seat. No invoice, no receipt, no howdy-do to the IRS.

Twenty-five grand for four hours' work!

And it was more fun than work. Taking the risk and getting away with it. What a rush, like being the last person standing in *Fortnite*.

Kip longed to tell Uncle Jake but knew he'd get salty and deliver a lecture.

"Dammit, Kip! Never sacrifice your integrity for the pursuit of money."

"In-teg-ri-ty." In his pious tone, Uncle Jake would pronounce each syllable as if the word belonged in a holy prayer.

So old school!

Slowing down to navigate a buckled stretch of asphalt, Kip heard a discordant sound and glanced at his rearview mirror. A metallic blue

Maserati, a growling beast, appeared in the mist a hundred yards behind. In seconds, the sports car closed the distance and pulled alongside, exhausts throbbing like symphonic horns. Kip glanced left, but the Maserati's windows were tinted a bottomless black, the driver a phantom.

Kip sped up and the Maserati kept pace, hanging there.

What? You want to race? That's cool.

His mind flashed to a video game he had played as a kid. *Road Fury.* Two cars zipping along a highway filled with hairpin turns. The goal: make the other car crash through a guardrail and fly over a cliff or drop into a raging river.

Kip punched the accelerator, pedal to the metal, and the Tesla instantly shot ahead, thrusting him back into the seat, an astronaut on liftoff. But the Maserati quickly caught up. Hurtling neck and neck, the two vehicles flew past low-slung gumbo limbo trees that crowded the scarred roadway.

The Maserati's windows rolled down, and Kip saw a driver and one passenger. What the hell! Both wore skeleton masks.

They must have seen him pick up the money at the fishing cabin.

They want to rob me!

And dump me into a mangrove.

Kip felt his throat tighten, and he struggled to remain calm as both vehicles picked up speed.

Think! Think your way out of this.

Then, a notion.

A Maserati GranTurismo. In the Glades?

Not the vehicle of swamp rats. A Chevy pickup with raised suspension was more like it. Then he remembered those rich-prick twins from Palm Beach, Niles and Teague, whose combined IQ wouldn't equal his. Their old man drove an Italian sports car. A Lamborghini or Maserati. Could it be them?

Sure, I punked Niles and owe him money. But playing chicken at high speed? Seriously?

Again, the Maserati was alongside him, music blaring through the open windows. Power guitar chords and heavy drums and a man's voice so hoarse he might have gargled with turpentine. Rasping, "I feel like killing you!" Cannibal Corpse, the death metal band.

Of course! The twins were metalheads. It had to be them.

A couple of twonks! Or, as Uncle Jake would say, knuckleheads.

The Maserati moved closer. The masked passenger lunged halfway out the window and swung a metal baseball bat, clunking the Tesla's side mirror and shattering the glass. Jolted, Kip veered off the road, and the Tesla's tires chewed through a patch of swamp lilies.

Kip yanked the wheel left and maneuvered the Tesla back onto the asphalt, but the Maserati now claimed the center of the narrow road. The cars were inches apart, and the Tesla's collision warning bleated like a frightened goat.

Again, the passenger leaned out, this time screaming over the music, "Keep your mouth shut, Lassiter!"

C'mon! That's what you want? As if I would talk to the feds.

Kip snorted a laugh, feeling the tension drain from him. But then his eyes darted to the road ahead. Something moving, the sun's glare turning it into a silhouette. Closer now, Kip made out a Florida panther, the color of sun-bleached saw grass.

The Maserati suddenly braked and fishtailed, sideswiping the Tesla and terrifying Kip, who fought the steering wheel, but his tires skidded off the road. Out of control, the Tesla slid down the embankment and splashed into the canal, taking on water through the passenger window.

The airbag deployed like a boxer punching Kip hard in the face and pinning him against his seat. Through the windshield, he saw fish the size of fingernails scattering in the brackish water.

Kip tasted blood and thought he heard the Tesla's horn wailing, but as the water reached his chest, he realized it was his own scream.

CHAPTER ONE
Generation Z Trauma

"Mr. Lassiter! Jake Lassiter!"

Milagros Soto, a court bailiff, called out to me, her voice echoing down the courthouse corridor. More urgent than necessary, I thought, for my being three minutes late for a hearing.

"Hey, Millie. Tell the judge I'll be right there."

"Hearing's cancelled. Why aren't you answering your phone?"

"I turn it off when I'm in the courthouse."

True enough. When I took the job with the Florida Bar, I started following rules I always ignored.

"Get over to Jackson Memorial right away," she said. "It's your nephew."

I froze, my chest crushed by dread, as if my lungs had suddenly filled with mud. "What's hap . . .?" I couldn't get the words out.

"I don't know, Jake. Just get to the trauma center, now."
Oh, Kip! Just when you'd turned your life around. Now what?

***

Fifteen minutes later, I was double-timing through the maze of Jackson Memorial, as Gloria Sanchez, a deputy administrator, filled me in. "I don't know why, Jake, but your nephew told me not to contact you. He said you weren't related."

"Aw, jeez. I thought the kid had outgrown that."

I'd known Gloria for twenty years, and she routinely gave me access to the inner sanctum of the trauma center so I could visit clients and witnesses, circumventing the rules. Either she liked me, or she was returning a favor. A while back, when her son was a junior at Coral Gables High, I got his marijuana possession charge dismissed. *Pro bono*, of course.

A sturdy woman in her fifties, Gloria kept pace, quick on her feet. She had probably traveled the circumference of the earth on the rock-hard tile of these chilly corridors.

"When EMS brought him in, I saw the name, 'Chester Lassiter.' I remember years ago you showed me photos of the boy. So proud of how smart the little fellow was. You raised Chester, right?"

I nodded. "He goes by 'Kip.' My half-sister Janet named him 'Chester' after her dad. She was too busy bouncing checks and jumping bail to catch the name of the kid's father."

Gloria led me into a room where Kip lay on his back, eyes closed, cervical collar around his neck, oxygen clips in his nose, tubes and wires sprouting from his arms and chest. Crimson scratches ran down both cheeks and across his forehead, and two black eyes gave him a raccoon look. A nearby monitor blinked with his respiration, pulse rate, and blood pressure.

In her professional tone tempered with motherly compassion, Gloria told me what she knew. First, not to be alarmed. Kip was sedated and "resting comfortably," as they say in the hospital racket. He was in intensive care only because that's what they do with head trauma. The brain scan appeared normal, but that didn't rule out a moderate concussion and a whiplash injury.

The headline: Kip had driven his car into a canal, and it was difficult to tell how long he'd been trapped, struggling to get out the shoulder harness and clawing his way through a window. The trauma crew had pumped a small amount of slimy water out of his stomach. No water down his airway thanks to involuntary laryngospasms, the throat constricting and sealing the trachea. Good thing because water in the lungs can lead to pneumonia, not to mention death.

I walked to the bed and clasped Kip's hand. Hundreds of times, I'd held him, hugged him, tousled his hair. I'd watched him grow. Taught him values. I'd marveled at his achievements and suffered at his stumbles. And now here he was, as helpless as the day he arrived at my home, my worthless half-sister shoving him out of the car. All his belongings—two filthy changes of clothes—stuffed into a Mickey Mouse backpack that looked as if Pluto had taken a dump in it.

Not a toy. Not a single toy.

He was nine with broomstick limbs, and no one had taught him how to throw or catch a ball, so we invented a game called "Ten." I'd toss him a rubber ball. If he caught it ten times in a row, he'd get a prize. A milkshake or a comic book or a pack of baseball cards. Soon he could catch it twenty or forty times without a miss, but we still called the game Ten.

When I'd come home from court, as soon as I walked in, Kip would say, "Let's play Ten." And by then, the phrase had taken on a meaning of its own. "Let's hang out" or "Let's watch a game" or "Let's talk." Our own private code.

Now, I squeezed his hand and whispered, "Hey little guy. I'm here."

Kip didn't respond.

"Give him a couple hours for the sedatives to wear off," Gloria said.

"Are you certain there's no permanent damage?"

"No hypoxia, no lack of oxygen to the brain. He was responsive and alert and answered our questions when EMS brought him in."

"Alert enough to say we weren't related." I gave a rueful laugh. "Any chance that was the result of head trauma?"

Gloria showed me a tolerant smile. "As a parent, I'd say it's more a case of Generation Z trauma. He's probably embarrassed. Maybe that hurts more than his head."

"Embarrassed about what?"

"His driving. Wrecking the car. Disappointing you. Who knows the mind of a 20-year-old man?"

Man?

I didn't think of Kip as a man. To me, he was still the terrified towheaded string bean I had raised. Maybe it was time I got up to speed.

Kip stirred and grunted in his sleep.

"Where exactly did the car go into the water?" I asked Gloria, thinking that Miami-Dade had hundreds of miles of waterways, a few not far from the hospital.

"In the Everglades," Gloria said. "Just this side of Ochopee on a Water District road north of the Trail."

That stopped me. "Way the hell out there? Who called 911?"

Gloria sighed. "I knew you'd ask, so I called the county. Male voice, a little agitated but not hysterical. Wouldn't leave a name but gave a precise description of the location. GPS coordinates. They don't get that very often."

"Did the county pick up a tower location?"

She shook her head. "Call was too quick. What do you think could have happened?"

My mind raced through possibilities, none of them appealing. "Jeez, Gloria, a deserted road in the Everglades. Nothing good goes on out there. Drug deals, human trafficking. I once had a case of illegal importation of macaws from Trinidad that ended up near Ochopee."

"You're letting your imagination run away with you," she said. "When your nephew's awake, I'm sure he'll tell you everything."

Kip stirred again, his eyes blinking, but he didn't awaken.

"Did the paramedics recover anything from the car?" I asked.

"One of them dived in, but just to make sure no one was in the vehicle. All we've got now is what Kip had in his pockets."

My look asked her a silent question, and her answer was to lead me to a room with two dozen small lockers. She used a master key to open one and handed me a plastic pouch containing a wallet and a passport, both still wet.

"Don't let anyone see you and put everything back." Gloria studied me a moment and asked, "Are you feeling okay, Jake? I heard you'd retired."

"Vicious rumor. I gave up my private practice three months ago. Now I prosecute shady lawyers."

She considered that and then said, "I read the sports section, so I know you're in that concussion study. I hope everything works out for you."

I mumbled my thanks, and she continued, "You look like you could still play linebacker."

"Ha! I still weigh 235, but it's repositioned itself."

"Aw, you're still a hunk, Jake." She gave me a playful chuck on the shoulder. "Your grizzled look with the playful eyes does appeal to women of a certain age."

"I'm not even gonna ask what age."

"And you've got all your hair, though it's turned . . ." She searched for the word. "Silver."

"You can say 'gray.' Silver reminds me of Oakland Raiders' pants, and I hate the Raiders."

She said goodbye and left, and I opened the passport and looked at the photo. Issued eleven months ago, a sly smile on Kip's face.

But what's this?

Five trips out of the country, five stamps, each with a little green turtle.

Cayman Islands, a British Overseas Territory.

All short trips, two to four days, including one last week.

What the hell!

Kip had never mentioned his travels.

I closed the passport and opened the wallet, which contained nine hundred eighty-seven dollars. Okay, that's more than I carry around, but so what? Kip had a small business tutoring high school students for the ACT and SAT exams.

I then pulled out a Florida vehicle registration certificate, expecting to find the paperwork for his ten-year-old Toyota Camry. Instead, it was the registration for a brand-new Tesla S.U.V., Model X with a personalized license plate, "EZ-1600."

I drive a 1984 Cadillac Eldorado ragtop, so I'm a little behind the times. But just how the hell did Kip afford this high-tech, space-age vehicle? The Tesla title was folded inside the wallet, too. No lienholder, meaning no loan. He owned the damn thing free and clear.

As for the license plate, I knew the meaning of "1600," which had nothing to do with Pennsylvania Avenue. As a junior in high school, that was Kip's score—perfection—on the SAT exam. So much promise. But then came the disaster his freshman year in college. An arrest, expulsion, and a humiliating trip home. And now what? The vehicle registration date was three months ago. I'd seen Kip several times since then. He had an apartment on Brickell, and on his occasional trips to my Coconut Grove house, he always was at the wheel of that old Toyota.

So, *the kid who used to tell me everything now buys a luxury vehicle with cash, and not only doesn't tell me, but goes to pains to make sure I don't know.*

I pulled Kip's driver's license out of its slot and studied the photo. Sixteen when it had been taken, and he looked about twelve. Straw-blonde hair falling into his eyes, a look of innocence, totally lacking in guile. I knew everything about him then. We had no secrets. So, was that him in the hospital bed or had space aliens taken over his body? Maybe all parents ponder that question one time or another.

So many threads that lead . . . where?
Why the Cayman Islands?
And what's with the pricey Tesla at the bottom of a canal?
Who called 911?

I replaced the items in the locker and walked down the corridor toward Kip's room. I would be there when he woke up. And we would talk.

Kip. This is your Uncle Jake. It's time to get reacquainted. Let's play Ten.

CHAPTER TWO
The Doctor Is In

Melissa Gold . . .

Jake's phone call rocked Dr. Melissa Gold. "Oh my God, Jake! Is he unconscious?"

"Sedated. It's probably just a concussion." He paused, then gave a rueful laugh. "I guess that's a little ironic, my saying, 'just a concussion.'"

Her fiancé, Jake Lassiter, had his own history of head bangers, which may have led to brain damage. Irony there, too. If not for Jake's traumatic brain injury, they never would have met. As a neuropathologist, she treated him. As a woman, she loved him.

"I'm with a patient," Melissa said, "but I can be there in an hour."

"Maybe it's better if I talk to him alone first. We need to reconnect."

"Has he strayed that far?"

"All my fault. I've let him get away from me."

Sadness and regret were heavy in his voice. She could practically see his broad shoulders slumping. Jake had given so much of himself so unselfishly, raising Kip after his mother had abandoned him. Jake's capacity for giving, in fact, had been one of the attractions for her.

They met when she was director of the Center for Neuroscience at UCLA's medical school. He had taken her deposition in a civil suit, and there was an immediate attraction. He said he liked long, leggy women who were smart and savvy. She usually didn't like wise-guy lawyers, but there was something solid about him. A strength of character to go with that barrel chest.

In her Left Coast days, she'd dated a number of eligible bachelors. Hollywood business managers in their Zegna suits and Italian silk ties, film agents in their Brioni suits and shiny shirts with no ties, even a couple of actors (*what was I thinking?*) in torn jeans and five-day beards. The men shared one personality trait: none could pass a mirror without pausing to admire himself. Los Angeles was awash with that kind of man, a Century City Narcissus worshiping his own reflection, waiting for his next project to be greenlit. Sure, a man of towering ego liked having an attractive, professional woman on his arm, but no more than that diamond-encrusted Piaget watch.

Then she met Jake, who was effortlessly natural and without pretensions, responsive to her needs, an excellent listener, and unaware of how rare a prize he was. He was something of a throwback. At a downtown diner, he drank his coffee black with a slice of apple pie, not a cinnamon cappuccino with a passionfruit macaron. In chi-chi South Beach, he remained a brew-and-burger guy in a paté and Chardonnay world.

"Do it, Jake. Talk to him first. You know him best."

"I thought I did, but what the hell happened?" He sighed into the phone. "When he went off to college, he had such promise."

"*Has* such promise. Jake, he's twenty! Didn't you ever get into trouble at that age?"

"I was almost kicked out of Penn State for throwing a refrigerator off a fourth-floor balcony. It was a twenty-dollar bet, and I'd already emptied the refrigerator of beer, so I knew I could do it."

"Just be gentle with Kip. He's sensitive and . . ."

"And I'm not?"

"No, you are, but in a different way. You grew up like Huck Finn, barefoot and rowdy. I doubt Kip ever free-dived to steal lobster pots."

"Only stole the lobsters. I left the pots on the ocean floor."

"I love you, big guy."

"I love you, too, Doc. Even when you stick needles in my butt."

"Call me as soon as you can."

"Will do."

She worried about both Lassiter men. Kip was a mystery. Just how did a kid who got a perfect score on the SAT, who never sweated through an academically rigorous private school, get booted out of college his second semester?

But her fiancé's medical condition had become her primary focus. Once Jake had been diagnosed with a precursor to Chronic Traumatic Encephalopathy, the fatal brain disease best known for afflicting former football players, he suggested—politely and sweetly—that they put off the wedding.

398

"I need a definitive diagnosis," Jake had said. "I don't want you to be a young widow."

When they spoke of marriage now, it was tied to a clean bill of health. Jake was in a study she was running at the University of Miami. Would the early indications of the disease that showed up on his brain scans morph into the full-blown killer that had stricken so many of his contemporaries? Or would they discover a cure for C.T.E. itself, saving him and thousands of others? No one knew.

Their personal relationship was much more joyful. When Chloe, her best girlfriend in Los Angeles, had asked how it was going, Melissa told her, "He gets me. Respects me. It's so easy, and we mesh so well."

"And in bed?" Chloe said.

"He takes my breath away."

"New lab project. Clone him!"

All of which raised a troubling question. When could she tell Jake about the new development in her life? Certainly not today, not until Kip was safely at home. She faced an issue so common these days that it had become a cliché. How could she manage both her relationship and her career? And perhaps the biggest question of all: Would Jake uproot his life for her, as she had done for him?

#

For more information or to pre-order, visit the "Cheater's Game" Amazon Page.

BOOKS BY PAUL LEVINE

JAKE LASSITER SERIES

"Jake Lassiter is great fun." – New York Times

"Lassiter is attractive, funny, savvy and brave." – Chicago Tribune

"Take one part John Grisham, two parts Carl Hiaasen, throw in a dash of John D. MacDonald, and voila! You've got Jake Lassiter." – Tulsa World

TO SPEAK FOR THE DEAD: Linebacker-turned-lawyer Jake Lassiter begins to believe that his surgeon client is innocent of malpractice...but guilty of murder. An Amazon Number One Bestselling Legal Thriller.

NIGHT VISION: After several women are killed by an Internet stalker, Jake is appointed a special prosecutor, and follows a trail of evidence from Miami to London and the very streets where Jack the Ripper once roamed. An Amazon Number One Bestseller in both the Serial Killer and International Crime categories.

FALSE DAWN: After his client confesses to a murder he didn't commit, Jake follows a bloody trail from Miami to Havana to discover the truth.

MORTAL SIN: Talk about conflicts of interest! Jake is sleeping with Gina Florio and defending her mob-connected husband in court. Then the hubby gets homicidal. Winner of the John D. MacDonald Fiction Award and an Amazon Number One Bestseller in Mysteries.

RIPTIDE: Jake Lassiter chases a beautiful woman and stolen bonds from Miami to Maui.

FOOL ME TWICE: To clear his name in a murder investigation, Jake follows a trail of evidence that leads from Miami to buried treasure in the abandoned silver mines of Aspen, Colorado. An Amazon Number One Bestselling Legal Thriller.

FLESH & BONES: Jake falls for his beautiful client even though he doubts her story. She claims to have recovered "repressed memories" of abuse...just before gunning down her father

LASSITER: Jake retraces the steps of a model who went missing 18 years earlier...after his one-night stand with her.

LAST CHANCE LASSITER: In this prequel novella, young Jake Lassiter has an impossible case: he represents Cadillac Johnson, an aging rhythm and blues musician who claims his greatest song was stolen by a top-of-the-charts hip-hop artist.

STATE vs. LASSITER: This time, Jake is on the wrong side of the bar. He's charged with murder! The victim? His girlfriend and banker, Pamela Baylins, who was about to report him to the authorities for allegedly stealing from clients. Nominated for the Shamus Award and an Amazon Number One Bestselling Mystery.

BUM RAP: Lassiter defends Steve Solomon in a murder case...and tries not to fall for Victoria Lord. An Amazon Number One Overall Bestseller and Number One Bestseller in Legal Thrillers.

BUM LUCK: After clearing a guilty client, a despondent Lassiter threatens to kill the man. Did Jake suffer one too many concussions playing football? All signs point to the fatal disease CTE.

BUM DEAL: With his CTE symptoms growing worse, Lassiter switches teams and prosecutes a murder case. There's just one problem...or maybe three: no evidence, no witness, and no body.

CHEATER'S GAME: Lassiter matches wits with the mastermind behind the college admissions scandal in a longshot effort to keep his nephew Kip out of prison.

SOLOMON vs. LORD SERIES

Nominated for the Edgar, Macavity, International Thriller, and James Thurber awards.

"Remarkably fresh and original with characters you can't help loving and sparkling dialogue that echoes the Hepburn-Tracy screwball comedies. A hilarious, touching and entertaining twist on the legal thriller." - Chicago Sun-Times

SOLOMON vs. LORD: Trial lawyer Victoria Lord, who follows every rule, and Steve Solomon, who makes up his own, bicker and banter as they defend a beautiful young woman, accused of killing her wealthy, older husband. An Amazon Number One Bestselling Legal Thriller. Nominated for the Macavity Mystery Award and James Thurber Humor Prize.

THE DEEP BLUE ALIBI: Solomon and Lord come together – and fly apart – defending Victoria's "Uncle Grif" on charges he killed a man with a speargun. It's a case set in the Florida Keys with side trips to coral reefs and a nudist colony where all is more –and less – than it seems. Nominated for the Edgar Allan Poe Award and an Amazon Number One Bestseller in Mysteries.

KILL ALL THE LAWYERS: Just what did Steve Solomon do to infuriate ex-client and ex-con "Dr. Bill?" Did Solomon try to lose the case in which the TV shrink was charged in the death of a woman patient? An Amazon Number One Bestselling Mystery and nominated for the International Thriller Writers Award.

HABEAS PORPOISE: It starts with the kidnapping of a pair of trained dolphins and turns into a murder trial with Solomon and Lord on *opposite* sides after Victoria is appointed a special prosecutor, and fireworks follow!

STAND-ALONE THRILLERS

IMPACT: A commercial jet crashes in the Everglades. Is it negligence or terrorism? When the legal case gets to the Supreme Court, the defense has a unique strategy: Kill anyone, even a Supreme Court Justice, to win the case. An Amazon Number One Bestseller in Hard-Boiled Mysteries.

BALLISTIC: A nuclear missile, a band of terrorists, and only two people who can prevent Armageddon. A "loose nukes" thriller for the 21st Century.

ILLEGAL: Down-and-out lawyer Jimmy (Royal) Payne tries to re-unite a Mexican boy with his missing mother and becomes enmeshed in the world of human trafficking and sex slavery. An Amazon Number One Bestseller in Legal Thrillers.

PAYDIRT: Bobby Gallagher had it all and lost it. Now, assisted by his 12-year-old brainiac son, he tries to rig the Super Bowl, win a huge bet… and avoid getting killed. An Amazon Number One Bestseller in Sports Fiction and Organized Crime Thrillers.

For more information and to purchase Paul Levine's novels, please visit his AUTHOR PAGE.

#

ABOUT THE AUTHOR

Photo by Doug Ellis

The author of twenty-two novels, Paul Levine won the John D. MacDonald Fiction Award and has been nominated for the Edgar, Macavity, International Thriller, Shamus, and James Thurber prizes. A former trial lawyer, he also wrote twenty episodes of the CBS military drama *JAG* and co-created the Supreme Court drama *First Monday* starring James Garner and Joe Mantegna. The international bestseller, "To Speak for the Dead," was his first novel and introduced readers to linebacker-turned-lawyer Jake Lassiter. He is also the author of the critically acclaimed "Solomon vs. Lord" series of legal capers. His latest book is "Cheater's Game," which digs deep into the college admissions scandal. He divides his time between Santa Barbara and Miami. For more information, visit his website or his Amazon Author Page or follow him on Facebook or on Twitter @Jake_Lassiter.

CPSIA information can be obtained
at www.ICGtesting.com
Printed in the USA
LVHW030429270722
724446LV00002B/227